end of days

ALSO BY MAX TURNER

Night Runner

MAX TURNER

end of days

ST. MARTIN'S GRIFFIN

NEW YORK

END OF DAYS. Copyright © 2010 by Max Turner. All rights reserved. Printed in the United States of America. For information, address St. Martin's Press, 175 Fifth Avenue, New York, N.Y. 10010.

www.stmartins.com

ISBN 978-0-312-59252-3

First Edition: October 2010

10 9 8 7 6 5 4 3 2 1

end of days

CHAPTER 1

BEING A TEEN VAMPIRE

I'm told vampires are popular in books these days. I'm not surprised. The perks of infection are pretty sick. Awesome physical power. Highly tuned senses. The ability to recover from almost any injury. Good dental hygiene. A simple diet. And that immortality thing—very impressive on a résumé.

My name is Daniel Zachariah Thomson and I'm living the dream. I have been for over nine years. Having said that—the first eight of them weren't what you might imagine. I was orphaned, living in a mental ward, and sick all the time from medications that would never cure me. Then I found out what I was, met a girl, fell in love, and died.

For a while afterward, I'd say life was almost perfect. Then I discovered that every silver lining has a cloud. Does this sound like a complaint? I guess it does. But being a vampire isn't a free ticket to Boardwalk. Those perks I mentioned earlier come with a heavy price tag. If you don't believe me, just think of all the wonderful things you did growing up. How many of them were outside on a beautiful day? For a vampire, the UV index never drops below *deep-fry*, and they don't make sunscreen for that, so once you get infected—no more warm, tingly skin on the beach, no more ocean sunsets, no more afternoon road hockey games, and no more sneaking into your mother's room to look at her Victoria's Secret catalogs. Actually, I guess you could still do that, but it would have to be at night. Still, you get the point. Life without the sunshine is tough. Just look what it did to Gollum.

And the sun is just the tip of the iceberg. I'm sure you've seen the movies. There are lots of ways for us to die, and some are pretty nasty. Forget about holy water and silver bullets. Water of the regular kind scares me, and bullets don't need to be silver, they just need to be airborne.

Then there's the angry mob. Scores of people armed with sticks and pitchforks and torches. They got the Werewolf. And Franken-stein's monster. And the Phantom of the Opera. They almost got Homer Simpson, too. For a vampire, fear of discovery, fear of the mob, is constant. It's why we work so hard to stay hidden. Vampire hunters are another reason. And they aren't all as cute as Buffy. In fact, most of them aren't human. They're vampires, which means most of us are killed by our own kind. Does this seem wrong? It certainly does to me. But if I understand it correctly, it's a matter of necessity.

Imagine a berserk gorilla. Now take off some of the hair and give it rabies. That's the future of every vampire in a nutshell. My father called it Endpoint Psychosis. The stuff of horror movies. No one really understands it. Some vampires get it right away, and others put it off for centuries. But eventually the stress of change, of hunger, of fear, and the loss of light and normal relationships—it unhinges us. Death is never far behind. A small number choose suicide, but as I said before, most are murdered by other vampires. Older ones who've lived for centuries and want our existence to remain a secret. They can be ruthlessly efficient at removing those who might give them away—or who might spread the infection care-lessly. To top it off, they really have it in for child vampires: at least, they did before The End of Days. I guess the theory was, a young vampire was pretty much guaranteed to do something stupid and give himself away. And young vampires had a history of spreading the infection too quickly. Given that I turned my friend Charlie last year, and he did the same to a girl named Luna on the same night—well, it would have been hard to argue our case.

Everyone imagines being a vampire would be cooler than joining the Justice League, and it is. You're practically a superhero. But you have to be able to cope with what you lose. It's a kind of culture shock. You need lots of support from family and friends. Sadly, when Charlie turned, he didn't have that. At the time, his father lived in Halifax and his mother was in rehab, his friends were still in school, and his girlfriend, Suki, lived with Luna in New Jersey. Without me, he would have been a hermit. He got angry often and it made him careless about keeping his condition a secret. I had hoped he would keep it together for a few more centuries, or at least until someone invented the jet pack, but at the rate he was going, a ride on the crazy train was just around the corner. Of course, you could argue he was a crackpot even before he turned, but guys can be loo-loo in a lot of different ways. He was giving up fun-loving-reckless for angry-young-man, and it had me worried. If he didn't get himself under control, someone was going to notice and take the *un* out of his undead. What he really needed was a *Chicken Soup for the Vampire Soul*. Something to calm him down and help him come to terms with what he'd given up. The sunshine. Safety. Sports. And school.

I know what you're thinking. *He had to give up school? What a heartbreaker! What could be worse, winning the lottery maybe?* Well, he didn't exactly love the place, it's true. But he was popular there. He was a great athlete, so he got to be in the spotlight often. He'd given that up for the shadows. And so Charlie Rutherford, Detention King of Adam Scott Collegiate, now talked about school as if it were the Land of Chocolate. If that's not a sign a guy's gone mental, what is?

I wasn't sure what to do to help him. Fortunately, I still had Ophelia in my corner. She was a vampire, too, and for nine years after my father died, she was the closest thing I had to a family. The night this story started, she was leaving to meet someone. I didn't ask whom. With Ophelia, if she wanted you to know, she told you up front.

Before she headed out the door, she reached up, pinched my cheek, and smiled. "You can't fix his problems overnight. Just try to help him reconnect with people. Take his mind off of things. But don't put yourselves at risk. If you sense he's getting a bit hot under the collar, get him home. I'll be out for a while, but I need to talk to you both before sunrise. It's very important."

I understood, so after I said good-bye, I wandered down to Charlie's room in the basement so we could work out a plan. Right after that, things started to go haywire, although as I look back, our problems really began long before that—with two murders in Toronto. Like a pair of dominoes, they set off a sequence of events that led to Peterborough and pretty much flattened everything in sight. But we didn't know that was coming so, for us, the End of Days started with a rave.

CHAPTER 2
PARTY CRASHER

Charlie was on his cell when I knocked on the door and stepped into our room. He'd been living with Ophelia and me for a few weeks now, ever since his mother checked into the clinic. She'd been fighting with the bottle and losing. After drinking herself into the drunk tank for the upteenth time, Children's Aid had given her two choices—quit the drink or lose custody of your son. She made the right decision and entered a rehab program. While she was away, Charlie was rooming with me.

"Sounds great," he said into his phone. He looked at me and quickly pointed to his bed. A black T-shirt was lying there, so I tossed it over. He slipped it over his head, then said, "Yeah . . . See you later," and hung up.

"What's going on?" I asked.

He turned and started sifting through his clothes. Like mine, they were in mixed piles all over the floor. I caught the smell of leather and looked up as he slipped his coat over his shoulders.

"There's a rave on River Road out past Trent," he said. "You feel like taking in some local wildlife?"

"You wouldn't rather go later? *A Fistful of Dollars* is starting in a few minutes." It was a Clint Eastwood duster. One of Charlie's favorites.

"Those old spaghetti westerns are on all the time. You'll like this better. You can work on your dance moves."

I'd never been out dancing before. My best move would have

been to find the closest chair. "I don't know how to dance, Charlie. You know that."

"Then it's a perfect night to learn." He smiled and headed for the stairs. "And you're going to love the scenery."

"Um . . . okay."

"You don't sound too keen."

I guess I didn't. I was worried that if he lost his temper, he'd have a fairly large audience. And I wasn't exactly thrilled at the prospect of dancing for the first time with a bunch of people watching. But this was what he needed—to get out and mingle.

"Come on, chowderhead. Fortune favors the bold. Get your boogie shoes on. This will be fun."

Well, it would be for him, and that was the main thing. I followed him upstairs and through the kitchen.

"Where's Ophelia?"

"She's gone to meet someone."

"Who?"

I shrugged. "She didn't say."

He didn't look surprised to hear it. Ophelia was a private person, and I wasn't one to pry.

We slipped out the front door and took off down Hunter Street. It was where we were living now—one of Peterborough's old west-end neighborhoods with huge trees and houses that were each different from the next. Some big. Some small. Some palatial. Some set back so far from the sidewalk it was a workout just getting to the door. Our place was a modest brick bungalow, the house on the block you were least likely to notice. Not too large or too tiny. Nothing fancy, but not uncommonly plain, either—or its plainness would have made it stand out. Around here, it was all about blending in.

"How far is it?" I asked.

Charlie set out at an easy jog. I let him set the pace so he'd be comfortable. "Close," he answered. He was right. Sort of. Maybe you know this, maybe you don't. Vampires are a lot stronger than normal people. We see better, hear better, move faster, heal faster.

We do everything better except suntan. So the two of us were across town and past Trent University faster than a Greyhound bus. About four miles. For us, it was barely a warm-up.

The rave wasn't quite what I expected. Speakers, lights, artificial smoke, the air so thick with body spray it was a wonder anyone could move. But people did. Perhaps a hundred. Maybe more. They jumped and danced and collided to music that thumped right through my chest. So much energy was in the place, even my hair was tingling.

I wasn't used to crowds, so I stood off to the side and watched for a few minutes while Charlie disappeared into the writhing mass of dancers. He was smooth. No herky-jerky. Like a normal person caught with a slow-motion camera, only he was moving at regular speed. Other people around me noticed, too, those on the periphery who were resting, or refueling, or looking for friends. A girl a few feet away was staring so intently I wondered if she'd forgotten how to blink. This happened often. It was the same way with Ophelia. When we went out shopping at night, even the blind gawked.

In little time, Charlie was surrounded by a group of people, mostly girls that I guessed were either friends or hopefuls. He looked at me and waved me over. I shook my head. I wasn't ready to brave the dance floor. Not yet, even though it didn't seem all that difficult. By the looks of things, the music and the crowd sort of pushed you around. Still, if there was a way to look ridiculous, I was sure I'd find it.

I pressed the charm of my necklace between a finger and thumb. It was a full moon fashioned of silver, etched and polished to a perfect shine. My father gave it to me when I was seven. I could still picture him bending down to fasten it around my neck. He pressed it against my chest, messed my hair, and stood. Then he left. And died. It was the day I became an orphan. And a vampire. Aside from a few old photographs, the necklace was the only thing of his I still had. There was another piece to it, a golden crescent that fit along one side, but that part was with Luna.

I thought of her and felt a smile creep up my cheek. Pretty soon my whole face was involved. I'd say I thought of her often, but it was more like I thought of her constantly and just got interrupted by other things. I wondered what she was doing, and if she was thinking of me. I pictured the two of us dancing. Would she have liked it here? I wasn't sure. Like me, she was comfortable when other people took the spotlight. It was even more true now that she was a vampire. Sadly, she was in New Jersey. A million miles away.

My smile faded. Then someone touched my arm, a tall woman with dark hair and black lipstick. She was carrying a tray of drinks. Her eyes wandered over me, then she offered me one. I raised my hand and shook my head. My drinking habits stayed at home. She wasn't gone a second when a strange feeling came over me. An absurd amount of body heat was being generated in the room, but for all that, I felt a chill. I was being watched.

I quickly located Charlie and his friends. They were in a tight circle, each taking turns dancing through the center. The guy in the middle, who might have been a lineman from Charlie's old football team, was doing something that I could only describe as the Cyborg Chicken. I scanned the rest of the floor. A guy with blue hair was jumping up and down like a spawning salmon. In another corner, a group of girls were dancing so close together it was a wonder their jewelry wasn't tangled. Farther on were a bunch of guys, some with spiked hair, others with shaved heads, who were all jumping up and slamming into one another. It was all alien to me. But certainly no cause for concern.

Then my eyes drifted upward. I thought I saw something in the lights. It was hard to tell. Even if you're from the planet Krypton, your eyes aren't much good with strobes flashing in them. But my instincts told me I was getting warm, so I made my way onto the dance floor to get a better look. I was staring up at the ceiling, not watching where I was going, when I bumped into a girl. Her red hair was cut like a lampshade and she was wearing high-heeled boots that went right up past her knees. Before I could reach out, her drink spilled. I started to apologize.

"That's fine," she said. She moved closer so we were almost touching. "Don't worry about it."

I offered to get her another drink, but she smiled and shook her head. She seemed cool with things. Her boyfriend wasn't. I hadn't noticed him at first. He stepped toward me with a scowl on his face. His hair was gelled down the center like a giant fan and he was wearing a Ramones T-shirt. The people around us backed away just enough that I could tell there was going to be trouble. Then Charlie slid in beside me. His eyes had the same look I imagine Roman gladiators wore when they went into the Colosseum. A kind of focused intensity that was a three parts anger and one part crazy.

"Back off, Romeo," he said. His teeth were starting to drop.

I felt the bottom fall out of my stomach. This was the last thing we needed. A free-for-all that would make the *National Enquirer. Teen Vampire Starts Riot at Small-Town Rave.*

"It's fine, Charlie," I shouted in his ear. "It was my mistake."

I think we could have made it out cleanly at that point if the girl I'd bumped into hadn't been staring at Charlie with a look of dazed euphoria. Whatever cologne he was wearing, it was working overtime. Charlie smiled at her. She smiled back. Then her boyfriend stepped closer so the two of them were chest to chest. *Here we go,* I thought. Charlie's eyes were like two black disks. I hadn't seen anything like it since Shark Week on the Discovery Channel.

Then something bizarre happened. A shadow fell to the floor on the far side of the hall. It happened quickly. With the lights doing a kooky flash dance above, I wasn't sure if I'd actually seen anything, but then the people on that side of the floor began to part. They were staring at a man who was moving toward us. With the light behind him, all I could see was a tall silhouette, but it was enough. His movements were fluid. Effortless. Perfectly balanced. Driven by tremendous strength. There was none of the stiffness you see with normal people. It was another vampire. He'd obviously spotted us. If he was one of those elders who didn't like kids, we were going to go straight from rave to grave.

I wasn't about to take any chances. "Charlie, we've gotta go." I grabbed the sleeve of his jacket and started pulling him to the door.

"That's right, pretty boy, take a walk," the guy with the fan-shaped hair said.

I'd hoped Charlie would just fall in step, but I should have known better. He resisted. Fortunately, I was a lot stronger and jerked his shoulder back. He shot me an angry look, but when he noticed I was staring past the guy with the fan-shaped hair, he turned and saw what I did. Right in front of him, the girl with the red lampshade hair was smiling and waving. Her boyfriend was smirking. Then the tall vampire, little more than a shadow, shouldered past a guy just behind them, spinning him like a turnstile.

Charlie looked back at me, panic all over his face. "Zack, that's a vampire."

"I know!"

We raced for the door.

"How did he know we were here?"

I had no idea. But it didn't matter. We'd been spotted. So we ran.

— CHAPTER 3

RUNNING SCARED

We were just outside when I heard a sound like a flag rippling loudly in the wind. I looked up to see a second shadow drop from the far corner of the building, about a hundred feet away. He was wearing something that might have been a cape, or a loose cowl. It snapped in the night air as he fell.

"There's two of them," I said.

Charlie put it into high gear and I followed. Neither of us spoke. We were both terrified. Our lives were at stake, no pun intended. Our fear was so strong I could smell the sharp tang of it in the warm night air.

To avoid being seen, we didn't follow the road, but stuck to the banks of the river. When we reached the Riverview Park and Zoo, we stopped.

"Are they following us?" Charlie whispered. "Do you hear anything?" He pushed so little air past his lips that it made less noise than a pair of moth wings, but to my ears, it was crystal clear.

I tested the air. Smelled sweat. Charlie's cologne. Zoo animals and rotting straw. Our strained nerves. The wind in the trees was loud. So was the babble of the river. I heard nothing else and didn't expect to. Vampires are predators. Fast, silent, and lethal. We wouldn't hear them until it was too late. Not if they were elders. Over time, the pathogen responsible for making us vampires changed us in ways that stretched the imagination. Talents, they were called, but they were more like the special powers you'd expect to read about in comic books and fantasy novels. Turning into mist. Blending into shadows. Reading people's thoughts. Shape-shifting. Even flying.

I scanned the treetops overhead, then started running again. In minutes we were downtown. We headed for the rooftops. Up and down, block to block. Trees, fire escapes, phone poles, and fences, we scampered over all of them, sticking to the shadows, jumping store to store, row to row, house to house. We were two foxes who knew the hounds were right behind.

We never made it home. About a block from our house, I stopped. Charlie was looking over his shoulder and nearly plowed into me. I tested the air with my nose.

"What is it?" he whispered.

I could smell blood. Normally, it has a distinctive odor—much like everything does. But because it's our only food, we'd never confuse it with anything else. It always set off a chain reaction, in me at least, that usually started in my mouth and spread like a jolt of electricity to every muscle in my body. But I wasn't reacting this way because the odor was a bit off. My mind took a few moments to sort out the reason why.

Charlie poked me in the shoulder. "Wake up, Sleepy Dwarf. Why have we stopped?"

"Can't you smell that?"

He tested the air. Then his eyes widened.

"I think it's from a vampire," I said.

"Yeah." He nodded. "Smells wrong."

The wind changed and the odor grew even stronger. I raced to the tallest house nearby, scampered up the wall, pulled myself up onto the roof, then perched on the chimney. Our place was just down the street. Ophelia's car wasn't there. Did that mean she hadn't returned? I was hoping so, because the odor of blood was coming from our driveway. A telltale crimson smear covered the asphalt.

I heard Charlie below me. He was climbing up the side of the house. I waved him off, then dropped as quickly as I could to the ground. Once I was hidden in the shadow of a tree, I pulled out my cell phone and called Ophelia. Her number was at the top of my call list, right under Charlie's. I hit send and waited. The ring sounded louder than a church bell. I figured every vampire from here to the moon could hear it.

"Can't you set the volume lower?" Charlie asked.

I shook my head. Then Ophelia's voice mail came on. "Call me immediately," I whispered. I nearly snapped the phone in half folding it up.

"Let's get home," Charlie said. He started off toward the house.

I grabbed his arm and pulled him the other way. "We can't," I said. "That's where the blood is coming from. I think they might have arrived ahead of us."

"What? Those vampires? How would they know to come here?"

I had no idea.

"Perfect. I knew this night was too good to be true. We were finally having a bit of fun." Charlie was starting to raise his voice. I waved for him to be quiet. The wind picked up and the smell of vampire blood intensified. "You don't think it might be . . . ?"

He didn't finish, but I knew where he was going. That the blood might be Ophelia's.

"I don't think so," I said. "Her car's not back. And I don't think she was planning to come home this early."

"Let's hope that's not wishful thinking." He stared up the block, then checked over each shoulder. What now?"

I had no idea, but standing still wasn't an option. I turned toward my old neighborhood, where I'd once lived with my father.

"Wait . . . not that way." Charlie pulled me around so we were backtracking downtown. "If we want to hide, the best place is somewhere they've already looked."

Did he mean back at the rave? We'd done this sort of thing once before, last year on Stony Lake when the police were looking for us. We went to a cottage they'd already searched. It seemed a good idea. I fell in step beside Charlie and we headed back to the rave, back to the rooftops.

"It's him, isn't it?" he said.

Him ... He could only mean one person. Vlad Tsepesh—the Impaler. His real name was Wladislaus Dragwlya, but to the modern world he was Dracula. Not a creature of fantasy but a scourge. When I'd first heard of him, he'd used an assumed name, the Baron Vrolok. My uncle Maximilian told me about him. That he'd killed my parents and infected me. Later, Vrolok tried to kill Charlie and me. And Luna. But, thanks to Ophelia, we'd survived. So had he, but only because I didn't have the heart to kill him. Now he was missing, or his body was. It meant he might still be out there. Although he'd almost burnt up in the sun, nearly dead for a vampire isn't really dead at all. Unless the head is cut off, or the body is incinerated, all it takes to bring us back is a bit of time and blood. Lots of it.

"We should never have stayed in Peterborough," Charlie whispered.

It was hard to disagree at the moment.

We ran over the downtown and sprinted along the river until we reached a picnic area between one of the city's hydro stations and a row of houses. Then the smell of vampire blood returned, stronger here than at the house. I slowed, then stopped. Charlie pulled up beside me. The way his nose flared, I could tell he'd noticed, too. His teeth were down and his pupils were two black disks again. Wide. Alert. Nervous. I felt the same.

I scanned the shore and the grass around the trees. A few picnic tables sat near a trash can. Drops of vampire blood ran past them in a straight line toward the river.

"Over here." Charlie pointed to a large bootprint in the grass a few steps away. "Do you think it's from one of those vampires at the rave?"

I had no idea.

"Look, it leads straight into the water."

In the mud on the lip of the bank was another print. I set my foot in it, then backed up and looked for another. Whoever it was, he'd lost a lot of blood here. Then jumped into the river. It made no sense. Blood doesn't clot underwater.

"What can do this to a vampire?" Charlie asked.

I shrugged. "A stronger vampire maybe."

He kneeled down and smeared his fingertips with blood, then raised it to his nose. He was about to stick it in his mouth when I grabbed his arm.

"Oh, right," he said.

I let go of his arm. He wiped his fingers on his pant leg and stood. A vampire's blood could be fatal to another vampire. I wasn't exactly sure why.

"He was motoring." Charlie stared at the bootprint in the grass. The other print, the one in the mud by the water, was at least twenty feet away. "You think he was being followed?"

My eyes swept over the grass. "I don't see any other footprints, do you?"

Charlie went back to the bank where the ground was softer and shook his head. Then he kicked off his shoes and waded out to his knees. A few seconds later, he pointed to the ground at the lip of the river. I saw a hollow depression. A few inches of water had washed inside, obscuring the bottom. We found several more. They were deep, as if someone had pressed a large tin can into the muck.

"What makes that kind of mark?" he asked.

I couldn't say. I stared at the round hole and tried to imagine what might have done it. It looked almost like a bear print, but was wider at the front, with no toe markings, though the river might have washed them away.

Charlie slapped my shoulder gently with the back of his hand. "Don't go catatonic on me now."

I wasn't planning to. But I often got quiet when I was thinking and sometimes forgot to answer people when they spoke to me. I'd picked up this bad habit from living in the Nicholls Ward. Half the people there couldn't carry on a conversation. They just muttered all the time or repeated themselves or completely ignored me. Since it didn't really make a difference what I said to them, I got used to keeping my mouth shut and thinking about things in my head. The busier my mind got, the less likely I was to say anything out loud.

Charlie gently punched my shoulder. "Say something, turkey meat. Your tongue's frozen."

"Sorry. I'm just trying to figure this out."

I tested the air. I could smell the damp grass, car exhaust, rotting sticks and leaves along the bank, my deodorant, vampire blood . . .

"What is it?"

"Wine," I said. "And a sweaty, leathery kind of dog smell."

We stood for a few moments, not speaking.

"You want to get your feet wet?"

I shook my head. I didn't like the water.

Charlie looked farther up the shore. "Should we keep checking along the bank? Whoever jumped in had to come out somewhere."

"If he came out at all. You really want to find him?"

Charlie shook his head. "Not really. But if he's injured, this might be the best chance we have. He's weak. If he feeds and regenerates, we're going to be in trouble."

I had a feeling we were already in trouble. I turned back to the street.

Charlie stayed for a few moments to tie up his shoes. Then he just stared out over the river. In his first life, he'd been a water baby. Swimming. Canoeing. Windsurfing. He used to be a sailing instructor. Before that, he raced Lasers, single-sailed boats you could skipper by yourself. It was all part of a life that belonged in the sunshine. It was gone and never coming back. I didn't know what to say to him. These were all things he'd lost because I'd infected him, and there was no easy way to set it right.

I heard him take a deep breath, then he turned so we were standing shoulder to shoulder. "Any more clues, Sherlock?"

Before I could answer, a howl ripped through the air. Another answered. Wolves. They were close, only a few blocks away.

"That's weird," he said.

And unsettling.

"Let's go." He started forward.

I didn't move.

"What is it?"

Did he really have to ask?

"We have an advantage, Zack. He's hurt."

"That only makes him more dangerous," I said.

"Or more likely to kill someone."

Charlie had a point. An injured vampire needed human blood to regenerate. If his hunger was strong enough, it might push him over the edge.

"Who else is going to do anything?" he added. "What if he's gone crazy?"

That clinched it. "You're right. We'd better check things out."

Charlie laughed.

"What is it?"

"You sound like you're auditioning for the part of Superman in the school play."

"Very funny."

Another eruption of howling. It sounded as if the entire cast of *White Fang* were having a feeding frenzy just up the street.

"Well, now is our chance, Clark. Up, up and away."

Charlie brushed past me, then raced off into the dark along the river. The howling continued.

CHAPTER 4

SURPRISE ATTACK

The Riverview Park and Zoo was less than a quarter mile down Water Street. And yes, they had wolves. Two of them. Whenever Charlie and I came by on a late-night run, they were always up, padding their cells, restless to join us on the hunt. They would have been disappointed. We never killed anything larger than mosquitoes. But tonight was different. We were hunting an injured vampire.

I took off. I'd been infected much longer than Charlie. Even though we'd been drinking human blood for about the same length of time, my transmission had a few extra gears. I wanted to arrive first, just in case there really was trouble. By the time he caught up, I was standing outside the wolf pen. It was empty. The chain links of the outer fence and the taller, inner fence had been ripped apart. The smell of vampire blood was in the air. I ran my fingers over the torn metal. I couldn't make sense of this. If a vampire was injured, why would it mess with two wolves?

"Why would someone do this?"

Charlie shrugged. "Like I'm supposed to know?" He nodded toward a hole in the ground. "One of the posts is missing."

We heard another howl. And a squeal.

"That way," Charlie said, nodding past the animal cages to a play area full of monkey bars and swing sets. He bolted. I got swept up in his turbulence. We passed a goat and donkey pen—they were bleating as if the world were going to end. Then we entered the kids' park. Every animal in the zoo was awake by this time. It sounded like the inside of Noah's ark. Then I saw the two wolves. They were dead. Both had deep rows of gashes along their flanks, as if they'd been run over several times by a lawn mower. I scanned the ground looking for footprints, then sniffed at the air to try to find any trace of where the vampire had gone. With so much blood everywhere, I couldn't tell what was what. My senses were on overload.

"He's definitely gone bonkers?" Charlie said. He had to raise his voice over the sound of the buffaloes, which were sounding off like a pair of foghorns.

I surveyed the mess and nodded. Most vampires hid their tracks. This one was advertising, a sure sign of Endpoint Psychosis. Whoever it was, Vlad or someone else, we had to catch him quickly or he might easily start the kind of pandemic you only saw in bad Hollywood horror films.

Charlie slapped my arm gently with the back of his hand, then flicked his fingers toward the edge of the park. "The prints lead that way."

The children's area was a sandlot. I could see a pair of boot markings—the same from the riverbank—leading past a tube slide to a set of steps that ran down the hill. The river was that way. As we were following the tracks, I heard the sound of sirens approaching.

"Hurry," Charlie said.

I took off at warp speed, following the blood trail to the bottom of the stairs. Then I slowed. I'm not sure why. Was it fear? Or perhaps a deeper instinct. Trouble was waiting ahead. The hairs on my arms were standing up, and the eerie chill I'd felt at the rave returned—as if I was being watched. Charlie was right on my heels. As I slowed, so did he. We crept along the path, then I felt his hand on my back. I flattened out on the ground so I was hidden in the long grass. Ahead, by the riverbank, we could see the silhouette of a man.

"Who is it?" Charlie whispered. "Can you see?"

I couldn't. He was about a hundred meters away, and the light of the moon was behind him, so his face was just a shadow. His hair was long. A mix of black and white and gray. He was wearing what might have been a cape, or maybe a long overcoat. As we watched, the man dropped to a crouch and looked back in our direction. By his movements, I could tell it was a vampire.

"It doesn't look like Vlad," Charlie said.

He was right. Vlad was short and thick with a neck like an ox. This man was taller. Leaner. This should have brought me some relief, but it didn't. Maybe because the vampire had the missing fence post—the one from the wolf pen—and was holding it like a baseball bat. He began to circle, his eyes scanning the grass where we were hiding. The trees to our right were suddenly looking like a much safer place to hide.

"I think he can see us," Charlie said. "What do we do?"

I didn't know. But if we didn't make up our minds soon, we were going to run out of choices. The vampire would decide for us. His eyes were still searching the shadows. Then he started toward us, first at a jog, then a sprint. I felt my stomach twist. Suddenly a shadow shot out of the darkness. It froze the air in my chest. I'd never seen anything move so quickly. I took it from Charlie's reaction, he hadn't either. He jumped as if I'd jammed a pin in his ribs. I wasn't even certain how the thing was running, on two legs or four. There wasn't time to tell. Whatever it was, it collided with the approaching vampire about a stone's throw in front of us. The two shapes rolled over the top of one another in a blur. A lethal dance started that was so quick, even my vampire eyes had difficulty following it.

"What is *that* thing?" Charlie asked, his eyes open wider than his mouth.

I couldn't decide what it was. It might have been another vampire, but it seemed too large, and the shape was wrong. Had I been able to see it more clearly, I might have been able to make up my mind, but it was moving too quickly. The vampire with the post was swinging for the fences as if this were game seven of the World Series. They were two overlapping ghosts. Snarling shapes that were impossible to separate.

I started creeping back to the stairs. Charlie was right behind me. We were way out of our league here. It was time to run. Then the fight ended. I don't even know how. I glanced up the hill toward the zoo and missed the grand finale. There was a splash in the river. When I looked back, the vampire was gone. The larger creature from the shadows craned his neck and let out a roar that would have scared the ears off a Kodiak bear.

"I think that's our cue," Charlie whispered.

As soon as he spoke, the thing turned and saw us.

Charlie froze. I didn't. I was the Night Runner. My feet were already moving. I grabbed an armful of his coat and hauled him back toward the steps. If we didn't slip it into overdrive, we were going to be next on the menu. We bolted up the steps. Ahead, at the zoo, the red and blue lights of police cars were reflecting off the leaves of the trees and sumac along the hill.

Charlie slowed when he saw them. "Are you sure you want to go that way?"

I wasn't sure about anything, but it seemed the safest place to go, and I said so.

"I don't think I'd feel safe in a bank vault right now," Charlie said.

The sound of soft footfalls behind us was all the motivation we needed. So we fled up the stairs in the direction of the police.

CHAPTER 5

INSPECTOR JOHANSSON

When Charlie and I topped the steps and entered the zoo play area, we nearly collided with a young officer who was standing near the mouth of the slide. He was stocky, with hair that would have looked perfect on a mannequin. When he saw us, he raised one hand in a "Halt" gesture. The other was pressing the buttons on a radio pinned to his shoulder. I felt Charlie tense up beside me.

"We should hustle," he whispered. "That thing is coming."

I quickly glanced around. Five other cruisers were in the lot, plus two more on the road, and three near the fountain. A group of officers were inspecting the wolf pen. Others were sealing off areas with plastic yellow tape. One was snapping pictures. At least a dozen officers had to be within earshot. And gunshot. Even Godzilla would have thought twice about making trouble up here.

"What are you two doing?" the officer asked.

Charlie looked at me. I looked at him. We both looked at the officer. There was no good answer for this. Fortunately, the conversation got cut short by a voice that crackled like a dry flame.

"I'll take it from here," a man said.

A dark shape hobbled out from behind a car that was more rust than paint. It was Everett Johansson. He was a police inspector and a good friend of Ophelia's—part of a network of supporters who helped supply us with blood so we didn't have to wander the streets at night looking for people to bite. He moved awkwardly, leaning hard on his cane. The injury was old, from when he'd worked as a homicide detective in Toronto. A bullet through the knee had helped him decide to get out before the locals learned to shoot a little higher.

"You sure?" the young officer asked him. "I was going to wait and turn them over to Baddon."

Inspector Johansson grunted. It might have been a yes, or it might have been a swear word. Then he started hacking. He had a smoker's cough from years of wine-tipped cigars. "Baddon's busy," he said. "I'll handle these two critters."

"They're all yours." The officer glanced at us once before walking away. I couldn't tell from his expression whether he felt relief or disappointment. It might have been heartburn.

I waited until he was out of earshot before speaking. "Thanks. I wasn't sure how I was going to explain this."

Inspector Johansson grunted again. He did most of his talking this way. Then he turned back to his car, one of those ancient muscle machines people bought before anyone knew what global warming was. For just a second, the streetlamp overhead lit up the bright pink scar under his eye. It made him look tough. I'd once mistaken him for a bad guy. He certainly looked the part. He cleared his throat, then pulled a cigar from a carton inside his coat pocket and lit up.

"What were you two doing here?" he said with the cigar pinched between his teeth. Without waiting for an answer, he opened the back door of his car and told us to get in. I slid through the door and across the seat. The inspector waited for Charlie to climb in, then closed the door and grunted his way into the front. Once settled, he rolled down his window and blew a plume of smoke from the side of his mouth. When he turned the key, I winced. The engine burped, hiccuped, detonated, then a cloud of black soot flew out the tailpipe. As soon as the car recovered, he slid it in gear and stepped on the gas. My whole body shook as if I were sitting on a paint mixer. It was easily 6.2 on the Richter scale.

"So?" Johansson said. We pulled out of the lot and turned onto Water Street.

"We were following a vampire," I said.

"Vampire?" The inspector pulled the cigar from his mouth and cleared his throat. "Are you crazy?"

After living eight years in a mental ward, I was pretty sure the answer was no.

"Do you know who it was?"

"I don't think it matters now," Charlie said.

A deep grunt followed. "Why not?"

"Because something showed up and carved him into fish food."

The inspector's eyes flashed up to the rearview mirror. He glanced at Charlie, then at me. He looked exhausted. His eyes were two slits. "*Something* showed up. *Something?* What do you mean *something?*"

"I didn't get a good look at it," I answered. "It was moving too fast. But we did see some weird footprints."

His eyelids rose to half-mast when he heard this. "Where?"

"The picnic tables by the hydro station," Charlie answered.

The inspector's hand disappeared into his overcoat and came up with a cell phone. He started dialing. When someone picked up at the other end, he said, "Yeah, it's me."

It was difficult to listen in. The car sounded like two chain saws trying to cut each other in half.

"Have you got them?" said a voice.

I looked at Charlie.

"Ophelia?" he whispered.

I nodded. It was her. It meant she was safe. She said something, but I missed it, then Inspector Johansson answered by saying he was bringing us home.

"That's a mistake," Charlie said.

The inspector hung up, then dropped the phone onto the seat beside him. "What was that?"

"That's a mistake," Charlie repeated.

"The vampires were there," I added.

"What vampires?"

"Two of them followed us from the rave. That's why we didn't go home. There's vampire blood all over the driveway."

"Great," grumbled the inspector. He hit the brakes and our heads jolted forward. He picked up the phone and made another call. No one picked up. "Well, that's not good," he muttered.

"What is it?" Charlie asked.

"Ophelia's place was under surveillance. An old friend of mine from Toronto. He's not answering." The inspector tried his car radio, but didn't have any luck with that, either. "Dammit!"

"What's going on?" Charlie asked.

"And where's Ophelia?"

Inspector Johansson ignored us. He just stared at the radio. "Let's hope he's at the hospital with his son," he muttered. I had no idea whom he was talking about. Then he turned so he could see us better. "What happened tonight?"

We did our best to explain. His eyes bounced from me to Charlie as we took turns running through the night's events.

"What do you think it was at the zoo?" the inspector asked me. "What killed those wolves? Was it the vampire? Or was it this *something* you were talking about?"

I shrugged. "I don't know."

"You said there were two vampires at the rave. What happened to the other one?"

I looked at Charlie. He shrugged, then glanced at the inspector. "You didn't answer my question."

Inspector Johansson responded by hammering on the gas pedal. The engine grumbled and we lurched forward. "What question?"

"What's going on?"

His eyes rose the rearview mirror. "The Underground is collapsing. No—let me rephrase that. It's going to hell in a handbasket."

"What does that mean?" I asked.

"The Underground has been compromised. We're under attack."

"*Underground?*" said Charlie. "You hanging out with mole men or something? What are you talking about?"

We drove in silence for a few blocks. The inspector was looking at his phone. He seemed to be debating another call. He put it down and sped up instead, then glanced back over the seat.

"Don't pretend you've never heard of the Underground."

"Who's pretending?"

The inspector grunted his surprise. "You've heard of it. You just never put the right name to it maybe."

"Then what is it?" Charlie asked.

"All the people who help look after vampires."

"Aren't they called the Fallen?"

Inspector Johansson started coughing. He hurried an answer in between a few loud fits. "That was a word Zack's father used, but it only applied to the bad ones. We're the good guys."

"You're part of it then?" Charlie asked.

"The Underground? Yeah. A small part."

"How big is it?"

The inspector put his lips together and frowned. "Global. But I only know what I need to know. A handful of names. Some are police. Some are vampires. Some are normal people. It's supposed to be a secret, but someone must have let the cat out of the bag. Our supply systems are falling apart. Blood has been tampered with. Poisoned. Other shipments have been stolen. A vampire in Havelock disappeared yesterday. Another in Lakefield last week. Bridgenorth before that. Just vanished. And they were good ones, like you two slack-jawed nincompoops."

He took his cigar out of his mouth. His hands were shaking—only a slight tremor, but I noticed. The window was still rolled down. He blew another lungful of smoke outside.

"Is that why the vampires showed up at the rave? Are they behind it?" Charlie asked.

"Who knows?" Inspector Johansson said. "Maybe they were trying to warn you."

I hadn't considered that. I looked at Charlie. Judging by the look of surprise on his face, he hadn't either.

The inspector stopped the car a block from our house. Then his phone rang. "Go," he said.

It was Ophelia again. She sounded alarmed. "Where are you?"

"I'm a block from the house with Tweedledumb and Tweedle-dumber. Looks like a hot spot. I think it's been compromised. Any other suggestions about where to take them?"

"Is Burnham safe?"

"I don't know if anywhere is safe, but it's probably the best option." He mashed his cigar into the tray under the radio.

"I need you to drop them off, then swing by right away," Ophelia continued.

"Where are you?"

"London Street."

"What's up?"

I held my breath and waited. Charlie was listening, too. For a few seconds, all I could hear was the sound of the car idling and the inspector, who was grinding his teeth and feeling about his coat pocket for another cigar.

"You need to come quickly," Ophelia said. "There's been another murder."

— CHAPTER 6

THE SAFE HOUSE

The inspector looked at his cell for a few seconds as if it were guilty of a heinous crime, then he disconnected it and tossed it on the seat beside him. A string of swear words erupted from his mouth. He pulled the last cigar from the box in his coat pocket and started chewing on the end of it. He didn't light up, he just rolled it from one side of his mouth to the other, then chucked the empty carton to the floor.

"Who just got killed?" Charlie asked.

The inspector shook his head. "I'll find out later. Once I've dropped you two off." He slipped the car into gear and headed back toward the downtown. We crossed the Hunter Street bridge, drove past a baseball diamond, then pulled onto a quiet side street.

"That's it." He nodded out the window toward a tiny brick bungalow that looked just big enough for a family of ants.

"We're staying *here*?" Charlie asked.

"Unless you had other plans . . ."

We didn't, so we followed Inspector Johansson around to the back door. He reached into his coat and pulled out a key ring that would have given Governor Schwarzenegger a workout. "Give me a second."

There were four dead bolts to unlock. As soon as he opened the door, I saw why. The place was like an antiques shop. It was packed floor to ceiling with swords, helmets, armor, busts, carvings, statues, old candlesticks, furniture, and carpets. Everything looked as if it had been stolen from a museum. Or a medieval castle.

"Where did you get all this?" I asked, bumping into a coffee table that might have belonged to Moses at one time.

"It's Ophelia's," the inspector said over his shoulder. He was punching numbers into an electronic box near the door. It must have been a home security system.

"Did you know about this?" Charlie asked me.

I shook my head. Ophelia wasn't into clutter. Our house had no knickknacks or collectibles. Not unless you counted books and music and the odd painting. This clearly wasn't a place she expected to be living in anytime soon. The sheer volume of stuff would have driven her into an insane cleaning frenzy—one that wouldn't have ended until nothing was left in the rooms but air and dried paint. But Luna would have loved it. And my father. He used to obsess over anything old. Or well made. Things that were lasting.

I don't know how long I stood there. Eventually, I felt the tip of Johansson's cane tap gently against the bottom of my arm.

"Come on," he said. "Ophelia's waiting for me."

I nodded, then followed him through the hall to the far end of the house. Just past the kitchen, a door led down to the basement. The inspector opened it for us, flicked on the lights, then nodded for us to go ahead.

If the first floor of the safe house was an antiques store, the basement was a Future Shop. Everything was state-of-the-art. High-def TV. Surround-sound stereo. A computer that looked as if it belonged on a spaceship. A weird sofa that had a thin, contoured back. A bed folded up against the wall. A funky reading chair with a spiral metal base that I was sure I'd seen in an episode of *Star Trek*. Several glass and wire bookcases with small lights built in. The only things that didn't look as if they were made in the year 3000 were the books. There were even game consoles. Charlie saw them and his eyes lit up.

"Now this is more like it," he said. "I could survive a zombie apocalypse down here."

"No windows," I whispered. Another plus.

"You aren't the first vampires we've had to hide." The inspector handed me a remote control. "Try not to break anything." He grunted and turned to go.

"Wait," I said.

He turned back. He was leaning hard on his cane.

"When will I see Ophelia?" I asked.

The inspector scratched at the stubble on his chin, then positioned his cigar at the side of his mouth. "We'll be back before dawn."

"She mentioned she wanted to talk to Charlie and me about something. Do you know what it was?"

"Yeah." He nodded. "A few things. The Coven was one of them."

The Coven . . . He meant the Coven of the Dragon, a team of powerful elders who were like the secret police of the vampire world. An invisible network of executioners. They were the most dangerous organization on the face of the earth, at least for Charlie and me, because they were the ones who were most likely to come after us. I didn't know much about them, only that their seat of power was overseas in Europe somewhere. Vlad had been their Grand Master. With him gone, I didn't know who was in charge.

"We weren't sure if the Coven were behind these disappearances," the inspector continued, "but I had my doubts, even before you saw that thing at the zoo."

"Why?" Charlie asked.

The inspector took out his cigar. "The Coven always impale their enemies. They cut off the head, stuff the mouth with garlic, cut out the heart, burn it, and put the corpse on display as a deterrent to others. The vampires who have died lately, they just disappear. Nothing is left but a stain on the sidewalk. And they were all stable. Discreet. That's not the way the Coven operate. They only go after the crazies. Or the ones who don't stay incognito. You were an exception. Vendetta. And an age thing. The Coven don't permit child vampires. But you knew that already." He grunted, then spoke with the cigar pinched at the side of his mouth. "And the Coven are in disarray right now. Infighting. Vlad is still missing. Even if he comes back, and let's pray he doesn't, he'll have a hell of a lot of reorganizing to do."

"What do you mean *reorganizing*?" I asked.

"Vlad's underlings are all fighting to see who gets to be the top dog. Vlad would have a lot to do to bring them back under control. Ophelia and I thought their lack of leadership would keep you out of trouble for a while."

Obviously not.

"So what happens now?" Charlie asked. He made his way over to the game console under the television.

"You two stay out of sight," the inspector said. "There's a phone by the bed, but I don't want you calling out. And don't answer it unless it's me. When I call, I'll let it ring twice, then I'll hang up and call again. Two rings, pause, pick up on the next one."

"Don't we have caller ID?" I asked.

"Yes, you do. But someone else might be using my phone. You never know. . . . Two rings. Pause. Then pick up the next call. Got it?"

"Yeah. I got it."

He grunted, then looked us over again. His head tilted forward a bit. I'd seen his expression on a lot of adult faces. *Be careful,* he was saying. Well, how much trouble could we get into in a one-room basement? I nodded back and he turned to go. Then he remembered something.

"One more thing. The alarm. It'll be on upstairs. If you try to leave the house, it will go off. So stay put. Is there anything else you'll need?"

"Yeah," said Charlie. "Could you send for some backup? Someone to watch the place from outside—raise the alarm if trouble arrives. We aren't going to see anything from down here. And once the sun comes up, we're toast if someone breaks in."

The inspector grunted a negative. "We're out of backup. Every cop

I know in the Underground is dead or missing. And I can't get anyone else involved on short notice. I have to keep you guys off the radar."

He walked over to me and reached into his coat. From the holster around his shoulder he took out his gun, a semiautomatic. He handed it to me. "The clip is full. The safety's on. You ever fire one of these things?"

I took the gun and shook my head. I'd never even held one before. Then a jolt of pain ran down my arm. It took root in my chest. My heart began to burn. I pinched my eyes shut, and when I opened them, everything was an agonizing haze. All I could see were spots. It was a few seconds before I could speak.

"Take it back," I whispered.

"I'll take it," said Charlie.

The inspector glanced down at the gun and removed it from my hand. Instantly, the pain began to ebb. Nerves stopped burning. My blurry eyes cleared.

I watched him reholster it. He was watching me intently. "You okay?"

I didn't know how to answer that, so I didn't. After a few seconds, he grunted a good-bye and started hobbling to the stairs.

"Two rings, pause, pick up," he reminded me.

I nodded and he closed the basement door. Then his footsteps clumped across the floor above. The back door opened and closed. The house shuddered. Dead bolts followed. A minute later, I heard his car roar. I could picture every animal in the neighborhood running for cover.

"What was that all about?" Charlie said.

"What?"

"With the gun. Your face . . ."

I rubbed my arm. It was still pins and needles. "It didn't feel right."

"You should have given it to me!"

I had no answer for this. I trusted my instincts. Something about that gun was just wrong.

"You want to play some?" Charlie turned the game console on. Then he started opening drawers in the TV cabinet, no doubt looking for games.

I wandered over to the desk. It was covered with open books. Loose-leaf pages were scattered everywhere. "There's a note here." A yellow sticky was pressed to the bottom of the computer keyboard: *Knowledge is your best defense.* The writing was tight and neat. I recognized it as Ophelia's right away.

"What does it say?" Charlie didn't look up from the drawer he was sorting through. "Man, all these games are old. We've finished them already."

I read him the message. "It's Ophelia's writing," I added.

"How long ago did she write it?"

"Beats me." He walked over and I handed it to him. He glanced at it, then down at the desk, and froze. I followed his gaze to the open book. There, staring at us from the page, was Vlad Dracula.

CHAPTER 7

PROPHECIES

Charlie and I stared at a picture of the vampire who had almost killed us.

"A little light reading, I guess," Charlie said. "Man, that dude is scary-looking." He closed the book.

Underneath was another note. The handwriting was larger than Ophelia's. Messier. More frantic.

THE END OF DAYS IS COMING.

Charlie picked up the note, read it over again, then handed it to me. "What kind of gobbledygook is this? The *End of Days*—isn't that an Arnold Schwarzenegger movie?"

It was. Not his best work. I started leafing through the other open books. One showed a page full of ideograms.

"Is that Chinese?" Charlie asked.

I shrugged. It might have been Martian. I couldn't read it, but Ophelia obviously could. Notes were in the margins. The writing was hers. I looked at the shelves. There were hundreds of other books. And more open on the desk, *Geschichte der Moldau und Walachei* The book beside it had a passage underlined: *i nu este revelat omul nelegiuirii . . .*

It meant nothing to me. I started looking at the others. I needed to know what the note meant. What the End of Days referred to.

"Oh, no, you don't," Charlie said.

"What?"

"Zack, it would take you ten years to read through this stuff."

I sighed. "Then I guess I'd better get started."

I didn't have much luck at first. Of all the volumes on the desk, only one was in English—the phone book.

After a couple of minutes, Charlie started walking back to the television. "I need to get doing something or I'm going to start gnawing on the furniture."

I gathered up Ophelia's notes. "Just wait a second. Give me a hand. I have a feeling . . . There's got to be something here." Charlie turned back and I handed him half of the pages.

"What am I doing, exactly?"

"Just look for something useful," I said.

"Like what? A recycling bin?"

I started flipping through the sheets. Charlie held his first one up. The page was covered in curvy letters that wound all over one another.

"What is this? Snake?"

"I don't know. Persian maybe."

Charlie gave me a look. "Zack, I'd have an easier time translating a Klingon war manual. Let's do some gaming."

"No. Wait wait wait." The words came out like machine-gun bullets. "I've found something."

Charlie reached over and pulled the top page down. The words on it were in English. Typed. A letter. It started in midsentence. I set it flat on the desk so we could both read it.

> ". . . bears a shocking similarity to 2 Thessalonians, chapter 2, verse 3, "for that day will not come until the rebellion occurs and the man of lawlessness is revealed."

The man of lawlessness . . . Who could that be?

Charlie nudged me. I read on silently.

The verse goes on to say that this man, presumably the Antichrist, is doomed to destruction, which is missing from Baoh's prophecy. The chapter continues by suggesting that the Antichrist will claim to be God, which Vlad has never done.

I hit the name Vlad and stopped again. So did Charlie. He looked at me. "Does this make sense to you?"

Not yet, so I kept going.

Regarding the other symbols, I have taken great care to translate them. I see definite parallels with the Revelation of Saint John the Divine, but there is no doubt in my mind that the prophecies of Baoh do not concern the Great Beast, the Antichrist, or the End of Days.

"Who is Baoh?" Charlie asked.

I shook my head. I'd never heard of him. But he sounded like a kind of prophet. Maybe he was a friend of Ophelia's.

Charlie pointed to the text at the end of the last sentence. "There's 'the End of Days' again."

I nodded and kept reading.

. . . but there is no doubt in my mind that the prophecies of Baoh do not concern the Great Beast, the Antichrist, or the End of Days. Not as it pertains to the human world and the Second Coming of the Messiah. Rather, I think these prophecies concern the fate of carriers, and more specifically, your ward.

Carriers. That was the word my father used for "vampires." Carriers of the pathogen. Those who were infected. My eyes gobbled up the rest of the text.

I have included my translations below. They are in no way complete. Even with the help of modern recording devices, we have been unable to decipher most of what Baoh said. I will forward more should we manage to transcribe them.

"The great hunter shall be sacrificed and make his son an orphan. The sun shall be given the power to scorch him with fire."

"The orphaned son who is and was and is to come shall not be hurt by the second death, though the sun will beat upon him."

"The Lamb will be their shepherd [indecipherable muttering follows] . . . a scourge. He will lead them to springs of living water . . . to destruction. Behold, he is coming soon."

And that was it. Charlie finished. We looked at each other.

"Are there other pages?" he said.

I started looking.

"We need to find more." He searched around the desk. On the floor.

I rifled through the stack one more time to be sure I hadn't missed anything. I came up empty. Charlie didn't. He found another from the mess I'd handed him. He waved the page like a winning scratch ticket.

"It must come right after." He spread it on the desk.

All of our far eastern agents are aware of Baoh's disappearance. Given his power and resources, it is unlikely we will find him. Rather, he will emerge at a time of his own choosing, though the Coven may possess the power to drive him out of hiding and compel his service. Whether they can do this without Vlad is doubtful. His whereabouts remain a mystery. No sign of him has been seen by any of our agents, in any corner of the world. If he has risen from his most recent death, he has chosen not to reveal himself.

The future of the Underground is uncertain. This would seem a prudent time to seek out those carriers with the power of prophecy and those who travel the Spirit Planes.

Be careful. You are now the rock upon which our future rests.

May God's blessings be upon you.

The name at the bottom was handwritten and difficult to read.

"What does it say?" Charlie asked. "Who's it from?"

I lifted the paper. Turned it sideways. Squinted. "I think it says Mutada."

"Mutada? Isn't that from *The Lion King*?"

"No, that's Mustafa. This is one of my father's friends. They hunted vampires together in Afghanistan. My father mentioned it in his journal."

"And this Mutada guy knows Ophelia?"

"It looks that way. We need to find the first page." I flipped through the rest of my pile. "I can't find it."

"Maybe she has it with her. Or it's in one of these books."

There was no way to know without a lengthy search.

Charlie was still staring at the pages. He spread them out so they were side by side. "I can't believe this stuff. This is about you, isn't it? You're the orphaned son. The Lamb. Ophelia's ward."

"Do I look like a lamb to you?"

"No. More like a reject from *Planet of the Apes*."

"Thanks."

"Don't mention it. I wonder who this Baoh character is?" he asked.

I did, too. He was obviously important.

Charlie elbowed me gently on the front of my shoulder. "You're off in la-la land again."

"Sorry. I was just wondering who he could be."

He picked up the note we'd found under the book on Dracula.

THE END OF DAYS IS COMING.

"That's the end of the world, isn't it?"

I wasn't sure. "We need to find Ophelia to see what all this means."

He nodded, then walked over to the phone. "Johansson said they'd be here soon. Why don't you call her?"

The inspector didn't want us calling. Not with the landline. But he didn't say anything about my cell. I picked it up and hit redial. Her voice mail came on straight off.

"It's me again. Please call me right away." I followed this with a text message, just for good measure.

"No luck?" Charlie asked.

"She must be talking to someone. I'm sure she'll call right back."

Charlie plopped down on the sofa and put his feet up. "We should phone the girls."

The girls. He meant Luna and her older sister, Suki. She and Charlie had fallen in love last July. If Stony Lake had been blessed with a tabloid, the two of them would have made the weekly cover. But she wasn't doing well, and it was largely my fault.

The past summer had ended in a night that belonged in a hack-and-slash horror movie. One of Charlie's close friends was brutally murdered. Shortly after that, I went berserk and got arrested. Suki had a front-row seat for most of it. Then, when it seemed things couldn't possibly get any worse, Charlie and Luna were abducted by my uncle Maximilian and handed over to Vlad, who wanted to impale them. Ophelia saved the day. I turned Charlie, and he turned Luna. But Suki was still human. And she was a mess.

I'd spoken to Luna about Suki many times since, and I know Charlie sent her lots of e-mails and called as often as he could afford to. But she just wasn't the same after *that night.* She felt like an outsider. With her living so far away, in Newark, New Jersey, there wasn't a lot we could do. I felt awful about it because I'd gone to

Charlie for help. If I'd done the right thing and stayed away from him and his friends, everyone would still be nicely tanned and living on easy street. Instead, I'd turned his world upside down. Suki's, too. There was no quick fix for this.

"You want to send her a text?" I said.

Charlie shook his head. "I could . . . I'd rather hear her voice. I haven't talked to her in a few days." He took my cell and started scrolling for the number.

It looked as if he was about to say something, but then the other phone rang—the landline that Johansson had told us not to use. We waited. Counted two rings. The pause was supposed to come next. It didn't. The phone just rang and rang and rang. Then it stopped. I waited to see if it would fire up again. It didn't. I snatched it out of the cradle.

"What does it say?" Charlie asked.

"One missed call."

"Can't you see who it was? There's a call display."

"All it says is *unavailable*."

"Who would call us?"

It obviously wasn't Johansson. Someone else from the Underground maybe. I set the phone back in the cradle. Then a loud boom shook the house.

Charlie and I stared at each other. "That came from upstairs," he said.

A second later the front door crashed in. Several people entered. Their footfalls were loud, as if they were wearing Frankenstein boots. An alarm started ringing. That had to be the home security system. They didn't have the password. Not good. Voices started shouting.

"What do we do?" I whispered.

"Look for something we can use."

We both glanced around the room. Charlie grabbed a table lamp. He unplugged it and wrapped the cord around the neck. Then he swung it, testing its weight. Ophelia's note sprang to mind.

Knowledge is your best defense. What did that mean? Was I supposed to hurl books?

The alarm stopped. More people came inside. It sounded like an open house. "Should we go upstairs?" I asked.

Charlie was still thinking. Listening. All I could hear was muffled chatter. And my heart. It was winning the Kentucky Derby. Several sets of footsteps walked across the floor above. They stopped at the door by the top of the stairs. It opened with a creak and the lights flicked on. First one police officer, then another started down the stairwell. Both were wearing bulletproof vests. And both had their guns drawn. The first officer saw me and aimed at my face. Another took aim at Charlie.

"Put that down," he said.

Neither of us moved.

The first kept his gun trained on me. The second stepped down into the room, then spoke into a radio attached to his vest near the shoulder.

"They're in the basement. We're going to need a few more bodies down here."

"Are you Daniel Thomson?" the first one asked me.

I nodded. Daniel was my first name. Only people who didn't know me used it.

"Get down on your knees and put your hands behind your head." The officer's voice was louder this time. He pointed to Charlie. "And you, drop the lamp and do the same. On the ground, hands behind your head."

"We haven't done anything wrong," I said.

"That's for the courts to decide," the policeman replied. "Now do as you're told. Down on your knees. Hands behind your head. You're under arrest for the murder of Everett Johansson."

CHAPTER 8
ARRESTED DEVELOPMENT

I'm sure you've seen this in the movies or on police shows. The bad guys or, in this case, our two innocent heroes get down on their knees, put their hands behind their heads, then get cuffed and hauled away to be interrogated. Things didn't quite follow the script. They never did with Charlie.

He set the lamp down and got on his knees. So did I. A second later, I felt the cold steel of handcuffs circle each wrist. Two other officers were coming down the stairs so that four were now surrounding us. I heard a loud ziplike sound and watched while Charlie's hands were cuffed behind his back.

"We didn't kill Johansson," he said. The end of his tongue was rubbing underneath his upper gums. I'm guessing his teeth were dropping. By the look on his face, he was trying to stay calm. I couldn't actually tell if he was nervous or scared. Then I realized he was angry.

"Deep breaths," I whispered. I made certain I was quiet enough that only he could hear me. "You have to fight it."

He kept his mouth closed. His jaw muscles were tense. His pupils were widening. He was snorting like a bull just before it charges the matador. The officers were watching him. I had to draw their attention.

"Where are we going?" I asked loudly.

No one answered. One of the officers took my elbow instead and lifted me to my feet. They did the same to Charlie. I thought he was going to freak, but he didn't. Then we got escorted up the stairs. One officer was in front of me and another was behind. Charlie was ahead, sandwiched between the two other officers. When he topped the last step, he dropped his chin and whispered so quietly I almost missed it.

"Let's ditch these turkeys. Right now. Come on. Follow my lead."

I heard a snap. It was the sound of Charlie breaking the chain of his handcuffs. He grabbed the officer in front of him, spun, and tossed him back so that he hit the officer behind, who hit the officer in front of me. Charlie was so fast, none of them had time to react. I did. I dropped a step and braced myself so I wouldn't lose my balance when they slammed into me. It was a mistake. I absorbed their momentum, and so the officer behind me wasn't affected by the avalanche. He had time to draw his gun. I caught a glimpse of Charlie's coat. Then the back door was ripped off its hinges. The pistol went off an instant later, right beside my ear. I had no doubt the officer missed Charlie by a mile, but the shock wave from the exploding bullet hit my eardrum like a wrecking ball. Sound disappeared. All I could hear was a shrill ringing. My head began to throb. The officer fired twice more. It made me so dizzy I fell into him. He must have thought I was trying to knock him over—to escape. He started yelling at me. I could see his lips move, but I couldn't tell what he was saying. Then electricity jolted through me. I was paralyzed. I tumbled down the stairs. Aftershocks followed. And more pain. I felt another powerful jolt. And another. Someone was hitting me with a Taser, or a stun gun. I couldn't breathe. I couldn't move. Then my head said, *Enough is enough*, and it turned out the lights.

My ears were still ringing when I came to. I was sitting in a chair, my arms behind my back. A table was in front of me. I tried to stand, but I'd been chained in place. I looked over my shoulder. The wall behind me was a mirror. I turned and gazed at my reflection. A young kid with a stunned expression stared back. His face was bruised. His lip was split. His eyes were bloodshot and tired. I took a deep breath, locked it in my chest, tensed my muscles, and tried to break loose. Iron bit into my wrists. Three or four sets of manacles had to be in place. I held my breath and tried again, but nothing happened. I tested the air with my nose. Smelled coffee and gunpowder. The room was small, off-white, square, with plaster walls, cheap ceiling tiles, and a cement floor.

My ears were still ringing from the officer's gun. It was all I could hear until footfalls approached from the hall. The door opened and a man wearing street clothes and tiny, round-rimmed glasses walked in. He was squat, maybe a foot shorter than me, totally bald, with tree trunks for legs and skin that was well tanned. He might have been a professional wrestler at one time. For just an instant, I was reminded of the Nicholls Ward. I wondered if I'd ever seen him there, then I realized it was his scent. Something on his clothes, like antiseptic or some kind of cleanser, made him smell as if he'd just stepped out of a hospital waiting room. He had a folder in one hand. In the other was a Tim Hortons mug. He raised his index finger, which was easily worth two of mine, pushed the frames of his glasses farther up his nose, and took a cautious sip of coffee. Then he set his drink on the table, pulled out the chair, sat down opposite to me, spread the folder open, looked at it, took a deep breath, and waited. After a cold minute, he looked up at me.

"You're Daniel Zachariah Thomson?"

I nodded. "I go by Zack."

"I've been told that. I'm Detective Baddon."

Baddon. I'd heard that name at the zoo. But I'd never seen this man and didn't know anything about him. He laced his fingers together and set them on the table. A wicked scar was on one of his wrists. I took a closer look at his face. He had to be in his forties. Tired, but alert. His eyes drifted up to the ceiling, then back to me.

"You know you were fingerprinted when you came in?"

I didn't know, but I said nothing. He took off his glasses and rubbed his temples, then slipped the glasses carefully back on. I noticed his eyes were watering. I couldn't tell if he was upset, furious, or just plain exhausted. "You're being charged with murder?"

I nodded. And swallowed.

"The top of Johansson's car was torn off. Like paper. Only a vampire is that strong, Zachary."

Vampire! I heard that word and my heart started to throw two-punch combinations against my rib cage. He knew what I was! I could feel his eyes probing. They were intense and focused. Searching for clues. My mouth was open. It had dried up like the Sahara. I had to clear my throat before I could speak.

"I didn't do it."

He didn't look convinced. "This is a complicated situation, Zachary. You're going to have to give me a little more than that." He flipped through the folder, then rubbed his hand over his head. "Why should I believe you?"

Why would he think I was guilty? Moisture started beading on my forehead. Isn't that just like the body? It takes all the water from your mouth and sends it to your sweat glands.

"Inspector Johansson is a friend."

I paused. He waited. His fingers were tapping on the plastic top of his coffee cup.

"That's it?" He leaned forward on the table again. "You've been accused of murder. You're not going to get a scolding and a slap on the wrist for this. . . . You have to give me more than that."

What else could I say? That the inspector was my supplier? Would that make sense?

"He dropped Charlie and me off at the house, then left. He was fine the last time I saw him. Well, tired. But he's always tired. He was going to look for . . ." I stopped to think. He'd gone to look for Ophelia. I wasn't sure if I should mention her name.

"For whom?" I waited just long enough that he answered for me. "For Ophelia?"

"Yeah."

He nodded and stared. His eyes ran over my face. He wanted to know if I was lying. Or if I knew something else. I looked down at the table and the file spread across its surface. A picture of me was paper-clipped to one side. I tried to see what was written there, but the words were upside down in messy writing. Not the best for a speed read.

"Why would your fingerprints be on his gun?" he asked.

My hand and arm twitched when he said this, as though they remembered the terrible discomfort I'd felt when I'd held the inspector's pistol.

"Did someone shoot him?" I asked.

Detective Baddon shifted in his chair. I'm amazed it didn't collapse from the weight of him.

"No. He fired several shots before the gun was taken from him. Everett said you were the fastest vampire he'd ever seen. Who else but you could have moved so quickly? My bet is, you snatched it away from him, which is why your prints are on the gun. Unless you have another explanation."

I did. But after living under Ophelia's watchful eye, I'd learned the value of keeping my mouth shut. Only a select few were supposed to know about us. I doubted Detective Baddon was one of them. Not if he threw the word *vampire* around. We weren't ever supposed to refer to ourselves that way. Ophelia and the inspector insisted upon that. Part of our secret. I wasn't going to tell him anything.

He waited for me to answer the question. When I didn't, he asked, "What were you doing at the zoo?"

We stared at one another. I wasn't sure if I should trust him. If I told him the truth, he might just use it to fabricate a story that would make me look guilty.

He looked down at the file, then up at me. "It says here you tried to run from the house. Is that true?"

There didn't seem to be any harm in denying this, but I was worried that if I started talking, I might not stop and would say something I wasn't supposed to.

"And your friend. He assaulted several officers and ran. Why would he do that?"

I'm guessing it was because he didn't want to wind up chained to a chair at the police station. I should have followed Charlie's lead. But the mention of his name got me thinking about what he would do in this situation.

"I want to make a phone call," I said.

The detective shook his head. "I can't do that. And you know why?"

I didn't know why, so he explained.

"You aren't a typical prisoner, Zachary. I'm not taking any chances with you. We're going to be moving you to a special detainment center until we get to the bottom of this. Given your special condition, you've been labeled a terrorist—a threat to national security. You won't be afforded the same rights as other prisoners."

A threat to national security. That was nonsense. Chained to this chair, I was about as dangerous as a wet paper towel.

He sat back and looked at me. "Everett trusted you. He was a good friend of mine, and now he's in pieces. I want to know why. I want to know why your fingerprints were on the gun. I want to know why you were at the zoo, and I want to know why Charlie ran. You answer some questions and I'll think about letting you make a phone call. In the meantime, you're going to stay chained up behind bars." He stood up, closed the folder, tucked it under one arm, then picked up his coffee and walked to the door. "I understand as a child vampire, you're an endangered species. Don't make things difficult for us, Zachary, or I'll do the worst thing imaginable. I'll let you go. Given what I know of the Coven, you won't survive a week."

He turned and left me alone in the room. I looked around. My instincts were telling me to pay attention, that I'd missed something on my way down to rock bottom. But my processor had more to consider than it could handle. Inspector Johansson was dead. For some reason, this hadn't really registered, maybe because I didn't see him die, or because I wasn't the one responsible, and so I'd been thinking of the whole thing as one big mistake. But now I was stuck here. And he was really gone. Poor Ophelia! She'd be sick with grief.

And worry. I had to get in touch with her somehow. I pulled the chains so they were tight between my wrists and tested them again. And again. The cuffs bit through my skin. I didn't care. I had to do something. But it was no use. Without a hacksaw or a magic wand, I wasn't going anywhere.

About ten minutes later two officers walked in. They were dressed up like grunts from a video game. Body armor, helmets with face shields. One was armed with a long stick—like a light saber. A Taser. The second one had a shotgun out. He did the click-click routine to get my attention. It worked. Then came the superzap. All I could think was *Not again.* Pain burned through every nerve. The room spun. I gasped and pitched forward. My head hit the table. It made a dull thud. Then my eyes closed and I went under.

CHAPTER 9

THE DREAM ROAD

The room was too bright. I turned away from the light and fell on the floor. It was either daytime or I'd been relocated to a tanning salon. I squinted and looked around. I was in a jail cell. Light spilled through a window set high in a concrete wall. A rough cut of cardboard had been crammed through the bars, but it stopped the light much like a screen stops air. Another wall behind me was made of cinder blocks. I sat up, still squinting. The light was unbearable. It made the skin on my face and neck itch. I could barely see, not that there was much in the way of scenery. A sink. A toilet. A narrow metal bench set into the wall. I had been lying on it until a second ago, before I rolled off onto the floor. I reached up to rub my eyes, but my hands were still chained together, manacled to my waist. My ankles, too. With three sets of chains. I guess Detective Baddon was being true to his word. He wasn't taking any chances.

The itch of my skin became a burn. I rolled underneath the bench set in the wall and pressed my back against the cold concrete. It was the only shaded place in the room. As soon as I was out of the light, the stinging began to subside and I was able to look around more comfortably. Outside my cell, at the near end of the hallway, was a desk. An ordinary-looking police officer was sitting there. His dark skin was wrinkled around his eyes, and his tight, curly black hair was receding up his forehead. He was flipping through pages on a clipboard.

I glanced at the window. It could have been noon or anytime

after. I wasn't going to last a day in this place. Then the light faded. I guessed a thick cloud was moving in front of the sun. It gave my eyes a much needed break. I tried to remember what I knew about jail from movies and TV. Then I stood up and walked over to the door of the cell and cleared my throat. I had to take advantage while the sun was hiding.

"I'd like to make a phone call."

The officer ignored me, so I said it again. And again.

Then he put down his clipboard and pen and stood from his desk to face me. His name tag said OFFICER M. LUMSDEN. "No can do."

"But I haven't called anybody, yet."

He grabbed another chart from his desk and examined it. Then he looked at me as though he'd just exposed a plot to overthrow the government. "Says here it's not permitted. I can't help you."

"Why not?"

He thumbed through his papers and shook his head. "Baddon doesn't want you calling out, plain and simple." He turned around and tossed his clipboard down on his desk. It sat near an exit. Like my cell, it had a door of metal bars closing it off from a short stretch of hallway behind. That meant to escape, I'd have to get through at least two sets of bars: the ones of my cell, and the one for the whole jail.

"It's one phone call. My family needs to know where I am."

Officer Lumsden picked up the clipboard again, then stopped and read for a few seconds. Whatever was written there made him scowl. "Says here you murdered Everett Johansson. Now why, if you killed a good friend of mine, would I reward you by breaking the rules?"

"You aren't breaking any rules. I get legal counsel. I get to talk to a lawyer. I get a phone call."

The officer snorted, then turned back to his desk. "You watch too much television. You got the right to sit on your butt and chill. Says here you're a terrorist. A threat to national security. That means no guests, no phone calls, no legal counsel, no chocolate pudding, no bedtime stories, and no favors."

"I didn't do it."

"Right. Like I'm going to take your word over Detective Baddon, who feeds my cat when I'm out of town. Whose son used to play minor hockey with my son. Who's an honest cop. Like Johansson was—before you killed him." Lumsden scowled at me. "You don't have a lot of friends in this place. Don't be bothering me again."

I wanted to tell him that the inspector was a friend of mine, too, but I sensed I would have had an easier time convincing him I was the king of Spain. "Can I have some water?"

I didn't get an answer. It didn't matter. What use was a glass of water? I'd be better off asking for some sunscreen. I went back to the metal bed and lay down on the cold floor underneath. With the manacles around my ankles and no pillow, it was about as comfortable as a bed of sharp stones.

Time passed. I drifted off. I dreamt I was back at our house running on the treadmill. My trial was on television. First I was accused of vandalizing the zoo. Then I was accused of killing Everett Johansson. I was also charged with breaking into his house and wrecking one of his lamps. As if that really mattered. The prosecuting lawyer was Clint Eastwood. He was wearing his cowboy outfit and riding on a mule. Every now and then he'd pull out his gun and shoot someone's hat off, and the jury would shout things like "What a classic!" and "Go ahead. Make my day." My lawyer was a Ken doll. The judge was charging him with contempt of court because he wasn't wearing any pants. Don't ask me what it all meant. I only mention it because one second I was sitting alone on my couch watching the fiasco unfold, and the next minute Ophelia was sitting beside me.

"Interesting program." She was dressed in her old nurse's uniform.

"They're about to announce the verdict." I turned back to the television. My stomach was trying to tear itself loose. I knew I was going to get put away for life if they found me guilty.

Ophelia stood up and turned the TV off. "Asleep or awake, television is generally a waste of time."

I sensed I wasn't dreaming anymore. I wasn't exactly awake, but dreams have a certain quality, and so does real life. I would have put this somewhere in the middle. Then the scenery changed. The walls of the room faded to black and the comfortable bedroom around me transformed itself to the outdoor play area of the zoo.

"What just happened?" I asked.

"I just turned off the television," Ophelia said. "And you changed the scenery."

I looked around. The two dead wolves were lying on the ground, their blood oozing into the sand. I could hear a rusty set of swings creaking in the wind.

"We're examining the crime scene." Ophelia kneeled on the ground and began inspecting the bootprints that led to the water where Charlie and I had seen the fight.

"That's not what I mean. I know where this is. But it's not right." I waved at the play structures and the teeter-totters.

"We are walking the Dream Road together."

"What's that?"

Ophelia smoothed out the folds of her skirt, then looked at me flatly, as though we were talking about the weather. "The Dream Road is one of our best-kept secrets."

That didn't tell me much. She kept everything a secret. My curiosity must have been obvious because she followed this with an unusual amount of detail.

"When you dream, your mind enters a different state of consciousness. One that allows me to enter your thoughts and direct them somewhat. It's my talent."

So that was it. Charlie and I had never been able to figure out what she could do. Vampire talents were a real fascination for us. Charlie thought Ophelia had the power to charm people, like vampires in the storybooks. They could often get people to do things with the force of their minds. Everyone did backflips whenever

Ophelia gave the order. We figured there had to be more to it than just good looks and a strong will.

"Why haven't you ever visited me before?"

. She smiled. "I used to do it all the time when you were young. It kept you from having nightmares when you first moved to the Nicholls Ward. But as you got older, there wasn't the same need. And it does involve a slight invasion of privacy, which became harder to justify. I only like to do it if it's necessary. And it doesn't always work."

"So you can visit people in their dreams? Anyone?"

She shook her head. "Not anyone, only vampires. Visiting normal people is forbidden. This is not something they can know about. But I can visit those whose minds I know well enough to navigate. It is a tricky business, getting in. And getting out. It's easy to become trapped."

I didn't get it, but I nodded anyway.

"Are you okay?" she asked.

"For now. But Detective Baddon says I'm going to stay in jail until I cooperate."

"*What?*" she shouted. It was so loud I was sure it shook the nearby trees.

"I said—"

"I know what you said. Are you telling me you're *in jail*?"

"Yeah."

"You're supposed to be in one of my safe houses! In East City!"

"I was, but I got arrested."

"For what?"

"For murdering Inspector Johansson."

I watched her face shift from surprise to shock. She looked at me carefully. My expression must have convinced her that I was perfectly serious, because her eyes drifted down and lost their focus. This happened when her thoughts turned inward. Charlie said it was exactly what happened to me. A second later, she reached up with one hand and started rubbing at her temples. I called this her headache pose. A short breath escaped her lips. I could hear two quiet words. "Oh, no." She didn't speak for another half minute. Then she came out of it and started asking questions.

"Are you sure he's dead?"

I wasn't, and I said so.

"When did it happen?"

"Last night. Right after he left Charlie and me."

"Why do they think it was you?"

"His car was torn apart. And my fingerprints were on the gun."

"How is that possible?"

I explained how he'd offered it to me because no one was available to watch over the house, and that touching it had caused me pain, so I'd handed it back.

Ophelia started chewing on the inside of her lip. "You are starting to develop a kind of instinct that Vlad had about things. Objects and their feel."

"Is it my talent?" I asked, surprised. I thought you had to be alive a lot longer for this kind of thing to happen.

"Not exactly."

I tried to keep my disappointment from showing, but Ophelia didn't miss much.

"It's something I don't really understand, Zachary. I get bad feelings about things, too. Nothing that approaches pain, but I've learned the hard way that these feelings shouldn't be ignored." She glanced around the children's playground, then down toward the river. "I need to know what happened here. Can you show me?"

"How?"

"Just think about what happened."

That was easy enough. I started with the rave. Being seen by the first vampire. And the second one that dropped from the roof. Running away. Arriving home and finding blood in the driveway, then again at the river. The torn wolf pen. Following the vampire's trail to the water. As I remembered things, the dreamscape around us changed. Everything I thought took on shape and color. It was like being in a movie, only it was my life happening around the two of us, unfolding just as it had. The creature emerging from the woods to attack the vampire. When she saw it, Ophelia was so startled she took a step back.

"What do you think it is?" I asked.

She shook her head and started chewing her lip again. "It might be a vampire. The pathogen does strange things in some people. But it's possible he's a lycanthrope of some kind. A shape changer. That is our best hope."

"A lycanthrope. You mean a werewolf?"

"Yes."

"I thought werewolves turned into wolves."

"I think, like vampires, the range of possibilities is broad. Your father once hunted a werewolf, did you know that?"

I did. My father had written about it in his journal. I wished I still had it, but it had disappeared from my uncle's office, along with Vlad's corpse. According to my father's narrative, he and my uncle Maximilian had used bear traps to catch it. In the end, because it wouldn't stop killing, they had to poison it with hemlock.

"Did you tell Detective Baddon about this?"

"It didn't come up."

"Well . . . He'll find out soon enough." She raised a hand and started rubbing at her temples again, then stopped to stare at me. "Where is Charlie?"

"I don't know. He ran when we were arrested."

"You don't know?"

"He ran off."

"Oh, no," she whispered. Her hand rose to her forehead. "That means he's alone. With that thing out there."

I'm ashamed to admit this, but I'd been so concerned about myself—that I was under arrest and in jail—I hadn't considered that Charlie might be in more trouble than me. "Can't you find him on the Dream Road?"

Ophelia's eyebrows rose just a fraction of an inch and she stared off into space. "It's possible, if he's sleeping. But I don't know him well enough to find him or get inside his mind. You'll have to do that."

"How?"

"I'll show you." She tipped her head down the street. "This way. We should hurry."

We started walking back in the direction of Trent University. "Where are we going?"

"To a window. Do you see it?"

A small patch of landscape was shifting in the air. It looked like shimmering water. That had to be it.

"When you visit someone on the Dream Road, you must leave a window behind, an exit, so that you can leave."

"That's a window."

She nodded, then stopped in front of it. The shimmering patch was about the size of her hand.

"So how do we fit through it?"

Ophelia smiled. She reached in with a finger, then pulled her hand down to the ground. It left a seam in the air, like a rip in the fabric of space-time. Stephen Hawking would have jumped out of his chair if he'd seen this. She stepped through as if she were walking behind a curtain.

"Quickly, Zachary, before it closes."

I followed. A film like a soap bubble passed over me. I reached up to touch my face, but it wasn't wet. A soft, warm glow was around me.

"I've been here before." My voice echoed through the light. I was walking, but nothing was under my feet but a hazy white glow. No walls were around me. Nothing above. Just the same pale glimmer. It was coming from a long way away, in every direction. I tested the air with my nose, but smelled nothing. It was like having a cold.

"Yes, you have been here," said Ophelia. "But not since you were a child. This is the Nexus of the Dream Road."

She was beside me. Shining, as I was. My skin and clothes were luminescent. We were two glow-in-the-dark ghosts.

"What is it?"

"The Dream Road? It's a series of conduits. Like highways that connect the minds of all sentient beings. The Nexus is where they all come together."

"I don't get it."

She smiled. "You don't have to. Just like the waking world, you are part of it, whether you understand it or not."

"This is some talent."

She laughed. Then she answered the question I was getting ready to ask. "You will discover your true talent in time, Zachary. Be patient. You're still young. It might be years before it is fully manifest."

Years? I didn't think I was going to last the week.

"So how do we do this?" I asked.

She looked away and closed her eyes. "Listen."

I strained to hear. My heart was beating. My lungs slowly expanded. Air rushed in through my mouth and nose, then rushed out again. Eventually I heard them. They were faint at first. Voices. Thousands of them. Their words were overlapping and impossible to separate. "Who is it?"

I heard Ophelia sigh quietly. Even with my eyes closed, when she spoke, I could tell she was smiling. "These are the Dream Roads, Zachary. Everyone who sleeps and dreams has a voice here."

"Are they all vampires?"

She shook her head.

"Is Luna's in here?"

"Stay focused, Zachary. Charlie is the one in trouble right now. Keep your mind on him."

I wasn't going to start a debate. Instead, I listened to the voices. Together, they sounded like hundreds of radio stations playing all at the same time. Everything overlapped. "How do you separate them?"

"You don't have to. We simply need to find one voice. Charlie's. Then you can follow it to his dream and speak with him."

"How?"

"Think of him, and listen."

"That's all?"

"I'll handle the rest."

I closed my eyes again and imagined Charlie as if he were standing in front of me. A bit shorter. Dark hair. Serious, but silly. Eyes intense. Smiling. I pictured the two of us at Stony Lake, bombing around in his tin boat. Nothing happened.

"I'm not having any luck," I said.

"Perhaps he's not asleep. Give it one more try."

I pictured the two of us with the girls, Suki and Luna, sitting around a campfire at their old cottage.

I heard a voice. It was faint. My mind zeroed in on it and I started floating away, don't ask me how. Ophelia was speaking behind me. She told me to wait, but I didn't. I felt a strong pull and let it carry me away. Ophelia's voice faded, and the one I was following got louder, clearer, more defined. And more feminine. The white light began to change and I passed through the soap bubble again. Everything was blurry, but I could see colors now. Like a scene through a film of water.

Window . . .

The word jumped quietly into my head. I almost missed it. Then I heard someone else.

"I didn't know there was a test today!"

Panic. I could sense it. I was in a classroom, right in the middle of a row of desks. A teacher was telling people to sit down. He had a suit vest on, and bifocals. A patch of hair was missing right on the dome of his head.

"Young man," he said to me. "Would you please show some consideration for your classmates and take your seat so that we can start the test."

I'd never been in a high school before. It seemed tense. No wonder Charlie had skipped so often. I glanced in the direction the teacher was nodding. An empty seat was waiting beside me. Beyond that, a wall covered in inspirational posters was taking shape. I remembered I had to leave a window, so I stuck my hand in the colors and shapes as they solidified. It felt as if I were touching the soap bubble again. It left a clear, shimmering patch in the wall. My exit.

"Please hurry. We need to get started," the teacher said.

I angled myself sideways to slip into the chair beside me, then realized I was being ridiculous. I wasn't here to take a test. I tried to imagine what Charlie would do. Believe it or not, it helped immensely. I looked the man square in the eyes and told him I'd take the zero. He made a face. I turned and walked to the other side of the class. Luna was sitting there. I was supposed to be in Charlie's dream, but my mind obviously had other plans.

Luna had a pile of books open in front of her on the desk and was frantically turning pages. "I didn't even know I was in this course." She was talking to a girl beside her with a blond ponytail and braces.

I closed Luna's books.

"What are you doing?" Then she looked up. "Oh, Zack. Thank God. Do you know what this test is on?"

I started to laugh.

"Young man," the teacher said again. "What exactly are you doing here?"

I had no idea what to say to this, but it was just a dream, so it didn't really matter. "I need to borrow this woman. She has information that is critical to national security."

Luna had gone back to flipping through pages. I turned back to her. "It's the summertime, you know? You aren't supposed to be here."

The pages began to turn more slowly.

"And you're a vampire now. You don't go to school anymore."

That hit a button. She looked at me. Her emerald green eyes were clearer than I remembered. This time last year, they'd floored me. She tucked one of her copper curls behind her ear. She looked stunning. I smiled. She smiled. We were smiling together. It was wonderful.

"How did you find me here?"

I waved a hand at the door. "Let's get out of here and I'll explain." Then I took one last look around. The faces were pure stress. It was exactly the way Charlie described it. "Man, why do people do this to their kids? It feels just like jail."

CHAPTER 10

CATCHING UP

I did my best to describe the Dream Road to Luna.

"I don't believe it," she said afterward. "This is incredible."

I didn't really believe it, either. But there we were. She reached up and cupped my face in her hands. I closed my eyes and pressed her fingers closer. I would have been happy to just stand like this for weeks. Then she changed the dreamscape. We were suddenly back at her old cottage. Her parents had sold it after *that night*. But it was exactly the way I remembered it, the last time we were all together. A porch swing was creaking behind us. Luna took a seat, then pulled me down beside her. She started playing with the charm on her necklace. The golden crescent. It fit alongside the silver moon I wore around my neck. The two pieces made one necklace, her slender, golden chain lacing through my thicker links of silver. I'd only seen them together once, the day Vlad had tried to kill us. They were old heirlooms and had once belonged to Ophelia. She'd gifted them to my parents. When they died, the two pieces passed to Luna and me.

"You seem anxious," she said.

I didn't know where to begin. "I was supposed to be looking for Charlie." I gazed out over the waters of Stony Lake. Near the dock, the image was clear. But farther from the shore, the dreamscape got blurry. Formless.

"Is he okay?" she asked.

I didn't know.

She squeezed my hand. I watched her do it, but the sensation wasn't quite right. Then I remembered we were in a dream.

"It can't be that bad," she said.

Our eyes met. My expression must have set her straight because she glanced away, nervously, then tried to force a smile. She knew Charlie had been struggling. We spoke about once a week, and it came up often. We used to text each other constantly, but her parents found out and took her phone away.

"He's missing," I said. This required a bit of an explanation. I should probably have started at the beginning and just told the whole story, but conversations don't really go that way. They sort of jump all over. We hit all the major topics. The rave. The zoo. The battle by the river between the vampire and the other creature. My arrest and interrogation. The Underground. Inspector Johansson's death. Even the letter Charlie and I had found with the prophecies. It took all day, and as I said before, the conversation bounced around like a rubber ball. She held my hand the whole time. She only had to ask me if I was serious about a hundred times. In the end, she was visibly shaken. She looked over the water, stood, then sat, then stood again.

"I guess this means I won't be able to come and visit. I was hoping my parents would let me go in a few weeks."

When she saw the look on my face, she reached down and touched my cheek again. "I'm sorry. I know we talked about it all year. Maybe you could come here?"

I wasn't going anywhere.

"Is there some way for me to get in touch with you? Get you a lawyer?"

I didn't think the regular rules were going to apply for me.

"This is a disaster." She sat down again. "Suki is already a mess. If she finds out Charlie's missing . . ."

"He wanted to call her," I said. "Maybe he managed it while we've been sleeping."

She nodded. "She wants to come up, too. I think . . . I think she wants to be turned. She's asked me to do it. I wanted to talk to Ophelia first. But I got the impression if I didn't get on it soon, Charlie would just go ahead and take care of it himself."

This was crazy. "Her timing could be a little better." I was going to mention that young vampires were an endangered species, but Luna knew this already. "What do your parents think?"

Luna shook her head. "They're helpless. Nothing is good right now. Suki has terrible nightmares. That's when she can sleep at all. Mom and Dad had to pull her from school this year, so she hardly spends any time around her old friends. She doesn't talk to most of them anymore. She says they don't understand her. And she's right. They don't. She sees a psychiatrist, but it doesn't make much of a difference."

"Does she think becoming a vampire is going to help?"

Luna looked at me. Her eyes were watering. "Could it possibly make things worse? Most days, I'm the only one she talks to. And she's madly in love with Charlie—from the minute she saw him. I'm not lying. He walked into the sailing club, and that was it. You know the goofy grin he has? He made some wisecrack and it was game over."

I'd heard this before. Charlie's version was much the same, only I seemed to recall his mentioning dimples and a pair of bronzed legs. I kept this to myself.

"So she knows you're a vampire?" I asked.

"Yeah. I know I was supposed to keep it a secret. But—I couldn't hide it from her. It just felt wrong." Luna pulled her foot up on the swing and rested her chin on her knee.

"Do your parents know, too?"

She took a long time to answer. "Not really. My dad knows what's wrong. And he knows he can't fix it. He tried a full blood transfusion, but it didn't do a thing. I guess the infection gets right into the cells."

I nodded. "Ophelia tried that with me. I used to have to get them every few months. God, I don't miss that."

"No. It was terrible. And he was crushed. He was so hopeful it would make all of this go away. But there's no cure, is there?"

I shook my head. "If there was, would you want to take it?"

She took a deep breath. Her answer took a while. "I'm not sure."

"But your father would want you to?"

"Definitely. My mother, too."

"What about Suki?"

Luna's head tipped to one side. "No. She'd rather be like me. Like Charlie. We talk about it. Joke about it. She stays up like I do so we can spend time together. Then she crashes and sleeps twenty hours in a row. It's driving my parents crazy. They fight all the time now. My dad . . . I imagine it must upset him a lot, having two daughters with problems he can't solve. He spends his entire day helping other people and he can't even help his own family."

I fell back into the swing and let my head slip down against the backrest. My stomach was a bed of thorns. It honestly felt as if I'd swallowed a cactus. I'm sure it was guilt. The mess Luna was describing came right back to me, and my decision to involve Charlie with my problems. If I'd stayed away, he'd be at Stony Lake right now, teaching sailing to kids with Suki and Luna. Instead of having to sell their cottage, Dr. and Mrs. Abbott would be up there, too, a picture-perfect American family.

"Is it serious?" I asked.

Luna took a deep breath. She put her fingers in her hair and combed it away from her eyes. Right away, it fell back. "I hope not."

"I hope not, too." I pushed my feet down against the porch to get the swing moving. I was hoping it might help unknot my stomach. It didn't work. I started feeling seasick.

"Are you all right?"

I didn't know what to say. With all the trouble I'd caused everyone else, it didn't seem right to say that I felt terrible inside, that I was feeling sorry for myself. Everyone else deserved sympathy, not me.

"I'll be fine," I said, "just as soon as I get out of jail."

Luna started to laugh. Our conversation had been so serious, I was a bit surprised to hear it.

"Of all the boys to fall for, I had to choose a vampire who ends up in jail. Boy, do I know how to pick 'em, or what?"

CHAPTER 11

VISITATIONS

Time is deceptive. Chain a guy to a chair in the police station and five minutes feels like five hours. But put the same guy on a porch swing with the girl of his dreams, and five hours passes in a heartbeat. Before I knew what was happening or why, Luna started to disappear. I remembered what Ophelia had said about getting stuck. I panicked.

"Quickly! Take us back to school."

Luna's eyes were starting to close. She was like a ghost now, slowly fading. I shook her shoulder gently. "Look at me," I shouted. "Take me back to your classroom."

Her eyes fluttered open. I could see the swing right through her body. "Your test," I said. "You still need to take your test."

That hit a note. The cottage and lake faded. Luna and I were sitting on a desk. She was reclined and falling asleep.

"Young man," said a voice. "Just what do you think you're doing?"

I felt something poke my shoulder. I turned. The teacher with the vest and thinning hair was jabbing me with a ruler.

"You make a mockery of the education system." He poked me again.

"Ah, sorry, but you managed that on your own." I reached past him to the window—the small shimmering patch I had left in the wall. The rest of the room was blurring. I pulled the window open as Ophelia had done in my dream, and I slipped through just as the teacher jabbed me one last time in the shoulder.

I woke up. Officer Lumsden was prodding me through the bars of my cell with a baton of some kind.

"Oh. I thought you were dead." He said it as if he was disappointed to learn otherwise. "On your feet."

I asked him why I had to get up, but he didn't answer. My wrists and ankles were still chained to my waist. My hands had fallen asleep and were starting to hurt. After moving unfettered through my dream, and Luna's, it was frustrating to be inhibited in this way and was a reminder of how much trouble I was in. I rose awkwardly and looked around. My fingers went all pins and needles. I clenched my teeth and waited for the feeling to pass.

A young boy about my age, maybe a little younger, was being admitted. I don't know why I had to be awake for this—maybe they didn't want me snoozing. I felt that I was on display. I probably was. The boy looked as if he was ready to have a nervous breakdown. I wondered what he'd done to get himself in trouble. I listened carefully to what the men were saying. All I caught above the rattle of my chains was that he'd stolen his neighbor's Porsche. Then Officer Lumsden signed him in, and an older guard with a mustache led him down the hall. His eyes were so wide and frightened, you'd think he was being marched to the electric chair. He slowed a bit as he walked past and looked in at me. The moment we made eye contact, the guard prodded him gently with a short baton.

"Hey! You keep your eyes to yourself, understand?"

I'm not sure which of us the guard was talking to.

The boy was taken to the farthest cell in the row. The officer waved him in, then locked the door.

"That kid down there is dangerous," he said in a quiet voice. "A cop killer. He's going away for life. You're lucky. You could have killed someone tonight. Then you'd be in the same boat."

I heard the boy swallow. He glanced my way again.

"Don't even look at him," the officer hissed. "Understand?" The kid nodded. Then the guard walked back with his baton out. It clacked against each bar in the row of cells. When he reached Officer Lumsden, he stopped.

"What is it with these rich kids?"

"Boredom," said Officer Lumsden. Then the phone rang. He picked it up and pressed a button next to the display. "Lumsden here." After a few seconds, he said, "Okay . . . sure thing." After hanging up, he looked straight at his colleague and made a face as if he'd just been canned. "You won't believe it, but that kid has a visitor already."

"Are you surprised?" the older officer asked. "The way parents bubble-wrap their kids these days. Mommy and daddy to the rescue. It makes me sick. Like they don't want him to be accountable. They probably have a high-priced Toronto lawyer who makes my salary in a day. So he gets off with nothing." The guard followed this up with a thorough description of where, exactly, he wanted to place his foot.

"So the kid's spoiled. He's still a saint compared to this other one." Officer Lumsden nodded in my direction.

"Yeah, keeps things in perspective, doesn't it?" The older guard scowled, stroked his mustache, then buzzed himself out. As he turned, I noticed he had a gun holstered to his waist. Officer Lumsden didn't have one. I wondered why.

Officer Lumsden went back to his seat and picked up his clipboard. A minute or so later his phone rang and he pressed a button. I heard footfalls coming from around the corner. The older officer reappeared with the kid's visitor a step behind. I rose and stood at the bars of my cell to get a closer look. Something about the smell wasn't right.

The two stopped at the set of bars closing off the jail from the rest of the police station. Officer Lumsden buzzed them through and I got a good look at the visitor. He was tall, even without the top hat, and was tottering on his feet as if the ground were heaving beneath him. He looked half-alive. His face was covered in short stubble, and his long hair, a mix of black and white and gray, was tangled as if a bomb had just detonated in his face. He was wearing a long, filthy overcoat. Worst of all was the reek of sweat and booze that preceded him into the hall. The older officer with the mustache started frisking him and had to turn his head away to breathe. The visitor seemed indifferent. He glanced around the jail. His eyes were pale blue, as if someone had bleached out most of the color.

I knew who he was.

I met John Entwistle last year when he stole a police cycle and crashed through the front doors of the Nicholls Ward. Then he helped me escape in a Ford Mustang—also stolen from the cops. This set off a series of unfortunate events that led to *that night*. He claimed to be the oldest vampire in the Western World—over six and a half centuries. It was hard to believe. He didn't look a day over two hundred. But he was supposed to be dead, firebombed by my uncle Maximilian. I realized when I saw him that he must have been the vampire from the river, the one Charlie and I had seen with the fence post.

He was plastered. He swayed on his feet as if he might collapse under the weight of his stovepipe hat. I felt as if I were looking at a ghost. I kept expecting him to acknowledge me in some way, to say something to dispel my shock, but he didn't.

"You here to see the Mowry boy?" Officer Lumsden asked.

"Yeah, I need to find a good car thief. I need a lift to Argentina. I hear they don't extradite." The old vampire gazed to the far end of the hall where the young boy was being held. "Yeah, that's him."

Officer Lumsden wrote something on his clipboard. Then he handed it to Mr. Entwistle, who put his signature on it. His hand was unsteady.

"You a relation?" Officer Lumsden asked.

"No. I'm his mentor."

Officer Lumsden shook his head back and forth. The old vampire started forward. "Wait," the officer told him. He reached out and stopped Mr. Entwistle with one hand. The other hand snatched a paper bag from the inside pocket of Mr. Entwistle's coat. "How did you get through with this?" Lumsden removed a bottle of whiskey from the bag and whistled in surprise. Then he opened a drawer of his desk and put the bottle inside.

"Do you have a coat check?" Mr. Entwistle swayed forward. The two men collided.

Officer Lumsden pulled his head back from the horrible smell that erupted from Mr. Entwistle's mouth and snapped, "Watch it."

Then he stood aside to make room for his colleague, the man with the mustache, who was to accompany the old vampire down the hall. I was still standing against the door to my cell.

The older officer had his baton out again and tapped it against the cell bars. He nodded for me to move away. "Back up."

Mr. Entwistle starting backing up.

"Not you."

The old vampire stopped. He was only a few feet away, but he pretended not to see me. Either that or he was seeing double and didn't know which version to look at. He took an unsteady step, then he fell down right outside my cell. His face crashed awkwardly into the bars. Something slid across the floor and hit the toe of my shoe. He was hacking too loudly for anyone else to notice. Without looking down, I stepped on it to keep it out of sight. It was thin. A coin maybe. Then he stood up. He was still swaying, but his eyes were clear and bright.

"I saw you trip me," he shouted to the guard behind him. "That's police brutality."

The older man just rolled his eyes. "Move along."

But Mr. Entwistle didn't budge. He squinted, then pointed at me. "I know you. You're the guy who murdered Everett Johansson."

"That's enough," said the escort. "Keep moving."

I looked over at Officer Lumsden to see what he was making of all this. He put his coffee down and grabbed the telephone on his desk. At the other end of the hall, the young boy was on his feet. Recognition was in his eyes. And fear. I would have bet my last night of freedom that he'd seen Mr. Entwistle before.

The old vampire started hacking as if he were going to drop dead. I wondered how he could be that drunk. Booze, I guess. He cleared his throat and wiped his mouth with the back of a glove. It was filthy. He would have been better off using the bottom of his boot. Then he glanced at me and winked.

"And you broke into that house and didn't even steal anything. All those priceless antiques. I don't care if he was a friend of yours, you could have made a fortune. Kids these days . . . Useless . . . You're worse than that Porsche-stealing vagrant down the hall." Mr. Entwistle's voice rose as he spoke.

I glanced quickly at the kid, who blanched and looked away.

"Don't worry, neighbor," the old vampire shouted, pointing a finger. "I'll get to you in a minute."

The escort swung his baton forward. It extended like a telescope into something the length of his arm. "Back upstairs," he said to Mr. Entwistle. "You're not visiting anyone tonight."

Officer Lumsden stepped away from his desk. Meanwhile, Mr. Entwistle looked back at me and shook his head as if he were totally disgusted.

"I hope they throw the book at you, boy." Then he turned to the two guards. "As a thief and a murderer, that kid is a total failure. I tell you, when they stopped strapping kids in school, this country went straight down the tubes."

He gave me one last look, then stumbled past both officers to the barred gate. He stood there, waiting for them to buzz it open, then bent over and started gagging as if he were going to throw up. Officer Lumsden glanced over at me, then pressed a buzzer to open the door. Mr. Entwistle gripped it by the bars and started pulling it toward him. A second later, he stumbled backward and fell to the ground. It ripped the bars of the gate right out of the wall.

"Oops." He stared at the ruined mess of twisted metal in his hands. "Made in China—I'd bet my hat."

Officer Lumsden put his hands over his head. Parts of the ceiling and wall pulled away. It filled the hall with dust and bits of concrete. The escort recovered sooner. He swung with his baton. Before it made contact, Mr. Entwistle dropped the gate, spun, and grabbed his arm. Then he tossed the man up against the wall. The old vampire kept a hand on his chest and forced out all of his air. The officer started to wheeze, then passed out. Mr. Entwistle eased him down. Then he kicked the ruined bars against the wall, walked over to the desk, opened the top drawer, and smiled.

"Almost forgot my booze." He took out his whiskey. "Hard to stay drunk without it."

Officer Lumsden reached under the desk. I heard a click. When he looked up, the surprise on his face was comical. Mr. Entwistle was holding a gun. He must have taken it from the other officer. How he did it without my seeing, I have no idea.

"Not a good idea—bringing guns down into a jail." The old vampire was suddenly sober. "All kinds of vermin down here. You never know what might happen."

Officer Lumsden put his hands up slowly. "Now don't do anything foolish."

"A bit late for that, wouldn't you say?" Mr. Entwistle waved the gun at me. "Well, what are you waiting for?"

I lifted my foot. Underneath was a key. I bent down and picked it up, then undid the cell door and waddled into the hall.

CHAPTER 12

ESCAPE

M r. Entwistle reached into his coat and pulled out another set of keys. When Officer Lumsden saw them, I thought he was going to fall over. While he gawked in despair, Mr. Entwistle undid all three of my manacles. Then he stepped aside so I could make my exit, but not before turning down the hall to address the kid in the far cell.

"You should be ashamed of yourself, Shawn, taking advantage of an elderly man."

The boy, Shawn, stood and grabbed the bars of his cell. He looked as if he was about to have a meltdown. "But you told me I could take it," he shouted. "You told me . . ."

Mr. Entwistle paused. "Did I . . . ? He scratched the side of his head with the gun barrel. "You know, I think you're right. I did tell you it was all right to take it. That must explain why I gave you the keys. Sorry, neighbor. I take back what I said—and all that stuff about your parents, too. I guess I'll have to drop the charges." Then he turned to Officer Lumsden. "Don't even think about calling up or setting off an alarm." He waved the gun for emphasis.

"Pull an alarm. Are you out of your mind?" Officer Lumsden said. "You're on closed-circuit TV. There's cameras all over the place down here. Everybody in the station can see you. They'll bust down here in about two seconds." He still had his hands up. He pointed one at the ceiling where two cameras were glued to both of us.

"Sneaky. I usually charge an arm and a leg to make a television appearance." Mr. Entwistle raised his hat to the cameras, then turned to me. "Do I need to say it?"

"Say what?"

"Run!"

I bolted past the broken gate and down the hall. What else could I do? My life had become too absurd to make any rational decisions. We rounded the corner. About a dozen officers were waiting at the bottom of the stairs. They were moving forward cautiously, guns out, all decked out in gas masks and bulletproof vests. The first two were carrying big see-through shields. A can of tear gas came bouncing down the hall. I started coughing. An officer started shouting from behind the shield men. He was holding a megaphone.

"Drop the gun. Down on your knees. Hands behind your heads. This will be your only warning."

Mr. Entwistle came to a stop right beside me. I couldn't see much else. I was hacking and my eyes were useless. Billows of yellow gas filled the air. The wall of police officers ahead of us became one big smear. I got down on my knees and put my hands on my head. I was getting good at this. In an instant officers were in front of me with shotguns. They were looking for Mr. Entwistle. He'd disappeared.

Several more cans of tear gas bounced down the hall and the two officers beside me started coughing. Their masks were gone. One got upended. The other turned and shot a cloud of bullets into the wall behind me. Another officer stepped forward, then flew into the air as if he'd stepped into the basket of an air balloon. I could barely see. The other officers were shouting at one another: "Where did he go?" and "What the . . . ?" and finally "Who's throwing that tear gas?"

Another can and another and another were suddenly bouncing along the cement floor. Half a dozen of them were pouring thick yellow vapor into the air. A gas mask landed near my feet. I put it on, then had to duck as a body went flying past me. Then someone grabbed hold of my collar and tossed me through the air. I flew over the other officers, the ones who were crouched at the far end of the hall. My appearance was so sudden, several had to duck to get out of my way. One shot at me with a pistol, and a bullet grazed my shoulder. Then I hit a door and took it right off the hinges.

I got up running. Somehow my gas mask was off. I'm guessing my unexpected trip through the door had ripped it loose. More shots echoed behind me. As I approached a set of stairs, a second bullet nicked my thigh. I stumbled. I might have tumbled down the steps, but Mr. Entwistle took hold of me again and I shot forward toward another set of doors. I was about to stumble through them, but they exploded into pieces just in the nick of time. Mr. Entwistle had darted past at the last second and taken them off the hinges. He was now in front of me, dressed like a one-man assault team, body armor and all. In the haze, with a gas mask on, he looked like one of them.

"The hall turns left," he said.

I slowed to take the corner.

"Oh, no, you don't." Mr. Entwistle grabbed me by the arm and pushed me forward. "The hall goes left, we go straight."

We did. Right into the wall. I turned and took most of the impact on my shoulder. A sharp jolt shot down my arm and I fell to my knees. Then Mr. Entwistle started a Bruce Lee routine that would have seen him nominated into the martial arts hall of fame. He hit the wall furiously with his fists. Cracks appeared in the mortar, then he rammed several cinder blocks out of place. In an instant, he'd made a hole. He widened it with his foot until it was big enough to duck through, then he grabbed me by the back of my shirt and pulled me along behind.

I found myself in an underground parking lot. Police cars were everywhere: SUVs, vans, cars, and paddy wagons.

"Are you all right?" he asked.

I had landed face-first on the pavement. Pain shot down my arm, and the bullet wounds in my leg and shoulder burned. I groaned.

"Is that *aaahhhhh* as in *good*, or *aaahhhhh* as in *bad*?"

"Bad," I muttered.

He reached down to help me to my feet. "Well then, boy," he

whispered in my ear, "let me make it up to you. Pick any car in the lot, any car, and it's yours."

I took a quick look around. I remembered our last ride together. It had ended with the car falling apart and the two of us spiraling into the Otonabee River.

"You leaning towards another Ford Mustang?" he asked.

I shook my head.

He snorted. "Been there, done that, eh? Well, I can respect a man who learns from his mistakes. I try to do likewise. The Ford does have muscle, but perhaps we need something with a little more heft. Just give it a minute, I'm sure the car you want will leap out at you any second now."

No sooner had he spoken than I heard a rumble like an earthquake. The garage doors in front of us burst inward. Something enormous punched through and bounced over the front end of a cruiser. It looked like a cross between a monster truck and an armored personnel carrier, the kind you see troops driving in missions overseas—angled plates of thick metal. Dust, cement, glass, and steel went flying everywhere. The car was coming straight for us. I fell to the pavement. Right beside me was a Humvee. I tried to roll underneath it, but the only person I know who can move fast after he's been shot twice is Will Smith. Then the armored car skidded to a halt in front of Mr. Entwistle.

He tucked the gun behind his back. "You coming?"

I didn't answer. My mouth was hanging open. He helped me to my feet. "This is yours?"

"Yup." His eyebrows rose and he smiled. "A testament to my near infinite capacity to err and learn. Quite something, isn't it?"

"I'll say."

He looked at me and laughed. "Well, just wait till you see my chauffeur."

CHAPTER 13

MR. ENTWISTLE

The old vampire reached down and took hold of my pants at the waist. Then he tossed me on top of the car. An instant later, he landed beside me. A round hatch was between us. He twisted a handle and pulled it open, then lowered me inside. The air smelled like motor oil and steel. I looked around. There, in the driver's seat, grinning ear to ear, was Charlie.

"Man, you look awful," he said. "Don't tell me you tried the prison food?"

I felt awful. Before I could say so, Mr. Entwistle dropped down between us.

"How did I do?" Charlie asked him.

"Ten out of ten, boy. You're a natural disaster." Then Mr. Entwistle turned and helped me over to a row of seats along the inside wall. "See. Told ya you'd be impressed."

I was incredulous. Charlie was the last person I expected. I didn't know he could drive.

"Here. Sit down." Mr. Entwistle eased me onto one of the molded side benches, careful to avoid the blood stains on my shoulder and thigh where the two bullets had grazed me.

"They're just nicks," I told him.

"The bleeding hasn't stopped on this one." He was looking at my leg. "I'd better take care of it." Then he turned to Charlie. "Get us out of here."

Charlie sat down. There was no windshield, just two viewers, each like the butt end of a pair of binoculars. Charlie pressed his eyes up against one, then reached down and took hold of two handles that stuck up from the floor, one on either side of his chair. "It's just like Cyber Sled," he said, laughing. That was a video game with two joysticks, one for each tread of your tank. The engine revved. It sounded like a hungry crocodile. Then it started pinging. I wondered if it was about to explode.

"What's that noise?" I asked.

"Bullets. They're shooting at us." Mr. Entwistle must have seen the concern on my face. "Don't worry, boy, the only thing that can penetrate this armor is parked in my underground garage."

Was he kidding? Before I could ask, Charlie pulled one lever and pushed the other. The car spun. The sudden movement pressed me hard against my seat. Then we lurched forward with a deafening rumble. Mr. Entwistle swayed on his feet, then turned and started nosing through a red case that was stuck to the wall. He pulled out a bandage, wrapped it carefully around my thigh, and cinched it tight. As I was figuring out how to quietly scream, he pulled a harness down around my shoulders, the kind stock car drivers wore on TV. I felt like a space marine. I looked at him. He smiled and winked.

"I thought you were dead!" I told him.

"I thought so, too. But it turns out, I was only at the Olde Stone Brewing Company. Best beer in town. You can't imagine my disappointment when I learned it wasn't heaven." He walked to the front, waved Charlie out of the seat, pulled a harness over his shoulders, then took over the controls.

"Didn't my uncle blow you up?" I asked.

"He tried. But why bother having visions if you can't see when the building you're in is going to explode?"

Visions. Mr. Entwistle sometimes saw glimpses of the future. And the past, too, if my memory was correct. It was his talent. I'm not sure how it worked exactly. He glanced back at me and smiled again. "You've been drinking the good stuff, I see."

The good stuff. With Mr. Entwistle that could have meant one of two things, human blood or Crown Royal. My guess was, he meant blood. When he met me in the mental ward last year, I'd never fed as a true vampire. Ophelia kept me alive feeding me hemoglobin from farm stock. Mostly cows. But the human stuff takes us to the next level. The longer we drink it, the tougher we get.

My friend walked back and strapped himself into a seat across from me.

"How did he find you?" I asked.

"I went back to the rave," Charlie said. "I didn't know where else to go. I was hoping my friends would still be there so I could find a place to crash. Figure out what to do. But Entwistle was there waiting."

"How did he know to go there?"

"Best way to find someone," Mr. Entwistle said, "go to a place they've already been. We are creatures of habit."

I looked at Charlie and he shrugged. I guess his theories about hiding needed some work.

"I still don't get it," I said to Mr. Entwistle. "How did you know to go there?"

The old vampire glanced back over his shoulder. "To the rave? I was there earlier, following another vampire. You can imagine my surprise when you two young bloods ran out of the place."

"He was the one outside," Charlie added. "The one who dropped from the roof."

"Then who was the other vampire?" I asked.

Mr. Entwistle pressed his eyes to the viewer in front of him. "The one inside. He was a Coven agent."

I looked at Charlie and swallowed. His pupils were expanding to a more frantic size. "They sent him to kill us," he said. "When we took off, he went straight to your house to wait. Entwistle got there before us, and the two of them started fighting."

"Is that why there was so much blood?" I asked.

The old vampire, grunted. "Not exactly. I was hoping to talk some sense into him. I guess I was bleeding a little. Then Mr. Hyde showed up and tore him to pieces. I've never seen anything like it."

"Who's Mr. Hyde?" I asked.

"That thing from the zoo," Charlie answered.

"What was it? It moved so fast, we could hardly see it."

Mr. Entwistle answered. "Mr. Hyde? I'm not sure, but I have my suspicions."

"Is it a vampire?"

"I doubt it."

"How do you know his name?"

"I don't, but we need to call him something. Thank God he hates the water. I damn near bled to death getting away. Even after a few pints of the good stuff and a day of sleep, I'm still not quite myself."

Well, Mr. Entwistle looked exactly the same as he had last year. A little messier perhaps. But not a day older.

"Where have you been all this time?" I asked. "I don't understand."

"Vampires my age are hard to kill, boy. Fire and sunlight might be the only sure ways. When that bomb of your uncle's went off, it buried me in rubble. I dug in deep. It insulated me from the worst of the heat. But I had to wait a few weeks to surface. My body was a mess. Burnt. Broken. It took weeks to heal. . . . The trouble was over by then, so I went home."

"Where's that?" Charlie asked.

"Merry old England. I needed information. But as soon as things started to fall apart here, I came back. That's John Entwistle in a nutshell—the best foul-weather friend you're likely to find."

"Why didn't you tell me?" I said.

"What? That I was alive. I'm telling you now. You're doing fine, aren't ya?"

The correct answer was no. I'd been gassed, shot twice, thrown through two sets of doors, and run full bore into a cement wall. My eyes stung from the tear gas, and the rumbling of the armored car had my body shaking like a pebble in a tin can. Everything but my eyebrows was sore. Still, I didn't want to complain. He'd just broken me out of jail.

"Do you have any blood?" I asked.

"No," Mr. Entwistle said. "I used the last of my stash after getting trashed by the fleabag in Round-Two-at-the-Zoo. I lost the first round near your house on Hunter. So my store is all tapped out. Except what's flowing in my veins, but that would probably kill you."

"Why? I've never understood that."

"I don't know exactly. I imagine it's because the pathogen behaves differently in different people. It changes us. And some changes just aren't compatible."

It made sense. Kind of. He eased up on one lever. I felt myself shift sideways as the car turned a corner.

"What was with the wolves?" Charlie asked.

"Reinforcements," Mr. Entwistle said. "I needed the help. But that creature is something else. Stronger than anything I've ever seen, and I've been to Venice Beach." He glanced back at me. "You sure you're all right? You look a little woozy."

He was starting to slide out of focus, but I didn't say anything. I had too many questions. "How did you know I was in jail?"

"I have a few contacts in the department. And I monitor the police radios."

"What was going on with that boy they brought in?" I asked.

Mr. Entwistle sighed. "Poor Shawn. I told him he could borrow my car, then called the cops and reported it stolen. Not very neighborly of me. But they wouldn't let you have any visitors. Some new terrorist legislation. So I needed to get someone else inside so I could visit them and scope things out."

That didn't seem fair to Shawn, and I said so.

"Oh, it won't do any permanent harm," Mr. Entwistle said. "I'll have the charges dropped, but it probably won't be necessary. The cops will put two and two together. They're not stupid. But don't lose any sleep over this. We've got bigger problems."

"Where are we going?" Charlie asked.

"Little Lake."

That seemed like an odd destination. There was nothing there but water. "Why?" I asked.

"This is an aquatic car. They won't be able to follow us."

"Are you joking?"

"You'll know when I'm joking. It will be funny. Didn't you notice the tires on this thing?"

I had. They looked big enough for a tractor. "Where did you get it?"

"The shell is military, special order. The tires are designed for a bulldozer. The electronics I did myself. The engine, too. One of the perks of being around since the preindustrial era. I've been able to follow the evolution of the engine from the steamship to the nuclear sub. Same for computers. It's what you have to do. Keep up with the times. An old dog who can't learn new tricks gets mired in the past. Then you get buried with it."

It was an odd message to hear from a guy who looked as if he'd walked straight off the set of *Oliver Twist*—with a detour through a mudslide. But I had no doubt it was true. If you were stuck in the past, and the past disappeared, where did it leave you? Floundering in an unknown world. That wasn't Mr. Entwistle. I'd once been in his house. For every old book on his shelf, he had a dozen magazines scattered on the floor. Computers, cars, science, business. Like Ophelia, he was interested in everything. It must have been how they stayed connected to the present.

The car lurched left, then right. We hit something hard and it tossed me back against the wall. Fortunately, a padded headrest was mounted right where it was needed.

"What was that?" I asked.

"Roadblock."

"Are we through?"

"Easily."

The car dropped and I heard a splash. The rumble of the wheels stopped. So did the jostling. We were bobbing, instead. "We're on the water now," Mr. Entwistle told me.

. . . on the water now. That sounded as comforting as "we're going back to jail." It wasn't that I hated the water. I just really, really, really didn't like it. Really. I unbuckled myself and walked to the front for a better view. When I pressed my eyes over the lenses, everything looked green. I could see the far shoreline, but that was it.

"Is there a way to see out the back, or to the side?" I wanted to know what kind of mess we'd left behind, and what the near bank looked like, the one that was closest to the police station.

"There are small windows on each side. You can take the helm in a second and I'll check things out." He started unfastening the harness that held him in place.

I put my eyes back to the lenses, then I started to get dizzy. The bleeding in my shoulder and thigh had stopped, but I was still sore. I was going to need blood. And a week of sleep. Charlie took hold of my arm. I hadn't even noticed him get up and step over.

"You look like you're about to pass out." He stared at me for a few seconds, then helped me into my seat.

The car was moving ahead by itself. Behind us, Mr. Entwistle removed something from his coat—the bottle of whiskey he'd brought into the police station.

"Saints preserve us!" he said, raising it to his lips. When he was finished, he walked over to the side of the cockpit and lifted a thin screen. It covered an elliptical porthole set above the bench. "Dammit," he snapped. He walked to the other side, uncovered the window opposite, continued to curse, then did the same at the back.

"What is it?" I put my hands on my knees and tried to push myself to my feet, but I wasn't feeling steady, so I stayed, unbelted, in the seat.

"The shore to either side is being monitored. Cruisers are everywhere. I'd hope to float down the river and exit farther along, where they couldn't be waiting for us, but there's a boat on the water. They can follow our every move. How could they have managed that so quickly?"

"It's the summer," Charlie said. "They always have a boat out this time of year. And usually a few Jet Skis."

"We can't outrun them in this. It's designed for power. Not speed." Mr. Entwistle took another sip of whiskey. "That Ford Mustang is looking pretty good right now."

"We wouldn't have made it out of the garage," I said. "And that roadblock would have stopped us cold."

"Quite right."

"Should we abandon ship?" Charlie asked.

Mr. Entwistle looked horrified. "There are twenty-four hundred horses under this hood. I'm not abandoning this treasure. That's blasphemy."

I stood up and looked through the window that faced the downtown. Under the streetlights a row of police cars were lined up bumper to bumper, their red and blue lights flashing across the neighboring buildings. We were crawling past.

Charlie edged in beside me to take a look. "We don't have a chance. We'd be better off getting out to swim. You can paddle a canoe faster than this thing."

"Yeah, but a canoe doesn't cost you all your Microsoft stock. Do you know how many beer bottles I'm going to have to collect before I can make another one of these?"

"So what do we do?" I asked. "Didn't you plan for this? I thought you could see the future."

Mr. Entwistle took off his hat and held it over his heart. "Of course I had a plan. My plan was to sink. I never thought these tires would keep us afloat."

"Sink?"

"Yeah. I figured we sink and swim out the top." He looked at the hatch, above. "It's why I brought the air tanks." He pointed toward the first-aid kit. I could see several small canisters strapped to the wall beside it. "The top is the only way out. You may be right. It might be time to get wet. We can leave the controls in place. That will keep the tires moving. We've got to take our chances in the water."

I was about as comfortable in the water as I was in the sun. "I can't swim."

"I know," he said. "I watched you nearly drown the last time we were in the river, remember?"

I did. It was part of our escape from the Nicholls Ward last year. It had nearly been the death of me.

"Don't worry," he said. "You can just walk on the bottom."

"Really?"

"Well, there's no harm in trying. . . . Here." He handed me his whiskey bottle. Then he started fiddling with the dash.

The engine's rumble turned into a quiet purr. Then something bumped into us. I heard a muffled sound, like someone shouting through a loudspeaker.

"Turn off your engine and come out slowly with your hands up. I repeat . . ."

"Just ignore them," Mr. Entwistle said.

"What can they do?" I asked.

He pursed his lips and thought. Then he reached out, yanked the bottle from my hand, took a deep haul, then wiped his sleeve across his mouth. "They don't have to do anything. We've got nowhere to go and no way to get there. We're going to run out of gas shortly. This thing drinks more than I do."

"Brilliant," I said. "So we're floundering in this sea cow waiting to get shot."

"Sea cow! Sea cow?" Mr. Entwistle threw up his hands. "Show some respect. This thing can bounce a plutonium-tipped warhead. We can't get shot in here."

"But we can't stay, either."

"Good point." He walked over to the hatch and undid it, then pushed it open. I moved closer and peered up through the open hole. There was nothing to see but stars and clouds. Then the beam of a searchlight bounced off the far side. Enough light leaked in that I had to squint.

"I don't suppose there's any point in waiting." He sounded painfully glum. "I don't normally get attached to things." He looked around the cockpit. "Well, I guess I owe them."

"Owe who?" Charlie asked.

"The Peterborough police. I trashed a police cycle last year, and that Ford Mustang, and a few more in that roadblock. And you de-moed at least three cars tonight in that underground garage, Charlie." Mr. Entwistle took a pull from his bottle. "I guess this makes us even." Then he grunted in disgust. "I really wanted to take this thing to the Warsaw Fair."

It seemed an odd time to get nostalgic. The police were still shouting instructions through a loudspeaker and I could feel the front of their boat bumping into the car. Mr. Entwistle reached up to the roof. I was hoping he'd pull out the controls for a laser cannon, or a giant slingshot, but instead he pulled down a short ladder that was hinged near the opening. It swung into place with a click. He gave it a shake to test it, then grabbed the waist of my pants with one hand and cupped the other one around his mouth.

"Here's your man!" he shouted to the police. An instant later, he raised me off the ground and flung me up through the hatch.

CHAPTER 14

WEED WORLD

I landed on top of the car in the blinding glare of a searchlight. Even with my hands shielding my eyes, and my head turned away, I couldn't make out anything but some blurry silhouettes— maybe four, on the deck of the boat. I could hear another vessel speeding over from the docks behind us. And I could hear Mr. Entwistle laughing in the cockpit of the car.

"Don't move. Keep your hands where we can see them," someone shouted.

I don't think they could have moved me with a keg of dynamite. I was petrified. I didn't want to get shot, and I didn't want to slip into the water, so I just stood there, not moving, and waited for further instructions. They never arrived. Instead, I heard a gunshot. It came from inside the car. Mr. Entwistle was firing the pistol he'd taken from the police officer in the jail.

The searchlight went out.

A pause followed that was just long enough for me to realize I was a dead man, then the police returned fire. I suppose I should have ducked behind the open hatch cover. It was bulletproof. But I couldn't do anything but flail my arms, largely because Mr. Entwistle had climbed the ladder and was pulling my feet out from underneath me. My head shot backward and I crashed into the lake. I started to flail in the water and managed to get my fingers into the deep treads of the back tire. They were still slowly moving and pulled me to the surface. I then pushed myself to the back in a space under the bumper. The police boat was on the other side of the car, so I had a few seconds to decide whether I wanted to stay with Mr. Entwistle or take my chances with the legal system. Then a blue flame arced out from the car. It was Mr. Entwistle's whiskey bottle. He'd set fire to it and sent it somersaulting through the air. One gunshot later it exploded, showering the top of the police boat with burning alcohol.

In that instant, Charlie leapt from the car with Mr. Entwistle right behind him. The old vampire was fast, but not fast enough. A barrage of bullets caught him in the back. His dive became a tragic belly flop. I reached out and pulled him over. He was sputtering and coughing. I felt the tire shift slightly as the front of the car dipped down. Someone had stepped on the top.

"They're coming," I said. "Are you all right?"

He nodded, thumping the chest of his body armour. "I'm fine." Then he patted the top of his head. "But I'll be better when I find my lucky hat." It must have come off in the water.

Charlie swam over beside us. He looked as if he was having the time of his life. "What now?"

"Duck." Mr. Entwistle put a hand on top of my head and pushed me under. I had just enough time for a quick breath, then I dropped as the smaller, faster boat sped past. The prop cut through the water with an angry whine. When it faded, we surfaced. I had one hand on his coat and another on the tire spinning slowly beside me. I didn't want to drown.

Mr. Entwistle had his top hat in one hand. He slapped it on his head so he could tread water with me hanging from his other side.

"Did you guys grab an oxygen tank?" he asked.

I looked at Charlie. He looked at me.

The old vampire sighed, then muttered something about youth being wasted on the young. He reached into his coat and pulled out one of the small canisters. "We'll have to share. Here's the plan . . ."

* * *

I don't know how much time you've spent walking on the bottom of a lake. My understanding is that our primordial ancestors just loved this kind of thing. Needless to say, after half a billion years of evolution, I was totally out of my element. My feet hit the muck at the bottom and I thought I was in Weed World. It was as if I were on a different planet. It wasn't just the density of the atmosphere, or the weird plants and soft earth, but that sound travels well underwater, and with the police buzzing overhead, I half expected a horde of giant hornet-men to descend and carry me off.

I started walking right away, although walking isn't the best description. You had to really push and lunge. It was tricky at first, because of the weeds. They made it tough to see and pulled at my body like strands of a giant, green spiderweb. The props of the police boats were loud, but as we walked farther through Weed World, the sound faded, and my fear of hornet-men disappeared. The frantic activity above us was all centered around the car, which they started to tow away. I could imagine the headlines in tomorrow's paper: *Drunk Mercenary Frees Terrorist from City Jail.*

We went single file. Charlie was first. He more or less swam, pushing off the bottom at irregular intervals. Mr. Entwistle went in the middle and helped us pass the tank back and forth. With his long hair flowing out in all directions and his overcoat, he looked like a dangerous hybrid of lion and manta ray.

Slowly, the water got deeper, and cooler. The plant life disappeared. I guess the sunlight couldn't get down this far. The lake bottom was silt so my feet raised little puffs of dirt with every step. To anyone watching, it would have looked as if I'd gone from the surface of a strange planet filled with exotic vegetation to a desolate moon with little gravity. The only hitch was that the temperature dropped quickly. The two bullet wounds in my leg and shoulder started to ache, and the pressure from the water grew so strong that it started to feel as if I had a nail sticking in both ears. Then Mr. Entwistle pinched his nose and puffed up his cheeks. He motioned for me to do the same. My ears popped and the discomfort went away.

We didn't make it all the way across before the oxygen tank ran out, but it didn't matter. The water got shallow enough for us to walk awkwardly with our heads clear. We had to tip them back so only our faces rose above the surface. Anything else and we would have been spotted. We were nearing the far bank, a good quarter mile from the opposite shore where the cluster of cruisers were still lined bumper to bumper.

"If we go farther upriver, we'll be able to make a clean exit," Mr. Entwistle said.

I knew the area well. It was just down the hill from a kids' park with play structures and a soccer field. I did a lot of running there, and on the bike path next to the water. As we got closer to shore, we heard the barking of dogs. A crew of police officers was patrolling the bank. Mr. Entwistle waved for us to stay low.

"Keep your heads down. We'll wait for them to pass, then we run. Don't hesitate and don't look back. Can you handle that?"

Charlie nodded. I wasn't sure. I was hurt, and the water at the bottom of the lake had been frigid. My joints felt brittle. I was sure if I tried to move quickly, they'd shatter. Normally cold doesn't bother vampires. With enough human blood in the tank, I could wander into a snowstorm with my clothes stuffed full of ice and I wouldn't have come home with so much as a goose bump. But I'd lost a lot of blood from my gunshot wounds, and the cold stiffness in my bones was a sign that I was getting weak.

We waited for the police to pass, then Mr. Entwistle pointed up the bank in the direction of the park. "This way. Let's get going."

I climbed awkwardly out of the water, my knees full of cement.

"Hurry," he whispered. Then he started off at a jog. In a few seconds, he was sprinting up the hill.

Charlie kept up, but I couldn't. Normally I could have outrun him dragging Moby-Dick and half the cast of *The Lord of the Rings* behind me, but now I was spent. My wet shoes squished like sponges as I struggled up the hill, the cadence of my footfalls much slower than it should have been. My body was shivering. I couldn't force it into overdrive. To top it off, my shoulder was bleeding again. The water had washed the scab free and so my shirt was covered with a deep red patch.

I wasn't at the top of the hill before I heard barking behind me. The police officers were a long way off. I doubt they'd seen us. But I'm guessing their dogs could hear my shoes and ragged breathing, because a few seconds later, as I crested the rise, I heard more barking. The dogs were off their leads and on the chase.

I could see Charlie ahead. A vanishing shadow. Mr. Entwistle had disappeared. I started across the field, then looked back over my shoulder. Two German shepherds were racing toward me. In no time, the first was nipping at my heels. Then I felt its teeth sink into my ankle. I pitched forward and hit the ground hard. It snarled and went for my throat. I got my hands up, then heard it squeal. Mr. Entwistle was back. He'd hauled it off the ground by a tuft of fur above its neck. Before I could blink the dog was hanging from the stump of a tree branch, the broken shard of wood resting cleanly under its collar. While it whimpered and thrashed, he turned to square off against dog number two. Both had their fangs out. I was thinking four out of five dentists would have been impressed. Then Mr. Entwistle spread his fingers like claws, hunched down, bared his teeth, and let out a hiss that made my hair stand up. They say police dogs are among the smartest of their species. Dog number two was no idiot. It fled.

Mr. Entwistle turned back to help me up. "Sorry, I had no idea you were so tired. Heavens, boy, you look like a bleached bone. And you're freezing."

I could barely hear him over my breathing. No matter how quickly I kept refilling my lungs, I couldn't seem to get enough air.

"Can you keep going?"

My hands were on my knees. I looked up and nodded.

"Good. Because this place is going to be crawling with cops in a few seconds."

Right on cue, the whir of sirens and the telltale red and blue flashes of their lights bounced up Parkhill Road beside us.

"Quickly, into the trees," he said.

He ran, half dragging, half carrying me through the kids' park and into a cluster of pines at the edge of the field. Charlie was waiting. His eyes were wide with excitement. We scrambled over a fence and started running through backyards. Our pace was slow, but it was all I could manage. At high speeds, a backyard could be an obstacle course. At the pace I was going, I wouldn't have outrun a fish, but at least I didn't stumble into a pool or impale myself on anyone's patio furniture. Soon my body started to warm, at least enough that my teeth stopped chattering.

We fled past a golf course to an area of town I didn't know well, dodging police cars and barking dogs all the way. Then Mr. Entwistle stopped in front of a split-level house near a strip mall. We slipped into the backyard and he jumped up into a tree. I scrambled up after, with help, then followed his gaze to the property behind. The two-story house was dark and empty. I listened, trying to make my breath soundless so that I could pick up anything unusual. After a few seconds, I tapped him gently on the shoulder, then silently mouthed, *Why are we waiting?*

He didn't answer. Instead he hopped down and made for the back entrance. He opened the outer screen door, then tested the knob on the storm door behind. It was locked.

"You don't have a key?" I whispered.

"It's not my house."

Wonderful. So I was about to add breaking and entering to my list of offenses.

"Whose house is it?" Charlie asked.

"It belongs to another vampire."

"Someone you know?"

"Not exactly, but rumor has it she's one of the good guys, even though she doesn't get out much."

Mr. Entwistle motioned for Charlie to bend down so he could step up on his back and reach the nearest window.

"No," I said. "There's no point. They'll all be locked." I didn't even bother keeping my voice down.

Mr. Entwistle looked at me. His forehead was creased with furrows.

"Our best bet's the doorbell." I pressed it. One ding-dong later, I heard the familiar click-clack of hard-soled shoes on the floor.

There was a short pause. The door had no windows, so I leaned in and waved at the small peephole. I heard a dead bolt slide in its casing, then a chain rattled, the door swung inward, and there stood Ophelia smiling like a sun.

CHAPTER 15

BY ANY OTHER NAME

Ophelia stared at me for a few seconds. My clothes were blood-stained, my hands chalk-white. Her smile evaporated. "Good Lord," she gasped. "What happened here?"

Before I could answer, Charlie stepped onto the stoop behind me. Ophelia saw him. Concern mixed with relief.

"Charlie? Thank heavens!"

I would have said something, but I was too busy staring at the revolver in her hand. It was like the kind you see in old gangster movies.

"Forgive me." She set it on a small table that was just inside the door. "I wasn't expecting company. I've been terribly worried about you two."

She hadn't noticed Mr. Entwistle. His back was against the brick wall beside the door.

"What happened?" she asked again. "Are you okay?"

I said I was fine, even though I wasn't. She moved aside so I could slip past. Charlie followed. Then Mr. Entwistle stepped out from his hiding place. Ophelia paused for just an instant, then tried to slam the door shut. Mr. Entwistle stopped it with his hand and forced it open, pushing her backward. She reached for the gun on the table, but he was faster.

"Excuse me," he said, "but I've been shot enough tonight."

I waited for Ophelia to say something, but she didn't. Instead, she stood there stunned while he examined the weapon. He opened the chamber, looked down the barrel, flicked it shut, then raised the hammer and gave the wheel a spin. "You've looked after this well." He switched his grip so that he was holding it by the barrel. Ophelia reached out and grabbed the handle. Her hand was a bit unsteady. He didn't let go until she met his gaze. Neither spoke.

Something odd was happening. Was this just the way it was when two vampires met for the first time—awkward, tense, uncomfortable? Then I remembered that the two had seen each other before. Just briefly the night Mr. Entwistle had crashed through the doors of the Nicholls Ward on that stolen police cycle. The police had been there, so he didn't stick around long, just enough to tell her to get me out of there. I don't know how much he knew about her, or she of him, but something wasn't right. I could feel it. I'd never seen her scared before. Not like this. When she pulled the gun away, her hand was still shaking, the barrel quivering slightly. She kept it pointed in his general direction, as if she wasn't sure if she should start shooting or not. I tried to see him as she would. Hair matted. Whiskers. Oversize boots and fingerless gloves. Weathered face. Intense eyes. Like a refugee from the Apocalypse. He took off his top hat and tucked it inside his coat. I wondered if he wanted her to see the armor he was wearing underneath. If this was a poker game, he was laying his cards down on the table, one at a time.

"How did I fail to notice?" he said. "But it makes perfect sense that it would be you."

Again she said nothing, but I thought something must have passed between them, because he nodded and a deep hum buzzed in his throat.

"The only relevant question is, what will you do now?" he asked.

Ophelia's hand was still shaking, and when she spoke it was with a quaver in her voice. "I appreciate that you've brought them back."

I couldn't remember ever seeing her this way before. Afraid. Uncertain. In the past, even when she was undecided about something and needed more time to think, there was a kind of certainty in her doubt, a confidence that she could work through the problem. Now she just seemed lost.

"It wasn't my intention to disturb you," he said. "I was told you were at your apartment on Clonsilla."

Ophelia stiffened. Her voice went cold. "How did you know about that?"

He reached into his coat and removed his flattened top hat. It looked like a black Frisbee. He started spinning it in his hands. "I've been very busy. Little happens in this city now that I don't find out about." He snapped his wrist and the top of his hat popped out. "I wouldn't impose on your hospitality, but I don't want to leave without some assurance that you can look after these boys."

"We've always managed."

"Things have changed. And they will only get worse. You know this."

Ophelia looked at the floor, then at me, then at Charlie.

Mr. Entwistle went on, "The Underground has been compromised. It's unstable. You can't depend on it. It's happening across the globe. The Coven has fractured. It is warring with itself. But they haven't lost interest in any of you. They sent an assassin to kill these two. If I hadn't shown up, they'd both be dead. And there is a creature out there killing vampires. It is intelligent and determined."

He stepped forward. Normally when he moved, it made me think of a wolf. He sort of loped. But now he was standing at his full height. I was surprised how tall he was, and how intimidating. Had I not known him better, I would have thought he was the King of Mean. Ophelia was holding a gun in her hand, but I sensed, as she must have, that the weapon was irrelevant.

"I am the oldest vampire in the West," he said. "Veteran of the Balkan Crusades, the Wars of the Roses, of World War II, and everything in between. I have never met anyone, man or beast, who was my equal in a fight. Not your husband. Not Maximilian. Not anyone—until now. This thing, the one I call Mr. Hyde, is positively lethal."

Ophelia glanced at me quickly. She must have understood that

Mr. Entwistle was the vampire from my dream. The one who had fought—and lost. The corners of his mouth turned up just slightly. It was almost a smile. Then his face flattened out and he spoke with unusual seriousness.

"I understand that you don't want me here. But how, in my absence, will you protect them?"

Ophelia's eyes were busy—alert. Her voice was quiet, but there was anger in it. "You are *reckless*. If you care about Zachary at all, about us, you'll turn around, walk out the door, and leave us alone."

Mr. Entwistle took a step forward so that the hall light was directly above him. It cast his face in shadow. His eyes looked like two empty holes. "I *have* left you alone. And since my little adventure last year with your ward, I have been traveling on my own, seeking answers to important questions. You know who the boy is. Now is not the time to isolate yourselves. Everything I have read and heard and felt and seen is consistent in this one regard—we are balanced on the head of a nail. One false move and we're finished. Now that Vlad is gone, a long-predicted war has arrived. The End of Days. And the boy has a part to play. We cannot lose him now. You know the price for all of us if that happens."

I was starting to feel like an extra in my own life story. Nothing Mr. Entwistle said was making sense to me. I looked at Charlie. He seemed as nervous and unsure as I did. As if the floor were falling out from under us.

"You have more problems than you can contend with. The Coven won't be in shambles forever. Once a new order is established, they'll come in force. For all of you. Not one assassin. An army. They don't approve of child vampires, or those who shelter them. And you've a more immediate problem—Mr. Hyde. Who else can help you? I'm your last best hope."

"No." Ophelia's voice had a tremor. "I'll take them away. We'll hide."

Mr. Entwistle's head tipped sideways just a hair. Pity was in his expression. "You can run, that's true. But where? And for how long?

Sooner or later they'll find you. Then they'll kill him, and his friends. Unless Hyde devours them first. He exists only to kill our kind. We have to make a stand. As time goes on, the situation here will only get worse."

Get worse? Unless we moved up north where there were twenty-four hours of daylight at a stretch, I couldn't imagine how things could get worse.

Ophelia was still holding the gun. She looked as if she might set it down, but she didn't. "You are asking me to trust you, and I don't. You might have changed your name and your clothes, but you are who you have always been." More certainty was in her manner as she spoke, but she was still a long way from the indomitable person who showed up to save my friends and me from Vlad.

Mr. Entwistle pressed his lips together and turned them up in a smile that had no humor or mirth. It expressed loss and disappointment. "Trust is irrelevant, Ilona. You can't protect him. There is only me."

Ilona. I'd never heard the name. But Ophelia's expression changed when she heard it. Her fear remained, and there was sadness, too. And what else? She was so practiced at hiding everything, I couldn't tell.

"Like you, I have reinvented myself. I am John Entwistle now. And I walk in the light. Well—in a manner of speaking."

Ophelia looked at me. Her expression softened. I smiled. Then she looked back at Mr. Entwistle. Her face could be an iron mask when she wanted, but not tonight. She was still shaken.

"I am not a trusting person. This is not a habit I plan to change. If you are being honest, time will bear you out. But until I am certain, I will not have you here."

Mr. Entwistle placed his top hat on his head. "I suggest you tell the boys everything. Now is not a time for secrets. Or for us to be isolated. Alone, the Beast will destroy us, one after the other." He nodded in farewell, then turned and walked out the door. I heard his footsteps on the back step, then the soft grass. A moment later he had vanished.

I glanced at Ophelia. Much of their conversation had been over my head, but it didn't change the fact that I owed him my thanks. If not for him, I'd still be stuck behind bars with the charming Officer Lumsden for company. This felt wrong. He shouldn't have left. My instincts told me he was right, and that we needed to stick together.

Ophelia must have sensed what I was thinking. "Let him go, Zachary."

"Why can't he stay here?"

"Give it a night. We can discuss matters. The situation is more complicated than you know."

Only because you never tell me anything, I thought to myself. I should have screamed it in her ear. But I couldn't. I was a bit old for tantrums. "I think you're wrong about him."

She let go of my arm. "He isn't who you think he is."

"What does that mean?"

She wiped her eyes again, then took a deep breath. "It is a common thing for a vampire to change his name."

"Is that why he called you Ilona?"

She looked at Charlie, then at me. "It was a name I used once, a long time ago, but it was never really mine."

I thought she might say more, but she didn't.

"Why don't you trust him?"

She looked at me, then at the floor, then pinched her forehead between her fingers and thumb and began massaging her temples. "Things are worse than you can imagine."

Since I could imagine the sun exploding and destroying all life on earth, this was saying quite a bit. "Then shouldn't we accept Mr. Entwistle's help?"

"Well, that's the rub, isn't it? Mr. Entwistle isn't really Mr. Entwistle."

"What does that mean?"

She fixed me with a sad stare. "When I knew him, his name was John Tiptoft. He had many titles. Earl of Worcester, Treasurer of the Exchequer, Deputy of Ireland, Constable of England."

A constable. Wasn't that like a police officer? It didn't sound so bad. None of it did. Ophelia must have sensed my doubt because she finished with a whopper.

"As a constable, he was essentially an executioner. The people hated him for his cruelty. They called him the Butcher of England."

CHAPTER 16

REVELATIONS

I knew Ophelia as well I knew anyone. She was a serious person. She laughed often, but rarely made jokes herself. She didn't kid people. What she said you could write in stone. She'd just told me that Mr. Entwistle was the Butcher of England. Mr. Entwistle, who preached forgiveness. Who believed even the worst vampires should be nurtured back from madness. Who had just saved me from the police and a murder charge.

I looked at Charlie. He was as shocked as I was. "What did you call him?" he asked.

"John Tiptoft. But that is not his name. Not the first. Who he was in the beginning only he can say. But he was John Tiptoft, the executioner for the House of York, when I learned of him. He was ruthless, Charlie. Ruthless."

I wondered how all of this was possible. I thought she might explain, but her eyes were staring at the back door, unfocused. She suddenly looked like a stranger to me. I realized I knew almost nothing about her. Where she came from. Her family. Even her real name. It wasn't Ilona. Did that mean it wasn't Ophelia, either? She might have been born centuries ago. From an age vanished in time.

She looked at me and smiled. There was warmth in it. And love. *No,* my mind told me, *this is no stranger.* People can have secrets, but they can't hide who they really are. This was the person I trusted more than anyone else in the world. Her name was Ophelia and she was the only reason I was still alive.

"I had hoped to talk to you earlier about things," she said. "It was why I asked you to come back with Charlie. I didn't expect things to get so out of control, so quickly. And I didn't expect to see John."

"I think you're wrong about him," I said. "I think we can trust him."

"He was a monster, Zachary."

"Wasn't Vlad?"

"At times. But he was never as bad as history would have you believe." She let out a tired breath. "He was a product of his time."

I wasn't sure what that meant. "Are you going to tell me what's going on?"

She laughed. "I'd tell you if I knew." She looked at me, then at Charlie, who I'm sure was feeling as confused as I was.

"There are clean clothes upstairs. And a laundry hamper. Why don't you two get cleaned up. I'll wait down here."

It didn't take long for Charlie and me to get our bearings. With Ophelia around, everything was always well ordered—fresh towels in the closet, beds turned down, clothes laid out, as if she'd been expecting us.

"This place is like a hotel," Charlie said when he saw new jeans and a T-shirt folded at the foot of his bed. "You don't suppose there's room service?"

I didn't think we should push our luck. I called dibs on the shower and left him in his room. He was making a call when I closed the door—probably to Suki. If I was lucky, I would have time to call Luna after I talked to Ophelia. So after the shortest, most painful shower in the history of personal hygiene, I hobbled down the stairs to the living room, where she was standing near the front window, her eyes far away. Light from a streetlamp filtered in through a thin white curtain, filling the room with a soft glow. I walked over so we were standing side by side, her head near my shoulder. It almost always surprised me how much smaller she was when we stood this close. In my mind, she filled the room.

"Thanks for the new clothes," I said.

She took hold of my arm with both hands and rested her head on my shoulder. "I hope you weren't attached to the old ones. I don't think they can be salvaged."

I didn't care and said so. "I'm sorry about Inspector Johansson. I know he was a good friend."

She didn't answer. She just wiped at her cheek with one hand. I hadn't noticed, but she'd been crying. I'd never seen her do this. Not in nine years.

"Is Charlie coming down?" she asked.

"No. I think he wants to talk to Suki. Things aren't too good for her right now."

A quiet *hmmm* escaped her lips—as if she understood. "That will change. She needs more time."

Or to become one of us, I thought. I knew that was how Charlie felt. I didn't want to mention it, knowing Ophelia would disapprove. At least until we were clear of trouble. If we were ever clear of trouble.

"I don't feel right about Mr. Entwistle," I said.

"I'm sorry. I don't think I ever forgave him for taking you away."

"From the Nicholls Ward?"

"Yes. Putting all that fear into your head so that you ran off. You can't imagine how scared I was. I searched for days. In the end, I was so desperate, I turned to Vlad for help, and so I found you entirely by accident. All this time, in the back of my head, I'd blamed him for all that worry. If he hadn't shown up . . ."

I never knew this. Of course, we never talked about it. We'd both assumed Mr. Entwistle was dead, so there seemed to be no point in blaming him for anything. "I think his intentions were good," I said. "I think they are now."

"I can't risk it, Zachary. I can't. . . . I'm sorry. There is an evil in some men, and no matter how hard they try to bury it, to cover it with new clothes and good manners, it stays." She looked me straight in the eye. "And I ought to know."

I couldn't argue with that. She'd once been married to a man who'd impaled people by the thousands. I never understood how she could have loved him, but I wasn't going to ask now. I was hardly an expert when it came to relationships. I'd fallen for Luna so fast, I'm still not sure what really happened.

"The sun is going to be up soon." She raised her head from my shoulder and walked over to a sofa that was sitting adjacent to a gas fireplace. We sat. "I need you to understand the trouble we're in."

"With this thing—Mr. Hyde."

"That is part of it." She drifted away again, chewing the inside of her cheek. Her eyes were deep and unfocused.

"Would you rather wait?"

She shook her head. "I just don't know where to start."

I was going to recommend the beginning, but I held my tongue.

"When Vlad disappeared last summer," she began, "it sent shock waves around the world. Before him there was nothing. No order. No law. No safety. Not for our kind. You can't imagine how terrible it was. . . . But he changed all that. The Coven of the Dragon changed it. And now that he is gone, all the jackals he chased into the shadows are free to run amok, and his generals—the elder vampires— are fighting amongst themselves."

"What does this have to do with us?"

She took a deep breath. "Everything."

That didn't tell me much. I waited. She sat thinking. I knew our time was short. The sun would be up in less than half an hour. "Have you learned anything about that creature?" I asked.

"Not enough. I wondered at first if he was an agent of the Coven, but I think not. I have spoken with other vampires who agree. They are all scared. Or they were."

I didn't know Ophelia was in touch with other vampires. "Can't we team up with them? Get more help?"

"No."

"Why not?"

"Because he's killed them all."

She looked at me with a flat expression on her face. But under-neath, I could see she was trying hard to keep herself level. I re-membered what Inspector Johansson had said, that other vampires had disappeared—good ones. No wonder she was so rattled. It was all the more reason to get help from Mr. Entwistle.

"Do you think we can beat it?"

Ophelia reached down and straightened the folds of her dress. "I don't know if it matters."

That made no sense to me, and I said so.

"Have you read The Book of Revelation?"

"From the Bible?"

"Yes."

I shook my head.

"It predicts that two Beasts will emerge, who, along with Satan, form an unholy trinity that will try to usurp control of the earth from God, His son, and the Holy Ghost. The Bible predicts that good will triumph in the end. That God will reestablish Himself as the absolute holy sovereign. Many vampires believe a similar cycle will occur in our world, but the ending isn't so certain. Order will fall into chaos and a new order will emerge. This creature you call Mr. Hyde is a being likened to the Beast of the Apocalypse, and so whether we beat it or not, many have taken it as a sign that the de-struction of the old order is upon us."

"Do you believe it?"

She looked at me, thinking, then gazed out the window. "It is hard not to believe it because it is happening. When Vlad was nearly destroyed last year, and disappeared, it was the first sign that the old order was failing. Now, his Coven is infighting and impotent, and the Underground is falling apart as a result. The appearance of Mr. Hyde is a sign to many that the destruction of the vampire world as we know it is at hand. Already, he is international news in the vam-pire world."

"Is this what Mr. Entwistle meant when he said a war has ar-rived? The End of Days?"

Ophelia nodded. "Vlad held the Coven together with an iron fist. Now that he is gone, the others are fighting for control. Most of this is happening overseas, so we've managed to stay clear of it. But the Coven has an interest in you. John is right. They will come for us."

"Because I'm a child vampire."

"Partly. But there's more to it than that. It has to do with your fathers."

She paused, so I could digest the word *fathers*. I knew what she meant. Every vampire has two kinds of parents. The normal human variety—and the vampire that turns them.

"You are Vlad's progeny," Ophelia continued. "And so they will fear you, because in time, you will come to have his power. But the Coven also feared your true father. And they fear you, because of him."

When she spoke about my true father, her voice changed. It always did when she talked about him—Dr. Robert Douglas Thomson, archaeologist and vampire hunter. I once thought that she must have loved him, but I wasn't so certain now. It might simply have been that she felt sorry for me. For my loss.

I felt her eyes on me again. Did she want to know if I believed her? Well, of course I did. Ophelia never lied. Never. So I believed her even when she didn't make any sense.

"I don't understand. Why would anyone fear my father? Or me?" This might seem like a stupid question considering my father's secret profession. But he never killed vampires, no matter how far gone, without giving them a chance to prove that they could be good—that they could live with the infection and not harm others. It made no sense that they would be afraid of him. He wasn't a threat unless they chose to do wrong. And I was seven when he died. Who would fear a boy that young? Only army ants and babysitters.

Ophelia managed a brief smile. It flickered across her face, then disappeared as she looked away. "The answer lies in an ancient prophecy. It concerns a messiah. A vampire who will overthrow the old order, emerge from the ashes of chaos, and re-create a new world. A better world."

Was this about the letter that Charlie and I had read the night of our arrest? About the Lamb? "What does this have to do with me?"

Ophelia sighed. "According to most versions, the future messiah of the vampire world is an orphan, the son of a great hunter. And this orphan would die and come back. Does any of this sound familiar?"

I caught myself swallowing hard. It was familiar. It fit neatly with what I'd read in that letter Charlie and I had found—about the sun scorching me with fire. And a second death that wouldn't harm me. That had happened last year. Death and rebirth.

I told Ophelia about reading the letter. "Do you believe what it said?"

"I'm not a prophet, Zachary. But there is something compelling in all of this. And I'm not the only one who thinks so. Vlad felt it, too. It was why he wanted you all to himself." Her eyes got their far-off look again.

My mind drifted back to *that night*. Vlad had wanted to kill my friends. To sever all of my personal connections so that the only future I had as a vampire was with him. And he'd wanted me to suffer, thinking it would make me stronger.

Ophelia stood up and stretched. She lifted the thin, white curtain hanging in front of the bay window and peeked outside at the sky, then across the street. "So you see why we're in trouble? It isn't just the Beast. It's the prophecy. All of the elders know about it. And so every power-hungry vampire who wants control will regard you as a threat because you are the orphaned son of a great vampire hunter. And you have died twice. Even if you weren't a child vampire, they would hunt you down. It is the only way they can ensure that you don't rise up against them, as the prophecy predicts."

I was stunned. I'd always known there were reasons for secrecy, but in the back of my mind, it was a temporary thing, based on my age. How much longer could I be considered a child, especially if I demonstrated I was stable and wouldn't attract attention or spread the virus carelessly? But if I was some kind of messiah—how could I outgrow that? I couldn't. I'd be stuck with it forever, even if it wasn't true, and it didn't seem to me that it was possible. I couldn't even keep my socks sorted.

"That makes no sense."

"That you're a messiah." Ophelia laughed quietly. "Chosen to establish and rule the new order." She reached down and took my hand, then helped me off the sofa. "Stranger things have happened. But if the End of Days for our kind is here, someone will emerge as the leader of a new Coven, because such an organization is necessary. And given what I know of our kind, I would much rather see you in charge than anyone else." She looked at me and smiled, then reached up and pinched my cheek. "But maybe that's just my prejudice." She glanced back at the window.

I could feel dawn approaching. It filled me with a mild unease.

"I think we should talk more about this later," she said.

I wasn't quite ready to end the conversation. I felt exhausted, but I knew I wouldn't sleep well until my questions were answered. "What are we going to do about Mr. Entwistle?"

"I wouldn't worry about him for today. I'm sure he can look after himself."

"But are we going to let him stay with us?"

"I don't want to have to decide anything just yet. I need to think about this a bit longer. He might be right. We might need him." She looked up at me. "I don't trust him, Zachary."

"Because of who he was?"

She nodded. "If you could have seen it—the things he did as John Tiptoft."

Well, I didn't know anything about that. I didn't want to. I liked him as John Entwistle. So did Charlie. And I think my father would have liked him. Luna, too. I'd never seen a hint of malice in him.

"I can't afford to take any chances, Zachary." Ophelia was watching me closely.

"So what are we going to do?"

She smiled, and shrugged. I couldn't remember her ever doing that. She always had a plan. And a backup plan. And a backup to the backup plan. Order. Routine. Structure. Careful planning. I fully expected that if an asteroid hit the earth and civilization ended, she'd have a spaceship handy and our destination mapped out on sticky notes.

"We'll talk some more later. Does that sound all right?"

I nodded and headed for the stairs. If I hurried, there might be enough time to call Luna. It had been a heavy night. I wanted to hear her voice. I was certain that would lift my spirits.

"Do you need anything else?" she asked.

Just a few minutes on the phone, I thought. And some blood would have been nice, but if she'd had any, she would have offered it by now. "No, but thanks."

"Sleep well. And try not to worry too much."

I said I wouldn't, which I hoped was true, then went upstairs to check on Charlie.

When I found him, he was lying sideways across his bed with his head hanging upside down over the edge of the mattress, his cell phone pressed to his ear.

"It's Zack. Just a second," he said to the person on the other end. Then he pulled the bottom of the phone away from his mouth. "What's up?"

"The Beast of the Apocalypse is on the loose and every power-mad vampire in the world wants to kill me."

"So nothing's changed?"

"I guess not. Is that Suki?"

"Yup."

"Is she doing all right?"

"Well, she's talking to me, isn't she?"

"Is Luna handy?"

Charlie repeated the question to Suki, then waited. A few seconds later he shook his head. "She went to bed. But apparently, she expects to see you in her dreams."

"Lucky me." Then I backed out the door and pulled it closed behind me.

CHAPTER 17

THE PROPHET

Growing up as an orphaned vampire in a mental institution, I missed out on a lot of things. Suntanning. Family picnics. Hand-me-down clothes. Popsicles. The list would fill an encyclopedia. Well, one of the things I'd missed out on was the thrill of nightmares.

As a little kid I got them all the time—lost dreams, being-chased dreams, scary-monster dreams, not-having-my-costume-ready-for Halloween dreams, Santa-missing-my-house dreams. But in the Nicholls Ward—nothing. Not a single nightmare. I understood now that this was Ophelia's doing. She walked the Dream Road to keep me safe, even while I slept.

So I was caught off guard when I found myself back at Iron Spike Enterprises, the office of my uncle Maximilian, having a nightmare. This was where my friends and I had been tormented by Vlad. Now, I was alone with the paintings and the statues and the antiques, the desk and the couch and the shattered windows. Everything was just as we'd left it.

I began to search for my father's missing journal, but I could feel that something was wrong. A restless presence, cold and evil, was approaching. I realized Vlad's remains should have been here. The sun had reduced his body to a roasted skeleton. I had to find it. I renewed my search, but the office kept changing. Every time I checked some area and looked up, everything else would have moved, so it was impossible to know where I'd actually looked. A sense of dread hung over me as I scrambled around. He was in this mess some-where, and I knew that the longer I took, the more likely it was that someone would bring him back—just as I had been brought back. Then he would find me and I'd have to relive the horror of *that night* all over again.

I started walking down a corridor—the secret passage my uncle had used to escape. Then I remembered—this was where I'd thrown Vlad's body. I sensed his evil here. It was approaching from behind. There was a door ahead. A way out. I started to run, but my legs were leaden, the injured one almost useless. It was bleeding and sore. The harder I tried to move, the slower I got. Vlad was getting closer. Right behind me. I wasn't going to make it.

"It's okay."

I stopped and took a deep breath. It was Ophelia.

"Thank God," I said. I ran my fingers through my hair and leaned against the wall. When I looked up, we were back at the Nicholls Ward. I had my scrubs on. I could tell by the sky outside that it was time to get ready for bed.

Ophelia had a look of relief on her face. There might have been some pity, too. "Are you all right?"

I sighed. "I am now." I started walking toward my room. Ophelia wasn't following me. "What is it?"

Her eyebrows rose and she tipped her head forward. "Zachary, you don't live here anymore."

That was true. I don't know what I was thinking. We lived together on Hunter Street now. No sooner did I imagine the inside of our house than we were standing together in the living room. "Are *you* all right?" I asked.

Ophelia nodded. "Yes. I'm fine. But I need to take you to see someone."

"Like a doctor?"

She shook her head. "No. Nothing like that."

I had hoped that if I was going to be traveling the Dream Road, I'd get to visit Luna again, but Ophelia obviously had other plans.

She asked me to close my eyes, then took hold of my hand. A warmth passed over my face. A glow.

"Can I open them now?"

"Not yet," she said, but I'd opened them anyway. I had been expecting her to say yes, so my eyelids slipped up just a crack. I didn't see much. Just soft, pale light. It was everywhere. We were back in the Nexus. I heard the voices again. A symphony of overlapping dream songs. I pinched my eyes shut.

"Now," said Ophelia.

When I opened them a second time, I was inside a dark building. I could hear birds singing outside, and the hum of insects. A huge set of double doors was open in front of me. A field stretched out to the edge of a forest, which receded down a mountain slope. The wind danced through the tall blades of grass and ruffled the pine trees. The sun was shining, but I wasn't afraid. Wildflowers were in bloom. I looked up at the decorated arches overhead. I'd seen a place like this before—in pictures.

"Are we in China?"

"No, this is Tibet, 'The Roof of the World.'"

I stepped onto the threshold so I could walk outside. Then I felt Ophelia's hand on my arm, stopping me.

"This way."

I turned and nearly tripped over a small gong sitting on the floor. Beside it was an open fireplace set deep in the floor.

"To him who overcomes, I will give the right to sit with me," said a voice.

I didn't know anyone else was in the room. My whole body jerked in surprise. I followed Ophelia's gaze to the far side of the temple. Although my eyes were usually good in the dark, I had trouble penetrating the shadows. Smoke was in the air, too, rising from two incense burners set on the floor. A pipe like a water pitcher with a huge stem was sitting between them. Only when the neck of it rose into the air did I see the man who had spoken. He was old and dressed in a robe that might have been orange at one time, but now seemed to reflect the shadows that surrounded him. He sat cross-legged on a matt. Smoke drifted in two slow ribbons from each of his wide nostrils, and more curled around his head, which was bald. His eyebrows were impossibly long and seemed to float in the air like insect wings. Stranger still were his eyes. They were missing. Skin grew over his empty orbits.

"For the Lamb will be their shepherd," he said. "And he will lead them to springs of living water." His voice was faint, but oddly musical. It was followed by a quiet sound. Almost a purr. It took me a moment to realize he was laughing. "I am Baoh, the Prophet. And you are welcome here."

Baoh—that was the name Charlie and I had seen in the letter we'd found at the safe house.

Ophelia bowed her head. "This is Zachary. Son of the late Robert Douglas Thomson, the great vampire hunter."

"You place us all in great peril, woman of the desert."

He raised a hand and waved for Ophelia to go. She was still holding my arm. She clung to it a moment longer, just so I would look at her. When I did, she nodded once, then walked toward the door.

"The first woe is past; two other woes are yet to come," the man said in a loud voice. His head was cocked to the side as though trying to get a better view of Ophelia as she disappeared across the field.

I wondered how he could see with no eyes. A few awkward seconds passed.

"Is she gone?" he whispered.

I was so surprised by his question and the change in his voice that I didn't answer. He didn't seem to notice. Instead, he rose to his feet slowly, as if his joints were stiff, and waved a hand in front of his face to clear away the smoke.

"You want a drink, gringo?"

I shrugged. "Um . . . okay." I glanced back at the temple doors. They were closed. When I turned back, the man was gone. I had a flash of panic. I didn't want to be stuck here alone. A second later he appeared at my side. The top of his head barely reached my shoulder. He had two gold goblets, one in either hand. He passed one to me. It had a red liquid inside. It might have been blood, but I couldn't tell. I sniffed at it, but my nose didn't seem to be working. He tapped the edge of his drink against mine, then raised it up.

"To eternal life. And miniskirts." He drained it in one go, then his head shook. "Whoa. That hits the spot."

I took a reluctant sip. It tasted sweet, and salty, and warm. Like blood mixed with something better than blood. I drank. A pleasant euphoria filled my limbs.

"Not, bad, eh?" Baoh said, placing his hand on the small of my back. He waved his other hand about the room as though the place was a colossal disappointment to him. "I don't know why she insists on these stuffy meeting places." He shook his head. "Poor Ophelia. Sooooo sad. Sooooo serious." He moved me gently to a door at the back. "But Baoh's a media man, eh. Give the people what they want! Doom and gloom. A little hope. Something from Revelation, maybe. And a way forward." Then he clapped me on the shoulder. His other hand reached into the folds of his robe and came out with a pair of sunglasses, which he slipped over his skin-covered orbits. "I gave up my eyes for true sight." His voice was suddenly melancholy. "And now look at me."

The door opened. Noise exploded inward. Cars. Horns. Loud music. Neon light. Wind and exhaust. Grease from a thousand deep fryers. Steam from a thousand soup kitchens. I found myself standing on top of a huge apartment building. Behind was a penthouse suite that looked to be made mainly of glass. Not a typical dwelling for a vampire.

"Ahhh, this is more like it!" Baoh shouted.

"Where are we?"

He laughed and spread his hands. His clothes had changed. He was now wearing a loose silk shirt and bell-bottom trousers. It did a perfect job of showing off his skinny legs and potbelly. "The center of the universe. Tokyo!"

"How did you do it?"

He laughed. "This is nothing. You should see me with a Ouija board."

He turned and reached for a tray. A waitress in high heels was holding it beside him. I wondered if she'd just appeared out of thin air. She had mascara plastered over her large almond eyes and was wearing less clothing than your average hamster. He reached up to a decanter, then filled two thimble-size glasses and handed one of them to me. "Drink up. You're with one of the old boys now."

My eyes were still on the waitress.

"Bah, don't mind her. She's not really here." He waved a hand and she walked away. "Come on inside." He downed his drink.

I was still looking at the clear liquid he'd handed me.

"He who hesitates is lost," he said. Then he took the drink from me, knocked it back, and tossed the empty vessel over his shoulder. I didn't hear it land. "One should never overdo opium on the first night. It can stop your heart faster than a long, tall woman in a black dress."

Opium? Was that what had made the blood taste so good? I wasn't sure if I should ask, so I kept quiet and followed him across the terrace, through a set of glass doors, and into an apartment that looked more expensive than the Vatican. At least a dozen women were inside.

"Out. Out. Out. Out. Out," he shouted. Once the room was clear, he put his hand beside his mouth and whispered, "Don't you dare tell them how old I am. It's hard enough getting a date when you have no eyeballs." He picked up a remote for the TV, which was about ten feet across and mounted on the wall.

"So, you want to talk to old Baoh, eh? Well, young man, there is a price. There is always a price."

I had no money. No valuables. This was going to be a short meeting.

"There are many ways of paying." He faced me so we were standing toe-to-toe. "I am of the ancient world—an age long past. But some things endure through time, and human nature is one of them. Pride. Courage. The need to prove oneself. Fear of failure. There are countless examples. Truths that don't change. You understand?"

I nodded.

"Cowardice, greed, selfishness. These also endure." His voice grew angry. Then he calmed. "So what kind of man are you becoming?"

I didn't have an answer for this.

"In my time, all men were tested by adversity. Pain, loss, struggle. There is less of this now. Life is too easy. But there is one arena in which a man's true nature could always be discerned, in this or any age. It is the crucible of war, of combat. You cannot know a man until you see him in battle. The truth of this endures also. And so you must be tested." He leaned forward. His voice grated against my ears. "Fail me, young blood, and you're doomed."

CHAPTER 18

THE PROPHECIES EXPLAINED

Baoh's back was to the television. The remote was still in his hand. Without turning, he reached over his shoulder and clicked it on. Then he nudged me to the side so we could stand shoulder to shoulder.

"You're a Microsoft man. I can tell." He handed me a Nintendo controller. "I prefer the Wii myself." When I accepted it, he bowed. "We shall see what kind of man you are becoming. The ancient sport of boxing. Or close enough. I much prefer this version. Less painful. But still a valid test. One you'll need to pass, if you intend to survive the End of Days."

I stared at the screen. This wasn't at all what I expected. I wondered if this was how Alice felt when she fell down the rabbit hole into Wonderland.

He turned to face the television as the game loaded. Then we chose our avatars, the little figures that would represent us in the fight. Instead of the usual dozens to choose from, there were only two—a blind monk with oversize eyebrows in an orange robe and a jogger in scrubs with a widow's peak. It seemed fitting.

As soon as the bell sounded, I stepped forward and threw a jab. I followed up with a right cross and left hook. He ducked and countered. I put up my guard, then dropped a good one on his nose.

"That was pure luck," he shouted.

I did it again.

"Take advantage of a blind man, will you? Shame! Shame!"

The third time I moved in, he pounded me back with a flurry of his own. "See? Hah. Thought you could get the better of old Baoh!"

His flurries continued. "I got you figured out, young blood. You're finished now."

He floored me. This happened again. And again. I struggled to my feet. Or, my avatar did. His eyes were crossed and he wobbled on rubbery legs.

"You're just being stubborn now," he said.

The fight ended a few minutes later with his icon, the monk, unconscious on the mat.

Baoh whacked his controller against his palm. "This thing's not working right. Must be a loose wire." He tossed it with disgust onto the sofa, then walked behind a counter and started pouring himself a cocktail. "You're not too shabby. Ophelia would be proud of you. Focused. Difficult to frustrate. Slow to anger. Little vanity. A good balance of aggression and self-preservation. Patience. Confidence. Little fear, just enough to keep you on your toes. You lack a recognizable game plan, but otherwise, she has done well."

It sounded like a compliment, so I said thanks.

"Courteous, too," he added, holding his drink up to the light. He lowered it under his nose. It wasn't quite right, so he continued to fiddle with the ingredients. "Combat, still the best test of a man. Even in a video game. Who you are—it comes through in all that you do, no?" He fixed me with his eyeless stare. "So . . . here is the real test! What did you learn about me?"

His question caught me completely off guard. I took a deep breath. What had I learned? That he could have used a bit of time in the Nicholls Ward. "You don't take yourself as seriously as I expected you to."

He nodded as if this was true.

"You've adapted to the times. You aren't stuck in the past."

"Keep going," he said.

"There's little bitterness in you." I glanced around the room. "You enjoy your life—being a vampire, having fun. You've surrounded yourself with things that are beautiful." Once I got going, I was on a roll. "You're good-humored. Observant. You see remarkably well for a man with no eyes. And you could have beaten me, but you didn't."

"And what does that tell you?"

"That you're willing to suffer a loss to learn something."

"Not bad. You missed a few things. My incomparable charm, for example. And superior intelligence. But I forgive you." He raised his glass as if he was saluting me, then took a cautious sip to test it. The face he made told me he approved. "So what did Ophelia want? Not just for us to meet, I think, eh? She had something specific in mind."

"I don't know. She's great at keeping secrets."

Baoh took a seat on the sofa. "Baaahhh," he scoffed. "All women are that way. Knowledge is power. Men have to learn it. Women know by instinct." I heard him crunch on an ice cube. "So what do you have to ask? Everyone has questions these days. Where do I invest my money? How do I lose weight without exercising or changing my diet? What's the best way to make my ex-lover jealous? You need help with your résumé?"

I shook my head. And thought. The first question that popped into my mind was *How did you get to be such a weirdo?* But it didn't seem appropriate. "Do you know anything about this Beast? The one that's going around killing off vampires?"

"What?" He spat out his ice and started hacking. It took him a moment to recover. "No one told me about this!" He looked over his shoulder as if the door to the living room were about to explode off the hinges. "I hope he isn't following you."

"No. He isn't." I had to pause to think. "You mean you don't know anything about this?"

"When you get to be my age, no one tells you anything. They just assume you know it all. Does this Beast have a name?"

"We call him Mr. Hyde."

"Does he have seven heads and ten horns?"

I shook my head.

"Well, that's a relief. Seven heads and ten horns would be bad. Where is all this happening?"

"In Peterborough."

"That is also a relief." Baoh wiped his shirt clean where he'd spilled his drink. "But not to you, I suppose. You live in Peterborough?"

"Yes."

"Is that the place with that big tower that spins?"

He must have meant the CN Tower. "No, that's in Toronto."

"Right, right." He took another drink, then pointed a thumb over his shoulder. "Want a rematch?"

I started shaking my head. "I thought you were a prophet. That you could give me some advice."

"I am! But what were you expecting? Prophecy is not an exact science. If it were, I'd have bought Microsoft stock back in the eighties. And I can't prophesy on the Dream Road."

"Oh."

"So you don't have any questions?"

I had tons, once I'd thought about it. "I need to know how to beat this thing. And how to deal with the Coven."

"Yikes. I'll need something stronger for that." He rose and went back to the bar. "Now where did I leave my opium pipe?"

"It's back in the temple."

His face sank. He started digging through a liquor cabinet.

"I read some of your prophecies. Some of them I didn't understand."

Baoh was pouring himself another drink. "I don't understand them, either." He waved his hand in a circular motion as if trying to remember something. "And those prophecies weren't really mine." He tested his concoction and made a face, then added more alcohol from the bottle he was holding. "No. They've been around for centuries. I just tweaked them a little bit. Creative license, eh. Not a bad job. Baoh aims to please."

I couldn't believe what I was hearing. Was this guy some kind of sideshow phony?

"Baaahhh. Don't get so upset. Prophecies are like that. Difficult to read. Over time, they change, or perhaps we change and see the signs differently. The originals bore no fruit, either. They were human prophecies for a human world. Or so we first thought, centuries ago. A noble hunter would die and leave his sons orphaned. It is over six hundred years old. Very close to the ones you read the other night." He reached into his shirt pocket and unfolded a piece of paper. Then he set it on the coffee table so we could both see it. It was the letter from Mutada.

"Where did you get that?"

"From your memory," he said. "This is a shared dream, after all.

"This is a mistake," he said, pointing to the page.

> The Lamb will be their shepherd [indecipherable muttering follows] . . . a scourge. He will lead them to springs of living water . . . to destruction. Behold, he is coming soon.

"Indecipherable muttering? You've got to be joking! I was as clear as the tax man." He waved a hand over the passage. "Amateurs!"

> The Lamb will be a shepherd or a scourge. He will lead them to springs of living water, or to destruction. Behold, he is coming soon.

He pointed to it, then took another sip. "There, that's better. And much improved over the original version. It was in Latin, you know, although I'm told there's a Han version that's older. No one can find it. Probably destroyed in the Cultural Revolution. But if you're a fan of irony, you'll like this little twist. In the fifteenth century, the prophets all lined up behind Vlad Dracula. Can you believe it? Your creator, no less.

"Vlad's father was a great falconer, a nobleman. One of the founders of the Order of the Defeated Dragon. And a mighty cavalryman. Dracul—the Dragon—he was called. He was assassinated, and so the great hunter died. He left many sons, the Sons of the Dragon, behind him as orphans. Vlad was a hostage of the Turks at the time. When he emerged from his prison, great things were expected. . . . Great things . . ." Baoh sipped his drink and shook his head. "But Vlad led the Western crusade against the Turks straight into the toilet." He paused and mumbled quietly to himself for a few seconds, lost in thought. "After his death, his head was taken by the Turks to Constantinople. Istanbul. My guess is, it must have been the head of a changeling. In any case, when he came back as a vampire and formed his Coven, he lost his interest in human history. It was too fleeting, too temporary for his liking. He became an alchemist, and the scourge of the vampire world. I'll bet my best tea set he's killed more of us than the Roman Catholic Church. He says it's to keep the spread of the disease under control, but I wonder . . ."

"Is he alive?" I asked.

Baoh shook his head. "Vlad? No—he sleeps, and it is always best to let a sleeping Dragon lie, eh? I hope no one wakes him, but I suspect the Baron Vrolock, Dracula, will rise again before the End of Days is concluded. But this is not the trouble you speak of, no? You mentioned a vampire hunter. A creature—Mr. Hyde. Do you think he is the Beast of the Apocalypse? The Beast that none can war against?"

"You mean he can't be beaten?"

"Yes."

"I hope not. But Mr. Entwistle couldn't beat him, and he claims to be the greatest fighter alive in the world."

"Who is Mr. Entwistle?"

"A vampire. John Entwistle."

"What? The bass player from the Who? He's come back as a vampire? Wow, that's cool! I always liked the Who. I'm a bit of a pinball wizard myself, you know."

I shook my head. This dream was getting a bit nutty, even for me. "Not the musician. A different John Entwistle. Ophelia says he was once John Tiptoft."

Baoh's eyebrows shot skyward. He swallowed an ice cube whole. I actually watched it go down his throat. "Are you certain? What does he look like?"

I did my best to describe Mr. Entwistle's appearance. His weath-ered features, scruffiness, and long, salt-and-pepper hair.

"You sure that isn't the Undertaker?" Baoh topped up his drink and sat back down on the couch. "Well, that explains it." He leaned forward and rested his elbows on his knees. "Ophelia insisted that we meet now—on very short notice. She is trying to hide her feel-ings, but not much gets past old Baoh. She is terrified. I haven't seen her that scared since your father died." He looked at me when he said this. With his sunglasses on, you could easily forget he was blind.

"I think she's worried about the Coven," I said. "And about Hyde. I don't think Mr. Entwistle is the problem."

Baoh swirled his drink delicately in his hand. The room was so quiet I could hear the sound of ice clinking against the edges of the glass. "I wouldn't assume that. No one knows who he really is. His past is cloaked in darkness. It was decades after his turning when he emerged as John Tiptoft, the Earl of Worcester. How many men he has been since that time, and how many men he was before, only he can say, but he has been a mercenary in his day, and an execu-tioner, a warlord, a murderer. The worst kind of vampire—ruthless and cruel. Death walks at his right shoulder. She would be wise to keep her distance from him."

I felt the blood drain from my face. Without Mr. Entwistle, we didn't have a chance. "He couldn't be as bad as Vlad."

Baoh's lips turned down as if he was puzzling it over. "As a man, a prince, Vlad killed with purpose. With great enthusiasm, to be sure, but always for a reason. He was not as crazy as history books would have you believe. As a vampire, he kills with equal enthusi-asm, or he did, but again, for a reason. To stop the spread of the disease. To silence those people who found out about us. Tiptoft was a different kind of monster. He killed for fun. For sport. To satisfy some sadistic craving." Baoh sat back and pursed his lips. "In the end, which is worse?"

I was speechless. Mr. Entwistle only spoke to me about forgive-ness and truth and doing what was right. This had to be a mistake.

I felt Baoh's hand on my shoulder. His sunglasses were off. I stared at his eyeless eyes. "He is ancient, Zachary. And there is only one reason God permits us old-timers to live so long. It is because the sins of our first lives are so heinous, it takes us centuries to atone, to redeem ourselves. If John Entwistle is John Tiptoft, is he atoning for his past sins?"

I nodded.

"Then he might be a changed man. Never underestimate the transformative power of pain and loss and time, of love and forgiveness and faith. People can change. Why, look at old Baoh. Two centuries ago I weighed five hundred pounds." He paused and settled into the sofa cushions. "Hard to believe, eh? I look pretty snazzy for a man of twelve hundred, wouldn't you say?"

I would say, and I did. He seemed pleased.

"Now, whether you can trust this John Entwistle or not, Baoh can't say. But I would advise you to be careful. You have a role to play in the future of our kind. It is your decency that makes you suitable. Be righteous, and if you survive, you will have earned it, and if you die, you will move into the next world with a clean soul."

"Is that what it says in the prophecies?"

"Baaahhh, who knows? They only make sense when they've already come true. That's the trouble with them. But this isn't a helpful answer, eh? Let me say that the prophecies you read are as accurate as I can make them. I check often for signs and portents. I meditate. I listen to the inner voice that speaks to me, and sometimes through me. It might be God. Might be the devil. Might be a restless spirit, good or bad. I might have a split personality. Baoh doesn't have all the answers. But I can tell you this: for decades those vampires with the power of true sight have witnessed the coming of the messiah. No two seers agree on all the details. No two visions are perfectly identical. But the essence remains the same. The greatest vampire hunter the world has ever seen will die, or has died—perhaps by his own hand. His son will be orphaned and will become a blood drinker. There is some disagreement about which comes first. What we all agree upon is that the future of our kind rests with him, with this orphan—the hunter's son. And he will be a saint, or a scourge. He will elevate our kind to new heights, or lead us to destruction. A time of change is upon us. Apocalypse. An end and a beginning. Perhaps only for vampires. Perhaps for the whole of the world. God only knows, and He is usually very quiet about His plans."

God only knows . . . I looked at the floor, thinking. My head was full of questions. "Am I that messiah?"

"That is for God to know."

"So what do I do? Who can I trust? This thing, this Beast, it seems unstoppable. And the Coven wants me dead. And my friends. They've already sent one vampire. Mr. Entwistle thinks they'll send an army of them once they stop fighting one another."

Baoh put his sunglasses back on, took a sip of his drink, and chomped down on another piece of ice. "A smart warrior fights his battles one at a time. Focus on the most immediate threat."

"That's Mr. Hyde."

He sat back and thought. "Any creature that bleeds can die. You must only hope that he is not one of us—a vampire. Only against a lycanthrope will you have a chance."

I wanted to ask what he meant by this, but I was starting to fade, literally. My body was almost see-through. I looked at my hand and saw a blurry image of the carpet coming through from underneath.

"What is happening?" I asked, but I already knew the answer. The same thing had happened to Luna when I went to visit her.

"You are waking up, Daniel Zachariah Thomson. But have no fear. All will be well, if you walk the righteous path, and do not do to others that which is harmful to yourself."

CHAPTER 19

AN UNEXPECTED GUEST

I awoke a few hours before the sunset, which was unusual. I was strangely alert. My heart was beating hard. I heard footsteps in the hall. Hackles started to rise on my neck. The footsteps stopped outside my door. A series of gentle knocks followed.

"Who is it?" I asked.

"It's me, boy. You up?" It was Mr. Entwistle.

"I'm awake, yeah."

The door opened slowly. Sunlight from the hall window filtered through the dusty air. It was faint, but strong enough that I had to squint.

"I was having trouble sleeping," he said, and stepped into the room. "I thought we should talk."

I was more than a bit surprised. He was supposed to be long gone. And it was daytime. The sunlight was still strong and there wasn't a mark on him. "How did you get in here?"

"Here? Oh, simple. I never really left. I've been sleeping here all day."

"I watched you go."

"Yeah. I did. I had to see a friend. But then I came right back and cut the glass out of a basement window. I couldn't risk staying away for long. Not with a creature as dangerous as Hyde running around. I had to stay close."

He started pacing back and forth in front of the window. It was shuttered with thick wooden slats. A blind and set of curtains kept out almost every photon.

"So you stayed?"

"Yeah. I figured if Ilona found out, I'd ask forgiveness. It's easier than getting permission."

Funny, that was Charlie's philosophy. It had helped him set the school record for after-class detentions. When I thought about it, the two vampires had a lot in common.

"Why do you call her that? Ilona."

He cleared his throat, but his feet kept moving. "Ilona is her name. Or it was, centuries ago. Why? What does she call herself now?"

"Ophelia."

"Ophelia." He paused for a moment, his lips pressed together, but his eyes stayed busy. "'To the celestial and my soul's idol, the most beautified Ophelia . . . Doubt thou the stars are fire; Doubt that the sun doth move, Doubt truth to be a liar, But never doubt I love.'"

He sat down on the edge of the bed, then stood up right away and started pacing back and forth in front of the painted window again. He did this for about half a minute. He was mumbling to himself.

"What is it?" I asked.

"I've been thinking. A lot. And I . . . Well . . . About your future and what's happening and what Ophelia said, and I think she's right."

I wasn't certain what he was referring to. What was she right about? It was hard to concentrate. His behavior was distracting— his voice, his restlessness, and the rapid movement of his eyes from the floor to me, to the window, to the door. He couldn't stay focused on anything for long. It reminded me of the first time I'd seen him, when he crashed a motorcycle through the lobby of the Nicholls Ward.

"You seem agitated."

"Yeah. Happens when I get visions. Can't sleep. And I could use a bolt or two. Haven't had a drink since our Little Lake adventure." He tapped his chest. "I usually have a bottle handy, but I sacrificed my last one during our getaway."

"Maybe Ophelia has something you can take."

He shook his head and waved a hand in front of his face. "No. No, I'm not into medication. My mind needs to be alert. That stuff turns you into a zombie."

He looked to be halfway there. If he hadn't been moving so quickly, I might have mistaken him for one.

"Has Ophelia spoken to you yet?" he asked.

I wondered if that was the real reason he was so restless, because he was worried I knew about him and about his past—that he'd once been a murderer and an executioner. "Yes. I have spoken with her, and I . . ." I didn't know how to explain about Baoh. It was just a dream, but it was more than a dream. I needed a second or two to think about what to say, but I didn't get time. He kept on talking.

"I have much to atone for. I've been many people in the past. Most of them bad. There are things I hope history will forget. Things you wouldn't understand. I was raised in a different age." His voice began to waver. He stopped long enough to look at me. His pale blue eyes were watering. "I have done terrible things. Unforgivable things." He looked away again. His fingers strayed to his forehead. "And no matter how often I change my name or redirect the course of my life, I can't escape them. . . . It is my cross to bear." He waved his hand and muttered something to himself. "But that is as it should be. And it's neither here nor there. What I came to tell you was this—I have tried to make up for it. To live my life, my recent life, in a way that is fair and good. That would be pleasing to a higher power . . ." His forehead wrinkled up and he lost his train of thought.

"I had a vision yesterday. I think it was meant to show me the way forward. I have been thinking about it . . ." He looked over at me again, then down at the floor. The pacing continued. "I think this Hyde creature is my penance. A thing I have to face, alone, to atone for what I've done. I don't think I'll survive. I don't think I'm meant to. But I have to face him anyway." He looked over to make sure I was following him. Or that I believed him. I kept nodding. "I have to, because no one else can. After that, there is only darkness.

But it doesn't matter. Do you know what matters?" His eyes found me again, then bounced away. I got the sense he'd forgotten the answer to his own question. But he kept talking anyway. "There are men out there who will judge us and kill us. And vampires like Vlad, who will do the same. I believe in balance. Yin and yang. You understand what I mean?"

I wasn't sure, but I said I did anyway.

"Well, there needs to be balance in the vampire world. A balance of perspectives. I don't judge people anymore. I used to. When men called me the Butcher of England. The Butcher . . . But I'm not like that now."

He sat down again. "What I'm trying to say is this. There has to be someone out there who doesn't judge. Who will try, no matter what, to be good to everyone, whether they're good or whether they're bad." He waved his hand in the air as if he'd just said something ridiculous. "Well, we're all good and bad. Everyone. You, me, Ophelia, Charlie. You know that." He stood up. "But sometimes the evil is more obvious. The good is buried. But it's always in there. Deep down. And you can find it—raise it up. Even in your enemies. You believe that, don't you?"

I did and I said so.

"Good." He looked at me and stopped again, but only for a second. "Good. You have to. You have to believe. Believe in goodness. And forgiveness. You have to. Because when I'm gone, there has to be someone left who will keep the balance. Who will see the good in all things. In all people. I think that someone is you." His eyes flashed over to me, then shot around the room. "No. I don't *think* it's you. I *know* it's you. It has to be you."

He stopped pacing and turned to the door. More footsteps echoed in the hall—light and quick. He sat down on the edge of the bed and whispered, "Listen carefully." Panic was in his eyes. "You're going to come to a crossroads. To a decision. I've seen it."

He was interrupted by a knock at the door. "Zachary, are you all right?" It was Ophelia.

"I'm fine."

Mr. Entwistle kept whispering. He waved a hand as he spoke. "Forget about her. Well, no, don't forget about her. She needs you. You have to stick together. Charlie, too. But just listen. The Apocalypse is upon us. For our kind, at least. And the one who leads us through the End of Days, who emerges in the aftermath to establish a new order, will be a saint or a demon."

A saint or demon? That sounded close to "a shepherd or a scourge." Was he was talking about the prophecies? He must have seen the surprise on my face.

"You know this already?" he said quickly.

I nodded.

"Good." I could feel his relief. It settled him down, but only for a second. "Like I said, you're going to come to a crossroads. To a decision. Do your best to be a saint. It's what the world needs. Lord knows, there are enough demons out there . . ."

As he was reaching for the knob, the door opened. Ophelia was standing in the hall, an alarmed expression on her face. "What are you doing here? The sun is still up."

If Mr. Entwistle noticed her fear, he gave no sign. He fished into one of the pockets of his overcoat. "Just bringing him this." It was a bag of blood. I was surprised all his pacing hadn't popped it open. "I got worried that if Hyde came and he was still injured, you wouldn't be able to escape." He fished in his other pocket. "I brought one for Charlie, too. And for you."

"Where did you get these?" Ophelia asked.

"From a friend. It's clean, if that's your concern. Harvested straight from the source. They haven't passed through the Underground, so there's no way for them to be tainted."

Ophelia took the bags from him and backed away toward the bed. He stepped into the doorway and turned to face me one last time. We made eye contact. He nodded. I nodded back. Then he closed the door and walked away.

I listened to his footsteps as they faded down the hall. He was talking to himself quietly. "'Yea, though I walk through the valley of the shadow of death, I will fear no evil: for thou art with me . . .'"

. . . thou art with me. The words felt like a quiet rebuke. This wasn't right. I opened the door. "Wait," I shouted.

He stopped. An uncovered window sat at the top of the stairs. The light was too bright so I had to step behind the doorframe. I don't know how he managed to stand there so calmly. Then I realized he wasn't calm. He was the opposite.

"Don't leave. Just wait downstairs. In the basement maybe."

I was worried Ophelia would object, but she didn't. I closed the door and listened. His footfalls descended two flights of steps. Ophelia moved toward me. I held up a hand to stop her. I wanted to listen—to see if he kept pacing. He did.

"Are you sure you're all right?" she asked.

"Yeah, I'm fine."

"How did he get here?"

I wasn't sure exactly what to say, so I said nothing.

"He seemed manic," she said.

"Yeah, he did. He was like that last year, too. When he crashed that stolen motorcycle through the lobby."

She looked at the door, then at the window. I'm not sure what she saw there, but she was thinking. "It could be a seasonal affective disorder."

I'd heard of this. Sad Stephen, one of the patients I used to know at the Nicholls Ward, had the same thing.

"Could you give him something?" I asked. "I think he just needs some sleep. He was worried."

"About what?"

"He says he has to face Hyde. Alone. He saw it in a vision last night. But he can't see anything after that. It's all dark. I think it means Hyde's going to kill him."

Ophelia looked at the door. Her expression changed. Worry became alarm. "Oh . . . Oh, no."

I didn't understand this. She'd booted him out last night and might have done so again just now, in broad daylight. "I thought you didn't trust him."

She sat down on the bed. She stared at the bag of blood in her hand. Her eyes were unfocused. "I don't know what to think." She looked at me. "What did Baoh say?"

"He said I need to be righteous."

"And about John?"

I looked down at the floor. His footsteps drifted up from the basement. From two floors up, they sounded no louder than the soft patter of a cat, but he was probably carving holes in the carpet. "He said that people can change."

"But can we trust him?"

"He didn't know. But he said I should not do to others that which is harmful to myself."

Her eyes returned to the window. For a time she just sat and stared, then she looked down at the bags of blood Mr. Entwistle had given her. "And what does your heart tell you?"

"I trust him. I think he's honest."

"A person can be totally honest and still not be trustworthy."

I didn't know what she was getting at. My expression must have told her as much.

"What if a person has poor judgment? For a person to be worthy of trust means you can count on them, not just to be truthful, but to be prudent as well."

I hadn't considered that. I sat down beside her. "Do you trust his judgment?" she asked.

"No. But that's why you're here."

Ophelia laughed. She didn't do this often. Not these days. The pleasant sound made it impossible not to smile.

"He told me you were right," I said. "That I had to stick with you. I guess he wants to protect us. He's going after Hyde alone."

"What else did he say?"

"He told me about the prophecies. He thinks I'm the messiah, too. That I need to see the good in people."

Ophelia squeezed my arm, then stood up. "Perhaps his judgment isn't so bad after all." She started moving for the door. "I'll see what I can do for him."

"Thanks." I eyed the bag he'd delivered. My gums started to tingle. It meant my teeth were going to drop.

"Ophelia."

She turned.

"I think we should stay together—all of us. I think he wants to be on his own to distance us from trouble, but it won't do us any good if he dies alone. I think this trouble will find us. That Hyde won't stop until we're all dead. And the Coven. We'll need his help for that, too."

She took a deep breath. "John's behavior is reckless, Zachary. He's a magnet for attention. That makes him dangerous to us, whether he means to be or not. We need to keep a low profile for the time being."

"Would you want me to be by myself with that thing running around out there?"

She shook her head. "No . . . but that isn't the situation." She looked at the clock beside my bed. A few hours of sunshine remained in the day. "I think you should get some more rest." She backed into the hall. "Take care." Then she closed the door behind her and went downstairs to look after Mr. Entwistle.

CHAPTER 20

A TRIP TO THE HOSPITAL

If you're a vampire, when blood enters your body, every system goes wonky. Energy courses through your limbs. Sometimes the rush is so intense you think your brain might catch fire. But when you're injured, it's a different game. The pain of your injuries gets concentrated into a few seconds of intense agony. After the burn comes the itch. I guzzled the blood Mr. Entwistle had given me, closed my eyes, and tensed every muscle. Ripped tissue mended. I hissed. Pain racked my body. Then the itch came. I started scratching at the bullet wounds on my thigh and shoulder as if I needed to take the skin off. When this faded, my mind went to heaven. I sat and enjoyed the pleasant aftershocks. When they were gone, I closed my eyes. I started thinking of Luna—how nice it would be if we could visit on the Dream Road every day. I carried this thought into a sleep that took me a few hours past sundown.

I woke up with Mr. Entwistle standing over me. His eyes were still restless, and his appearance was so haggard, if you'd told me he'd been hit by a train, then dragged along the tracks for a few hundred miles, I would have believed you.

"Did you get any sleep?" I asked.

"No, but I'll be fine."

"Are you leaving?"

He nodded. "I'm going to see if I can find the Fleabag."

I didn't think it was a good idea for him to go after Mr. Hyde alone, and I said so.

He looked at me for a few seconds, his teeth clenched, the muscles at the sides of his jaw twitching. "I understand your concern, but there are greater things at stake than the life of John Entwistle."

"Where's Ophelia?" I was hoping she could talk him out of going after Hyde alone.

He handed me a note. "This was downstairs on the dining room table."

The writing was Ophelia's.

> *Zachary,*
> *Detective Baddon has asked for some assistance regarding*
> *the investigation of Everett's death. I thought it might help*
> *to clear your name. I see no sign of Mr. Entwistle. Should*
> *he return, please exercise caution. Don't leave the house.*
> *There is exercise equipment in the basement and a*
> *collection of books and movies. My recommendation is*
> *rest. I should be back from the police station in a few hours.*
> *O*

"It says here you left," I said.

"Yes, I did. I had to see someone about a lead. Before I go after Hyde, I thought it would be a good idea to put you in touch with someone who might be able to help out in my absence. Come on. We're going to the hospital."

"I'm not supposed to leave."

I held up the note with one hand like a raffle ticket. I hadn't meant for him to read it, but I guess the way I was holding it suggested otherwise, because he snatched it from my fingers and glanced it over.

"'Exercise caution,' huh? That's great advice. So . . . you coming?"

"But it says—"

"Look, boy, the toughest vampire on planet Earth is leaving. Are you safer with me or here by yourself?"

He had a point.

"There's the spirit of the law, and the letter of the law. Always go with the spirit, Zack, the spirit. Always. Ophelia wants you to be safe. You're safer at the hospital. Plain and simple." He clapped me on the shoulder and headed down the stairs. "We're going to be tight for time," he added over his shoulder, "so hurry. I'll be in the garage."

"What about Charlie?"

"He's waiting for us downstairs."

I should have known. If trouble was brewing, he'd already have his nose in it.

I was dressed and downstairs in a flash. The place was dark and empty. I made my way to the garage. I walked in and found Mr. Entwistle and Charlie digging through a toolbox. The old vampire pulled out a small tommy bar and handed it to my friend, who stuffed it into a backpack. Before he closed it, I spied the head of a hatchet and a coil of white rope that was woven with red. It made me think of a candy cane.

"What's that smell?"

"Lighter fluid," Charlie said.

"So where exactly are we going?"

Mr. Entwistle shouldered the pack. "Civic Hospital."

He stepped past me, then quietly opened the back door of the garage. Fresh air wafted in and the smell of dusty motor oil mixed with a blast of cedar. I closed my eyes. Even without looking, I knew that it was going to be a perfect night for running. The air had the right weight. Fresh and clear. Mr. Entwistle peeked outside, scanned the neighbors' yards, then nodded for us to go ahead.

"After you," said Charlie.

A second later the door was closed and we were approaching the sound barrier. I was much faster this time. Instead of struggling after, I let Charlie set the pace and tried not to run him over. We made good time and didn't let up until we were in the parking lot of the new Civic Hospital.

"Hold up." Mr. Entwistle took off the backpack. "I need to ditch this." He stowed it in the shadows against the wall, then smiled at me. "You looked better tonight. That blood did you wonders."

"I'd say so. And thanks."

"Don't mention it. But you might want to consider getting some body armor." He slapped the plate over his chest.

"How much would it cost me?"

He took off his top hat and mulled it over. "More than you're likely to make selling your life story, that's for sure. Now come on, I've got a lot to do tonight."

"How are we getting in?" Charlie asked.

"I'm using the front door. Did you have another strategy in mind?"

Charlie shrugged and we entered the lobby. A hand-wash station was set up just inside the door. It must have looked ridiculous to the people in the waiting room when Mr. Entwistle cleaned his hands. He would have needed to swim in a vat of sanitizer to get all the germs off. He looked like a dried-up mud puddle. When he was finished, a nurse at the reception desk asked us if we needed help.

"I just got a call to pick up my son," Mr. Entwistle said. "He's in detox again. Can you believe it?"

The woman took one look at him. He could have been the poster boy for a life gone wrong. "Down the hall and to the left," she said.

"Thanks."

Mr. Entwistle headed for the elevators.

"We aren't really going to detox, are we?"

"Now would a guy like me need directions to detox? No, we're going to radiology. Fourth floor. Actually, you're going. I'm meeting another contact to see what I can learn about where Hyde holes up. He has to have a den or lair somewhere." Mr. Entwistle pressed the button that would bring us an elevator, then handed me a slip of paper. It had a number scribbled in blue ink: 412.

"So we're staying here by ourselves?"

"Not counting a few hundred patients and hospital staff, Charlie, and Agent X, yes, you're all alone."

"Who's Agent X?" I asked.

"The man in room 412."

"But what about the spirit of the law—and being safer with you?"

"Didn't you spend eight years in a hospital ward? What could possibly happen here?" The elevator doors opened. He put his hand inside to keep them from closing. "Just make certain when you boys leave, that you take the stairs. Got it?"

I couldn't imagine why this was important, but I wasn't about to argue with a man who could see the future. "Got it."

He pressed the button for the fourth floor, then stepped back as the doors closed. The elevator started to rattle its way up.

"Man, that guy's a piece of work. Can you believe it, *my son's in detox again*?"

I nodded. Mr. Entwistle was a disaster. But he was also our best hope for staying alive. I wished he weren't leaving.

"Do you think he really was a butcher—like Ophelia says?"

I looked at Charlie. He knew my answer was yes. I didn't have to speak.

"Well, I'd hate to be in your shoes when we get home."

I imagined Ophelia coming back from the police station and finding the house empty. I should have left a note. "She's going to kill me, isn't she?"

"You have to die somehow."

I could have called her on my cell, but I couldn't stand the thought of hearing the disappointment in her voice. Or worse, that she might be scared. Or angry.

The elevator stopped on the fourth floor. It opened, and I followed the signs to room 412. The door was closed.

Charlie peeked in through the window. "Looks empty."

The lights were off.

I reached past him and knocked on the door. There was no answer. I hadn't been told what to expect, so I opened the door quietly. "Hello," I whispered. The room was dark except for a small red light that came from a machine of some kind. It was set beside an empty bed. I could tell by the wrinkled sheets that someone had recently been sleeping there. I listened. A tap was running in the bathroom. I could smell the chlorine in the water, clean sheets, men's aftershave, and disinfectant. I quietly entered and knocked on the bathroom door.

I heard a click and a whoosh, followed by a surprised "Ow!" I looked over at Charlie. His hand was on his neck. He looked at me, then his eyes rolled up and he collapsed into a heap on the floor.

I heard a swish of fabric at my back. Then the light flicked on and I turned my head. A man in a white hospital robe was standing behind me. He was holding a semiautomatic pistol in one hand. He took his other hand off the light switch, used it to steady the gun, then cocked the hammer and backed away, all in one fluid motion. He was just far enough from me that I couldn't lunge and disarm him quickly. He knew exactly what he was doing.

I was shocked. I'd been betrayed once before, and the feeling wasn't pleasant. My stomach felt as if it were falling out. The same question that had popped into my head the last time made a sudden reappearance: *How did I get here?*

"Hello, Zachary. I've been expecting you."

The man looked different than I remembered. Skin hung more loosely over his large muscles now, and his head was completely bald. But his eyes were just as intense as ever.

"Hello," I replied. The word barely made it out.

Then my uncle Maximilian, the vampire hunter, stared down the barrel of his gun, stiffened slightly, and pulled the trigger.

CHAPTER 21

AGENT X

In the movies, when a hero gets shot, he usually has time for some last words. The villains, if they don't drop dead like a stone, usually stay alive long enough to look dazed and confused—as if they're stunned that good could ever triumph over evil, as if it never happened in Hollywood before that one, shocking moment. I think I went out like a villain—stunned. I wasn't instantly dead! What a surprise! I reached up to my neck expecting to find a gushing wound. I didn't. Wonder of wonders! Something about the size of a cigarette butt was sticking out of my throat. What could this be? I pulled it out. A sting followed. Then I dropped, no wiser than before. Dazed and confused.

My uncle caught me. Pain was radiating up and down my neck. It turned from a burn into a warm rush. This passed after a few seconds and a feeling of pleasant euphoria took over. Lightness filled my limbs. I'd felt something like this before. A runner's high, it was called. When you run long enough, your body starts to produce natural painkillers. They act a bit like morphine. But I would've had to run to Pluto to feel this good.

"Forgive me," he said. "But all hell's broken loose. Good people are dying out there. I can't take any chances right now."

Forgive him? For what? This was heaven. My body was turning into air. The only thing that stayed heavy was my head, which was starting to feel like a medicine ball. If I didn't lie down, it was going to roll right off my neck.

"Just ride it out."

I managed to whisper the word "What?"

"Nothing fancy. Mostly sodium thiopental and a mild opiate."

I smiled. Why hadn't I tried this before?

Maximilian led me to a chair, then sat me down. I melted into it.

"Are you okay? Can you hear me?"

I could hear him, which I assumed was good, so I kept smiling. Questions formed. "Are you going to kill us?" The words came out in slow motion.

He shook his head. He was starting to look fuzzy around the edges. "Of course not. Charlie's going to have a little sleep, and we're going to talk."

"Thaaaat's goooood."

He sat on the edge of his bed and slipped something under his pillow. Then he started talking about Vlad, and how dangerous he was, and that he wasn't supposed to hurt anyone *that night*. I had trouble listening. I was staring at my hand. It looked interesting. So did my other hand. I waved them in front of my face. They were like two blobs of ice cream with peach-colored birthday candles sticking out the top. A birthday ice-cream cone . . . Why hadn't anyone thought of this?

My uncle gently brushed my hands away. Then he rolled up my sleeve and drew out a syringe. "Can you hear me?"

I had forgotten how to speak, so I just hummed—like R2-D2.

"The Coven doesn't want people to know about vampires. Only the Underground is exempt, and they are selected with great care. When Charlie and Luna found out about you, the only thing Vlad was willing to do was absorb them as agents, or make them vampires. I would never have guessed he was planning an execution."

"Two executions." My voice was coming back, at half normal speed. I held up two fingers in case he didn't understand me, but it might have been four.

"I'm going to set things right." He snorted. "Ironic. In the end, you all wound up vampires anyway. And Vlad is finished."

I shook my head.

"What do you mean?"

"His body went missing," I said slowly. "It disappeared." I spread my hands for emphasis. It felt as if I were rising out of my chair, so I flapped my hands slowly a few more times to see if I could really fly, but the weight of my head made it impossible. It tipped forward. My uncle seemed to take up my entire view. "You look terrible."

He cleared his throat. It sounded like rocks breaking. "It's the cancer treatment. If the chemotherapy doesn't kill me, the radiation will."

"I hope not."

For a long time he looked at me without speaking. I tried to stare back and nod so that he'd know I was being honest, but it was hard to focus on anything because my eyes wouldn't open all the way. The room seemed to be shifting, as if I were seeing it through a hazy waterfall. It made him sound far away.

"Are there any rumors of him? Of Vlad? From Ophelia or Entwistle?"

I shook my head. "Nothing."

"Do you know why the Coven wants you and Charlie dead?"

I tried to focus. It seemed this was important. Why did they want us dead? There could be only one reason. "They just don't know us very well. We're actually really nice guys."

"What can you tell me about this creature—this vampire hunter?"

He must have meant Hyde. "Ophelia and the others are hoping he's a werewolf. I don't know why. We call him Mr. Hyde, although he doesn't hide. He attacks people with these huge claws."

"Why does she hope he's a werewolf?"

I hummed for a while—until he repeated the question. "I don't know. No one tells me anything."

My uncle rose from his seat on the bed and started lacing up a pair of heavy black boots. When he took off his gown, I could see scars on his torso. He had lost a bit of weight, but he still looked like a powerhouse. He slipped on a shirt.

"What is Entwistle planning to do?" he asked.

"He wants to face Hyde on his own. He told me I needed to survive."

"You will. That's a promise. Why does he have to face Hyde alone? He didn't mention it to me."

"He saw it in a vision. He's going to die."

My uncle stopped. Whatever he'd put under his pillow he removed and tucked into the back of his jeans. "He told you this!"

I nodded.

"Did he say when? Or where?"

I tried to remember if he had. Nothing was coming back to me, so I shrugged.

"What did Ophelia say about this?"

"She doesn't trust him because he's a murderer."

"Who's a murderer?"

"Mr. Entwistle. But his real name is John something or other. Or it was. He was the Barber of England."

"The Barber of England?"

That didn't sound right. "No. The Butcher of England."

My uncle was putting on a windbreaker. His moving blur became a stationary blur. "John Entwistle is really John Tiptoft? The executioner for the House of York?"

"Yes. Well, not anymore."

"Who told you this?"

"Ophelia did. And Baoh."

My uncle moved closer. His face took up the whole screen. The words seemed to echo in my head.

"You met Baoh? The prophet? *Unbelievable!* So he does exist!"

"We played Nintendo. I beat him, but only because he let me win." It was funny—our little men pulverizing one another.

"What did he tell you?"

I wondered what my uncle was talking about.

"Baoh. What did he tell you?"

He told me lots of stuff, but one thing stood out. "To be righteous."

"That's it?"

I sat up. My uncle's tone was serious. "The End of Days is here. I have to die with a clean soul."

My uncle reached down to a black bag that was on the floor. "You're not dying on my watch." He took out something in a thin leather case. "I'm leaving this with you. Be extremely careful. It's lethal."

"What is it?"

"It's a knife. The blade has been treated with dioxin. It's sixty thousand times more potent than cyanide, so leave it in the sheath until you need it."

I looked at the knife. The blade was buried inside a narrow leather sleeve, but it must have been about the same length as my hand. My hand . . . It really did look like an ice cream cone, especially when I made a fist. Then I lifted my other hand and the two started waving to each other.

My uncle dug back into his black bag. This time he pulled out something that looked like a space gun I'd once seen on Teletoon. "This is going to cause some swelling." He put the gun against the back of my shoulder blade and pulled the trigger.

I felt a jab of pain. Right away the area under the skin started to bulge. It felt like a pimple.

"Don't pick at it."

"What's that for?"

"It's a microtransponder, so I can find you if I need to." He took out a small case and removed a syringe. He screwed a needle into the end and stuck it in a small bottle. After drawing some fluid into the syringe, he told me to roll up my sleeve.

"Is that poison?"

He shook his head. "No."

He helped me roll up my sleeve, then injected my arm with something.

"You're going to sleep for a while, but you'll be safe here. The door's locked. Mr. Entwistle will be back before the sun comes up.

I'd stay, but this Hyde creature appears to be nocturnal. I have to see if I can find it before Entwistle gets himself killed."

Was he crazy? My head slumped forward. It was too heavy to lift again. My eyes were starting to close. I fought against it. There were things I had to know. "How can you kill this thing?"

He grabbed my arm and pulled me out of the chair, then slipped his shoulder under me and tipped me onto the bed. "Poisons work best. Cyanide, arsenic, or dioxin. I've used *Conium maculatum* effectively in the past, but your father preferred venom from *Hydrophis belcheri.*"

Hydrophis belcheri? What was that? It sounded like a burping water dragon. "Do you have any?"

"Only what I've given you. The dioxin. It's the Cadillac of poisons." He was moving toward the door.

The Cadillac of poisons? What I needed was the bulletproof, floating Cadillac of poisons with huge tires and twenty-four hundred horses under the hood. Then I could drive back to Weed World. Hyde would never find me there. I laughed. Why hadn't I thought of that before? I was full of good ideas tonight.

My uncle was leaving. I needed to ask something else. "Where have you been all this time?" I hadn't seen him in a year. He was sliding in and out of focus.

"Hunting a werewolf."

"Was it Hyde?"

"No."

Now he was a complete blur. "Did you catch it?"

He said something, but I couldn't make it out. I wanted to ask him to repeat his answer, but my tongue got all tied up and my eyes just wouldn't open. I heard the door. Then it closed and I fell asleep.

CHAPTER 22

ABOVE THE TILES

I awoke feeling like death. My tongue was sandpaper and my head was a swollen wound. I couldn't move. I wondered for a minute if this was what a hangover was like. Charlie had once described one to me, but they couldn't have been this bad or no one on earth would have risked taking a drink. The thought of moving made my stomach tremble and my brain scream. I didn't want to move a muscle, but the clock on the wall said 4 a.m. I'd been asleep for several hours. If I fell asleep again and didn't wake up in time, I'd wind up on fire.

I sat up. This required I wait a few minutes while my head adjusted to its new elevation. *Why are you doing this to us?* it asked. It repeated the question when I stood. Then I noticed the knife on the bedside table. A parting gift from my uncle. I would say this for him, he was a hard guy to figure out. I picked it up and examined the handle. It was molded and had a compass built into the knob on the end. I wasn't wearing a belt, so I stuck the sheath in my back pocket and pulled my shirt over the top to keep it out of sight.

Charlie was asleep on the floor beside me, a towel balled up under his head like a pillow. I gently touched his shoulder.

"Ohhhh," he groaned. "Go away."

"Charlie, wake up," I whispered. "We have to get going. The sun will be up soon."

That got his attention. His eyebrows rose on his forehead as if he were trying to force his eyelids open. "What happened?"

I wasn't sure what to tell him. I suppose the truth would have worked, but Charlie hated Maximilian, and his feelings were well-founded. "You were shot with a tranquilizer."

I heard footsteps outside. Then the window in the door darkened. I ducked around the curtain—the one that you see in most hospital rooms that hangs around the bed to create the illusion of privacy.

"Charlie, someone's in the hall. We need to hide." He seemed not to hear me.

"Whose idea was this anyway?" he asked. "Can't you give me five more minutes? I feel like I just stepped off the Time Warp at Canada's Wonderland."

I heard the rattle of the door handle. It was locked, but someone clearly wanted in. We were in no condition for a confrontation. I looked for a hiding place. There was none. At least, none in the room. But the false ceiling had tiles hanging on a plastic frame so that ductwork and plumbing could easily be accessed. They had the same kind back in the ward. I'd once used it to hide. No reason it wouldn't work again.

"Keep it down," I whispered. I quietly hauled him up to his feet. Then I stepped up on the bed, onto the machine beside it, and slipped a ceiling tile out of place. Overhead were the heating vents, wiring, and plumbing for the hospital. I grabbed a pipe and pulled myself up, then hooked my legs over so I was hanging upside down like a three-toed sloth.

Charlie stepped up onto the bed, then took my hand so I could pull him out of sight. As soon as he had a hold on the plumbing beside me, I slid the tile back. My coordination was a bit off, so I didn't get it set right. It left a slender crack open.

An instant later, I heard a key twist in the door lock. A man whispered, "Thank you," and walked in. The privacy curtain slid back and he stepped into view. He was short, bald, with legs that belonged on a rhinoceros. Detective Baddon. His head was angled to the side as though expecting to find someone in the bed. When he saw no one there, he sighed, disappointed. He moved closer, checked around

the bed and table, then noticed a depression in the center of the mattress. A footprint. He gazed up at the ceiling, drew a gun from a
holster strapped around his shoulder, then turned and reached for a
chair.

Well, I wasn't sticking around for a shoot-out. My best projectile
was a spitball. I slipped the tile down.

"We've got to move," I whispered to Charlie. Using my hands, I
pulled myself away. I tried to be quiet, but I think the detective
must have heard us because he was looking in our direction when
his head popped up above the tile. He'd used his gun to lift the near
end up out of the frame. It was pitch-black. I was hoping it was too
dark for him to see. We didn't stick around to find out. I kept moving until I heard the tile drop. The faint light coming in from the
room below disappeared. I stopped and listened.

"Did he see us?" I asked.

Charlie was staring back through the darkness. "Well, he didn't
shoot, that's the main thing!"

We were above the hallway. I could hear Detective Baddon's
footsteps as he exited the room. Another set, moving faster, swish-
ing on the floor like slippers, was coming toward him.

"Oh, hi there," said a female voice. She sounded friendly, but
surprised. "Sleepwalking again?"

I heard a gentle laugh. "No," said Detective Baddon. "I was hoping to talk to a patient, but he appears to have checked out."

"Did you want me to look into it for you?" I assumed the woman
was a nurse.

"No. He's definitely gone. I'm just going to check in on my son.
Who's on call tonight?"

"Dr. Bell. Do you want me to send for him?"

"If you don't mind. I was hoping for some news, but I don't have
much time tonight. I'm not staying long."

"Oh, of course. I read the news about the police station. I hope
no one was hurt."

"Not seriously."

"Have you found the boy?"

"Not yet, but we're hopeful." The tone of the detective's voice changed. I couldn't see him, but it sounded as though he was looking up. I had a flash of panic, as if he knew we were here. Sweat started to break out on my hands and forehead.

"I'll be down the hall," he added. "I'd appreciate an update as soon as possible."

"I'll pull his charts," the nurse said. "Someone will be in to see you right away."

He said thank you, then the two headed off in opposite directions.

My mind was racing. The detective had been looking for Maximilian. Why? It must have had something to do with Hyde.

"What do we do now?" Charlie asked.

The dawn was nearing. It was time to get going. "We should split," I whispered.

Charlie nodded, but he didn't move. "What's he doing here?"

I didn't know. But there was one way to find out—follow the footsteps as they faded down the hall. Common sense suggested we should leave. Ophelia would definitely want us to play the safe card and get home. But Charlie wanted to stay. What to do? Follow the Detention King of Adam Scott Collegiate, whose decisions had, arguably, driven his mother into rehab, or go with the most responsible person I'd ever met, whose levelheaded decision making had kept me safe for almost ten years?

Naturally, I went with Charlie.

CHAPTER 23

SICKBED

Something about hanging upside down must have been benefi-cial because my grogginess vanished once I got moving. My head started to clear and my strength returned. I followed Charlie, hand over hand, down the hall in pursuit of the detective's heavy footfalls. We were quiet. The only real danger seemed to be the dust. I was worried one of us might sneeze and give ourselves away. But I'd never read about a vampire being thwarted by unclean plumb-ing, so we slothed onward.

The detective quietly entered one of the rooms farther down the hall. We had to take a detour around a heating duct, which took an extra minute. By the time we were overhead, he'd settled himself into a chair beside the room's only bed. I eased a tile up just a fin-ger's breadth and listened. A boy was asleep in the bed beside him. He might have been six or seven. Judging by his features, he must have taken after his mother—slight, with fair hair and skin. Tubes ran into his arm and nose. The detective was sifting through a stack of what looked to be magazines. Only when he took one out of the middle did I see they were children's books. I recognized the picture on the front. It was *Where the Wild Things Are*, by Maurice Sendak—one of my all-time favorite stories as a little kid.

Detective Baddon pushed his glasses up on his nose, turned on the bedside light, angled it away from his son's face, and started to read out loud. I thought it was odd he would do this with his son sleeping. He was just turning a page when a knock came at the door. The detective stood. A man entered. He was wearing a collared, short-sleeve T-shirt and a pair of slacks that were pulled up too high. He looked to be a bit older, in his sixties maybe. He was flipping through pages on a clipboard. I guessed this was the boy's doctor. After a few seconds, he peered over his glasses. "You get any sleep this week?"

"Not much. Things are a bit crazy at the moment. Any news?"

"Yes. Good news." The doctor stared at the pages a moment longer. "The cancer's gone."

The detective looked down at his son. He removed his glasses and rubbed his eyes. "I don't get it. I thought we were starting a more aggressive treatment tomorrow. You said his chances were low. That the cancer was spreading."

"I can't explain it, Adam. The cancer is in total remission. His blood sample came back from the lab clean. The tissue biopsies came back this afternoon. Also clean. His white blood cell count is off the charts. Given the medications he was taking, it should be low, almost nonexistent. Not high. I've never seen anything like it. No one around here has."

Detective Baddon rubbed a hand over his scalp. I noticed the scar on his wrist again. A nasty swath of pink skin, as if he'd been burned or cut open. He looked exhausted. His eyes were red-rimmed and bloodshot, with deep ditches underneath. He slipped the arms of his glasses back over his ears, then stared at his son. When he started to speak, his voice broke. It took him a few moments to pull himself together.

"Is he ever going to wake up?" he asked.

The doctor didn't answer right away. He looked at the charts in his clipboard one last time, then slipped them into a tray at the base of the boy's bed.

"Usually I tell people in situations like this that you can't tell. All you can do is wait. But your son's a fighter, Adam. He's not a big kid, but . . ." The doctor shook his head. "Most people would have died from a head injury like that. The MRI came back and it looks like we were off with our first assessment, because his brain tissue is in better shape than we thought. His heartbeat is more regular. His breathing's stronger. It's all good news, Adam. The only problem is his red blood cell count. We can't keep it elevated. I've sent samples to a few specialists in Toronto. We should hear back soon."

"Do you need me to leave you with some more?"

"Give it a few days. We'll see what happens to his hematocrit levels. If he needs more blood, I'll let you know."

If he needs more blood? I looked at Charlie. He looked at me. Was he thinking what I was thinking? I examined the boy more carefully. He was emaciated, his features well-defined for a child so young—just as mine were when I was that age. Was he was one of us? A vampire? His blood was our first clue. He'd obviously had cancer, then it had gone away. Could he be carrying the pathogen? That would get rid of his cancer. It would also heal a damaged brain, which wasn't always possible for a normal person.

"You need to get some rest," the doctor said. "When did you eat last?"

The detective looked as if he was about to respond, but was interrupted by the old theme song from *Hockey Night in Canada.* He frowned and reached to his belt, then unclipped a cell phone and read the display.

"I have to take this. Who's in tomorrow?"

"Dr. Spink."

The detective nodded, then pulled the cell phone away from his ear to hear the last thing the doctor said.

"You should take a day off, Adam. You look like the walking dead."

The doctor turned and left the room. Detective Baddon waited until the door was closed before he answered the phone.

"Baddon here. What's up, Matt?" There was a pause. "Good." He tipped his wrist to check his watch. "Can you give me half an hour? . . . Perfect." He snapped the phone closed and clipped it back to his belt. A lock of his son's hair had fallen over his eyes. The detective brushed it away with a thick finger, then bent and kissed the boy's forehead. A few seconds later, the book was in his hand and he was reading again.

I started backing away. This was a private moment between a man and his son. It didn't feel right to hang around. The sun would soon be up. Charlie took one last look, then followed. I turned my head to see the best route out, then reached over to a neighboring pipe. It must have been all the dust in the air because I didn't see the jagged end of the bracket holding the pipe in place until I scraped my wrist against it, cutting my skin. It caught me by surprise. I pressed my teeth together to smother a snarl. I didn't want to give myself away. Because I was hanging upside down, I couldn't use my other hand to cover the gash, so I pressed it against my mouth instead in hopes that it would quickly clot. It was little more than a scratch. The taste of my blood got me thinking about the detective's son. If he was one of us, the scent of his blood would give him away. I could probably have picked it up from his arm, where the needle was inserted under his skin. But there wasn't enough time to wait for Detective Baddon to leave.

"Why are you waiting?" Charlie asked.

"I cut myself."

"Yeah, I can smell it."

I gave the cut a few seconds to start drying, then I began crawling, hand over hand back to my uncle's room. Once there, I exited the ceiling the same way I came in, by stepping off the machine and onto the bed. Through the window, I could see the dark night sky growing lighter at the horizon. Sunrise was about a half hour away.

"What do you make of that?" Charlie asked, dropping quietly beside me.

"What? The boy?"

"No—the plastic flowers by his bed. Of course the boy, you dough head!"

"I think he must be one of us."

Charlie crept to the door. "Exactly what I was thinking." He glanced up and down the hallway, then nodded. "The coast is clear. Let's go."

We slipped out without a sound and headed for the elevators.

"What was he doing in the room?" Charlie asked.

"What?"

"That bald dude. How did he know to look for us there?"

He hadn't been looking for us, he'd been looking for my uncle. "He must have been looking for Agent X."

Charlie hit the button for the elevator. "Well, this was a wasted trip."

A bell dinged and the door in front of us slid open. Charlie stepped in and I followed. He hit *L* for "lobby."

"What is it?" Charlie said. "You look like you lost your brain."

My brain was actually right where it belonged. It just wasn't working particularly well. I couldn't decide if I should tell Charlie that Agent X was really my uncle. And I was worried about Mr. Entwistle. Why wasn't he here? At the same time, a vague uneasiness had settled over me, as if I'd forgotten something important. Did it have to do with my uncle? Our conversation was difficult to recall. Like remembering an old dream. I reached back to scratch behind my shoulder. It was sore for some reason. Itchy. The skin raised like a blister. The doors closed, and the floor indicator started dropping from 4 to 3. Had I missed something?

"Speak up," said Charlie. "You're worse than a rock sometimes."

"Sorry, I'm just thinking."

"Well, I know that, Brainiac. When are you not thinking?"

Never was the correct answer, but I didn't get a chance to say so, because the top of the elevator exploded. The overhead lights burst and an alarm started to ring. The wall behind Charlie folded inward, knocking him against the door. The elevator jerked to an instant stop, buckling me at the knees. Then Mr. Entwistle's words came back. "Just make certain when you boys leave, that you take the stairs. Got it?" Not the best thing to forget, apparently, because the elevator was flying apart. A corner of the roof above me disinte-grated, creating a hole that brought the elevator shaft into view. Hairy fingers, half again as long as mine, reached down through the opening and tore it wider. Through the smoke and spark of burning wires I glimpsed an enormous, man-shaped shadow. It snarled, then dropped down beside me.

CHAPTER 24

THE BEAST THAT NONE CAN WAR AGAINST

From a distance, you might have mistaken him for the world's largest vampire. His shape was human. And he was clothed. Tattered leather jacket. Harley-Davidson belt buckle. Jeans that were way too short, like Hulk pants. But the odor was wrong. Even with the elevator wires sparking, and the stink of burning plastic everywhere, I could tell he wasn't one of us. He smelled musty—like an animal. And he was huge. Seven feet at least, and so wide at the shoulders he filled the elevator. Something about his shape was off. His arms were heavily muscled, but just a bit too long. His fingers, too. The nails of each were black and tapered to a sharp point. So were his toenails, which clacked on the elevator tiles when he landed. The floor lurched and my knees gave way. It gave me a good view of his feet. His arches were all stretched up so that he seemed to be perched on the balls of his feet, his ankle a foot above the floor. It made me think of the paw of a dog, or a wolf.

He bent down and glared at me with his large, yellow eyes. They were set wide apart on his face, and the irises were covered with flecks of red, like tiny drops of blood. The rest of his face was only vaguely human. The skin, where it wasn't covered in hair, looked as if it had been pulled back, so his nose was broad and flat against his skull. His nostrils flared with each breath. His forehead sloped backward, as did his ears, which were long and pointed. The top of his head was covered with coarse, black hair. It ran down each jaw, and even down his neck, but the whiskers didn't stretch across his chin, so they looked more like long sideburns. His thin lips pulled back and a low rumble leaked from his mouth. I could see a row of teeth not unlike my own. Incisors, long and pointed. They would have been right at home in a dinosaur exhibit. It made the hair on the back of my neck stand up. Then he growled. The sound was like electricity. It rippled through the bones of my chest. I glanced at Charlie. He'd been knocked flat and was crouched behind Hyde's feet. He looked as if he'd been hit by lightning.

I had one chance—the knife my uncle had given me. It was still in the back pocket of my jeans. I reached for it, but before I could get it free, Hyde snapped out his hand and took hold of me around the throat. He was so fast, I'm not even sure I saw it. It was more like my mind took its best guess from the blur of movement and then, afterward, tried to patch together what had happened. I felt myself rise, then the air flew from my chest as he pushed me up against the elevator wall. Charlie got to his feet. I have to give him credit. He wasn't looking for the exit. He balled a fist and swung. Like his dancing, it was smooth. But Hyde reacted as if his eyes were on the back of his head. He quickly shifted his body. Charlie missed. I saw a blur of movement, followed by a dull thud, and Charlie collapsed.

Hyde turned back to me. He leaned closer, so his teeth were a few inches from my face. A hoarse, guttural sound crackled up from his throat. He might have been speaking, but I couldn't make sense of the words. Then he hissed and slammed me up against the elevator wall a second time. I couldn't breathe. Or cry for help. I glanced down toward Charlie to see if he was all right, if he could do something to help me, but I couldn't angle my head properly. The Beast tightened his grip and my eyes started to go spotty. He started to speak to me again, but I still couldn't tell what he was saying. His teeth gnashed together and his head turned sideways so I could see straight into one of his yellow eyes. He loosened his grip and tried to speak a third time.

I answered with the knife.

While he was slowly strangling me, I'd been working it free of the sheath. I was blacking out as I swung. He blocked the stroke, but the blade must have cut through his skin because his body stiffened. The only explanation I could think of was the poison my uncle had smeared on the blade. It must have been as lethal as he said, to work so quickly. Then I noticed something around Hyde's neck—a nylon rope, white and red threaded together like a candy cane. My eyes followed it up through the darkness to the top of the elevator. Mr. Entwistle was leaning in from the hole above. He held the rope tightly in both hands like a garrote. He'd slipped it over Hyde's head and was trying to tighten it, so that the Beast's face was red and the veins of his neck bulged. That explained why Hyde had stopped moving. He was suffocating. This should have brought me some relief, but I was still suffocating myself. It was hard to feel anything but panic.

"Quickly, boys," Mr. Entwistle shouted. "Get out."

Get out. Happily. But I still couldn't breathe, let alone move. And I thought Charlie was unconscious.

Hyde's fingers dug into my throat. The knife clattered to the floor and my eyes started to go spotty again. I clawed at his hand, but it was no use. I couldn't pry it loose. Then he let go. I dropped to the floor and took a desperate gasp of air. By the time I could see clearly, the candy-cane rope was in pieces beside me. Hyde was snarling and staring upward. Just past his shoulder I caught a glimpse of Mr. Entwistle's overcoat disappearing into the shadows above. As my eyes improved their focus, I could see the old vampire retreating up a set of rungs set in the elevator shaft.

In an instant, Hyde was in pursuit. He pulled himself up through the hole, then launched himself into the air. Using the cables and the wall, he scrambled upward with a strength and speed that were dizzying. It was both awesome and terrifying. My whole body started shaking. How had Mr. Entwistle faced this thing down so many times? All I could do was cough and sputter.

I rose, still trembling, on legs that felt hollow, and moved over to where Charlie was lying in a heap on the ground. His arm was twisted awkwardly underneath him, and his eyes were glazed. One of his feet was twitching, and a huge welt was on the corner of his forehead. I straightened him out, then checked to make sure he was breathing. His heartbeat was strong. His eyelids started to flutter and his head shook slightly as he came to. Then a quiet moan escaped his lips.

"Don't . . ."

I wasn't actually doing anything. He must have been worried that I might move him. I stood up to give him some breathing room and stared through the hole in the top of the elevator. I could see the entrance to the next floor—sliding doors that led to the hall above. They had been torn back. Light from the upper corridor spilled into the dark space, illuminating the claw marks Hyde had scratched into the steel and concrete. I listened for sounds of a scuffle, but all I could hear was the pop and crackle of the still-burning wires that sparked around us, filling the small space with a nauseating odor. I felt weak, and my ankle was burning. I wondered if I'd landed on it funny when I'd fallen to the floor. I looked down and spied the knife lying beside my foot. I picked it up. Blood was on the blade. Perhaps I'd cut him after all.

Don't celebrate yet, my mind told me. *Get moving.*

I looked at the mess above, uncertain. I didn't know what to do. Mr. Entwistle was up there by himself. If I jumped and grabbed a cable, I could shimmy up to the floor above, but it meant I'd have to leave Charlie behind.

The floor tilted and I lost my balance. My ankle was definitely burning. Something was wrong. I heard the sound of steel grinding, and the elevator jumped down a foot. Then another. My first thought was that it was going to drop. Then I heard a loud bang beside me and the doors shifted apart. A slender ribbon of light appeared between them. I could see a shadow moving beyond. Someone was prying the doors open. Whoever it was, he was snarling through clenched teeth. I raised the knife in my right hand and got ready to move quickly. My head was surprisingly dizzy. A fire was spreading up my calf. I fell into the doors. The end of a small crowbar appeared between them and the ribbon of light widened. Then the smell of wine and lighter fluid mixed with smoke and Mr. Entwistle stuck his head through.

"Going down?" he asked.

He was standing below me. He'd somehow pulled the elevator closer to the floor he was on, but it wasn't quite level.

"Here, let me just"—he put his back against one door and pushed so the gap was almost shoulder width—"finish this. . . . There!" He dusted off his hands, then reached for his backpack.

My heart was frantically beating. I started forward in a daze. The burn in my calf was spreading up my leg. My whole body began to sweat.

"What is it? Did he bite you?" Mr. Entwistle was looking up through the hole Hyde had made in the ceiling. "He doesn't mess around, does he?"

I fell past him into the hall, then slipped to a knee. My balance was off.

"Watch that!" he said.

I felt him pry the knife out of my hand, then I reached forward and tumbled to the floor. Standing was impossible. It was easier to roll onto my back. Not as dizzy that way.

Mr. Entwistle was standing over me. The knife was under his nose. His face twisted in revulsion, then he crouched and set the blade on the floor. In a blink the backpack was off his shoulder and he was sifting through it, his hands a blur.

"Did you get cut? Did he cut you with the knife?"

I was having trouble speaking. The liquid fire was spreading to my chest, making it hard to breathe. Pins jabbed inside my lungs and ribs. I looked down at my leg. A small cut was on the side of my ankle. It must have happened when the knife dropped. That explained the burn. There was poison in my body. *Sixty thousand times stronger than cyanide.*

Mr. Entwistle pulled out a hatchet. My tongue was paralyzed, but I turned enough so that I could see the cut on my ankle. The edges of it were black.

"Dammit!" he snapped.

He grabbed the end of my shoe in one hand and pulled it down so that my toes were pointed. Then he put his knee on my shin and raised the hatchet. "Don't move."

Was he crazy? He was about to cut off my foot. I wanted it left where it was, thank you very much. I shifted as he swung. The head of the hatchet sparked and a chunk of tile popped out from the floor.

Mr. Entwistle swore again. "Stop squirming." He was glaring at me. Then his head started shaking back and forth. "No, no, no, no, no." He repeated it over and over. The ax clattered to the floor. His hands slid under my legs and shoulders. "No. No, you don't. Don't you dare . . ."

I wasn't about to do anything. I could barely breathe.

He stood with me in his arms and started running. I felt myself shaking. Burning. Pain froze the air in my chest. *Don't leave Charlie behind,* I wanted to say. *He's helpless.* But I couldn't talk.

Mr. Entwistle stopped. I shifted in his arms, then heard a loud bang as he kicked open a door. He turned sideways and stepped through. Then he was airborne. He didn't go down the stairs, he dropped from landing to landing. Each one rattled the air from my chest. I was suffocating. Then he stopped again. I could sense something was wrong even before he set me down. It might have been in his body language. The way his eyes widened when he looked up. It might have been the smell of fear. And something else. Something feral.

Hyde was waiting for us. I sensed him before I heard him. Another growl echoed up and down the staircase. I was lying on my back. Burning. I raised my head to take a look around. All I could see was darkness. Then suddenly, everything was on fire. My body must have been playing tricks on me. The walls, the floor, the ceiling, the stairs. And me. All of it in flames. I started to convulse. Orange, red, and yellow blurred into a smear of light. Then it got quiet. At least inside. Outside it was noisy. Like two dogs fighting over a bone. But that quickly faded. I listened, knowing I should have been able to hear something. Anything. The sound of the fight. Of air leaving my chest. My heartbeat. But they were gone. So was the burning. It had faded, too. Only the light remained. It was far off, down a long tunnel, but I knew if I was patient, I would reach it. That it would welcome me back. So I left the vanishing world of sound and fire and sped toward it.

CHAPTER 25

REUNION

People generally regard dying as a downer. I assume it's because they've never tried it. Of all earthly phenomena, death is probably the most underrated. Imagine not having to worry about anything. How do I look? Where did I leave my wallet? Why do I get so many pimples? All that vanishes in a snap. So does your pain. Aches and bruises and burns. They all disappear. In the end, there is only the light. And the light is full of hope and love and all things good. And it was receding. A terrible sense of isolation came over me as I slipped away. As if I was being disconnected from something much greater than myself. I reached out so I wouldn't get separated, but it was too late. The light was gone.

I heard a faint voice. It was familiar. The person was right beside me, but he sounded light-years away. *"Clear."*

A shock went through my body. It made me want to scream. My mouth was too dry. I needed more air.

"Did it work?" asked another voice. It was also familiar. The words were packed anxiously together.

"Not yet. . . . *Clear.*"

It happened again. A powerful jolt. My eyes opened. The light was blinding, with no warmth in it. I sucked in an icy breath. It stung.

"It's working. His pulse has steadied. That's all we need."

I felt a sting in my elbow. Nothing happened, then a warm rush crept up my arm. A feeling of heaviness followed. A man stepped into the light. His shadow fell over me. I saw black hair streaked with white and gray under a hat like a chimney pipe. "Get some sleep, boy. You've had a busy night."

His advice seemed reasonable, so I slept.

When I woke up, it was dark. I came out of my sleep slowly. Comfortably. My arm was a bit numb. It was tied to the metal rail of the bed I was in. I was alarmed at first. The thought of being tied up scared me, then I realized it was only surgical tubing. It was to keep my arm from moving. A machine beside the bed hummed quietly, pumping blood through a needle and into a vein near my elbow. Something brushed against my cheek. It made me jump. I heard a quiet laugh.

"Sorry. I couldn't help it."

It was her. Luna. She was crouched over my bed. "It's you," I whispered. My voice was hoarse, my throat dry.

She left her hand on my cheek and smiled. "Yes. It's me."

I felt the floor shift. Then a door opened. It made an odd metallic sound. Cool night air rushed inside the room. It smelled of concrete and wet paint. I heard city sounds. Distant feet on pavement. The hum of cars. The creak of trees nearby. Then Mr. Entwistle appeared. He had to take off his top hat to step inside. The ceiling was low. I realized why when he closed the door.

"Are we in a truck?" I asked.

"No. An ambulance," he said. "I borrowed it from the hospital."

"Borrowed?"

"Well, I'm thinking of it more as a trade-in. The hospital lost an ambulance, but the police got a pretty good aquatic car out of the deal." A stool was beside him. He handed it to Luna, then slumped down to the floor and let his head fall back against the wall, which was actually a medicine cabinet of some kind.

"Thanks." She slipped the stool beside the bed and sat down.

"How did you get here?" I asked her.

"Charlie called and said you'd been poisoned. I had my sister drive me up right away. The two of them are inside with Ophelia."

"So he's okay?"

"Charlie? Yeah. He's going to be fine. He was in here until a few minutes ago."

I felt the air rush from my chest. A breath of relief. My face stretched into a comfortable smile. Everyone was safe. And Luna was here.

"I can't believe your parents let you come." I wasn't one of their favorite people. It wasn't hard to understand why. Thanks to me, one of their daughters was a vampire and the other was in therapy.

Luna eyes flicked nervously over to where Mr. Entwistle was sitting, then she looked back at me. By the expression on her face, I would have bet a stolen ambulance that her parents had no idea where she was.

"We're just sorting that out now." Mr. Entwistle smiled, spinning his hat in his hands. I'm not sure why he found this so amusing. If Luna's parents found out that she and Suki were here, the Beast of the Apocalypse would be the least of my problems.

"They already hate me," I said.

"Who hates you?" Luna asked.

"Your parents."

"*Hate*'s a strong word, boy. They might dislike you—"

"No, they hate him." Luna was smiling now, too. I couldn't see what was so funny. "Don't sweat it. You have enough to worry about."

This was true. And lying around here wasn't going to fix anything. "Why am I not inside?"

"Ophelia didn't want to risk moving you," Mr. Entwistle explained. "And I wanted to be mobile if Agent X raised the alarm and we had to split in a hurry."

"Who is Agent X?" Luna asked.

"Someone from the Underground. He's helping with security. Zack knows him. He's walking the perimeter. I'm sure he'll want to talk to you, boy, once you're feeling better."

I was feeling better, and I said so.

Mr. Entwistle laughed. "Zack, you were clinically dead. Anything else is generally considered an improvement."

With Luna beside me, I wasn't going to argue. "How did I get here?"

"We drove," he said.

"No. I mean, how did we get out of the hospital?"

"We ran."

"Helpful, isn't he?" said Luna.

Her tone was playful, which surprised me. She couldn't have known him more than a few hours, and he looked like Jack the Ripper. If I'd seen him coming down the sidewalk, I would have crossed the street.

"My guess is, Ophelia kicked him out of the house for being a smart aleck," she added.

The old vampire smiled. "Well, at least you said *smart*." Then his smile vanished and he wiped his forehead with his sleeve. "She wasn't happy with me for dragging you out of the house last night."

I remembered the note she'd left me, advising me to stay home. I should have listened. "Was she angry?"

"Angry!" said Mr. Entwistle. "Men get angry. Women get something else. I don't think they've invented a suitable word yet. . . . But I settled her down eventually."

"What did you say?"

"That I'd made a mistake. And that I was sorry. And that we were recruiting help from Agent X—which she appreciates."

Agent X. The alias made me think of my father's journal. He always referred to people with letters. Only Maximilian and Mutada were mentioned by name. Everyone else was Dr. Q, or N, or C. I guess it was to protect people's identities.

"Aren't you going to tell me what happened?" I asked.

"At the hospital? Sure. Just let me fuel up." Mr. Entwistle took a bottle of red wine from inside his coat and downed a good mouthful. "So . . . where did I lose you?"

"You were about to chop off my foot."

"Right." He took another swig. "You would have grown it back, you know. It only takes a couple of weeks."

"How comforting."

"I didn't want the poison to reach your heart."

"Poison?"

"Yeah. From the knife. You're lucky. Not every guy is fortunate enough to stab himself in a hospital. How did you get it, by the way?"

"The cut? I think it happened in the elevator. I dropped the knife. It might have nicked me on the way down. Or maybe I fell on it."

"No," he said. "I meant the knife. Where'd you get it?"

I had to think. My memory was usually dependable, but my brain was still warming up. "It was a gift from Agent X."

Mr. Entwistle took another sip and nodded. "Should have guessed. . . . That was bad luck, getting cut like that. But that knife is our best protection right now."

"What about Mr. Hyde?" I asked. "He caught us, didn't he?"

"More like he was lying in wait for us. But, yeah, he was there." Mr. Entwistle cleared his throat, then smiled. "But he doesn't like being lit on fire. It looked a bit uncomfortable. We'll have to re-member that trick. Then Charlie showed up. He had the hatchet I'd dropped. He came in swinging like a madman. Not even the walls were safe. He's got guts, that boy."

He was certainly brave in the elevator. When Mr. Entwistle car-ried me off, I was worried that he'd get left behind, but his was the voice I'd heard in the ambulance earlier. *Did it work?* he'd asked. Mr. Entwistle must have been the one shouting *Clear.* I'd watched enough television to know what he'd been doing—fixing my heart-beat with those paddle-size electrodes you see doctors using when a person flatlines.

"You saved my life."

Mr. Entwistle stood. He had to bend at the waist to keep his head from hitting the roof. "I'm more than just a pretty face, boy. But it was really the knife that saved you. In the end, that was what scared the fleabag away. The poison is lethal. And as you found out, it only takes a scratch. Agent X really came through with this." He tapped his waist.

"You have it?"

He nodded. "I'm going to hang on to it. At least until you're feeling better. I promised Ophelia. She's not happy we have it. Woman's intuition maybe. She was insistent I keep it as far from you as possible. *A bad feeling* is what she said."

A bad feeling. A lot of those were going around.

"What is it?" Luna asked. "Are you all right?"

I could feel that my eyes wanted to close. But this wasn't the time for sleep. "I had something important to tell you," I said to Mr. Entwistle. "It's on the tip of my tongue."

"Was it about Hyde?"

I couldn't remember. Then more questions popped into my head. Why had he wanted me to meet with my uncle? And how had the two of them met up and reconciled? But I didn't want to mention any of that with Luna right there. To her and Charlie, Maximilian was a villain.

"I'll be inside," Mr. Entwistle said. "You can tell me later." He tapped the side of the metal bed frame several times with his knuckles. "I'll give you two a minute alone, but you might want to consider making an appearance soon. We have a lot to discuss. And a few important decisions to make." He flicked the bottom of his hat in way of farewell, then opened the door and stepped out. The ambulance sank, then rose again.

Luna was looking at me, biting her bottom lip. She rested her hand on my arm. I was sure she meant to comfort me, but I could tell by the expression on her face that she was nervous about something.

"What is it?" I asked.

"I just don't know what's going to happen when my dad finds out I'm here. He's going to flip. So is Mom. But I couldn't risk staying home. If something had happened to you, I would never have forgiven myself. I needed to be here."

"I'm glad you came."

She smiled. "Me, too. I just don't want to have to turn around and go back home."

I didn't want that either, although it might have been much safer for her not to stay. "Take me with you if you go," I said.

"I'd have to sneak you in the trunk."

That sounded perfect, so long as there was room for two.

Luna stood and checked the machine at the bedside. "There's not much left."

"What's that?"

"Blood. This is the last of it. There's only about a half liter left."

She tilted her head so our faces were in line. It was dark inside, but some light from the streetlamps managed to sneak in through the tinted windows. Enough that I could see her emerald green eyes, her copper curls. She reached up and touched my fingers. Suddenly they were on fire, but in a good way.

"Do you want to go in?" she asked.

What I really wanted was to stay here with her, but if plans were being made, I didn't want her to miss out, especially if it meant she might get to stay longer. Then I remembered what I had to tell everyone—that Detective Baddon's son might be a vampire. I sat up. The room spun. Luna must have seen the look on my face.

"Better not push it." She put her hand on my chest and I flopped back down.

"Wait." I nodded toward the machine. "You can turn that off."

"Are you sure?"

"Yeah." I sat up, more slowly this time. The dizziness came back, but I toughed it out. Sleep would have to wait. "There's a faster way." I pulled the needle from my arm, snapped the surgical tubing, removed the bag of blood from the machine, and drank. It wasn't quite enough. My ankle and calf were still itchy. Some stinging remained. My head was clearing, but I didn't get the usual urge to go marathon running. "That's all we have? Is that what you said? This was it?"

Luna slipped in front of me. We stood facing each other. Like Mr. Entwistle, I had to duck to keep my head from hitting the roof. It brought our faces closer together. Enough that I could feel her breath on my cheek.

"That's the last of it," she said.

"You didn't bring any up with you?"

She shook her head. "Sorry. The last batch I got was tainted. I was hoping to find more here."

"And did you?"

She moved a bit closer. "No. But I'll be all right for a while. I didn't get poisoned last night."

"Last night? What time is it?"

"Almost midnight. You've been out for about twenty hours or so."

Asleep for twenty hours? That meant I'd been out all day. But it also meant there were a good five hours or so before sunrise. I had a pretty good idea how I wanted to spend them. Then I heard footsteps outside the door. It opened a crack and Charlie's face appeared.

"Room service." He smiled when he saw I was out of bed. "He lives." He opened the door and stepped inside. "I hate to spoil the party, but Luna's father is on the phone. He was so angry it almost blew apart. You two need to come inside."

CHAPTER 26

SECURITY

I looked at Luna. I could see she was feeling the same disappointment I was. It was probably good that I didn't have a driver's license, or I might have put the ambulance in gear and made a run for the Mexican border. Charlie was obviously worried, too. He stepped out, leaving the door open behind him.

Luna didn't move. "It's funny."

"What?"

"Just how becoming a vampire changes things so much. I don't mean the sun and food and everything like that." She was standing close to me. It made it hard to concentrate. "I mean the way you feel changes."

I didn't know what she was trying to tell me. I swallowed.

"I get upset more often now," she said. "The things people do . . . I don't know why. And I feel . . . lonely, in a way I never used to. Especially at night. I don't like it."

I understood. Vampires are complex creatures. We thrive in darkness. The setting sun awakens a deep restlessness in us. A hunger for the hunt, but also for the things that regular people want, including the company of friends. The night can be empty. Without Charlie and Ophelia, things would have been much worse for me. Luna was the only vampire in Newark, at least the only one we knew about. She was alone too often. But I was hoping to fix that.

She was still looking at me. "And some things don't change at all." Her eyes were wide. Almost luminescent. I've described them before as emerald green, but that isn't really true. Eyes are never one color. Hers had ribbons of amber in them. And olive streaks. The overall effect was shocking. And beautiful. I watched, spellbound, as her gaze fell to my necklace. She stepped closer and took the charm in her fingers. The full moon. With her other hand she took out the golden crescent that had belonged to my mother. "Some things are a perfect fit."

She looked up at me. I smiled. She smiled. We were smiling together. Again. It was nice.

"I've missed you," she said. She somehow got a bit closer. This might have been her talent.

The door was still open. Charlie leaned in. "Sometime tonight would be nice, you slowpokes. Suki's in the hot seat by herself. It's torture in there."

I backed up and stood aside while Luna slipped past. For just an instant we were side by side. Her hand slid down my arm. Her fingertips gently grazed the back of my hand as she stepped down. I held the door, then followed her out.

Charlie was looking at me funny. He had the same smile on his face when he was planning trouble.

"What?" I said.

"Nothing." But he kept smiling.

"No really. What is it?"

"It's nothing. Seriously."

I let the two of them go ahead. I didn't know exactly where to go. We were parked in a lot behind a row of three-story apartments. I had expected us to be back at Ophelia's safe house, the one we'd left to go to the hospital, but obviously, we'd had to move. I glanced back at the ambulance. It was covered, top to bottom, in a sloppy layer of black paint. That explained the smell I'd noticed earlier. It was still drying. Even the lights on top had been done. From up close, you could still see the brushstrokes. A monkey with a stick would have managed a better job.

"Who did this?" I asked.

"Me," Charlie answered.

"You missed a few spots."

"Who do I look like, Picasso? The sun was coming up. We needed to camouflage it. I was in a hurry."

I guess we wouldn't have stayed hidden for too long with a stolen ambulance in the driveway. It looked more like a hearse now.

Charlie strolled up beside me. "Come on. I don't like it out here. I got the heebs."

The breeze picked up for a second and carried away the smell of drying paint. My hackles started to rise. The same feeling had come over me at the rave the night all the trouble started. As if I was being watched.

"Do you see anything?" His eyes were busy scanning the backyards.

I didn't. Nothing unusual.

Luna opened the back door. "Come on, you guys."

Charlie started in and I followed. Then I spotted the watcher. Or rather, the man stepped out of the shadows and revealed himself.

I waited until Charlie was inside, then I hesitated on the back step and said, "Just a second." Before he could object, I closed the door and hopped the fence into the neighbor's yard.

The man waiting there was wearing a commando outfit—all black. He looked like a graduate from the school of ninja. The only difference was his headgear. To his attire he'd added some kind of tight-fitting helmet with lenses. He might have borrowed it from Cobra Commander. Even without his face showing, I could tell it was my uncle Maximilian. Agent X. Something in the way he moved, like a stone golem, gave him away.

"You feeling better?" he asked.

"Yeah. A lot. I think I just need some more sleep."

"See that you get it."

He was holding a heavy gun in his hands. The barrel was unusually large. I'm sure it could have fired a shell to Florida. He flipped it up on his shoulder just as a car turned the corner. There was just enough space between the houses that we could see it. He stepped behind a tree before the headlights could pass over him. My eyes followed the car as it rolled gently to a stop. Then the brake lights went off and it kept on moving. It was a police cruiser.

"Don't worry," he said. "I've set up motion detectors around the property. If anything larger than a cat approaches the apartment, an alarm will sound inside the house."

That was just like my uncle. One step ahead.

I glanced back over my shoulder at the apartment complex. "Do the others know you're here?"

He crossed his arm over his chest. "Not exactly. I agreed to stay out of sight, just in case. I won't be here for long. My last radiation treatment is tomorrow morning, and I'm a bit short on sleep. It's probably better if I stay out of things for now."

He didn't need to explain why. After handing us all over to the Prince of Darkness last summer, keeping his distance was probably a good idea.

"Are *you* all right?" I asked.

"As much as can be expected. I'll be fine if all goes well at the hospital." He nodded a good-bye and turned.

"Wait," I whispered. "I thought you should know a few things. After you left the room, Detective Baddon came looking for you." This led to a conversation about the detective's son and what I'd seen with Charlie in the hospital. "I think the boy might be a vampire."

"Possibly. His condition does seem very unusual. I'll look into it. If his son's infected, then we have every reason to expect Hyde will go after him, too. He'll need protection."

I agreed, and I said so. I sensed that my uncle was about to go, but I had a few questions. "When did you leave the hospital?"

"Right after I talked to you. Why?"

"Have you seen this thing?"

"No."

"But you've hunted werewolves before. Do you think that's what he is?"

He shrugged. "We shouldn't assume he is. To be honest, this thing sounds different. Faster. Stronger. More intelligent. Entwistle says it can talk. I've never heard of a shape changer that could do that. Not as a beast. But I've only seen two. Lycanthropes are very rare."

"Why?"

My uncle took a deep breath. His head tipped up, as if he was thinking. I could imagine his eyes, focused and intense, under his helmet. "They're not like vampires. They aren't immortal. Lycanthropy doesn't bring them back from death. Quite the opposite, in fact. It ages them quickly. And most werewolves kill their prey, so they don't spread whatever virus causes it. But I think the main reason is the Coven. When word of a lycanthrope gets out, they move very quickly to neutralize it."

I wondered why the Coven hadn't done anything about Hyde, but I guess I already knew the answer. They were fighting among themselves.

"We'll be all right, Zachary, if we keep our heads screwed on straight. We just can't afford to make any mistakes, that's all."

No mistakes. That sounded painfully simple. And tragically impossible.

"You need to get some more sleep," he said. "I can see it in your eyes. Your father used to get that way when he was tired and had too much to think about. You'd better get inside." He nodded a goodbye. I watched him return to the shadows, where he stopped to examine a small device staked to the ground. A motion detector, I was guessing. I heard a latch behind me and turned. Luna was waiting at the back door of the apartment. She held it open for me. She looked upset. Her eyes were watering.

I sprinted over. "What is it?"

"I'm sorry, but we have to go home."

CHAPTER 27

THE HUNT BEGINS

I felt my lungs deflate. Through the open back door I could hear Ophelia talking with Mr. Entwistle. He was ranting about the stupidity of anyone under the age of two hundred.

"Does he really think she'll be safer there?" he asked. "What protection can he offer?"

"He's still looking for a cure," someone said. "He thinks if he works hard enough, he can make her better." I didn't recognize the voice, but I figured it had to be Suki.

Luna and I walked in through the back hall, past the kitchen, and into the living room where everyone was waiting.

"I tried that route with Zachary for almost eight years," Ophelia said. "There is no cure."

I remembered this. Ointments and pills and injections and blood transfusions. Most of it just made things worse.

"It's not his speciality," Suki said, "but he thinks one of his colleagues can help. A blood specialist in Toronto. They went to school together. My dad thinks he might be close to something." She was sitting on the couch, her feet drawn up on the cushions and her knees bent so her head was resting on top of them. It seemed as if she were trying to take up as little space as possible. The change in her appearance was so dramatic, if I hadn't expected her to be sitting there, I wouldn't have recognized her. The long blond hair of last summer had been cut short and dyed black, and she had piercings above each eye. Her skin, normally bronzed, was pale as alabaster. Charlie was beside her, a foot of space between them. Last year they would have been wrapped up like two pretzels.

"Do you think we can talk him into letting you stay?" Charlie said.

Suki looked away and rolled her eyes. "Good luck."

I moved farther into the room toward the only empty chair—a La-Z-Boy across from the sofa Charlie and Suki were in. I offered it to Luna, but instead of sitting down, she pushed me into it. My body flopped back against the cushions. I could easily have fallen asleep.

Ophelia was leaning against the kitchen counter, a phone in her fist. Both she and Mr. Entwistle looked frustrated. He was standing beside the window, peeking past the blind, his face grim.

"Are you serious?" I asked Suki. She seemed a bit nervous, a far cry from the bubbly, bouncy person I'd met a year ago.

"Yeah. He wouldn't let us stay here if it was the last place on earth."

She didn't have to explain why. After what had happened last summer at the Abbott family cottage, I wasn't exactly at the top of their Christmas-card list. Dr. Abbott wouldn't want his daughters anywhere near me. It was unfortunate. With Mr. Entwistle here, this was the safest place next to the White House, but that wasn't what I'd been asking about.

"No. I mean about the cure. Is someone really close?"

Suki shrugged.

I glanced at Charlie. He was scowling. "Would you really want one?"

Would I want a cure? I wasn't sure. Of course, I could imagine being human—or at least being able to go out in the sun. But I'd been a vampire for most of my life. I didn't really know what it meant to be a normal person.

Luna sat down on the armrest of my chair. "I'm not going any-where." Her words and tone surprised me. She wasn't normally rebellious. That was more Suki's domain. It was what made her so compatible with Charlie.

"I'm not going to shelter you here without your parents' approval," Ophelia said.

Mr. Entwistle was still holding the same wine bottle that he'd had in the ambulance. He swallowed a mouthful and frowned. He looked like an undertaker raised from the grave. "If we let Luna leave, we'll be killing her. The Coven are already sending their drones here. Hyde killed one in your driveway. When word of that gets back to head office, some higher-ups are going to send in the troops. If we don't stick together, we'll be finished."

"I'm more worried about Hyde than the Coven," Charlie said.

"You should be worried about both. But Hyde's a local problem. The Coven is global. It's just a matter of time before they're here in force. If we allow Luna to become isolated, she'll be killed." Mr. Entwistle turned and looked her square in the face. "Your father can't protect you."

"I know. I don't want to go home. No one there really understands what I'm going through."

I looked over at Suki when she said this. A hurt expression was on her face.

"When is your father coming?" I asked.

"He's leaving now. He'll be here tomorrow."

"And then what?"

Ophelia looked uncertain. "We'll see. Perhaps we can talk him out of leaving right away."

I looked at Luna, then at Suki, to see if any trace of hope was in their faces. There wasn't. No one moved. Then something beeped. It was coming from downstairs.

"What is that?" Luna asked.

"An alarm," Ophelia explained. "I'll be right back."

She disappeared downstairs. The room was as quiet as a church while she was gone. A few seconds later she returned. Her eyes were on me. "Detective Baddon just pulled into the laneway."

"What's he doing here?" I asked.

She moved past me on her way to the door. "He's here because I invited him."

"He thinks I killed Inspector Johansson."

Ophelia raised her hand to her forehead and started massaging her temples. "He doesn't think that anymore. And we need his help."

"Do you trust him?"

"Absolutely. He was Everett's best friend. They worked together in Toronto for over twenty years. The man's a saint. And he's had a very difficult year."

I wasn't sure if I should mention his son. Maybe Ophelia knew already. But I got cut off by the doorbell. She was already moving to answer it. After a brief exchange of pleasantries in the hall, she and Detective Baddon came in for a round of introductions. He obviously wasn't expecting a crowd. Ophelia noticed, too.

"You can speak plainly, Adam."

"I don't have much to tell you." He adjusted the waist of his pants. With legs the thickness of a phone pole, I was amazed they didn't stay up on their own. He looked even more exhausted than the last time I'd seen him. His eyes glanced over at me, but he didn't say anything. Then he rubbed his hand over his head, as if he needed to wake up his brain. "Do you mind if I sit?"

"No," said Ophelia. "I'll put some coffee on."

"Could you make it a decaf? I'm hoping to go to bed shortly."

Ophelia walked into the kitchen. She answered over her shoulder, "I'll see what I have. Go on. I can hear you perfectly from in here."

Officer Baddon didn't know whom to talk to. He looked around the room and settled on Mr. Entwistle. The old vampire was still standing beside the window, peeking occasionally past the blind as if he expected trouble to arrive at any moment.

"I don't have much time," the detective said. "We found some hair at the zoo, and some clothing fibers. The lab results came back. Nothing useful. The hair isn't human, so they couldn't match it to anything in the data banks. The clothing fibers are just regular jeans. Nothing special about them. But we got him on a security camera at the hospital. It picked him up on the way out."

"Do you have a copy?" asked Mr. Entwistle, his eyes still focused outside.

"Not here. But I've seen it. A blur in two frames. Seven feet at least. I'm guessing between three and four hundred pounds. Tough to tell. He's moving like a bullet." He paused. Ophelia came in from the kitchen. The detective glanced around the room. "A phone call came in to the station yesterday just before sunrise. An elderly gentleman on Gilmour. He was reporting a trespasser in his yard. A car was sent. Usual procedure. They got a description. Big and fast. It only came across my desk tonight because of the timing. So I followed up. He didn't have much more to say when I checked in, but he let me see his backyard. The tracks there speak volumes. Same as the zoo. We have a trail. I considered putting some dogs on it, but it was sixteen hours old. I figured it was too cold. At the speed that thing moves, I'm not sure if it even leaves a scent."

Mr. Entwistle rubbed at his stubble. "We can start there. If it goes nowhere, we're no worse off."

He actually wanted to go after this thing. I didn't want to run into Mr. Hyde again unless I was flying in an F-15.

Detective Baddon placed his hands on his knees and started to rise. "Well . . . I need to check in at the hospital and get home for some sleep. I'll call in the morning if anything comes up with the night crew. Please let me know if you find anything tonight. And try to keep it quiet. People are asking questions, and I don't have answers. At least none that any sane person would believe."

"Are you sure you won't have some coffee first?" Ophelia asked.

"One for the road, if you don't mind."

While Ophelia got his coffee ready, the room quieted again. I felt as if I were standing in a funeral parlor. No one spoke until she got back.

"Is there anything else you can tell us?" she asked.

Detective Baddon accepted a mug of coffee, then turned to me. "I'd like to have a word with you outside, if you don't mind." He took a sip, nodded his thanks, then turned for the door.

I looked at Ophelia.

"It will be fine," she whispered.

The words were for me only, although I don't doubt Charlie, Luna, and Mr. Entwistle heard them, too. I gulped. Then I felt Ophelia's hand on the small of my back directing me to the front entrance. She opened the door quietly, then closed it behind the detective and me.

We stood in the narrow hall. I'd never been in this apartment, but I'd seen ones like it. It was basically three separate units, all stacked on top of one another. Beside me were a set of stairs leading up to floors two and three. On the other side was the main door that led out to a front walk.

Detective Baddon sipped his coffee, then said, "I owe you an apology. I shouldn't have behaved that way back at the station. I can't believe this thing. What it did to that elevator."

I understood. It was hard for me to believe it, and I'd been right there.

"I shouldn't have brought you into the system. I think I was just angry. Everett was a close friend. When your prints were on that gun, and in his car, I . . . Well, I'm sorry."

"It's all right."

"Technically, you're still a fugitive. I'm supposed to arrest you on sight."

"You know I didn't kill the inspector."

"Yes, I do. But there is a small matter of a ruined jail, and some injured police officers, and a number of flattened cars."

I wasn't sure what to say. None of that was really my doing.

"I think what I'm saying is that I can't make this mess go away just because you didn't kill Everett. I need help. Off the record. And you know why."

I did know why. He couldn't afford to expose his son. Or any of us. If he was part of the Underground, silence was the rule.

"That was you at the hospital in your uncle's room, wasn't it?"

I nodded.

"Well, you need to keep a lower profile. Any police officer who sees you or John is going to try to arrest you. If you resist, they'll shoot. So be careful. No more public spectacles."

He reached into his coat pocket. I could see his automatic hanging in the holster. He pulled out a card.

"I need to talk to your uncle. My understanding is, he's the only man in this part of the world who's ever caught and killed a werewolf. Is that right?"

I accepted the card and read over Detective Baddon's contact information.

"A werewolf—is that what you think it is?"

He yawned and shook his head. "No idea. But it doesn't matter to me. Whatever it is, we have to catch it. I'm hoping your uncle can help."

"He can. He and my father caught a lycanthrope in England. They used bear traps."

The detective nodded. "That probably won't work in the city. But I've a few things to discuss with him. Sooner is better."

"Is there anything else?"

"Just help me get this thing." It might have been fatigue, but his eyes were starting to water. "We're running out of time."

He backed out the door, then turned and started down the steps. "Have your uncle call my cell," he said over his shoulder.

I wondered if I should have told him that my uncle was patrolling the grounds, and that we were calling him Agent X, but the detective seemed to be in a hurry to leave. And it didn't seem fair to Maximilian. He liked to do things on his own terms. And as selfish as this will sound, I wanted to get back to Luna. I turned and walked back to the door. Ophelia opened it for me.

"Did you hear any of that?" I asked.

Her eyebrows lifted a bit and she nodded. She was chewing the inside of her lip. "He wants to meet with your uncle?"

"You know they were both at the hospital?"

She nodded.

"He told me about the sensors he set up."

"We're trying to keep his involvement under wraps," she said. "If Charlie finds out, he might overreact."

"I thought you didn't trust my uncle."

"I didn't. But while you were in the ambulance, he was convincing. And John feels he has your best interests at heart. I think we were meant to work together. It's the only way we'll survive. War does make strange bedfellows."

This seemed a bit out of character for her. She wasn't a trusting person. "What did he say?"

She paused. Her eyes drifted up while she considered what to tell me. "We talked about the night he betrayed you to Vlad. We talked about mistakes and misconceptions. He was badly used, your uncle. And deceived." She took a deep breath. "The situation is complicated, but it's hard to say no to a dying man." She reached out and pinched my cheek. "Now if we could just get Gerald on board."

"Gerald?"

"Dr. Abbott."

"Do you think he'll let them stay?"

"I think the good doctor is seriously rattled. But we may have a chance to impress him. The alarms and security cameras will help. We almost seem like we know what we're doing. Leaving Luna in our care is certainly the best thing for her. If he's a reasonable man, he'll come around. Luna is a child vampire, just like you are, and so the threat is constant. Going back to Newark won't make it go away."

"Does he know that?"

"I don't think so. But that just means we'll have to be more convincing." She slipped her arm through mine and we walked back into the living room. Everyone stopped talking when we entered. Luna looked upset. Her eyes couldn't settle comfortably on anything. Mr. Entwistle was still looking out past the curtain. He let it fall.

"I'd like to leave as soon as possible," he said. "That trail isn't getting any warmer."

Ophelia nodded. "Can you let me get Luna and Suki settled on the top floor? I'd like to have a word with you before you go."

The old vampire nodded. Charlie helped Suki to her feet. He pulled her into a hug, then reluctantly let her go.

"You did the right thing coming here," I told her.

She smiled. Dimples formed at the sides of her mouth. For just a moment, she looked like the old Suki.

Then Luna bumped past me. She didn't look over, but I saw her lips move. Just enough breath was behind them for me to hear her words: "Meet me on the roof."

My ears started to burn. Then Ophelia led them upstairs. I listened as their footsteps faded to the second floor, then the third.

"What a ham," Charlie said. He must have meant Dr. Abbott.

"Don't underestimate Ophelia," Mr. Entwistle said. "If the doctor has an ounce of sense, she'll bring him around."

He had a point. No one I'd ever met could say no to her.

"And it's what both his daughters want," the old vampire added. "Although you two might have to sleep in the ambulance."

I didn't think that was funny. Charlie didn't, either. Mr. Entwistle was trying not to laugh. But the mention of the word *ambulance* reminded me of something I had to say. "I forgot to mention this to you before. When I was at the hospital visiting—"

"Agent X," Mr. Entwistle interrupted.

"While I was visiting Agent X, he had a visitor."

"Who's Agent X?" asked Charlie.

He seemed to have forgotten. I wondered if it was the effect of being drugged in the hospital. I wasn't sure what to say about this.

Fortunately Mr. Entwistle answered for me. "He's an old friend who's agreed to help us. He was the one that you and Zachary met at the Civic."

Charlie shot me a questioning glance. I felt myself blush.

"He shot you with a tranquilizer," I explained.

"That was my fault," Mr. Entwistle said. "I forgot to say there would be two of you. He was only expecting Zack."

"So you talked to this guy?" Charlie asked.

I nodded.

Mr. Entwistle cut in again. "He set up the alarms and cameras around this apartment. We're keeping his identity a secret, for his protection."

Charlie made a face. He'd want an explanation later. I told my brain it had better come up with something good, then I explained about Detective Baddon's son—and what Charlie and I had seen in the hospital. Ophelia entered about halfway through and asked me to back up and start over. When I did, it was clear she'd had no idea the boy was sick.

"I can't believe he never mentioned it! I wonder if Everett knew."

Mr. Entwistle removed the top hat from inside his coat and started for the door. "If Baddon's son is in danger, too, it's all the more reason for me to get going. I couldn't find a trail last night. I'm losing time. If I can follow Hyde's footprints from that house on Gilmour or pick up his scent, we might be able to figure out where he goes each morning. If I need to, I'll call in for some backup."

"Do you think leaving is the right move?" Ophelia asked.

"I won't be gone long. If anything comes near the place, you'll know. Agent X is on call. And with these two young bloods handy, you're well protected."

"I was more worried about you," Ophelia said.

Mr. Entwistle laughed. "I'll be fine. You have my cell number?"

Ophelia nodded.

I looked at Charlie. Disappointment was etched clearly in the lines around his mouth. He was restless, and with his girlfriend asleep upstairs, he clearly didn't want to spend the rest of the night indoors. My bet was, if he stayed housebound, he'd wear the carpet down to threads pacing the room.

"Why don't you take Charlie, just to be safe," I said.

Ophelia stiffened slightly, but the damage was done. With that one suggestion, I'd severed my friend's shackles.

"Sounds good," Mr. Entwistle said. "If we need you, we'll be in touch."

Charlie brightened up immediately. He gave me a shot in the shoulder on the way out. "Don't die of boredom while I'm gone."

I wasn't planning to. The hunt for Hyde could begin without me. I had a date on the roof with Luna.

CHAPTER 28

ON THE ROOFTOP

Ophelia wasn't thrilled to see Charlie go and let me know the minute he was out the door. "He's just as reckless as John. We'll be lucky if those two don't set the whole town on fire."

I thought this was a slight exaggeration. They wouldn't set it on fire so much as knock it down. "He's got a lot of restless energy," I said. "He can't work it off in here. You know how he can get?"

"One night inside won't kill him."

"No. But it might kill us."

Ophelia shot me a look, then headed for the basement. "I've some research to do. Watch your step on the roof."

She must have heard what Luna had said. Fortunately she was already at the top of the stairs, or she would have seen my face turn flammable red. A second later, she poked her head around the corner again. So much for hiding my embarrassment.

"I almost forgot. I'm setting you and Charlie up on the second floor. It's furnished, but there's no bedding. Why don't you come down and I'll get you some sheets."

I followed her downstairs to the basement. This simple living space had a laundry room near the back. A small office was on one corner, with the door open wide enough for me to see a long desk inside. It was covered in computer monitors. Every few seconds, the view through one would change. It didn't take long to recognize the street outside. These must have been where the security cameras were hubbed.

Ophelia retreated to a storage closet, then came out with several sets of linens. "They're a bit dusty. The key's hanging in the rack by the front door." She handed me the bedsheets. "Please don't do anything foolish. We're going to have enough trouble with Dr. Abbott as it is. And a bit more rest wouldn't kill you either."

I said my thanks and headed for the stairs, then stopped. "Are you going to be talking to my uncle?"

"Only if it's necessary. He has a cancer treatment tomorrow. Why?"

I handed her Detective Baddon's business card. "He wants Maximilian to call him."

Ophelia took the card and read it over. "I'll take care of it."

I scampered up the stairs. "He said to use the cell number," I said over my shoulder.

"Got it."

I made my way to the front door, grabbed the key to the second-floor apartment, and took the steps two at a time. I'd never had a place of my own. It was exciting just opening the door. I was making up one of the canopied beds when I heard a knock at the window. Luna was outside, hovering in midair. It was like a scene from *Harry Potter*. All she was missing was a broom.

"How are you doing that?" I asked.

She laughed and started flapping her arms like wings. Her body was bobbing gently from side to side. "Flying is my talent."

I couldn't believe it. And of course it wasn't true. She was standing on a fire escape. Her knees were bent and she was shifting her weight gently from foot to foot to make it look as if she were floating.

"You coming out sometime tonight, or were you planning to scrub the floors and vacuum the carpets?"

"Would it impress your father if he knew I was house-trained? Maybe you could take a picture and show him when he arrives."

"I think he'd just assume you were trying to steal the vacuum cleaner."

I walked over to the window and wound it open. I popped out the screen and stepped onto the fire escape. Luna grabbed my hand and nearly pulled my arm out of the socket hauling me up the steps. They led to a flat roof that was covered in pea gravel. Our feet made crunching noises on the stones. A chimney along the side made a perfect backrest. We sat. She still hadn't let go of my hand, not that I was complaining.

"Is there any chance your dad will let you stay?" I asked.

Luna's lips pressed together and one side of her mouth curled down. It was a perfect I-don't-know-but-probably-not face. "He might let Suki and I visit the lake while he meets with his colleague in Toronto. But he . . . well, he'll want us to steer clear of you. As far as he's concerned, you and Charlie are the real danger."

"Do you think he might be right?"

"What do you mean?"

I had to choose my words carefully. "I hate to say it because I want you to stay, but it might be safer for you to get away from us. At least until we've dealt with Hyde."

Luna let go of my hand. "That's not fair."

I didn't understand. What did fair have to do with it?

"If I were Charlie, would you want me to stay?"

"I already said I want you to stay. But I also want you to stay alive. This thing . . . I don't know what to tell you. You remember how terrifying Vlad was. Well, Hyde's a hundred times worse."

I didn't think she believed me, which wasn't at all surprising. Vlad was a live horror show. "Honestly. Until you see him, you won't understand."

She looked away, shook her head, stood up, and started pacing. When she spoke again, her hands were on her hips. "It's because I'm a girl."

I was totally confused at this point. I'd never had a problem with the essential girlness of her. In fact, I was pleased about it.

"If I were Charlie and I said I was leaving to go hide in New Jersey, you'd think I was a coward."

I hadn't thought about it that way.

"Ahhh, see. You know it's true. I can see it in your face."

I stood and dusted off my pants. "You're right. If you were Charlie, I would think badly of you if you left."

She put her hands in the air and started doing a victory dance. I had to admit, she had some pretty good moves. Definitely rave material. Then she started shadowboxing with me.

"You don't think I know how to fight?" She followed this question with a few jabs. Had she punched anything harder than shaving cream, she would have broken a wrist.

I waited for an opening, then slipped inside her guard and took her down to the roof. I twisted so she'd land on top of me, then I rolled over for the pin. It took about half a heartbeat. Just enough time for her to yelp.

"That was fast!"

"I had to move quickly. I was worried you might accidentally hit me and hurt yourself."

I rolled to the side, then let her up. She pulled me back to the chimney so we could sit side by side and look up at the stars.

"You've changed," she said.

"How?"

"You don't seem as shy. You were so funny at the cottage. So polite."

"What's wrong with that?"

"Nothing. I like polite." Her hand snuck into mine. "You seem a little . . . I don't know."

"I think it's the poison. Maybe I need more blood. And a bit more sleep, too."

She glanced at me and smiled. It made her eyes pinch shut. I remembered this from last summer—this smile. But seeing it was something else.

"That's not what I meant. You seem more confident. And don't take this the wrong way, but you're a little more like Charlie. I think he's rubbing off on you a bit."

Rubbing off? What did that mean? Was it good? I suppose I shouldn't have been surprised. I spent more time with Charlie than with anyone else. But I didn't think we were alike at all.

"Did I spoil things?" Luna's smile sagged a little and she looked up at the night sky.

"No. Not at all. It's wonderful to see you."

She was still holding my hand. For a moment we just stared at the arrangement of our fingers. Both pale. Hers slightly shorter, leaner, more delicate, but still strong. Years of weight lifting had built thick calluses on the inside of mine, and along the top of my palm. I had to use the back of a finger to feel how soft her skin was.

She looked at me and her face turned serious. "Could you show me how to do that . . . that thing that you just did."

"You mean how to fight?"

She nodded, then bit her lip and smiled again.

"I don't really know much," I said.

"Maybe you're a natural."

"Maybe."

She cleared a lock of hair away from her eyes and squeezed my hand. "It's wonderful to see you, too."

I took a deep breath and closed my eyes. I felt her lean into me. Her head fell onto my shoulder. We sat for a time saying nothing. I just enjoyed the feel of her beside me. Her hand in my hand. The pleasant smell of her. I could happily have frozen my life right there. Just stopped the clock and been in heaven forever.

"Are we going to be all right?" she asked.

I didn't want to spoil the moment by being honest. I tipped my head to the side so that it was resting gently against hers. She turned just enough so that our noses were almost touching. Then they were. I thought she might move away, but she did the exact opposite. Her breath was suddenly on my lips. Her hand came up and cupped the side of my face. In that instant, I promised myself two things. The first was that I wasn't going to let anything happen to her. That I would die first. The second was that I was going to find out how to properly kiss someone, because I never had.

My teeth started to slide down. I couldn't stop them. I glanced at her mouth. Her teeth were down, too. It pushed up her lips, made them look fuller. Her eyes were closed. Her chin rose a little, bringing her mouth closer. I understood in that moment why people said things like "these two have electricity." We weren't touching, but I could feel her getting closer. Even before her lips parted, I could sense them moving. Making my skin tingle.

"Hey! Get away from my daughter!" shouted a voice.

Luna shrieked. I jumped. Then I heard laughter.

Luna picked up a rock and tossed it hard at the fire escape. Charlie was standing on top. He barely ducked in time. When the rock flew past him, he put a hand on his stomach and started laughing even harder.

"You should have seen your faces!" He could barely get the words out as he wiped at his eyes. They actually had tears in them.

Luna reached for another rock. "You jerk!"

I was so relieved that it was Charlie and not Dr. Abbott that I didn't think to complain. Instead, I helped Luna to her feet. She pulled me close. Her lips brushed gently against my cheek.

"You make sure you pay him back," she whispered.

I wasn't going to suggest otherwise, but a part of me was grateful. In a way Charlie had just got me off the hook. If Luna knew I was a lousy kisser . . .

Charlie slapped my shoulder. He was breathing as if he'd just done a six-mile dash. "I hate to break it to you, Edward, but you aren't in Forks anymore. The love-in is over. We're going after Mr. Hyde."

CHAPTER 29

OF VILLAINS AND VAMPIRES

Charlie disappeared down the fire escape. It was a prudent move. Luna looked angry enough to stone him to death. Since nothing but pea-size gravel was on the roof, it would have taken her a while.

"I'd better see what this is about," I said.

We both started down the stairs. Luna stopped outside her window.

"Is it a good idea to have this here?" She shook the railing of the fire escape. "Couldn't that thing climb up?"

"It wouldn't make a difference. If he wants to get inside, he'll just plow through the wall."

Her eyes widened. "Are you serious?"

"From time to time."

We stood there for a few moments just looking at one another. Then Charlie called. I really didn't want to go.

"I should come with you."

I shook my head. "I don't like the idea of leaving Ophelia and your sister here by themselves. Will you be awake later?"

She nodded.

I turned and started down. I didn't get far. She took hold of my shirt and spun me around.

"Don't be too long," she whispered. "You still owe me a kiss."

When I heard that word, *kiss*, my brain stopped working properly. Instead of formulating a witty response, all it could do was change my face from pale to crimson. It might have been a survival thing. If I was blushing enough to produce my own light, I'd be less likely to trip on the stairs and fall to my death.

"Be careful," she added.

I nodded, then got myself turned around and slipped down to the driveway. Charlie had circled around the corner of the building. When I caught up, he was waiting with Mr. Entwistle, who was talking on his cell.

"How did things go at the house on Gilmour?" I asked. "You weren't gone very long. Did you find a trail?"

Charlie shook his head. "The owner cut the grass today. The tracks were gone and all we could smell was chlorophyll."

"Where does that leave us?"

Charlie was about to answer, but he was cut off by Mr. Entwistle, who snapped his phone closed and announced we were leaving. "Ophelia just got off the phone with Baddon. Hyde was at his house." Mr. Entwistle pulled off his hat, ran his fingers through his hair, then turned and started moving down the street.

"What about the others?" I didn't want to leave them by themselves.

"Ophelia isn't worried. It was her suggestion we go. I think she wants some time alone with the girls." He put his top hat back on and nodded to Charlie, who smiled and fell in step.

I shuffled after slowly. I wasn't sure I should be going. "I still feel awful. I think I'll only slow you down."

Mr. Entwistle laughed. "That's why I wanted you to join us. You might still have some traces of poison left in your system. This will flush it out. The best thing for you. A good run."

He sped up more. We turned a corner and started east on Sherbrooke. We were heading downtown.

"Here. Off the streets." He led us over a fence and into a backyard. He moved like a character from *The Matrix*. I kept looking above him to see where the strings were attached.

"What do we do if we find him?" I whispered.

Mr. Entwistle jumped off a tree and landed in the next yard.

"Hyde? We don't really want to find him. We want to follow him. And hope he really is a werewolf."

His words dislodged something from my tired brain. Baoh had said something similar. It didn't make sense to me at the time, and it still didn't.

"What do you mean *hope he's a werewolf*?" I asked.

Mr. Entwistle hopped another fence and stopped. He was in a crouch. I was reminded again of how wolflike his movements were. Steady, smooth, dangerous.

"Well, we don't have a lot of choices. He's one of us, or he's a lycanthrope."

"What difference does it make?" Charlie asked.

"All the difference in the world. You've seen the movies, read the stories. Every kid has." Mr. Entwistle pointed down the block. "That way's a shortcut." We took off again and he continued, "Vampires of ancient lore are creatures of pure evil. Very human, but stronger. Implacable. Almost indestructible. And in my case, uncommonly handsome."

"We're not evil," said Charlie.

"You aren't a vampire. Not in the traditional sense." Mr. Entwistle slipped through a cedar hedge. We followed, the smell of the evergreen thick in our noses. "No, boy, a vampire is an archetype for a villain. In real life, they don't exist."

"What do you mean in real life we don't exist? This is real life." Charlie gave a me look. *This guy's a nut*, he seemed to be saying.

"No, Charlie. I mean villains don't exist. In real life, everyone is both good and bad. Everyone. Whether someone is a villain or not just depends on whether they're for you or against you."

"Are you saying Hyde's not a villain?"

Mr. Entwistle didn't answer. He stepped off a lawn chair, shot up onto the roof of a shed, ran silently across the top, then launched himself into the next yard.

"Wow, he's smooth," Charlie whispered. Mr. Entwistle was already over the next fence. We hurried to catch up.

"Hyde is a villain, Charlie, but only to us," Mr. Entwistle said. "From his point of view, we're probably the bad guys. That's what I mean. Villainy is about perspective. Always has been."

We ran past a pool, crossed Momaghan Road, turned north, and started along another row of backyards.

"You still haven't explained what you meant," I said. "About wanting him to be a werewolf."

He hurdled a hedge, then stopped. Charlie and I pulled up beside him. All three of us were breathing heavily.

"Right . . . a werewolf. Well, lycanthropes are like vampires, Zack. They're blood drinkers. But they have two personae. Two aspects. One good. One bad. Like the movies. There's a guy with a normal life, then a full moon comes around, and presto! We've got a hairy-faced monster with an appetite for destruction. We want Hyde to be a werewolf, a creature that changes. That way, we don't have to deal with the Beast. He'll rip us into atoms."

I understood. If Hyde was like a vampire, if he never changed, then he was never vulnerable.

"So we're really looking for a man?"

"Not necessarily. We can't assume Hyde is a lycanthrope just because he looks different than we do. But to deal with a man would be much easier, assuming there's anyone around who fits."

"What does that mean—*fit*?" Charlie asked.

"Well, there's no getting around the laws of physics. Matter cannot be created or destroyed, only transformed. Whoever Hyde turns into, he has to be huge. Someone who would tower over us. Three to four hundred pounds of human that becomes three to four hundred pounds of werewolf."

Charlie shook his head. "Wait a minute. I knew something about this wasn't right. It wasn't a full moon the night we were at the zoo. Or when he went after Zack in the hospital."

"True enough," said Mr. Entwistle. "But there's more than one way to trigger a transformation. That full-moon stuff might be claptrap anyway. It dates back to the fertility cults of early history. They usually performed their rites when the moon was full. The Christians demonized them. Made them out to be full-moon monsters. But many myths contain kernels of truth. A full moon might do the trick, but if memory serves, they are other things that turn a lycanthrope from human to beast."

"Like what?" I asked.

"Bright lights—like a meteor shower. Injury. I read about a werewolf who changed because he took a sip from a silver cup and the purity of the metal exposed him. Probably balderdash. Heard of a man who turned just before he was hanged at the gallows. The monster inside didn't want to die. Blood might do it, too. Bring out the inner beast. For all I know, it's different for each of them. But it doesn't have to be a full moon."

Charlie looked up at the sky. A slender crescent hung overhead. "So what makes Hyde change?"

Mr. Entwistle put a hand on Charlie's back as he walked past. "No idea. Assuming he does change. It might just be wishful thinking. We want Hyde to have an alter ego. Someone we can deal with." He took off his hat and rubbed his hands through his hair. "But it all hinges on the same questions. Is he a werewolf or not? Does he change? Is he like us and vulnerable to the sun? Or just an abomination of some kind—a Beast with his own set of rules?"

I remembered Ophelia's note from the first safe house I was taken to, where the police had arrested me. *Knowledge is your best defense,* she had written. We knew little about Hyde. Who he was. What he was. Why he wanted us dead. So our best defense had more than a few holes.

"Why have we stopped?" Charlie asked.

Mr. Entwistle slapped the hat back on his head. "That's the detective's street. His house is farther down."

"Are we supposed to wait here?"

Mr. Entwistle didn't answer. Instead, he lifted his nose slightly. The wind picked up. I could smell the same canine odor I'd noticed at the zoo. Leather and wet dog. Just a trace.

"I'm just giving you a second to catch your breath," he said. "That smell could mean trouble."

I looked at Charlie. He looked at me. This was it. I let my teeth drop. He did the same.

"You two ready?"

We nodded, Charlie, then me.

Mr. Entwistle turned, then bounded through two yards, back-to-back, crossed the street, and stopped on the far sidewalk.

"It's quiet," he whispered. He pulled out his cell, punched in a number, then waited. A second later someone picked up on the other end. "We're outside your front door," Mr. Entwistle said. Then he turned down the nearest walk. "Get your game faces on, boys. This is it."

CHAPTER 30
FAMILY PORTRAIT

Detective Baddon's house was a small, two-story dwelling. Set back under an arch was the front door. In the center near the top was a small, circular window. The detective's face appeared behind it. He pushed the door open and stood aside so we could enter.

"No need," he said to me when I bent to remove my shoes. "We're going straight out the back."

When I looked up, I could see the barrel of a pistol at his side. A large wheel gun. His hand wasn't steady. A sharp smell was in the air—one I'd noticed a lot at Charlie's when his mother had her drinking spells. When the detective led us through the living room, I saw why. A bottle of alcohol and a shot glass were on the coffee table. We passed through a kitchen to the back door. Before he opened it, he turned and looked at all of us. I thought he was going to say something, but he changed his mind and hit the latch. Mr. Entwistle stepped out and we followed.

After witnessing at the hospital and the zoo what Hyde could do, I was surprised when I saw the backyard. I'd anticipated much worse. Tracks dotted the ground. The doors on a small shed at the back were pulled open. That was it. No scorched earth or torn-up sod. No debris or nuclear fallout. The lawn furniture on the patio was still sitting right where it should have been, looking old and bored.

Mr. Entwistle bent to a knee and examined the ground. Then he started touring the yard. Every now and again he would bend down to examine the grass more closely. When he was finished, he stuck his nose inside the shed.

"What do you see?" Detective Baddon asked him.

"Nothing as dramatic as I'd expected." Mr. Entwistle pointed to a spot near his foot. "He landed here from that yard." He indicated the fence. "He went straight to the shed, got a bit rough with the doors, looked inside, walked toward the back door . . ." He grunted here and examined the flattened grass more carefully. "Looks like he changed his mind, turned, and left that way." He gazed toward the backyard behind us.

I moved over to examine the prints. They were shaped just as I remembered them. Round and deep. The nails had left long scars in the lawn at the point of takeoff. "How long ago did this happen?" I asked.

The detective was still standing on the back step. "With the exception of the ten minutes I was at your place, and a short trip to the station, I've been at the hospital all night. It could have been anytime."

"There's a second set of footprints here," Mr. Entwistle said. "I assume that was you."

"Yeah. I wanted to see what he'd taken from the shed."

"And what was it?"

"Well, that's just it. He didn't take anything—not as far as I can tell."

The old vampire closed the doors. One of the hinges was broken, so they didn't fit together properly. "So he didn't find what he was looking for?"

"It looks that way."

Mr. Entwistle returned to the back step. "So the question is, what did he want? Why come here?"

"I have a theory." The detective rubbed a hand over his eyes.

"Let's hear it."

He took a full chest of air and let it out. "Before Hyde appeared,

Everett was very worried about the Coven. Apparently they don't approve of child vampires, and the rate at which the pathogen is spreading here. Everett was worried that there'd be trouble, so he brought me into the Underground to help."

"Your timing could have been better," Charlie said.

The detective snorted a laugh. "You're not kidding. He thought he was doing me a favor. I was struggling in Toronto. We both thought a change might help." He sighed. I took it from his expression that the scene in his backyard wasn't quite what he'd had in mind. "Neither of us knew that Hyde was coming down the track. He's not just going after vampires. He's taking the whole Underground apart. So when this thing killed Everett, it put me at the top of his list."

"You think Hyde is after you?" Mr. Entwistle asked.

Detective Baddon nodded. "Yes."

"Is that why he was at the hospital?" I asked.

"Maybe. Unless he was after you. Or John. It could have been any one of us."

"That doesn't explain the shed," said Charlie. "Why bother with it?"

"I was doing some work in there yesterday. My wife never liked it when I cleaned my guns in the house. My guess is, he followed my scent there." The detective adjusted his glasses and stared at the footprints all over the grass. "I don't think there's anything else in there of interest."

He held open the back door of the house and we walked inside. Just past the kitchen was a small living space with a couch and some chairs. He took off his glasses, rubbed his eyes, led us through, and sat down. Then he started unscrewing the cap on the bottle he'd left on the coffee table.

"You want one?" he asked.

The old vampire shook his head.

"Do you mind?"

"Go ahead."

The detective filled a shot glass and drained it.

"I want to get on that trail while it's still fresh," Mr. Entwistle said. "Anything else you can tell us?"

Detective Baddon shook his head. A photo was on the coffee table. A family portrait. I recognized him and his son. The woman at his side must have been his wife. Like the boy I'd seen in the hospital, she was fair and slight. Tall as well, and happy. There was another boy, too, clearly older. He was short and thick, like his father.

Mr. Entwistle started fidgeting with his hat. I could see that he was impatient to be going. He had the same restless look in his eyes I'd often seen in Charlie's.

"Do you think this has anything to do with your son?" Mr. Entwistle asked.

The detective thought for a moment. He was spent. He sighed and tipped his head so it was resting on the back of the sofa. "I don't think so."

"Is he a vampire, like us?"

He shook his head, then reached behind his back and pulled out his gun. He set it on the coffee table beside the open bottle and photo of his family. It was a grim still life. "I wish he were a vampire like you. It would certainly solve his problems."

"What do you mean?"

"He's been in a coma for six months. He took a hit to the head that did a lot of damage. God—to think I could just give him an infusion of blood and he'd regenerate the way you three do. But it's not like that. Then he got diagnosed with leukemia, like he wasn't in enough trouble. It spread to his bones, liver, and kidneys. I thought he was going to die. The cancer's gone now, but it probably doesn't matter. I don't think he'll ever wake up."

"I'm sorry to hear that."

"So am I." The detective's eyes were on the coffee table.

"And the boy's mother?" Mr. Entwistle asked.

"She died. My older boy, too." His hand reached out and fell upon the bottle. He lifted it and started pouring another shot.

Mr. Entwistle put a hand on the detective's arm. "Why don't you stay with us at the apartment? If Hyde knows you live here, you're safer with us. You can get some rest and see your son in the morning."

"I won't get any sleep tonight. I haven't been able to string more than two hours together in the last six months."

"A change of scenery might help."

"It can't hurt." Detective Baddon stood and stepped past the old vampire, then proceeded into the kitchen. When he came back, a small box was in his hand. It rattled when he set it on the coffee table. He sat and flipped the gun open, then started sliding the bullets from the chambers in the wheel. When it was empty, he opened the box in front of him and pulled out a shell. It caught the light of the room's only lamp and lit up like a new coin.

"I ordered these the night Everett was killed. Silver." He started to reload the gun with the silver bullets. "I'm not taking any chances." When the gun was full, he snapped it closed. His hand stretched out of his sleeve just enough so that the scars on his wrist were visible.

"What happened there?" Mr. Entwistle asked.

The detective looked at his wrist, then pulled his hand back so that the row of scars disappeared under the fabric. "I was attacked."

"Can I see?"

He pulled up his sleeve. A large swath of pink scar tissue ran across the tendons just under his hand. "Ended my power-lifting career."

"What happened?"

"I don't remember exactly. But I read the report after I got out of the hospital. We walked in while someone was robbing the house. I didn't see him in time. I got my hand up though. I'm told it saved my life." He held up his arm so it was resting against his forehead. A smaller scar that I hadn't noticed was on the top of his head. It lined up perfectly with the ones on his wrist, like pieces of a grisly puzzle. "He had a bottle. When it broke, it slashed through the tendons. Knocked me out."

I could imagine a bottle breaking against his head and wrist. He lowered his hand and picked up the picture. He stared at it for a long time before he continued. "He was more thorough with my wife and son. That little guy in the hospital is all I have left . . . I don't know what I'm going to do if I lose him."

"We won't let anything happen." Mr. Entwistle spoke with such confidence, I found myself believing him. He put a hand on the detective's shoulder as he passed. "I'm going to stop this thing if it kills me."

He looked at me squarely when he said this. We both knew what he'd seen in his vision—the darkness that was coming.

"Good luck tonight. Call me and let me know what you find." The detective pushed himself up from the sofa and started to rise.

"Don't get up. We'll see ourselves out." Mr. Entwistle nodded to Charlie, who fell in step behind him.

"Wait, Zachary," Detective Baddon said. "I need another word with you, if you don't mind."

I stayed behind. Charlie held the back door, but I raised my index finger. "One minute," I whispered. He nodded and let it close.

"I know you have to go, so I'll be brief." The detective's hands were shaking. "If something happens to me and my son is still in his coma . . ."

I didn't think he was going to finish. He reached for the bottle on the table, then set it back and stood up so we were face-to-face.

"Would you consider . . ." Again he stalled.

I could smell his fear. I looked into his eyes. Saw his jaw clench. Then I realized what he was asking me.

"Would I consider infecting him to keep him alive?"

"Yes." We walked to the back door. "Just think about it."

"If I infect him, he will wake up, but the Coven will come after him. They want to kill us—Charlie, me, Luna. There aren't supposed to be child vampires."

"I know." He took a deep breath. It was a miracle he was standing. He looked like a man who'd run the Daytona 500 dragging his
car.

"But the alternative . . ." Again he didn't finish, but there was no
need. I understood his fear. That his son might never wake up. Well,
I'd died before. It wasn't as bad as everyone thought. It might be
better than waking up alone, confused, in a strange place with his
family gone.

The detective reached past me and opened the door. "Be careful."

"I will." Then I stepped out to join the others.

Charlie waited for the door to close, then walked over beside
me. "Everything all right?"

"Yeah."

"What did he want?"

"He just wanted to make sure we'd look after his son if something happened to him."

Charlie took a deep breath. "Man, that's heavy. His kid would be
an orphan, just like you."

Not quite like me. But I understood what Charlie was saying.

Mr. Entwistle started talking into his phone. "Yeah, you need
to send Agent X over here. Baddon's a mess. Trust me, I'm an expert when it comes to nervous breakdowns. I have one every few
years just to stay in practice." There was a long pause. "Yes, he was
here. He was looking for something." Another pause. "We don't
know. Baddon thinks Hyde was looking for him. . . . We've got a
trail to follow." Mr. Entwistle looked at us and held up his hand—
Stay right there, he seemed to be saying. "It means he knows where
Baddon lives. We can't let him stay here. Hyde might come
back. . . . Because he might not. . . . I'm going to follow this
trail. . . . No, they're safer with me. . . . Then he can meet up with
us. If there's trouble, he can drive them back. . . . Sounds good."
Then Mr. Entwistle said good-bye and flicked his phone closed.

"What did Ophelia want?" I asked.

"She wants you two home."

Charlie started to protest.

"Don't worry. You're with me. She's just worried that if you leave, Hyde will find you; if you stay, Hyde will find you; and if he doesn't find you, you might find him instead. But I think she knows you're better off with me. Agent X might join us later if we need him."

"Or if you need to send us back," said Charlie.

"Or that," said Mr. Entwistle. "Don't forget, Luna and Suki are back there. If Hyde pays them a visit while we're hopping backyard fences, you're going to have a disappointing homecoming."

CHAPTER 31

THE TRAIL ENDS

We followed Hyde's trail east toward the downtown.

"Do you really think Hyde was going after Baddon?" Charlie asked.

Mr. Entwistle took a few backyards to think about it. "Probably. Hyde killed those other officers. He obviously has an interest in bringing down the Underground. I just hope we're following the right trail."

I hadn't realized there were others. When I asked about it, Mr. Entwistle hurdled a doghouse, ducked a clothesline, then answered over his shoulder, "We could have followed the trail backward and seen where Hyde had come from."

I hadn't considered that. "So why did we pick this one?"

"I was worried he might be heading for the apartment."

Charlie grimaced as we turned down an alley. Neither of us was keen to see Hyde do an about-face and head back to Ophelia's. Fortunately he didn't. The trail was clear. Nothing erratic, just a straight line out of town. Either he didn't expect to be followed, or he didn't care.

"Those silver bullets Baddon was putting in his gun, do they make a difference?" Charlie asked.

Mr. Entwistle shook his head. "Would it matter if I shot *you* with silver bullets? Anything traveling over two hundred yards per second is going to hurt. I don't care if it's a lima bean."

"So why do all the werewolf movies have that in them?"

Mr. Entwistle slipped between two sections of a cedar hedge, then slowed to explain, "In ancient stories about vampires and were-wolves, all you needed to kill us was metal. Regular iron was just fine. It had to do with the mysteries of metallurgy. Most people didn't really understand how iron was forged. To the average person, it was a mystical process, and it represented a kind of triumph. Man rising above nature. And above the supernatural. I remember ghost stories as a boy about men who killed restless spirits with iron knives. Then when metal was more common, and less mysterious, silver became the new iron. At least in the stories."

"Why?" Charlie asked.

Mr. Entwistle took a detour around a patio party. Someone had a stereo blasting, so Charlie had to repeat his question.

"Silver doesn't corrode like other metals. It gives it an aura of purity. It's all poppycock, of course. If I shoot you with silver, steel, lead, or Botox, it's going to do some damage."

In the next backyard he stopped. A large addition to a two-story house was in front of us. He took off his top hat, flattened it to pancake dimensions, and stuck it inside his coat. His hair looked fresh from a Jell-O mold. He rubbed his fingers through it, then wiped his forehead on the sleeve of his coat. He started scowling and his head swung back and forth in disbelief.

"What is it?" I asked.

He was looking down at the ground. I could see a deep footprint. Then he nodded toward the roof of the house. "I think he must have taken this in one stride."

"What do you mean?"

"I mean he jumped straight up onto the roof." He looked at me with his eyebrows high on his head, as if I ought to be impressed.

I was. "You having second thoughts?"

"No. I'm way past that. More like tenth or eleventh?"

Charlie looked at me. He was incredulous. All of us were.

"Think happy thoughts," said Mr. Entwistle, then he started up again.

"Happy thoughts," Charlie repeated, shaking his head. "Where did you find this guy?"

I hadn't found him. He'd found me—in a mental institution. That was before Hyde. Before Vlad. Before *that night.* Those years at the Nicholls Ward were starting to look like the glory days.

We were moving east down Parkhill Road by this time, away from the city and into an area with lots of farms. Mr. Entwistle picked up the pace. With no cars on the road, we really dropped the hammer. I bet we broke the speed limit. I spent the whole time thinking about Luna and what she would think if she could see me. I looked like the Michelin Man. My shirt was puffed up like an air balloon. It was the only thing that kept it from catching fire. We were that fast. After a few miles, Mr. Entwistle slowed. We were far out of town. I couldn't smell the Quaker Oats factory anymore.

"Why are we stopping again?" Charlie asked.

Mr. Entwistle was bent at the waist. His breathing was heavy. I was panting, too, and I wasn't running in body armor. He was so smooth and fast, I often forgot he had it on under his overcoat. It was a wonder he hadn't melted.

"Why? Because if we catch up to Hyde panting like overweight geriatric patients, he's going to slice us into small pieces." Mr. Entwistle was looking at the ground. "And because he stopped here himself." The old vampire started hopping from foot to foot. He looked like a drunk sailor trying to master an awkward version of hip-hop. Then I realized he was putting his feet in Hyde's footprints.

"What is it?" Charlie asked.

"He left the road here," Mr. Entwistle said.

I wondered why. "To avoid a car maybe?"

"Maybe."

We followed the trail off the road and into a pasture. There we found another set of tracks. These ones led back into town. Mr. Entwistle bent down to inspect them. His nostrils flared. "The ones heading back in are fresher. The scent on them is stronger."

"Did he turn around here?" Charlie asked.

Mr. Entwistle shook his head. "No. He continued that way." He pointed in the direction we'd been running—out of town. "He must have done an about-face somewhere ahead."

"So what do we do?" I asked.

Mr. Entwistle peered skyward. A few hours of night remained. He paused for a moment to think. "If we follow the first trail, we might find his lair. Or at least where he turned around. But, obviously, if we're out here, and he's back in town . . ."

"We need to find out where he lives. Where he hides," said Charlie.

"Yes, we do. Eventually. But these tracks won't disappear overnight. We can follow the first set again if we have to and see where they lead."

Charlie nudged me on the shoulder. "What are you thinking, boy genius? I can see the gears grinding."

I was thinking that Hyde knew he was faster than us. Maybe he planned for us to follow him out here. Then he could double back and do whatever he wanted in town because we were wasting our time chasing shadows. I looked at Charlie, then at Mr. Entwistle. The old vampire seemed to know what I was thinking. I heard his teeth grind. So we turned and took off in the direction of home.

"Do you think the others are all right?" Charlie asked.

"I'd better call." Mr. Entwistle pulled out his cell phone. "Thank God for technology. Can you imagine how easy life would have been for the Hardy Boys if they'd had these things?"

Charlie looked at me and mouthed, *Hardy Boys?*

I shrugged. I had no idea who they were. Pioneers maybe.

The old vampire slowed to talk. I heard Ophelia's voice on the other end. "Yeah, it's John. We're turning around. We followed tracks to Douro, but found another set heading back into town. They're fresher, so we're following those. Keep your eyes open. Hyde might be heading your way. Are Agent X and Baddon there?"

I heard Ophelia say no. They were at the hospital. I remembered what my uncle had told me. That his last radiation treatment was in the morning. He must have gone in early with Baddon so the detective could be with his son.

"Call if there's trouble," Mr. Entwistle said, then hung up. "They're alone. Let's motor."

"Why did Agent X leave?" Charlie asked.

"He was taking Baddon to the hospital. My guess is, they'll both be staying there."

Charlie shook his head. We hurdled a farm fence. Mr. Entwistle sped up and we followed. I was starting to falter. I hadn't recovered from my visit to the hospital. I loved few things more than running at night, but my gas tank was down to fumes.

"I had a bad feeling about him," Charlie said.

"Who?"

"Agent X. Who did you think I meant? Did anyone else shoot me with a tranquilizer? How do you trust a guy when you don't even know his name?"

I didn't have an answer for this. I looked over at Mr. Entwistle. He was listening, his eyes busily scanning for the next footprint.

"When you get to be my age, boys," he said, "you discover there are reasons not to trust everybody. You can twist your mind into a pretzel thinking about it. Trust, I wouldn't get too hung up on it."

I was surprised to hear this. The way Ophelia made it sound, trust was one of the founding principles of the universe. Trust and order.

"You mean you don't trust anybody?" Charlie asked.

Mr. Entwistle shook his head. "It isn't about trust. It's about understanding. Should I trust you?"

"Yeah. Of course."

"Okay. Imagine this scenario. Hyde has Suki as a hostage. He asks you to betray me, or he'll kill her. Should I still trust you?"

Charlie started to answer.

Mr. Entwistle cut him off. "Think. Is your first loyalty to her or to me? Now what about Baddon? You know how he feels about his son. What do you think he might do if something happened to the boy, if the Coven took him, for example? Would the detective sell your soul to get his son back? Count on it."

The old vampire looked at us and laughed. "See what I mean? You could go nuts worrying about all the possibilities. All the reasons not to trust people. Me, Baddon, Agent X."

I was pleased he didn't add Ophelia to that list. Or Luna or Suki for that matter.

"So don't focus on trust," he told us. "Focus on understanding everyone's situation. Everyone's point of view. And what they want. Hyde. Baddon. Dr. Abbott. Agent X. When you know what people want, and how they plan to get it, you can stop thinking about trust and focus on what you need to do to help them, if it's the right thing, or how to stop them, if that's the right thing."

"What does Agent X want?" Charlie asked.

"To stay alive," said Mr. Entwistle. "He's part of the Underground, so his interests are our interests. You can count on that."

The old vampire looked up at the sky, then sped up. He definitely had more fuel to burn than me. I did my best to follow. The pace he kept made it impossible to talk. Maybe that's what he wanted. The sun would soon be up. We were running out of night.

Eventually, Hyde's trail took us around to the south side of the city.

"This is good," said Charlie.

I agreed. It meant Hyde wasn't heading for the apartment.

We entered the land of sidewalks and roads and it got more difficult to follow the trail. At Hyde's speed, he didn't leave much of an odor behind. All we had to go on were his footprints, and with all the pavement, clear ones were often half a block apart. It was slow going. Eventually, we wound up on Neal Drive. Mr. Entwistle pointed to a set of Dumpsters sitting beside a long building. It looked like a series of miniature garages sitting side by side. The sign in the driveway said Peterborough Multiple Storage. He made his way over, crouched in the shadows, and stared at the building.

"What are we doing?" Charlie whispered.

"Thinking. Now quit stealing all my oxygen."

I tried to quiet my breathing. It was just starting to settle when Mr. Entwistle stood up and crept along the back of the storage units. He stopped outside one in the center of the row, number 6.

"Is he in there?" I whispered.

Mr. Entwistle nodded. He put a finger over his mouth and quietly tested the knob. It was locked. He paused. His eyes rolled up slightly while he considered what to do. Then he drew out the knife—the one Maximilian had given me—and kicked the door in.

CHAPTER 32

MONKSHOOD

The doorframe buckled under the force of Mr. Entwistle's boot. Pieces of cinder block scattered as the housing for the dead bolt tore loose from the wall.

"Well, there goes the element of surprise," Charlie muttered.

The old vampire laughed. "The way you two breathe, he could hear you through six feet of concrete." He stuck his head in the doorway. "Honey, I'm home." His voice was remarkably steady.

I listened, but heard nothing but the sound of dust settling on cardboard. The room was full of packing boxes and not much else.

"Well, let's see what Old Yeller was up to." Mr. Entwistle moved carefully into the room.

I stopped in the doorway. There was nowhere else to go. The room had cardboard boxes piled floor to ceiling along each wall. The only place to walk was a path down the center that ended at the far side.

"You sure he's gone?" Charlie asked.

"Unless he taped himself inside a box," Mr. Entwistle replied.

I started forward. He stopped me with his hand. He was inspecting the floor. Then he turned his attention to the labels on the boxes.

"Sorry. You can come in. I just didn't want you walking all over his footprints until I had a chance to check them out." Mr. Entwistle reached up and pulled a box down. It said CLOTHES on it. He started picking at the tape. Then he shook his head. "Here. Let's get those ones down."

"What are we doing?" I asked. I thought if Hyde was gone, we should be hightailing it. He might have been anywhere in town by now, including the apartment.

"I want to know what he came here for."

"Is all of this his?" Charlie asked.

"Not unless his name is Nancy." Mr. Entwistle pointed to a box. "That's our winner, right there." On one side the words NANCY—COSMETICS were written in black marker. The tape wasn't sticking to the cardboard properly, as if it had recently been pulled loose. Mr. Entwistle lifted the box down and opened the top, then he whistled as if he'd struck gold. Charlie and I stuck our heads closer to see inside. It was packed with makeup cases, lipstick rolls, mascara, perfumes. Enough to keep Kiss in costume for a decade. Sitting on top were a bunch of yellow flowers. They'd dried somewhat, but were still fragrant. Mr. Entwistle was staring at them.

"What are they?" I asked.

"Monkshood," he said.

The name fit. The flowers looked like tiny hoods.

"Why would he want these?" Charlie reached in.

Mr. Entwistle stopped him. "You mean you've never heard of monkshood?"

"What, like I work for FTD?"

"A simple *no* will suffice."

"Well then, *no,*" Charlie said. "I've never heard of monkshood."

"It has another name. Wolfsbane. You heard of that?"

Wolfsbane. I had heard of it. Charlie and I used to play Dungeons & Dragons. I wasn't sure if I should admit to this or not. But poisons were part of the game. Wolfsbane was right up there with hemlock and belladonna.

"You mean you never played D & D as a kid?" Mr. Entwistle asked. "Too bad. Great game. I guess you two didn't hang out with the cool kids in the neighborhood. If you had, you'd know that wolfsbane is lethal. Back when I was your age, people nailed it to their doors to keep wolves and lycanthropes away. It's deadly stuff."

"I'll try to remember that when I roll up my next half-orc assassin," Charlie said.

"I prefer human wizards, myself." Mr. Entwistle stared down inside the box, then started humming to himself and scratching at the whiskers on his chin.

"What is it?" I asked.

"More questions . . . What is this stuff doing here? What does Hyde want it for? Whose storage unit is this?" Mr. Entwistle glanced around at the other boxes. "We should call in the morning and see if we can find out. I wonder . . ."

"You wonder what?" Charlie asked.

"Well, if this is registered to a man, it might be his alter ego."

"The man he turns into?" I said.

"Yeah, his Dr. Jekyll."

"What do you mean, Dr. Jekyll? Like the guy from that horror movie?" Charlie asked.

"It was a book first. Great werewolf."

"He wasn't a werewolf!"

"Not literally," Mr. Entwistle explained. "Weren't you listening earlier? I'm speaking figuratively. In the archetypical sense, Dr. Jekyll was the good persona, Mr. Hyde was the evil one. Why do you think I picked that name?"

Charlie shrugged. "Body hair? *Hide*—you know. A hairy hide."

Mr. Entwistle looked at him, then at me.

I had thought Mr. Entwistle picked the name because we couldn't ever find him, and that his secrets were hidden, but I was too embarrassed to say.

The old vampire shook his head. "How did you two nincompoops get out of elementary school?"

"I stopped going to school in grade two," I said.

"And I think I got promoted so my teachers wouldn't have to see me again," said Charlie.

I didn't think he was joking, but Mr. Entwistle laughed anyway.

"Right. Well, I think we can leave now. With any luck, we can find out who rents this unit. Hyde must have used a key. He got in without breaking the door. That's a good sign."

He started to fold the box closed.

"Don't we want to take that with us?" Charlie said.

"Charlie, that would be stealing! Zack, what kind of company are you keeping?"

All of this from a guy who'd stolen a motorcycle and a Ford Mustang from the police, and an ambulance from the hospital. I checked his face for signs that he was joking. It was like reading a cement wall. He would have been deadly in a game of Texas Hold'em.

"Do you think the Almighty would forgive us if we just borrowed a sprig or two?" the old vampire asked. "You can give some to Luna and Suki."

Yes, he was definitely joking.

"I'd rather give some to Hyde," Charlie said.

"Only if we have to. Now how should we carry it? Just one scratch and it's game over."

"It's that strong?" I asked.

"Yup."

"The box is full of makeup bags," Charlie said. "Can't we just put some in one of those?"

"And to think I called you a nincompoop. Grow a few more brain cells, Charlie, and I'll upgrade you to genius." Mr. Entwistle looked at me and smiled, then reached into the box and pulled out a purse. The outside was covered with grotesque floral patterns. He tipped it upside down and the stash of makeup thingamabobs spilled out. Then he folded the bag over the bouquet of monkshood. He was careful not to touch any. Once it was zipped shut, he handed the bag to Charlie and pushed him toward the door.

"Why do I have to carry this thing?"

"It's part of that boyish charm that got you through school. And it matches your eyes." The old vampire herded us out the door, then did his best to close it behind us. It was bent and the housing for the dead bolt had torn free from the cinder-block wall. "If only we had some duct tape," he muttered. Then he reached into his coat, pulled out a plastic bag, and jammed it under the door so that it was wedged closed. "Plastic bags—a million and one uses. Now, a million and two."

I smiled. Charlie was still trying to figure out what to do with the handbag.

"Quit fussing," Mr. Entwistle said. "Look on the bright side. If Hyde tries to kill us on the way home, you can fend him off with your purse."

"Yeah. Great. If only my friends could see me."

"Be careful what you wish for." Mr. Entwistle fished into his pocket and came out with his cell phone. "Cheese!" He snapped a photo, then started out across the lot at a slow jog. "Yeah, I'm definitely tagging you on my Facebook page."

Charlie was still staring at the handbag. "Where's a good half-orc assassin when you need one?"

"I heard that," the old vampire said. "Let's go."

"Where?"

"Good question. Can you find the trail?"

Charlie and I tested the air. All I could smell was garbage and dust and cooling asphalt. I checked the ground for prints, but saw nothing. "Where did he go?"

Mr. Entwistle snorted. "No idea. But we're out of time. The sun will be up in an hour, and I forgot to bring my stolen ambulance with me. We'd better get back. You two ready?"

"Yeah."

So we headed for home.

CHAPTER 33

INFIGHTING

H ope is a funny thing. It can be totally unreasonable—bone dumb, in fact—and a part of it still clings to your brain. I remember as a kid hoping to find a light saber in my Christmas stocking. After reading my first *Marvel Tales* comic, I hoped that I might get bitten by a radioactive bug and receive the full range of superpowers you'd expect from such a miracle. You can bet all that hope came to nothing. But other times hope is dead-on. Like when you hope the winter will soon be over and it's already late April. That's the kind of hope you want to have. It's less disappointing.

All the way home, I was thinking of Luna. I was hoping she'd be awake and that I could see her. And I was hoping that my hope wasn't too unreasonable. When we reached the apartments, my first thought was to find her and head up the fire escape. Sadly, fate had other plans. The trouble started with our greeting in the backyard. My uncle was there in his ninja garb, Cobra Commander helmet and all. Mr. Entwistle clearly wasn't expecting to see him.

"I thought you were at the hospital with Baddon?"

"I was. But I thought the greater threat was here, so I came back. I also wanted to know if you'd found Hyde." Maximilian glanced over at us. If he noticed the purse Charlie was carrying, he said nothing. I was about to make a wisecrack about our failure to find my friend a decent set of matching high heels, but the look on his face told me it was best to shut up. He was looking at Maximilian intently, his pupils wide and his nostrils slowly flaring.

In some ways, vampires are closer to dogs than humans. Humans trust their eyes more than anything else. If I showed you a chunk of hot fudge, you'd think it was hot fudge, even if it smelled like strawberries. A dog wouldn't be fooled. A strawberry is a strawberry because it smells like a strawberry. Charlie was sniffing the air as if he smelled a rat. You can bet that raised my blood pressure. He had good reason to despise my uncle—and if he figured out that Agent X was Maximilian, well then, I was sure episode one of *Charlie Goes Homicidal* was going to happen right there in the yard. I took a deep breath through my nose. The faint odor of hospital cleanser still clung to my uncle's skin and clothes. No surprises there. He'd just delivered Detective Baddon to see his son. I casually walked past my friend and took hold of his elbow, spinning him toward the door. If it sounds like an aggressive move, it wasn't. I was just trying to get him focused on something other than Maximilian.

"Come on, Charlie," I said. "The sun will be up soon. Let's get inside. Maybe the lovely Suki Abbott is awake."

Charlie fell in step beside me, but kept his head turned and his eyes on my uncle. Mr. Entwistle was giving him a play-by-play of our evening.

"We'll be inside if you need us," I said.

The old vampire nodded, then continued his narrative. Charlie and I navigated the front hall, then stopped outside of Ophelia's first-floor apartment.

"Something about that guy isn't right," Charlie said. "I don't care what Entwistle says about trust. There was no reason for him to shoot me."

I didn't know the best response for this. Any answer would have prolonged a conversation I didn't want to have, so I said nothing. I wanted to see Luna, and the sooner I checked in with Ophelia to make sure she knew we were safe, the sooner I could go knock on Luna's window.

"You know," Charlie said, "I've been thinking. If Hyde is a

werewolf, and Mr. Entwistle is right, he needs to turn into someone huge."

I wondered where Charlie was going with this.

"So. Look at Agent X. He's could be a WWE wrestler."

I must have looked incredulous. I'd never for a second considered it.

"And he was at the hospital, then left, just before Hyde showed up. And now he's snooping around here and he's supposed to be with Baddon."

Could this be true - that my uncle was Mr. Hyde? I was dumbstruck. And Charlie didn't know the half of it. Maximilian had been hunting a werewolf earlier this year. He might easily have been bitten. It would explain why he'd never seen Hyde. Why they were never around together.

Why hadn't this occurred to me? I had to warn Mr. Entwistle. But how? He and my uncle were talking outside.

Charlie nudged me in the ribs. "What's going on in that steel trap you call a brain?"

My steel trap was undecided. Was it really possible that my uncle could be trying to help us as a man and kill us as a monster? I tried to remember what I could from the movies. It seemed to me that the man rarely knew about the beast he turned into. Even if he did know, he could never remember what he'd done when he wasn't human.

"Earth to Zack. You okay? You look like you just got tagged on the chin."

I needed more time to think this through. "Maybe we should mention it to Ophelia."

Charlie nodded, then we entered the first-floor apartment. Ophelia was pacing the room. She looked pale. I couldn't tell if she was worried or furious.

"What is it?" I asked.

"Did you know anything about this?" Her voice was stern.

"About what?"

I looked at Charlie. His expression changed. It might have been guilt. It might have been nervousness. I couldn't tell. I looked back at Ophelia, but had no idea what to say.

"Charlie?" she said.

"Hey, don't look at me."

"What are you talking about?" I asked.

"The girls are gone." I sensed Ophelia was about to start a barrage of questions, but she didn't say any more because Mr. Entwistle and Maximilian were coming through the front door, laughing. Her attention shifted to them.

Mr. Entwistle's nose must have told him something was wrong because the humor disappeared from his face before he looked over. "What is it?"

"The girls have left," Ophelia said. "I was in the basement. I heard them on the fire escape. By the time I realized they were leaving and got to the door, they were already taking off in their car. I had hoped they'd be back by now."

Mr. Entwistle looked at me, then at Charlie. His pale blue eyes probed my friend's face. "Tell us what you know."

Charlie glanced at me. I expected him to look nervous. The old vampire was still staring at him. So was Ophelia. I would have melted under their gaze. But Charlie was used to being in trouble. He was simply irritated.

"Neither of them wants to go home," he said. "They won't be coming back here."

I thought for a second Ophelia was going to attack him. "Charlie, you have no idea how thoughtless this is."

"There wouldn't be a problem if you hadn't called Dr. Abbott."

I hadn't realized that Ophelia had placed the call. But looking back, it was the only thing that made sense. Luna was with me, and Suki wouldn't have called her father, knowing he'd get angry.

"Every parent has the right to know their children are safe."

My uncle stepped between them. "Where have they gone?"

As soon as he spoke, Charlie glared at him. I felt myself cringe.

I'd once compared Maximilian's movements to those of a stone golem. Strength and purpose were in everything he did. He was still carrying his gun, the one that looked as if it had been stolen from a Klingon war chief. I wondered if Charlie was right. If my uncle was Hyde. He swung the gun up so that it was resting on his shoulder. His other arm was folded across his chest in a familiar pose.

"My guess is, they've gone to their cottage," Ophelia said.

"They sold the cottage," I told her. "They don't own it anymore."

She turned to Charlie. "Where are they?"

He wasn't going to answer. I could see his pupils getting wider. His eyebrows knotted.

"Charlie," Mr. Entwistle said, "we can deal with Dr. Abbott. We can't deal with Hyde. Neither can the girls. We have to get them back. The sun will be up soon. There's not much time."

Charlie looked at the ground, then at me. I wish he'd told me Suki was planning to go. I could have asked Luna to talk her out of it. Perhaps she'd tried.

"They're going to the lake."

He must have meant Stony Lake, where Charlie's cottage was.

"Where exactly?" Mr. Entwistle said.

"The camp."

"You mean Camp Kawartha?" my uncle asked.

Charlie glanced at me, then said yes.

Ophelia had assumed her headache pose—fingers and thumb rubbing opposite sides of her forehead. She looked at Mr. Entwistle. "Can you go now? Is there time?"

He didn't have an answer.

"I know the place," Maximilian said. "I can't go. I'm due at the hospital first thing, but you can take my car."

At the sound of the word *car*, something happened in Charlie's brain. You could see it. His face went from thoughtful, to certain, then to rage.

"This is crazy," Mr. Entwistle said. The word *crazy* hung in the air like a challenge. Then Charlie attacked my uncle. I can only assume that he figured out who Agent X really was. Perhaps it was his tone of voice. Something in the way he moved. Or dressed. Or the mention of the word *car*. My uncle had a rocket on wheels. Last year, he'd taken Charlie and Luna hostage and driven them to Montreal in the trunk while I'd sat in the cockpit, totally oblivious.

Maximilian was caught completely by surprise. He turned just in time to have Charlie knock his gun away and slam him up against the far wall. I was already moving. I threw myself at Charlie, shoulder first, in what would have been a textbook tackle if he hadn't ducked. I slipped over the top of him and hit the side of his head with my knee. To Charlie's credit, he rolled with it and came up swinging. He was actually so angry, he'd forgotten about my uncle and was attacking me. I had to play the Artful Dodger for a few seconds until Mr. Entwistle jumped over and tied him up in a bear hug.

Charlie shouted the entire time. "I knew there was something about him. I knew it. I knew it!" He mixed a few swear words in for effect. His eyes were like two black pearls. Hell hath no fury like a demented vampire. I'm sure Shakespeare said that somewhere.

My uncle rose to his feet and pulled out a stun gun.

"There's no need for that." Ophelia was right beside him, her hand on his arm.

I felt like a lost tourist in a haunted house. My friend had finally snapped. Luna was gone. Hyde was still out there, and now we were fighting among ourselves.

My uncle started coughing. His helmet had been knocked loose, and he was spitting up blood.

"You okay?" I asked. "Can you breathe?"

He nodded, then started looking around. His eyes fell to the floor. Then he stumbled over to where his gun was lying and picked it up.

By this time, Mr. Entwistle had taken Charlie to the floor. "Control . . . deep breaths," the old vampire was saying.

I don't know if Charlie was listening, but it was hard to go ballistic with a 650-year-old vampire slowly choking you in a sleeper hold.

"What are you thinking?" Ophelia snapped. Her voice was school-teacher angry.

Charlie couldn't answer. It took most of his effort just to breathe. Mr. Entwistle slowly let go. My friend sucked in a few deep breaths and started rubbing at his neck. Then another cascade of profanity tumbled out of his mouth. He described my uncle's character, his behavior, what he wanted to do to him, and just about anything else you could slap between two swear words. Or two hundred. If it had aired on the radio, it would have been one continuous beep. Then Charlie looked at me.

"You knew. You knew! It's why he shot me in the hospital. You knew he was here the whole time and you didn't say anything. If Luna was here, she'd murder you."

He might have been right. I knew she blamed my uncle for *that night*. For what happened to her. And to her sister. I didn't know what to say to Charlie. This was a disaster.

"Let go of me," Charlie said. "You may trust this bozo, but I don't. He's a backstabbing turncoat. He betrayed all of us."

"Actually, he's more of a front stabber," said Mr. Entwistle. "And if I can forgive him for blowing me up, you should be able to forgive him for trying to keep you alive."

"That's a bunch of baloney," said Charlie. "He drugged us and turned us over to that freak. We should be dead. All of us."

"It wasn't supposed to be that way," Maximilian said. "Vlad said he would accept you in the Underground. Swear you to secrecy. That way, you wouldn't be killed for knowing about Zachary and his condition. Instead, you'd have the protection of the Coven, which Zachary and I were to join."

My uncle turned to me, his face sad. And frustrated. "Vlad wanted to talk to you first, to see if you were ready to assume such an enormous responsibility. That was the arrangement I made with him. So you wouldn't lose your only friends. But Vlad broke his word. I had no idea he'd try to kill anyone."

"I don't believe you," said Charlie.

"That changes nothing. Not the present. Not the past. Nothing." My uncle lowered his gun and looked around at all of us. His eyes settled on Mr. Entwistle. "I have to go to the hospital shortly. If you are serious and really want to get the girls, you can take my car."

Blood was still at the sides of my uncle's mouth. He suddenly looked gray. A kind of exhaustion had settled over his features. I'd never seen him this way. Vulnerable. Corpselike. He did things with such self-assurance, it was easy to forget he was dying of cancer.

"It's all right," Mr. Entwistle said. "There isn't time. I'll take the ambulance once the sun goes down."

My uncle nodded. "I'm sorry about what happened. My loyalty is to my nephew. I have always kept his interests at heart."

"And your own," Charlie hissed.

"Believe that if it helps you. But I'm no good to anyone if I'm dead. Dealing with Vlad and joining the Coven—it seemed the best way at the time." Maximilian's eyes passed over all of us, then he turned to go.

"That's it? After all he's done, you're just letting him go?" Charlie shouted at us.

My uncle stopped in the doorway. For a man who'd been attacked and vilified, he had remarkable composure. "What reason would I have for hurting you?"

We all waited.

Charlie stared at him. His mouth started to move, but nothing came out. A voice in my head told me I should write this down. It was the first time in my life I'd ever seen him speechless.

"You're a one-man soap opera, Charlie," Maximilian said, reaching for the door. "You're lucky your friends are so patient."

A second later the door closed.

"We can't let him go," Charlie said.

"Why not?" Ophelia asked.

"I think he's Hyde," Charlie said. "I think he's the one we've been looking for."

Mr. Entwistle looked at Ophelia. I could tell they both thought Charlie was right out to lunch. I understood his anger. He didn't want Suki to go back to Newark. He wanted to make her a vampire so she could be one of us. That couldn't happen if her father took her away. I felt so bad for him, I started talking and didn't stop until I'd mentioned all the reasons my uncle might have been the Beast. His size. The year he'd spent hunting a werewolf. His sudden appearance in our lives—timed perfectly with Hyde's. The fact that he'd never seen Hyde, and we never actually knew his whereabouts when Hyde was around. In the end, I'd convinced everyone, even myself.

Mr. Entwistle moved to the window and started peeking from under the blind. Ophelia sat down.

"Do you really think it's possible?" she asked.

I didn't know. But if it was true, it meant he knew where we were. He knew our defenses and how to get past them. And he knew Luna was unprotected at the camp.

Charlie rose to leave.

"Where are you going?" I asked.

"I'm going to bed, *buddy*." He said the last word like a curse.

I guess, like me, he just wanted this night to be over. I opened my mouth to say sorry but he cut me off.

"Don't bother."

Then he walked out the door and slammed it shut behind him.

CHAPTER 34
PARTING WAYS

Mr. Entwistle looked at me. The muscles in his jaws twitched as his teeth ground together. "This is bad," he said.

"Tell me about it."

"There's more at stake here than a summer romance, boy."

I knew this already.

Mr. Entwistle's face relaxed. He took a deep breath, apologized for losing his temper, and headed for the back door.

"Are you leaving?" I asked.

"No. Just checking on your uncle."

I'd just assumed he'd left. When I said so, Mr. Entwistle shook his head. "If I know Maximilian, he'll walk the perimeter once more just to make certain the motion detectors are working. He wasn't lying when he said he has your best interests at heart."

The old vampire slipped out the door, leaving me with Ophelia, who was chewing her cheek, her eyes lost. A few seconds later, I heard the sound of an engine starting. It was the painted ambulance in the driveway. Did that mean Mr. Entwistle was leaving?

"I'll be right back," I said.

I slipped out the back door. Mr. Entwistle was pulling out of the drive. I wondered if he'd been lying. If he hadn't been talking to my uncle at all, but was really leaving to go after Hyde. He'd said he would have to face Hyde alone. But it was so close to dawn. And he hadn't even said good-bye.

Then the garage door started to open. Two headlights lit up the apartment. It was suddenly brighter than Broadway. I heard a sound like a jet engine, and my uncle slowly pulled forward in his car. I slipped to the side of the driveway and he stopped beside me. Although I'd seen it before and had even ridden in the front, the sight of his car was still shocking. Jedi knights didn't get to drive in things this cool. It was half bat mobile, half spaceship, with doors that opened upward and a spoiler like a whale tail. The window slid down.

"Is he leaving?" I gazed at the ambulance, which was backing out onto the street.

My uncle shook his head. "No, just moving so I can get out."

I suddenly felt foolish. But life is like that sometimes. You get so used to bad news, you just expect more.

"Are you okay?" I asked my uncle.

"Tired . . . I got sloppy. I shouldn't have pushed my luck—coming in the house like that. Thoughtless . . ." Pain was in his voice. He let his head fall back against the seat rest.

"I'm sorry." It sounded lame, but I meant it.

"Don't apologize. I had that coming." He took a moment to adjust his seat belt, a double-shoulder harness.

"Your father had a belief that we should put the job ahead of everything. I put myself first. And I lied to myself. I said I was doing it for you. That if I died, I couldn't protect you from the Coven, couldn't continue your father's work—our work. So I negotiated with Vlad. It was foolish. . . . And I have paid. We all have."

He started coughing. I could smell the blood in his mouth.

"You're dying."

He nodded. "Yes. Nothing is working. I've one last option."

"What is that?"

"Biotherapeutics."

I had no idea what that meant.

"You take a nonlethal virus and use it to kill the cancer cells in your body," my uncle explained. "But I still have one more radiation treatment. I'm afraid I won't be much use for the next little while. I've never been this exhausted." His eyes drifted up to the eastern horizon. It was growing lighter. "You should go. Make sure Charlie's okay. I know he's angry with you, but this will pass. He'll come around. Just give him time." The words tumbled out slowly. He sounded tired, but sincere.

I thanked him and he slowly pulled away. The car engine whined. I could feel the power of it resonate in my stomach. A second later Mr. Entwistle pulled the ambulance back in. I didn't wait for him. The light was faint, but it still made me uncomfortable, and I was worried about Charlie.

When I came in, Ophelia was in the kitchen returning the phone to its cradle. She had the ugly purse with the wolfsbane in her other hand.

Mr. Entwistle entered a second later. "Where is he?" I guessed he meant Charlie.

"He's on the roof," Ophelia answered. "I heard him go up while you were outside."

Mr. Entwistle nodded and headed for the stairs.

"What are we going to say to Dr. Abbott when he gets here?" I asked.

"I'll call him now and tell him where his children are. He'll probably be relieved. It means he won't have to come here and talk to any of us."

This was true.

"I had no idea they were going to leave."

Ophelia nodded. "I could tell." Then she held up the purse. "Why did you bring this awful thing into the house?"

I quickly explained about the storage unit and the monkshood. I was expecting her to be impressed. We'd acquired a new poison, perhaps one that might prove useful against Hyde, but if anything, the mention of it just made her nervous. "What's wrong?" I asked.

"Wolfsbane is lethal to vampires, Zachary. And to people. If Hyde has this, it only makes him more dangerous."

I don't know why this hadn't occurred to me. I guess it indicated how poorly my mind was working.

"I'll have to call Detective Baddon," she said, "and see if he can find out who that storage unit belongs to."

"Do you think Maximilian might be Hyde?"

She sighed and zipped open the purse, then carefully examined the tiny hooded flowers inside. "I hope not. I was counting on his help. But if it is him, at least he knows us as a man and trusts us. Perhaps we could find a way to help him."

I looked away and nodded. I didn't want it to be true. I didn't want my uncle to be that thing.

"You should get some sleep. You look beat."

She was right. It had been a long and tiring night. I said good-night and made my way up to the second-floor apartment, sealed the window shutters in my room, pulled the blind closed, and shut the curtains. Then I settled on the bed and listened for Charlie.

It wasn't my intention to doze off, but it happened anyway. I woke up to the sound of someone knocking at the door. I hoped it would be him, but when I said "come in," Mr. Entwistle entered.

"You're not asleep yet. Good."

I sat up and asked if Charlie was okay.

"He's fine. Just talking to Ophelia now. They're in the apartment upstairs."

"Is something wrong?"

"He'll be fine. I just needed to explain to him why it was so important that your uncle be involved. And that he be forgiving. Are you all right?"

"Yeah. You?"

His movements were restless, his eyes busy. He strayed into the doorway, his hat tucked under his arm. The hall light was behind him, so his body was like a tall shadow. "As good as can be expected. I wanted to speak to you about a few things, but I . . ." He waved his hand through the air as if it wasn't really that important.

"No, tell me. What is it?"

He hesitated. "I just wanted to . . ." A few quiet seconds followed. "I've been trying to find a solution to this Hyde dilemma."

"Do you think Charlie's right? That his alter ego might be Maximilian?"

He started shaking his head. "I'm not convinced. It just doesn't fit."

I didn't know what he was talking about. It seemed to fit perfectly to me. But he didn't say anything else about it. He just sat down on the bed and looked at me over his shoulder.

"I believe he's a lycanthrope, Zack. Hyde, I mean. Not your uncle. But no matter how I reason it out, I can't get past the reality of the Beast, and that I have to face him. I've seen it too many times. . . ."

I realized as he spoke, as I watched his eyes move around the room, that he was terrified. I understood. Hyde terrified me, too.

"You don't think you can beat him?"

He took his hat off. It trembled in his hands. "I can't."

"Are you afraid of dying?"

He looked at me. His clear blue eyes were piercing. His forehead knotted. He looked offended. "Of dying? Me? Heavens no. I've never been afraid of that." He stood up as though I'd somehow restored his confidence. Then he seemed to sag. His face. His shoulders. It was subtle, but I didn't miss it. "But when I die, who will deal with him?"

Is that what scared him? That he would die and leave us helpless?

"I can't beat him. I've faced him several times now, and John Entwistle is no match for this thing. I can't. John Entwistle can't . . ."

When he said his name that way, I suddenly understood his fear. The air of defeat around him. He wasn't afraid of Hyde or of dying. He was afraid of himself.

"John Entwistle can't beat him," he continued, "but the Butcher can. The Butcher can kill anything."

So that was it. I was right. He was afraid he would become John Tiptoft, the Butcher of England. The man he used to be.

"I don't think you're meant to be that person," I said.

"I can't see any other way. I keep asking myself, *How can we survive?* There is no cure for lycanthropy. Only death stops the curse.

To atone for the sins of John Tiptoft I must face the Beast. I know that. But how can I atone for my sins by committing murder? How can I atone by becoming a monster myself?"

There was only one answer. He couldn't. I suddenly understood why he wanted to face Hyde alone. He didn't want us to see him becoming the thing he most feared—the Butcher. He wasn't just trying to protect us from Hyde, but from himself.

He sighed, turned, and opened the door. "You're a good kid, Zack." His voice sounded sad. It dropped to a whisper. "I had a son once . . . little boy . . . died of plague. . . . Had he grown up, I would have wanted him to be like you . . . would have been proud of that."

He put his hat on his head and closed the door. I listened to his footsteps. A great swell of pity rose up in my throat. I wondered how he could have been anyone but Mr. Entwistle. And I wondered how Luna was. And Charlie. I decided to wait up so I could ask him, but when I put my head down, I fell into a deep and dreamless sleep. Some days are like that.

I awoke at dusk to the sound of gentle knocking. It was coming from the window. I got up, drew the curtains, raised the blinds, and pulled back the shutters. A faint strip of yellow light was fading on the western horizon. The sun was gone, but I still had to squint to see.

Charlie was standing on the fire escape. A pack hung loosely over his shoulder. He looked at me. I knew what he would ask before he opened his mouth. *Are you coming?*

"Where?" I asked.

"Stony Lake."

"You mean the camp?"

He nodded.

I started looking for my shoes. Once I'd slipped them on, I climbed out onto the landing. Charlie hadn't moved.

"You should have told me," he said.

He must have been talking about my uncle—that Maximilian was Agent X.

"Yeah. I know. I'm sorry. I kept thinking there would be a good time, but stuff kept happening. . . . Are we good?"

Charlie turned and started down the steps. "Yeah. But still—you should have told me."

I closed the window and followed him to the street. "You know they'll see us leave. And it won't take a brain scientist to figure out where we're going."

He nodded. "Ophelia said the same thing last night. She wanted me to know that if I left, she'd notice. But I don't care."

We started off down the street. Then my mind started wandering. What if we ran into Hyde? Or worse. What if he followed us to the camp? I slowed. Then stopped.

"Don't tell me you're bailing already?"

"We need to go back."

Charlie looked as if he were ready to bite me. His voice was angry. And disappointed. "You want to go back to the apartment?"

"No. I want to go to Ophelia's safe house on Burnham. The one with the antiques—the weapons. If Hyde shows up, I want to be armed with more than just running shoes."

Charlie smiled, exposing his long incisors. "Now you're talkin'!"

CHAPTER 35

THE VAMPIRE'S KISS

The trip to Stony Lake was exhausting. Running with a two-handed sword isn't as easy as it looks. Video games can be deceiving that way. The thing was five feet long and weighed forty pounds. I was flushed and famished by the time I arrived. Charlie was, too.

We approached the camp from the road. Because it was just down the channel from Charlie's cottage, I'd assumed it was on Stony Lake, but he explained on the way in that it was actually on another one, Clear Lake, though the boundary wasn't really clear at all. It looked like one large body of water. It was around ten by this time, and the place was settling down.

I'd never been to a summer camp or even seen one before, so I was a bit surprised by the number of buildings scattered through the woods and along the shore. There were playing fields for football and soccer. And even a rope course.

"This place is awesome," I whispered.

Charlie laughed. "Aren't you a bit old for camp?"

Obviously not. It looked like paradise to me. We passed a rock-climbing wall, then a basketball court. You'd never get bored at a place like this. It was like Disneyland, but without the threat of anyone spontaneously bursting into a corny song.

"Where do you think the girls are?" I asked.

"My bet is, they're at the docks. Just one second." He pulled out his cell.

One text message later we were heading for the waterfront. There, on the docks, Luna and Suki were sitting side by side, their feet dangling in the water.

Charlie and I crouched in the shadows of a boathouse. We didn't want to brave the lights. Several were illuminating the shoreline. A swirling cloud of moths hovered around each lamp. From time to time, the familiar shape of a bat darted through.

Charlie raised his chin and whispered into the wind, "Hey, Luna. The president of your fan club is here."

As soon as he spoke, she turned, then smiled and tapped Suki on the shoulder. A second later they were walking toward our hiding place. Luna's expression changed from pleasure to alarm when she saw the weapons we were carrying. My sword was almost as tall as she was, and Charlie had a voulge on his back—a pole arm with a head like a halberd's, a combination of spear and cleaver with a few extra barbs and hooks thrown in for good measure. It was over seven feet long.

"What are those?" she asked.

"Security," answered Charlie. He was watching Suki. She seemed sedate and uncertain. I could smell it on her skin and see it in the anxious movement of her eyes.

"Are you expecting trouble?" she asked.

Charlie reached out and took her hand, then raised it to his mouth and kissed it. "Only the trouble I plan to make."

She smiled, then tugged at his arm and started to pull him away from the boathouse toward a trail that led through the woods. He resisted, his eyes staring out over the lake. He lifted her hand then kissed it again.

"I miss the water," he said. "Is there somewhere we can go without spotlights? I'd love to get my feet wet."

"There's a beach this way," Luna said. "Let's get out of here before someone sees you guys. You look like a pair of assassins."

"Wait. I've a better idea." Charlie tipped his head toward the boathouse. "There's got to be some canoes in here. Why don't we take one out?"

Suki shrugged, then smiled. A mischievous spark was in her eyes. A trademark of the old Suki. "I'd love to go for a midnight paddle."

Charlie laughed, then pulled her closer, which made her giggle. Then he saw the look on my face and laughed even harder. He knew I didn't like the water. I felt his hand slap the center of my back.

"Don't worry, Captain Nemo. Hyde hates the water, too, remember? It's what saved Entwistle. So at least you'll be safe for a few hours." Then Charlie looked at Luna. "Well, safe from him, at least."

A canoe is a tricky beast. It looks stable until you get in, then, just when you relax, it tries to throw you overboard. The secret, I've learned, is to stay low and let the other person do most of the work. I had never paddled before, so Luna had me sit in the bottom with my back against the piece of wood across the middle. She told me it was called the thwart, which was a perfect name, since it thwarted me from getting anywhere near her. In the end, I crawled to the front and sat facing backward so I could look at her without having to peer over my shoulder.

"Why didn't you tell me you were leaving the apartment?" I asked.

Luna raised her paddle as if she were going to hit me with it. "I didn't know anything about it. It was Suki's idea. I couldn't talk her out of it. I didn't really want to go, but the thought of going home with my dad was too depressing."

"What's going to happen when he shows up here?"

"What do you mean when he shows up? He showed up this afternoon and flipped out."

"What happened?"

Luna shrugged. "Suki's words, not mine. I was asleep in the trunk of the car."

Those didn't sound like the best sleeping arrangements. When I mentioned it, Luna shrugged it off. "Better than the alternative."

She took another stroke. I noticed that she turned her thumb down each time. It made the blade twist in the water so it acted like a rudder.

"I thought your dad wanted to take you home," I said.

"He does. But he wants me to see a blood specialist in Toronto first."

"Where is he now?"

"Who? Dad? He's asleep in the infirmary. The camp doctor is an old friend of his. After driving most of the night and morning, he's exhausted."

"So how long will you be here?"

She shrugged. "We'll drive to Toronto tomorrow night—that would be my guess."

For a time, neither of us spoke. I just watched the muscles in her arms and shoulders at work as she paddled us down the shore.

"Does anyone know you're here?" she asked.

I shrugged. "It won't take a rocket surgeon to figure it out."

"And then what?"

"Who knows? I don't want to think about it. I can't believe you're leaving."

Her eyes softened and she smiled sadly. "We have tonight. . . ."

I glanced over my shoulder. Charlie and Suki had already paddled farther down the shore. I think they were planning to go to his family's cottage. It was on an island down the channel.

"You look much better," Luna said.

I didn't feel much better. I needed more sleep, and another dose of blood. But mostly I just needed to hear some good news.

"Have you talked to your sister about Charlie?"

"What do you mean?"

I let my hand fall into the cool water, where it left a long V-shaped trail across the surface. "About turning. Becoming one of us?"

"A bit. I think she wants to. But she's afraid. Now might not be the best time. Why? Has Charlie said something?"

"Not lately. Not to me. But things have been crazy. I'm sure he wants to."

"Yeah, like we aren't in enough trouble." She put the paddle down across the gunnels and started sliding forward. "Don't move for a second."

I wasn't going to move if a whale breached under us. I wasn't wearing a life jacket, which for me was like skydiving without a parachute. As soon as she started toward me, I gripped the gunnels so hard I felt the wood begin to creak. Luna stopped when she crossed the thwart, then turned and backed up so that she was leaning against me.

"You seem nervous," she said. She took my arms and wrapped them around her waist, then let her head fall onto my chest.

We looked up at the moon. At the clouds. It was a perfect night. She nestled in a little closer. Then she turned so that her face was right in front of mine.

"You still owe me a kiss," she said.

My brain was starting to sizzle. The smell of her hair. The closeness of her. I'd read about moments like this. Seen them in movies. The kiss that would make some patients at the Nicholls Ward roll their eyes and others sit up in their seats. A part of me, my heart I guess, was screaming, *Yes, yes, yes, yes, yessssssssssss.* But another part of me was saying, *No, no, no, no, nooooooooooo,* because my teeth were up to their usual tricks and wanted to get busy. My whole body started to buzz. And my eyes—they kept straying to that part of Luna's neck right under her ear where her muscles formed a perfect contour. It was inviting all kinds of mischief. I couldn't figure this out. I knew I wasn't supposed to bite another vampire. Her blood might be fatal. So why did I want to so badly?

Her eyes closed. Her chin rose. A quiet breath leaked past her open mouth. I should have just kissed her, but I didn't want to mess it up.

"Don't be afraid," she said.

"I'm not afraid."

"You're shaking."

"I'm not shaking." I'm not sure why I said this. It wasn't true.

"What are you waiting for?"

I wasn't sure. I just didn't know what I was doing. Her teeth were down like mine. One started to tease the front of her bottom lip. It made a gentle indentation against her skin. I was going crazy. I wondered if she felt the same.

"You think too much," she said.

Her face was close enough to me now that I could feel the warmth of her. One of her hands strayed to my chest. She turned and her other hand slipped around my neck. She tightened her grip. It surprised me. She was a vampire now, much stronger than the first time we'd been like this—last year, at her cottage. Almost kissing.

"Don't think," she said. Her eyes closed again. Her head tipped back. Mine tipped forward. "Just do what comes naturally."

So I bit her.

I took it from her yelp that this wasn't exactly what she'd been expecting. Fortunately she wasn't loud, or the whole shoreline would have woken. I'd finally get to meet an angry mob, or at least the summer-camp version. The rush I got from the taste of her blood sent shock waves through my body.

Luna gasped. Then she tightened her grip and drew me in closer. I felt her head shift. Pain jabbed my neck like two hot nails. The skin burned. Then an airy feeling filled my head. I couldn't think of anything but the rush. It was thrilling. And horrifying. She was drinking from me, and I from her. I was getting weaker. We both were. My vision went blurry. My hand was on the back of her head, my fingers massaging her warm skin. I could feel her pulse. It was quickening. My head fell back and the stars overhead started to swim. I had no strength left. I had to lie down. Somehow we managed it together so we were resting in the canoe. I closed my eyes and felt her body lying against mine. Her breathing was like my breathing. Slower now. Her heartbeat was more settled, but still strong. One hand remained on my chest, and her head nestled in the space between my arm and shoulder.

"What just happened?"

She hummed a soft sigh. "I don't know." Then her eyes opened. They were warm. Glowing. "But we have to do it again sometime." Her teeth were still down. The same one as before had strayed outside her lip and was pressing against the front of it.

"I think I need a minute," I said, and looked up at the stars. They were back in their usual arrangement. I took a deep breath and smiled. The rush was passing, but with no feeling of disappointment, of ending. Instead there was only deep contentment. A warm restfulness. Not even dying felt this good.

"You mean that?" Luna asked. She nestled her head a little deeper into my shoulder. I kissed the top of it.

"Do I mean what?"

"That this is better than dying?"

I must have been thoroughly exhausted. I was certain that I hadn't spoken a word.

"I heard you," she said.

An honest mistake. I was zonked.

"That's a funny word," she said.

I knew I hadn't spoken that time. This was odd.

I felt her hand pinch me. "What's so odd about it?"

She raised her head so that her chin sat gently against my chest. I smiled. Nothing about this was odd. It was perfect. She was perfect. I saw her smile. It was beautiful. Just for me. Then her eyes popped to full width, then somehow got bigger.

"I can hear you," she whispered.

Unbelievable!

Her head shook back and forth. Her mouth started to move as if she were going to say something, but nothing came out. Her hands were touching me. I could almost feel what she was thinking. Surprise. Wonder. Then fear. *She could hear my thoughts.*

I was stunned. Then embarrassed. Her beautiful neck was still in front of me. The two puncture wounds I'd put there were healing. To see them, and smell her blood, made me ravenous. I knew it was wrong, but I couldn't help it. Nor could I hide it. She could read my mind. I felt my face heating up. A smile crept back onto her lips. Her eyes sparkled. Beautiful shades of olive and pale emerald. They were moist and happy. Then mischievous.

That's nothing to worry about.

"I'm not worried." I realized as the words left my mouth that she hadn't spoken out loud.

I didn't.

The thought was as clear as the sound of my own heartbeat. I wasn't imagining this. It was real. I could hear her thoughts, too. I looked at her face and pulled my hand through her long, beautiful hair. This was really happening.

Yes, it really is, she thought.

She smiled, and my senses were suddenly flooded. Her hands found my sides. She squeezed me. I couldn't imagine it was possible to feel more complete than I did at that moment.

I love you, she thought. And I thought the same. And she held me tighter.

CHAPTER 36

MISSING IN ACTION

I think I must have slept, although I'm not sure, because I didn't dream. I just thought of Luna. We didn't speak. There was no need. But a kind of physical paralysis had come over me. I wasn't aware of it until I felt Luna's breath on my neck again.

You still owe me a kiss, she thought.

I wasn't sure that I could pull it off.

Why? she asked.

I thought of my answer before I had a chance to stop myself.

You've never kissed anyone? She paused. Her smile was electric. "Oh, that's so cute."

Cute. I had nothing against the word, but it had never been an ambition of mine to be described that way.

You'll get over it, she thought. Then she leaned in and kissed me.

I'm not going to say it wasn't pleasant. The whole lip-smushing experience was quite exciting. It didn't compare to the thrill of our vampires' kiss, but I soon discovered that kisses of the normal kind had an addictive quality all of their own. After one, I found I needed another. And another. I was beginning to feel as if the canoe were just about the best invention since God made air. I could have spent weeks like this. The whole time we shared thoughts. Well, one thought, over and over. But that was all right. It was a good thought. We were in love. It was nice to say it, and better to hear it, and better still to feel that it was true.

Just before midnight, we were interrupted by the sound of our canoe banging against something solid.

Luna sat up.

"What is it?" I asked. I peeked over the gunnels. The water had pushed us into a dock down from the camp. We were bumping up against a large powerboat.

"I'd better get us back," she said.

I let her go, thinking how terrible it was that some moments had to end.

"That's very romantic," she said. Then she climbed into the back of the canoe and started paddling.

Do you want to try?

I didn't, and I let her know.

This is going to take some getting used to.

You're tellin' me. I wonder how long it will last.

I have no idea, Luna thought. *But I like it.*

I did, too.

She smiled, then paddled us back to camp.

Charlie and Suki were on the farthest dock along the shore. I could see a huge waterslide beside them. It looked like fun, except that it involved landing in the water.

You just need more practice swimming, Luna thought.

This was true. I needed practice with lots of things.

"Not as much as you think," she said. "Not that we won't practice more anyway, but we should check in with those two first and see what's up."

I glanced down toward Charlie and Suki. They were sitting together, holding hands, their feet dangling in the water. I wondered if he'd bitten her.

I hope not.

As we got closer, I could hear Charlie whispering. "Man, I miss this . . ."

I felt a pang of guilt. And then sympathy. This had come from Luna.

Charlie saw us coming and put his hand in the water, then scooped a handful and splashed it our way. "I was starting to think you two lovebirds were going to float down to Burleigh Falls."

Should we tell him? Luna asked.

No, I thought. I didn't want him to know about this. Not until I was sure that things with him and Suki were solid. I was worried that he might get jealous. It was bad enough that his girlfriend was struggling and wasn't one of us. If we told him about this connection, it would just be one more thing that Luna and I shared that Suki and he couldn't.

"How were things at your cottage?" Luna asked.

"We didn't stop in," Charlie said. "But I gotta tell ya, it would be a perfect place to hide from Hyde."

"But?"

"But Dan is there with his family."

Dan was one of Charlie's older brothers. He had a gaggle of kids. I doubt he would have wanted us showing up to make things even more chaotic.

"So what happens now?" I asked.

Charlie shrugged, then he saw the marks on my neck. And on Luna's.

"You didn't! Isn't that supposed to kill you?"

"It hasn't yet," I said.

"Let's hope Daddy Abbott doesn't notice."

My stomach wasn't thrilled with the idea. Fortunately Charlie got the conversation rolling in another direction.

"I think we should call," he said.

I assumed he meant Ophelia.

"We should get back to the apartment," he added.

"Who? All of us?" I glanced at Suki, then at Luna.

Charlie looked as me like I'd just won the village idiot award. "Well, I didn't come here to work on my tan."

Are you cool with this? I asked Luna.

What? With leaving? You bet! I don't want that thing showing up here. We need to stick together, and get someplace safe.

I agreed, and pulled my cell phone from my pocket, but I couldn't get a signal.

"What is it?" Charlie asked. "Is the battery dead?"

"No. I'm not getting any coverage."

I felt Luna's hand come to rest on my arm. "I could have told you that."

I guess it explained why I hadn't heard from Ophelia. I felt a twinge of guilt in my stomach. She must have been worried sick.

"So what do we do?" Suki asked.

"Do you feel up for a drive?" Luna asked her.

A drive?

How do you think we got here? We'll just take our car.

What do we tell your father? If we just leave, he'll murder us!

No, thought Luna, *he'll murder you.*

Suki was the only one with a license, which meant Luna and I were crammed into the back of the car. It was a BMW—90 percent engine and 10 percent tire. The backseat was like an afterthought, small, cramped, with just enough leg room for a small house cat, but that was okay, it kept us close. There was a lot of nervous energy in the car. No wonder Charlie broke the rules so often at school. It was fun.

Until the phone rang. Everyone but Luna checked their pockets.

"That's me." I scanned the display. Ophelia was calling.

Are you going to answer?

I hit the button with the green phone on it and said hello.

"Oh, Zachary, thank heavens. Why did you turn your phone off?"

"I didn't. We came up to the lake to get the girls. There's no reception up here."

"So Charlie's with you? And Luna?"

"And Suki."

"I suspected as much. Is everyone all right?"

I said yes.

A wave of relief poured through the speaker of my phone. "I need to speak to John."

John? I thought for a second Ophelia must have meant Luna's father, then I remembered his name was Gerald. "You mean Mr. Entwistle?"

"Yes. I need to speak with him."

Luna was listening. So was Charlie. I looked at both of them. Charlie shrugged. Luna didn't. She was wondering what I was wondering. Why would Ophelia think Mr. Entwistle was with us?

"He's not here," I said.

There was a short pause. "So who's driving?"

"Suki."

Smart money would have bet she was in her headache pose right now.

"So is John following you? He's not answering his phone."

"No. We haven't seen him all night."

This time the pause was longer. "I beg your pardon."

"We haven't seen him all night."

It might have been static, but I could have sworn I heard a faint "Oh, no."

"What is it?" I asked. "What's going on?"

"I don't know. John left to get you just after sunset. He took the ambulance. That was hours ago."

I looked at Charlie. I heard Luna's thoughts running parallel with mine. Mr. Entwistle had left for the camp to get us and hadn't arrived. There could only be one reason. And I knew what it was.

CHAPTER 37

HOMECOMING

Get home right away," Ophelia said. "I mean here—to the apartment."

I said we would. Then she hung up. I felt another surge of sympathy from Luna as I put my phone away. And fear. She didn't know Mr. Entwistle well, but she could feel my distress and was worried.

Charlie was watching me closely. "He knew where we were going, didn't he?"

Probably.

"So Hyde got him."

I didn't think so. My guess was, he had told Ophelia he was coming to find us, but instead went after Hyde knowing we wouldn't be able to follow. It would have explained his odd behavior and the things he'd said when he came to see me that morning. It was his way of saying good-bye.

Do you think so?

I do.

Luna squeezed my hand. "Step on it," she said to her sister.

Suki didn't disappoint. The engine roared. What would have taken Charlie and me almost an hour on the Shoe-Leather Express she covered in about twenty minutes. The only thing that slowed us down were all the fire trucks on Clonsilla as we approached the apartment. Police cars and ambulances were gathering, too.

"That's smoke," said Charlie.

It was. It got thicker as we got closer to home.

"Hurry," he said.

"I can't," Suki exclaimed. "There's police everywhere. You want to get pulled over and spend the next few hours explaining why we have a car full of medieval weapons?"

She had a point. The two-handed sword and voulge were tucked along one side of the car. They were too long to lie flat against the floor, so the handles of both would be obvious to anyone who looked in.

As we rounded the corner near Gordon Avenue, I could see the apartment. It was being consumed in a pillar of fire. Gouts of flame burst from the windows, and a thick, billowing cloud of black smoke poured from the roof. The fire trucks were setting up. Men scrambled with ladders and hoses. The police were there. Someone in a paramedics uniform was waving for us to turn down Victory Crescent instead of driving past the building.

"What do I do?" asked Suki.

"Pull over up there," said Charlie.

We turned off of Clonsilla and Suki slid in along the curb. Charlie had to get out first so I could climb past his seat. I heard Luna's voice in my head: *Call her.* I dug out my phone. Found Ophelia's number. There was no answer. I started running. Several officers tried to stop me, but I was moving too quickly. Then I reached the front walk. The heat from the building was so intense, I couldn't get near the door. I felt someone take hold of my arm, a firefighter. He started talking to me.

"It's my house," I said. "My mother is inside."

I don't know if he answered me, but he let go. I guess he knew I wouldn't be able to get any closer. I just stared at the inferno. If Ophelia was in there, it was going to take a time machine to save her.

Charlie caught up a moment later. Luna was with him. *Listen!* she thought.

I looked at her, then realized Charlie was talking to me.

". . . be around."

"What was that?"

"If Hyde did this, he might still be around. We need to get out of here."

"What about Ophelia?" I couldn't leave until I knew if she'd made it out okay.

Luna took hold of my arm. *She would want you to get somewhere safe.*

That was true.

Luna started pulling me away from the crowd that was gathering on the sidewalk to watch. I didn't resist. Men and women in uniform were trying to move everyone to the other side of the street.

Then my phone rang. I checked the display. Iron Spike Enterprises. It was my uncle. He would know what to do. I picked up and said hello.

"Zack. What a relief! Everything okay?"

"No."

"Are you here—at the hospital?"

It was just up the hill. "I'm down the street at the apartment."

"What's going on? It sounds like a circus."

I told him about the fire. He swore. "I'm still at the Civic. It's crazy here, as well." I could hear him stumbling around. "Wait. I can see it from the window. Did Ophelia make it out?"

I couldn't answer. He repeated the question. Luna moved her mouth closer to my ear and told him we didn't know.

"Zachary, listen. This is important," he said. "Hyde was just here. He's taken Baddon's son."

I thought of the small, frail child and a part of my mind snapped awake. It was angry. "Is he still there?"

"Who? Hyde? I don't think so. I can't get near the room. Security has it cordoned off. I was asleep when he broke in and didn't get down the hall in time. Dammit, I can hardly move."

"Are you hurt?"

"No. It's the radiation treatment. Burns your insides. . . . Poor Adam. I think he might be dead."

Who's Adam? Luna asked.

Detective Baddon.

For a few seconds all I could hear was static and the sound of sirens and chaos.

"Get somewhere safe," my uncle said. "I'll find you. Just get out of sight."

Somewhere safe? Unless he had a spaceship and could ferry us to Mars, we weren't going to be safe anywhere. And I had to look for Ophelia. She had to be somewhere. My uncle started talking again. I couldn't really hear him. The hand I was using to hold the phone had dropped to my side, and the sirens were making a lot of noise.

"Zack. Zack, are you still there?"

Luna took the phone. "We're here. We'll call you once we're clear."

My uncle said something to her, then she hung up and handed the phone back to me. I felt Charlie's hand on my back. He'd opened the door to the car and was guiding me in.

"What's going on?" Suki asked.

She and Luna and Charlie started talking. I didn't follow their conversation. My mind was too busy trying to figure out how to find Ophelia. If she'd made it out, where would she go? Would she stay here knowing we'd be back? Did she have another safe house I didn't know about? Would she try to find Mr. Entwistle or go to the hospital to get my uncle?

Suki pulled out of the parking spot and Charlie fed her instructions. I didn't pay attention. Not until the car stopped.

We were outside of town on Highway 4. A familiar pasture was beside us. It was where Mr. Entwistle, Charlie, and I had followed Hyde's trail the night before. Charlie got out. So did Suki. I felt Luna nudge me gently. I climbed outside and she followed.

Where is this? she asked.

I told her.

What is Charlie thinking?

That we have something to take care of. I turned to face my friend. He was talking to Suki.

"Then we followed him out here. His trail is just off the road."

He reached into the car along the side of the seat to where he'd stashed our weapons. He handed me the sword, then pulled out the long-handled voulge.

"What are we doing?" I asked, although I already knew the answer.

Charlie looked at me. His pupils were widening. I saw his tongue flick up against his gums, a sure sign his teeth were dropping.

"We're going to follow Hyde's tracks," he said. "You and I. We're going to find his lair and wait for him there. Then when he comes back, we're going to kill him."

CHAPTER 38

SCORCHED EARTH

My thoughts seemed to be stuck in slow motion. Luna's were racing. There was fear. Uncertainty. Questions. About me. About Mr. Entwistle. About Ophelia. About Hyde and the stupidity of two young boys who thought they could deal with him using weapons that were out-of-date three centuries ago. I didn't have answers. I only knew Charlie was right—we had to kill him.

I hadn't spoken to him much about the prophecies—about the son of the hunter, the messiah. The End of Days. Not after we'd read the letter together. But Luna and I had covered them thoroughly when we'd met on the Dream Road. Since then, I'd spoken to Ophelia, to the prophet Baoh, and to Mr. Entwistle. It came down to this. None of it mattered. Not one pinch. Was I special? Well, sure. Isn't everyone? We're all the heroes of our own life stories. We try to be good. To do what is right. And we have to live with ourselves. With what we do. And what we don't do.

Hyde had stolen a man's son. The boy was finished if we didn't find him. I didn't even know his name. But if Maximilian's hunch was right, his father, Detective Baddon, was dead. I thought of all that had happened in the last few nights. I heard Baoh's voice in my head. *Be righteous. And do not do to others that which is harmful to yourself.* What could be more harmful to a person than being left in the hands of a beast like Hyde? In my mind's eye, I could still see the boy as he'd appeared in that hospital bed. He reminded me of myself. I was his age when Vlad had infected me. It was just after my father died. I'd spent weeks in a coma. But I hadn't been alone. Ophelia had saved me. But she was gone now. So was Mr. Entwistle. My uncle was a walking corpse, a man just waiting for his cancer to kill him. That left only me. And Charlie. And Luna. She moved closer to me. I could feel the nervous energy in her.

Are you sure about this?

I was. And I wasn't. Our chances weren't good. The words *snowball in hell* came to mind. But maybe two snowballs have a better chance than one, and a kind of certainty comes from having a purpose, even if the odds aren't good that you'll make it to the finish line. I knew that if I balked—if I ran and hid—then every bad thing that Hyde did would, in some way, be my fault.

You aren't to blame for any of this.

No, I thought. *I'm not to blame. Unless I do nothing.*

"You girls better get going," Charlie said.

Luna looked at me. Her eyes were burning. *I'm coming with you.*

I shook my head. I remembered what she'd said on the roof. That if she were Charlie, I'd have different expectations. That was true, but what could I say? I had a double standard.

Charlie was saying good-bye to Suki. He had his arms around her. Her head was tucked under his chin. He kissed her once, then let her go and walked over to the two of us.

"Get her someplace safe," he said to Luna. "Don't let anything happen."

"She'll be fine on her own," Luna said. "I'm coming with you guys."

Charlie looked stunned. He glanced at me.

I shook my head. "No, you're not."

"Try to stop me."

"I don't have to," I said. "I'll just outrun you."

I thought she was going to hit me.

That's not fair.

Is it fair to Suki if she loses her boyfriend and sister in one night? You haven't seen this thing. We have no chance.

You have a better chance if I come with you.

I didn't think so. But she quickly reminded me of what had just happened back at the apartment.

You had a brain freeze. What if that happens again?

I grasped the handle of my two-handled sword and felt the leather grip twist and creak beneath my fingers. I understood what she was thinking—that my mind often strayed, so I wasn't always in the moment. Well—that wasn't going to happen again.

I thought back to our meeting on the roof, when she'd asked me to teach her how to fight. I didn't have anything to teach her. Fighting wasn't my forte, and it certainly wasn't hers. But I was the fastest and the strongest, so I had the best chance. And if I was going to be some kind of messiah—didn't I have to earn it?

Not by getting yourself killed!

Getting killed wasn't the plan. I wanted to find Detective Baddon's son and bolt. But if Luna came, and she got into trouble, I wouldn't be able to run. I'd have to stay and fight a losing battle. Did she understand? I could see her following my thoughts, but her mind was suddenly closed. I didn't know how she'd done it, but I couldn't hear her anymore.

I handed Charlie my sword. He shot me a puzzled glance. Then I reached up and undid the clasp of my necklace. In nine years, I'd only had it off twice, once to show Luna and once when Vlad took it from me. I slipped the two ends of the chain from around my neck, then took hold of Luna's hand.

Don't you dare give that to me! The sudden eruption from her mind was painful. She tried to pull her hand away.

I grimaced but didn't let go. Instead I put the necklace in her palm and folded her fingers around it. *Give this back to me tomorrow.*

Her eyes closed. A deep breath followed. *Just get the boy and get out. Don't try to fight with Hyde. Promise me you won't.*

I couldn't promise her anything. I had no idea what might happen. I looked at Charlie. He handed back my sword, then nodded that he was ready. It was time to go.

I love you, she thought, and I thought the same.

As she looked up at me, I studied at her face. Her chin, her mouth, her eyes. Every line. Every contour. Just so I wouldn't forget.

She turned and got in the car. Her mind was closed again. A few moments later, she pulled away.

"You didn't even say good-bye," said Charlie. "If I did that, Suki would kill me."

He jumped the ditch at the side of the road and started across the field.

"Come on. We're losing time."

I watched the car disappear down the highway, then followed him. We quickly found Hyde's tracks. They led farther out of town. We ran like two wild wolves. Never had I set such a fierce pace and maintained it for so long. In the city, we were always having to slow down, but now we were in the darkness, with nothing around us but farms and fences and the cool night air. So we reached our destination with a few good hours to spare before sunrise.

"I should have known," Charlie said. "Where else would Hyde go?"

Field had given way to forest. We crossed a road, then came to a parking lot. The sign at the entrance said WARSAW CAVES. I remembered what Mr. Entwistle had said about darkness. For a vampire, it is never total. The moon and stars are too bright. But the deep earth would be different. Dark like the grave.

Charlie pulled up beside me, then reached out and slapped my arm gently with the back of his hand. I looked up. He was pointing to a black van. It was streaked. Poorly painted. The ambulance Mr. Entwistle had stolen from the hospital.

"He's here," Charlie said.

We rushed over. The parking lot wasn't paved. I could see the marks of Mr. Entwistle's boots where he'd stepped out onto the stone dust.

"You smell that?" Charlie asked.

I could. The faint trace of wine and sweat that clung to Mr. Entwistle's body armor.

Charlie looked at the ground carefully. "Do we follow Hyde or Entwistle?"

Did it matter? They would probably take us to the same place. "Mr. Entwistle," I said. "He might still be alive."

Charlie looked doubtful. He took the voulge from his back. I followed his lead and drew my sword. The metal, dark and scarred, made an odd rasping noise, like an angry serpent, when it rubbed against the leather sheath.

"I'll go first," I said.

Charlie nodded, then followed me into the woods.

We weren't running long before Hyde's tracks and Mr. Entwistle's overlapped. And soon after that we caught the smell of blood. The first splattering was across the rocks under our feet. More showed up on the trunk of an oak. Then on the soil and the carpet of needles underfoot. On low-hanging leaves and needles, and the long grasses that grew in clumps where it was too rocky for trees to take root.

"They must have fought for hours," said Charlie.

It was impossible to know. The ground was torn up. Small trees had been uprooted or snapped at the trunk. Rocks were overturned. The bark of the tall pines was scarred. Lichen and moss were shorn loose. Every aspect of the landscape had been altered in some way.

"Have you ever seen so much blood?"

Only in a nightmare.

We followed the smell, and their footprints. We looped back again and again. Soon our own tracks were everywhere.

"We're going in circles," Charlie said.

He was panting heavily. So was I. Neither of us had expected to do so much running. I would happily have traded my sword for an inhaler.

"We must have missed something," I said.

"Yeah. The fight of the century."

We slowed and tried to follow their footprints more carefully. Still, we wound up back at the same rocky clearing.

Charlie shook his head. "We need to do something. If we take much longer to find them, there won't be time to get back before the sun rises."

I took out my phone.

"Who are you calling?"

I scrolled until I found Mr. Entwistle's number, then I hit send. Ophelia had said he wasn't answering his cell. It didn't mean it wouldn't ring.

"What are you doing?"

"Just listen." I tucked my cell into my pocket to muffle the noise.

I didn't hear anything. Neither did Charlie. So I started running. After a few moments, I pulled out my cell phone, hit redial, then started moving again. Charlie followed. I listened. A far-off river gurgled gently. The wind swished through pine and oak, cedar and maple. Crickets buzzed, quieting only when our footsteps drew close. I could hear Charlie's breathing, and mine. Our footfalls. Then I heard it. Electronic notes. *Hallelujah.*

Charlie tapped my shoulder. "It's coming from behind that rock."

We were in a clearing. Just one of the many areas where the rock was exposed. We'd passed this way several times already. A large lip of limestone rose up beside us, walling off the clearing from whatever lay behind. No prints led in that direction, but a leap would have taken Mr. Entwistle over the top. Or he might have been thrown. . . .

Charlie zipped past and scampered up the rock face. It was about twelve feet high. Once he cleared the top, he looked back. "Call again."

I did, then bounded up after him. The ringing started again. We followed it down a tree-covered slope to the edges of the Indian River. And there, on the bank, chained to a huge stone, was the body of Mr. Entwistle, lifeless and bloodied, just waiting for the sun.

CHAPTER 39

HYDE'S LAIR

I stuck my sword into the soft earth of the riverbank, then bent to examine Mr. Entwistle. He was chained to the rock so that his hands were stretched out to the sides—as if he'd been crucified. The stone behind him was scorched. Ashes were all over the ground underneath him. His coat was torn in a dozen places. Blood was caked on his face and in his hair. The knife I'd been given by my uncle, the one with the dioxin, was buried right up to the hilt just below his chest. Teeth marks scarred his neck. Were they from Hyde? Mr. Entwistle's words came back to me. That werewolves were blood drinkers, too.

"He's dead, isn't he," Charlie said.

I nodded. The eyes were dull. Dry. Lifeless. I wondered who had actually died here—Mr. Entwistle or the Butcher.

Charlie handed me something: Mr. Entwistle's lucky top hat. Bloodstained, torn, crumpled. Its luck was spent.

"He'll go up like a Roman candle when the sun comes up."

"Unless we can move him in time." To the east, the sky was still dark, but I could tell by the stars that dawn was only an hour or so away. By the look of things, more than a few vampires had been chained here. The rocks on the ground were stained black, the bushes nearby burnt. I reached out and took the pole-arm from Charlie's hand. Then I set about breaking the chains. It was noisy work. And time-consuming. But I was furious, and hammered steel, even the old stuff, is tougher than poured iron, so the links gave way under my assault.

"We'll never get him back to town before the sun comes up."

I agreed. "We'll have to find a cave and wait it out." I handed him the voulge. The blade looked as if I'd taken a can opener to it. Somewhere in Western Europe, a medieval blacksmith was rolling over in his grave.

"This was an antique," said Charlie.

"It still is." I lifted one of Mr. Entwistle's arms and drew it over my shoulder, then picked him up. "You still feeling confident about your plan?"

Charlie shook his head. "Not really. I wasn't counting on the mess of tracks back there. I felt like a mouse in a maze. It really slowed us down. And you just made more noise than a five-man electrical band. Unless Hyde's got six inches of wax in each ear, he'll know we're here."

I figured as much. But the sun was certain death, so we had to get underground. "Don't forget my sword," I said. The tip of the blade was still stuck in the earth. It made the arms and the pommel of the hilt look like a cross. More like a grave marker than a weapon.

Charlie pulled it out and wiped the blade clean in the long grass by the water. "Okay," he said. "Let's see if we can find that boy and scram."

The area around the river was dotted everywhere with caves. It didn't take long for Charlie to find one.

"What do you see?" I asked.

He was peering down a hole that looked wide enough for us to hide in. "Ice." Then he got on his stomach, slid the weapons down in front of him, and crawled into the darkness.

It wasn't at all what I'd expected. I'd only seen caves on television. It turns out Bruce Wayne's Batcave was the Hilton compared to the dump we found ourselves in. It was cold. Moldy. Wet. The ceiling was three feet high, so it was impossible to stand. White ice covered the floor. Within seconds of crawling in, I was soaked.

"Should we leave him here?" Charlie said.

I nodded. Without a system of mirrors, the sunlight wasn't going to get in. And I didn't want to move him farther underground. It would have been too difficult in such a cramped space.

"These weapons are going to be useless in here."

True enough. There wasn't enough space to swing a flashlight, let alone a five-foot sword.

Charlie was eyeing the knife still protruding from Mr. Entwistle's chest. "We should take that."

I felt a bit squeamish about removing it, but he was right, so we worked the blade free. It was wedged between two plates in Mr. Entwistle's armor. I examined the blade. No trace of the dioxin was on it.

Charlie stared the slender wound the knife had left. "You know, you're about the same height as him. A little shorter, maybe, but I bet that armor would fit."

I hadn't considered it. It seemed wrong to take the clothes from a dead man.

"He'd want you to have it."

I nodded. "Yeah, he would."

It wasn't easy stripping down on an icy floor with a roof three feet overhead. And the armor was a bit tight. It amazed me that Mr. Entwistle could move so smoothly with it on. By the time I was finished, my fingers were frozen. Not a good sign. It meant I was tired.

"I've never had more sympathy for penguins than I do right now," said Charlie. He was shivering, "What happens now?"

We had to find the detective's son. We couldn't look outside; the daylight was arriving. That left only one option.

"Let's move," I said. "Maybe we'll find a clue down here."

So we began to crawl. Eventually, we hit a dead end. Charlie started swearing. It poured out of him like gangster rap. I didn't recognize half of the words he used.

"Did we miss something?" he asked.

It was too tight in the cave to turn around, so we had to creep our way backward. It was a good thing neither of us was claustrophobic. There was barely enough room for a mole rat.

"This is worse than a coffin," Charlie said.

Then he found what we had missed. There was a scrape along the rocky floor where an enormous stone had been moved. I would have needed Yoda's help just to lift it. A faint odour of wet fur clung to its surface. Judging by the smell, Hyde had dragged the rock away some time ago, perhaps several days. It exposed an opening barely large enough for us to snake through. The way the wall was angled, the hole was hard to spot when you were approaching from the front.

Charlie looked at me, then down into the shadows below. I knew what he was thinking. We were wet, cold, tired, and underarmed. Anyone with a lick of sense would have stayed put.

"Do you think that boy's still alive?" he asked.

I didn't know. But it didn't matter. If there was even a chance, we had to keep going.

"I'll go first," I said. But Charlie was already ahead of me.

We squeezed through the hole and emerged in a cavern. It was long, as if a giant worm had plowed its way through the solid rock. At least now we could comfortably stand.

"This is more like it," Charlie said. A trickle of water ran along a groove in the rock floor down the center of the tunnel. He put his hand in it, then shook the droplets from his fingers. "Freezing." Then he looked around. "Must have been bigger at one time."

"What do you mean?"

"This little stream. It must have been a full-blown river at one time to have carved this out."

I nodded.

"Can you smell that?"

I could. Like leather and wet dog. It was much stronger here.

"I think it's coming from that way." The tunnel led in two directions. Up to the right or down to the left. He was pointing down.

"Are you ready?" I asked.

He held up the knife. The blade looked purple against the black cave walls. "Yeah," he whispered.

The patter of padded feet echoed up the tunnel. Long strides. Hyde was coming.

I swallowed. "Is it too late to discuss strategies?"

"How about you attack him, and I slip out the back?"

"That's not funny."

"Or you could distract him somehow. Why don't you try dancing? You might as well do it once before you die. Or—die again."

I shook my head. This was no time for jokes. I needed Charlie to put his gladiator face on.

"I think you should try to get around him," I said. "See if you can find the detective's son. I've got the armor. I'll do my best to keep Hyde off your back."

Charlie nodded, then turned to look me squarely in the eyes. His teeth were dropping. "Zack." He didn't bother keeping his voice down. "You can't make him good."

"What do you mean?"

"I know you. You want to make everyone good. You can't. Do you understand? This thing is going to kill us unless we kill it first. All that talk of Entwistle's about villains and evil. I don't care about that stuff. This is about Hyde and us. You can't hesitate. You can't wonder if you're doing the right thing. Attack, attack, attack. Like a berserker. Like Alexander."

I nodded. We were both big on Alexander the Great. Attack, he believed, even in defense. It seemed reasonable. But I'd only been in two fights before. In one I got trounced. In the other I died. Not a great track record. And I remembered clearly what Baoh had told me: *Do not do to others that which is harmful to yourself.* It didn't seem like the best fight strategy. But I had no more time to consider it.

Hyde had arrived.

CHAPTER 40

HELL HATH NO FURY...

The darkness around us was complete. There is no light underground. Not unless you burrow right through the crust to the molten rock below. Hyde was a shadow. A black shape against a black background. But Charlie and I could see him. Our eyes were built for it. He stood to his full height and stepped forward. He looked like a demon. Huge. Taloned. Emanating anger. One eye was swollen shut. The other looked like a hollow pit. A tooth was chipped, and he walked with a slight limp. Mr. Entwistle had done some damage. But for all this, Hyde still smiled. I heard his throat rumble—it might have been a laugh. Then he spoke. This time, the word came out like a raspy gargle. I understood clearly.

Welcome. . . .

Charlie shifted beside me. We were shoulder to shoulder. I understood his strategy. Be like a berserker, those Viking warriors who charged fearlessly into battle. No thoughts of self-preservation. No hesitation. Just relentless assault. Well, that wasn't me. I had no idea who Hyde was. What he wanted. Why he'd done the things he'd done. A part of my mind insisted on understanding.

"Where is the boy?" I asked.

Hyde stopped. His head snaked forward, his good eye narrowed. He squinted at me, then at Charlie. He must have seen something he didn't like. He attacked. I expected a lunge. A charge. Something similar to what Charlie and I had witnessed that first night at the zoo, when he'd ambushed Mr. Entwistle. But Hyde must have understood the value of unpredictability because he did the last thing I'd expected him to do. He jumped straight up. His arm snaked out and he smashed off a stalactite, one of those cone-shaped rocks that was hanging from the top of the tunnel. Then he wound up and hurled it at me.

I twisted and the chunk of rock shot past. It was moving with the speed of a bullet. In the meantime, he closed the space between us. After watching him limp down the tunnel, I hadn't expected him to move so quickly. He pushed Charlie aside, then hit me flush on the chest with his fist. The punch lifted me cleanly off my feet. An instant later, I smashed headfirst into the rock wall behind me. I felt a shock wave run down through my spine. Pain followed, and the kind of paralysis you feel when your nerves are on fire. My eyes swam. I was on my back. A few seconds passed before I could move. I rolled over and pushed myself slowly up to my knees.

I could see Charlie. He was attacking Hyde with reckless abandon. Like a berserker. No thoughts of self-defense. The knife swung back and forth in wild arcs. Had it still been poisoned with dioxin, he might have had a chance. But his opponent was stronger. Faster. And patient.

Hyde backed up, circled, waited. Charlie swung again and again. Then he overextended himself. Hyde shot forward, caught my friend around the wrist with his long fingers, twisted the knife loose, then slammed him against the wall. Bones snapped and Charlie sagged to the ground.

I rose awkwardly to my feet. The back of my head was burning. I could feel blood running down through my hair and along the skin on the back of my neck. My legs were unsteady.

Hyde picked up the knife and came toward me. The sight of him was terrifying. There was death in his eyes. It made my whole body shake.

Get around him, a voice in my head told me. *Stick to the plan. Get the boy.*

It was Luna. She must have come back. The sound of her voice was like a jolt of electricity. I snapped to attention.

Hyde was only a few steps away, limping. It gave me an opening. I ran for the near wall, jumped up off the rocks, and soared past him. It almost worked, but I jumped too high. I'd expected Mr. Entwistle's armor to weigh me down more than it did. My shoulder scraped against the top of the tunnel. It slowed me enough that Hyde was able to spin, reach up, and get a hand around my ankle. Then he introduced me to the floor. My eyes sparked. Spots dotted the darkness. I rolled over onto my back and gasped from the pain.

A new shadow flitted across my vision. Darkness within the darkness. In that instant, I had an epiphany, more sudden than a spark. First, Mr. Entwistle's words came back to me. *Be a saint,* he'd said. Then Baoh's eyeless face drifted through my mind. *Do not do to others that which is harmful to yourself.* Just like that, I knew exactly what to do.

Hyde stood over me. I rose and started shouting as if my pants were on fire. I knew I'd never beat him, but I might have been able to outrun him. He was hurt. It gave me a small edge. But that would mean leaving Charlie and the detective's son if he was here somewhere. That wasn't what saints did. Instead, I kept my eyes on the knife. The handle, too small for his large fingers. The blade—slightly curved, like a half moon that angled to a point. He swung. I stepped back. The knife whistled past. He punched out with his other hand and knocked me flat. I stayed down. It would make things easier. An instant later his fingers closed around my throat. I flailed. I kicked. I pushed and squirmed. It didn't matter. Escape was impossible. But escape was not my plan.

Hyde drew the knife back a fraction of an inch, then his whole body exploded toward me. He aimed for my heart. I managed to deflect his hand low. The point of the blade hit an armor plate and stopped. I kept struggling. He aimed a second time. The knife sparked, but stopped again. Then he got wise and worked the tip of the knife to an area between the platinum plates. He must have done this before in his fight with Mr. Entwistle. An instant later he rammed the blade through. I had just fractions of a second before the pain arrived. Fortunately I'd told my hands what to do ahead of time, so they were already on the move. I grabbed his wrist and hung on. He wasn't going to get the knife free. Not in time. Then the pain paralyzed me. Locked my fingers in place. I squeezed as hard as I could and prayed it was enough. And I kept shouting.

Hyde twisted the knife. My shout became a scream. He pulled. My hands were too weak to stop him. The blade slipped out slowly. Metal on metal. I ran out of air. For an instant, I felt despair. And the fear of failure. I needed to make more noise and couldn't. But I'd held on long enough, and I'd filled his ears with my screams. Mr. Entwistle would have been proud. I had martyred myself—like a saint.

The shadow I'd seen earlier was now beside us. I heard a hiss like that of an aerosol can. Then Hyde jumped back. His hands were over his eyes and face. He snarled. Then I felt Ophelia's hand on my chest.

"Don't budge," she whispered.

I couldn't have moved with a team of oxen helping me. My stomach had a hole in it. I was in pain from head to toe.

Hyde stood. Whatever Ophelia had sprayed in his face was working. His eyes were horrid. Bloodstained yellow. Furious. Then he fell to his knees. His hands rose up to the sides of his head and he let out a howl. He started to change. His arms shortened. Thickened. His fingers, too—from long and clawed to thick sausages. His teeth receded. Hair disappeared. Not just from his body, but from his face. Even the top of his head. But the greatest change was in his legs. They went from long and lean, feet stretched up at the arches, to something that looked like a pair of tree trunks. And there lying on the ground beside us was Detective Baddon.

CHAPTER 41

THE WEREWOLF

Ophelia stared at the detective, unspeaking. I tried to sit up. Her hand was still on my chest.

"Just lie still," she said. "I know it hurts, but it won't be fatal."

"Where's Luna?" I asked.

Ophelia looked surprised for a moment, then glanced over her shoulder. "She's not with me."

"She was here. She must have been. . . ."

Ophelia shook her head.

Had I imagined it? I was certain I'd heard her voice.

Beside us, Detective Baddon moaned.

"What did you do to him?" I asked.

"I used the wolfsbane."

"Will it kill him?"

She shook her head. "No. Wolfsbane is lethal, but not to werewolves. It doesn't kill them. It transforms them. There were teeth marks on the flowers Charlie brought me. I think Hyde chewed it when he needed to turn back into Adam."

Amazing! And more impressive, Ophelia was able to turn this knowledge to our advantage. I guess it was true—knowledge was our best defense. Or in this case, our best offense.

"Did you know it was him?" I asked.

"I wasn't positive, but you never can be." She turned to face the unconscious detective. "But I suspected it was him when his son was taken from the hospital. The boy isn't a vampire, so why would

Hyde care about him? And Adam was nowhere to be found. He would have called or at least put up a fight."

My mind started putting the pieces of the detective's story together. It started by answering the most obvious question. How was this possible? Only one explanation fit with what I knew. The day he'd been attacked in his house, back when he lived in Toronto, it hadn't been a robber with a bottle. The police must have fabricated the story. If they were part of the Underground, they wouldn't have wanted him to know the truth. That he'd been attacked by a werewolf. Perhaps the same one that Maximilian had been hunting. The boy must have been infected, too. It explained his illness. Like his father, he must have been a lycanthrope.

Beside us, Detective Baddon began to stir. He had his hands on his head. As soon as he came to, he started groping around as if looking for something. "Where are my glasses?" he muttered. He was totally confused.

"Are you all right?" Ophelia asked.

At the sound of her voice, the detective jumped as if someone had kicked him. He couldn't see. "Who's there? Where am I?"

"It's Ophelia. And you're underground. You won't be able to see. There's no light."

I heard him take a deep breath. "My leg is killing me. Was I sleepwalking again?"

"Not exactly."

He was on his hands and knees. He stood and started to wobble. Ophelia reached out, took his arm and helped him to sit again.

"Where is my son?"

Ophelia wasn't certain.

"He might be farther down that way." I pointed in the direction Hyde had come.

"Who was that? Is that Charlie?" asked the detective.

"No." Ophelia still had a hand on his shoulder. "No. It's Zack. He's hurt. It would probably be best if you two stay here and let me go ahead."

I hoped she was kidding. I didn't want her to leave me alone with Detective Baddon. What if he changed back? With Charlie lying nearby helpless, and me with a hole where no hole should be, Hyde would find himself with a handy meal right at his feet. Ophelia was obviously thinking the same. She stepped over to me, then bent down and put her mouth next to my ear.

"I'm leaving these with you," she whispered. "Just in case." She put a small aerosol can into my hand. It was the wolfsbane. She must have made a serum of some kind from the monkshood we'd brought home. In my other hand she placed the knife, the one Hyde had rammed into my stomach. Then she stood and started up the tunnel. She stopped when she saw Charlie lying across the small rivulet of water.

"Dear Lord . . ."

I could hear her shifting him carefully. "Is he dead?" I asked.

"No, he's breathing. But the base of his spine has been shattered. . . . Don't worry. We can fix it."

"What about Mr. Entwistle?"

"Did you find him?" she asked.

"Yes. We dragged him into a cave. It's right above us."

"Is he dead?"

"Yes."

"It doesn't matter. We can heal all of you. We just need to get you out of here. Give me a moment. I'll be right back." Then she took off in search of Detective Baddon's missing son.

I clenched my teeth. It was getting harder to hold my stomach together. As the pain intensified, the feeling of weakness in my limbs grew. I was starting to feel cold. This was definitely spoiling my first visit to the Warsaw Caves.

"Is it bad?" Detective Baddon asked.

"No, it just hurts."

"Stomach?"

"Yeah."

He nodded. "I've heard it's the worst place to get shot."

I could imagine at least one place that would top it, but I kept that to myself. Still, there had to be something to what he'd said. Whenever a samurai committed suicide, he sliced his belly open because the pain was off the charts. It was the only way to restore lost honor. I guess that was more or less what I'd done. Committed a kind of suicide. But Ophelia had arrived just in time.

The detective was still rubbing his neck. Funny how wrong I'd been about him. About Hyde's alter ego. I'd imagined someone ten feet tall. But Detective Baddon was probably three hundred pounds of solid muscle, most of it in his legs. We hadn't considered that he might be Hyde. He probably hadn't considered it himself.

"How did I get here?" he asked.

I took a few breaths to ready my body for speech. "You ran."

The detective didn't understand. He rubbed a hand over his head. "So I *was* sleepwalking."

I shook my head. Pain ran down my neck and back.

"Where did you say Mr. Entwistle was?" he asked.

I didn't get to answer. Detective Baddon started coughing. I heard him muttering something about the air not being right. His voice was off. I turned. He was standing. Stumbling. His hands were pressed against the sides of his head. Then he started to change. His eyes got bigger. Blacker at the center. They yellowed, then focused on the canister in my hand.

There's more than one way to trigger a transformation, Mr. Entwistle had said. Obviously, whatever it was that made Detective Baddon turn, it was in this tunnel. As I watched, he lengthened. Thinned. His teeth descended. Hair rose on his head and arms and face. He looked over to where Charlie was lying beside him. He smiled, then he stepped toward me.

I raised the can and pointed it at his face, but before I could press the nozzle, he turned and fled. I took a deep breath. Would it be an overstatement to say I'd just dodged a bullet? Maybe—but that same bullet was heading straight for Ophelia.

I rolled over onto my side. Blood from the wound in my stomach mixed with the thin stream of water on the tunnel floor. It must have been worse than Ophelia thought. I was weak. Too weak to stand. I started crawling.

"Ophelia . . . Ophelia!" I shouted her name as loudly as I could. The effort caused me to black out. Like a sleeper who nods and wakes up, I came to as my head sank. It happened twice more. "Ophelia!"

She'd be trapped with Hyde by herself. Her only defense was the canister of wolfsbane in my hand.

I reached Charlie. Ophelia had straightened his body so it lay flat and straight on the ground. His breathing came in shallow fits. My movement and shouting must have roused him from unconsciousness. His eyes fluttered open. He saw me and groaned.

"How did we do?" he gasped. The words were hard to make out.

"Not well."

"I feel cold . . . I can't move."

"Your back is broken."

He seemed to take this news remarkably well. "Hyde?"

"He's going after Ophelia."

His eyes started to water. He must have known we were finished. "Any more good news?"

I laughed, then coughed up a mouthful of blood. "Yeah. I'm afraid I'm going to have to kill you."

His head moved just a little. "What are friends for?"

My teeth were down. One of them was broken. I rolled up Charlie's sleeve.

"Wait," he said. "Are you sure this won't kill you?"

It hadn't with Luna. I still didn't understand why. But what did I have to lose?

Charlie started sputtering. Tears were spilling out of his eyes. They were crimson. "Don't hesitate this time. Do what you have to do."

I wasn't going to argue. Instead, I drank. Charlie gasped. I took what I needed and left him with a slow pulse. I told myself this was necessary. That one of us had to be strong or Hyde would finish us all. Permanently. It didn't change the feeling of wrongness about it.

But what choice did I have? My stomach was in knots. Actually, it was in sliced-up knots. They started to twist and burn. The pain in my chest and limbs disappeared. So did my doubt—the feeling that this was a mistake. Ophelia was alone with that thing. Was he evil? Did he deserve to die? It didn't matter now. Not to me. So I picked up the can and knife and sprinted down the tunnel.

CHAPTER 42

CAVE-IN

I ran down a steep slope and around a corner. I could have tracked Hyde by his scent but it wasn't necessary. He was shouting. The sound was ferocious.

Where is my son?

His voice was coming from a smaller enclave that branched from the main tunnel. I ducked inside. The entrance was low and braced with thick logs. So were the walls. It looked like a cave-in that hadn't finished collapsing.

Hyde was holding Ophelia off the ground. He had one hand around her neck. In the other was a hospital blanket.

Where is he?

His voice was quiet now, but still terrifying. He could easily have killed her, and she must have known it.

What are you waiting for? Tell him where his son is, I thought.

But she didn't know.

Hyde turned my way. He saw the canister in my hand.

Drop that.

"No." I ran straight for him.

I was a terrible poker player. I couldn't bluff. Some people can hide what they think and feel. I can't. So the only way I could bluff was to not bluff. If he snapped Ophelia's neck, she'd die. But I could bring her back. And if he did that, I'd blast him with the wolfsbane and turn him back into his human self. He couldn't allow that. As Hyde he was invincible. As Adam Baddon, he wasn't.

He thought Ophelia knew where his son was. He knew I didn't. That made me expendable. So he did what I expected him to do. He attacked me.

I assumed he'd drop his son's blanket. It was useless to him, or so I thought. But instead, he flicked it at my face, the way a kid flicks a towel. It snapped like a whip over my eye. It didn't slow me down, but instinctively I turned my head, so I didn't see him kick out with his leg until it was too late. I was raising my hand so I could depress the nozzle of the canister when his foot hit my chest. It knocked me back toward the cave entrance. The canister flew from my hand. It hit the rock wall and ripped open with a loud pop. The poison leaked out onto the floor. It was useless now.

Hyde growled. Then he turned back to Ophelia.

Where is my son? Where?

My nose and ears told me the answer. I smelled disinfectant. And I heard the careful steps of heavy boots. I should have guessed. I rose to my feet as noisily as I could, coughing and scuffing my shoes against the stone floor. I even pretended to slip, scattering loose pebbles across the ground. It was loud enough that Hyde didn't hear my uncle until he'd ducked inside the room. Maximillian smelled the way he always did when he got back from the hospital—like cleanser. He'd traded in his gray skin for white. His face was so drawn and pale it practically glowed in the dark. But his eyes were alert and intense, his pupils wide. And his timing was perfect—as always. He had Hyde's son cradled in one arm. The boy was unconscious, his breathing irregular. Shallow. Strained. In Maximilian's other hand was a gun. It was pointing at the boy's head, right at the base of his skull. Before anyone could blink, he cocked the gun. The trigger was already pulled back all the way. If anyone breathed on him too heavily, his thumb would slip, the hammer would slam into the cap of the next bullet, and the boy would die.

"Put her down and step back." my uncle said.

Hyde stood to his full height. His eyes moved between his son and the man who was about to shoot him. He roared.

Maximilian kept his face expressionless, his eyes level. He pushed the tip of the gun barrel more firmly against the back of the boy's head. "Whether he lives or dies is up to you. Now put her down and move back."

Was this a bluff? My uncle knew the stakes. He was a cunning man. Obviously smart enough to figure out that Detective Baddon was also Hyde—that they were two halves of a single person. Like Ophelia, he must have figured things out at the hospital.

"My friends and I are walking out of here," my uncle said. "I'll take your boy back to the hospital. You can visit him there, as Adam. I won't deal with you."

Hyde growled.

Baddon is weak. How can he protect the boy from others like you?

Maximilian stared at Hyde's face. What was he looking for? Some sign of reason or compassion?

"Is he in there?" my uncle asked. "Can Adam hear this? Does he know about you?"

Hyde didn't answer. He probably didn't know. But I'd seen Detective Baddon's face and heard his confusion after his transformation back in the tunnel. It was genuine. He didn't know about this—that he was Hyde. A beast that hunted vampires.

Leave my son and I'll let you go.

"I won't turn him over to you. I'll turn him over to Adam. That's the best offer you're going to get."

Hyde glared at him. Seconds passed. It felt like forever. Then he snarled and let Ophelia drop to the floor. Once her feet were set, he turned her toward the entrance. I couldn't believe it. That he was agreeing to this. But he wasn't. It was just a distraction. As soon as she moved in front of him, he pushed her hard at my uncle. Then he lunged. It was a bold move, but it made sense. My uncle wouldn't kill an innocent child, and Hyde must have known it.

But people always underestimated Maximilian. Was it because he was human? Because he had one foot in the grave? We were all wrong about that. He had both feet in the grave. I don't know if it was because of my fear, or the desperation of our situation, but my mind wasn't asking itself the questions it should have about him. Where did his confidence come from? The guy was underground with a bunch of vampires strong enough to knock his teeth out through his ears, and he wasn't a bit intimidated. Most humans were afraid of the dark. How could Maximilian even see?

I got my answer as soon as Hyde attacked him. Maximilian dropped the boy and fired a round that grazed Hyde's shoulder. In the next instant, his gun got knocked away and he was pushed back through the entrance of the lair. Even though Hyde was faster, Maximilian's movements had changed. Nothing like a stone golem. He was fluid. Perfectly balanced. Like a vampire. Don't ask me how he'd done it, but he was one of us now. I should have guessed that he'd do this. Mr. Entwistle had given me the first clue when he'd told me and Charlie to focus on what a person wanted. Maximilian wanted to live. To hunt vampires. This was the only way. Biotherapeutics, he'd said. Killing cancer cells with a virus. Well, he'd used the heavyweight champion of contagions. My guess was he'd taken my blood—in the hospital maybe. But I suppose it didn't matter how he'd done it. What mattered was that he'd dropped Hyde's son, and so we'd lost our leverage.

But my uncle always had a plan B. He put it into action as he stumbled back into the main tunnel, still reeling from Hyde's assault. Not a bad bit of multitasking. He was a talented hunter. Always prepared. And he loved his toys. Guns and Tasers and things that go bang in the night. I shouldn't have been surprised to see the detonator appear in his hand. He'd used one just like it to stop Vlad. A year ago, he'd blown out some windows and let a little sunlight into our lives. This time, when he pressed the magic button, the wooden supports around us exploded. He must have done a quick wiring job while the rest of us were out in the tunnel, fighting and talking and stumbling around.

Without the wooden timbers in place, gravity went to work. A huge column of broken stone started to slide down. I leapt for the opening. So did Ophelia. We were close enough to make it easily, and my uncle would have known that. But as always, Hyde was fastest. He grabbed us both, hurled us back, and used the momentum to throw himself into the entrance. It put him directly in the path of the largest chunk of falling rock. The weight of it was unimaginable. It would have flattened Superman. But Hyde stopped it. Or slowed it. He was forced to his knees. He had his arms straight over his head, but the immensity of the stone forced him to lower it across the back of his shoulders. He crouched across the doorway, his son on the ground in front of him. The two were blocking the exit.

Then Hyde started to change. It started in his arms and legs. His hair began to vanish. It was the wolfsbane. The shattered canister was right beside him, the air around it fragrant with the smell of monkshood, the flowers Ophelia had used to make the poison. If Hyde became human, we'd be doomed. Buried in a grave of stone and dust. The rock column forced him onto his hands and knees. His son was trapped underneath him. He was like a bridge. And he was breaking.

Hurry . . . your knife. Hurry!

He was looking more like Detective Baddon with each passing moment.

I still had the blade in my hand. It was well-balanced with a keen edge, but was about as useful for stopping a rockslide as a handful of pudding.

Cut yourself. Hurry.

Was he serious? Before I could come up with an answer, Ophelia snatched the knife, dragged it over the palm of her hand, and stuck it under Hyde's nose. He started to change back.

Blood might do it, too. Bring out the inner beast. For all I know, it's different for each of them. But it doesn't have to be a full moon.

Mr. Entwistle had said this to Charlie and me. Vampire blood was Hyde's trigger. That must have been why Detective Baddon said the air in the tunnel wasn't right. And why he had changed in the hospital. I'd cut my wrist on a piece of metal above the ceiling as I was leaving his son's room.

Hyde growled. The rock was crushing him. He raised one hand. I assumed he was trying to get out of the way, but he grabbed Ophelia by the arm instead.

My boy . . . get him out.

The words were scarcely louder than his breath. He could barely get them out. The strain of holding up the stone avalanche had every vein in his neck bulging. He couldn't even raise his head. His eyes were glued on his son.

Not his fault . . .

Ophelia nodded. Sympathy was one of her strong points. It made her the perfect person to ask.

Hyde let her go. She crouched and slipped past. Then she turned and pulled his son free. I wondered if this was going to be my tomb. If he'd let me leave as well.

Get out.

I couldn't believe what I was hearing.

Adam chose you. . . . Now go.

Adam chose you. What was that about? That he'd asked me to look after his son—to infect him? There wasn't time to ask. I dove for the opening. My head was barely out in the tunnel when I felt Ophelia's hands pulling at my arms. She helped me to my feet. The boy was lying on the ground beside her.

I looked around for my uncle. He was gone. A thick cloud of dust obscured my view ahead. I heard a loud crack above. The cave roof was shifting.

"Come on," Ophelia said.

She bent and scooped Hyde's son off the ground. As she straightened back up, I slid my hands underneath him so he was draped across my arms. I nodded, and we raced back up the tunnel.

CHAPTER 43

THE PROPHECY REVISITED

Ophelia and I didn't get far. As we rounded the corner, we could see my uncle ahead. He was supporting Charlie with one hand and had a bag of blood in the other. Luna was crouched beside them.

"Come on!" Maximilian said. "Or we're going to spend the next hundred years digging up your friends."

The air was charged with panic. Charlie was unconscious and most of the blood was dribbling out of his mouth. As Ophelia and I approached, my uncle glanced over.

"We're okay," I said.

Luna stood. *Thank God.*

You can say that again.

She slipped over beside me. I set the detective's son on the ground and Luna and I sort of melted into one another.

I was sure I'd heard you. That you were here somewhere.

She looked at me and smiled. *Did you think an army of were-wolves could have kept me away?*

I should have known better than to underestimate her resolve. *How did you find us?*

I drove back and followed the trail. Why did you guys run in circles for so long?

I wasn't sure how to answer that. We certainly hadn't meant to.

I was climbing over that pile of rocks when I heard your voice in my mind. You were talking to Charlie. You must have been moving away from me because your thoughts faded almost right away. But it led me to that cave.

She thought of Mr. Entwhistle and a wave of pity spilled out of her. But it was all right—we were going to make it out now. All we'd need was more blood, then we could restore his ruined body. Charlie's, too.

I heard your voice, I told her. *I wasn't sure if I'd imagined it because I didn't hear you again.*

I don't really understand any of this, she thought. *When I got closer to you, I could feel your panic. I was above, and tried to reach out—to keep you moving, but I wasn't sure if you could hear me. After that, once you got slammed to the ground, I couldn't get through. And it took me a while to find the hole that led down here.*

She was standing beside me, with her arms wrapped around my waist. She pulled me a bit closer. *I'm sorry it took so long.*

I thought of what had happened with Hyde. How he had closed in on me with the knife—his mind bent on murder. I'd frozen.

Your timing was perfect, I told her.

She looked away. *I know you're exaggerating, but I appreciate it.*

I wasn't exaggerating. If she hadn't restored my focus at the moment Hyde attacked me, things might have turned out differently. But it looked as if we were all going to be okay. I had Ophelia and my uncle to thank, as well. She was hovering over the detective's son. Maximilian was trying to get Charlie to swallow more blood.

"How did you know where we were?" I asked him.

Maximilian lay Charlie flat. "The transponder."

Transponder? Then I remembered. I reached back and felt a small bump on the top of my shoulder blade. My uncle had put it there with his Teletoon gun during our conversation in the hospital.

He looked up at me. Relief washed over his face. Deep lines of worry around his eyes and mouth disappeared. "I expected you to come out right behind me. When you didn't, I nearly had a heart attack. I came back here to get reinforcements."

"It was Hyde," Ophelia said. "He stopped us."

"How is the boy?" Maximilian asked.

"He's alive," Ophelia said. "But weak."

"How did you get him out?"

"Hyde held the door."

My uncle looked surprised. He was about to ask another question, but was interrupted by Charlie. He started to hack and cough. A fine mist of air and blood exploded from his mouth. Then he began to convulse.

"Get your hands on his shoulders," Maximilian shouted.

Ophelia and Luna took his arms and pinned him to the rock. I steadied one of his legs, my uncle took the other. Then my friend's eyes popped open. His teeth were down. He looked around at all of us.

"What are you doing to me?"

He seemed to be past the worst of it, so the others rose to give him space. He wiped blood from around his mouth. The bruises on his face were clearing. A second later they were entirely gone. He reached for my hand so I could pull him to a sitting position. "What happened?"

I started to answer but he waved for me to stop. "I need more blood."

"I have more in my car," Maximilian said.

"Where did you get it?" I asked.

"I stole it."

I thought about what Inspector Johansson had said. That shipments of blood had disappeared from the Underground. I'd assumed this was Hyde's doing, but my uncle must have been behind it. I guess it was a good thing. I was going to need a few gallons myself.

I felt Luna's hand on my arm. *I have something to give you first.* She took out the necklace. The two parts were attached, the chains woven together. She gently separated her crescent from my silver moon, then slipped the chains apart. I bowed my head and she clasped the necklace into place. I felt her hand on my chest. She was beaming.

Now everything is as it should be.

Not quite, I thought. I looked down at the boy. He was still un-well. His breathing was shallow. And Mr. Entwistle was still in the cave above.

My uncle moved over beside us, then pointed down the tunnel.

"I came in another way. That direction. It would be faster, unless the path is blocked."

I looked back the way we'd come, but there was so much dust in the air, I couldn't see far.

"I'm sorry about what happened in there," he added. "One thing your father and I learned the hard way—nothing ever goes accord-ing to plan."

"We would have made it out if he hadn't taken hold of us so quickly," Ophelia said. "I've never seen anything so fast. I was cer-tain that cave was going to be our tomb."

"Well, you wouldn't have been buried long," my uncle replied. He was looking at her intently. Something was wrong. I'd been so fo-cused on Charlie, I hadn't noticed, but I could see it now in her eyes.

"What is it?" I asked her.

"Can you go back and get Hyde? He might still be alive."

"Where is he?" Charlie asked. He started to cough again. He tried to stand up but couldn't manage it.

My uncle offered him a hand. Charlie paused, then he took it and rose unsteadily to his feet. I couldn't help but smile. My uncle and Charlie. Both vampires.

Hyde's son stirred. His breathing was still ragged. He looked awful. Pale. Emaciated.

"Do you know what's wrong with him?" I asked.

"Later," said Ophelia. "You have to save Adam. Quickly."

"Are you certain that's what we want to do?" my uncle asked. "I know Adam was a good man."

Charlie turned and nearly fell over. "Adam? You mean Detective Baddon? What are you talking about? What is he doing here?"

"Detective Baddon was Hyde," I explained.

Charlie looked at all of us. Then at Maximilian. "I'll be

damned . . ." Charlie's surprise quickly turned to alarm. He looked at the dying boy lying on the tunnel floor. "That means he's Hyde's son."

As soon as he said this, I had my second epiphany of the night. A personal best. I looked at Ophelia. She understood, too. She was crouched over the boy, her finger gently touching his neck. She was taking his pulse.

"Go," she said.

I turned and started running.

"The whole tunnel is unstable," my uncle said.

"Then hurry," I shouted back. We had to save Adam. I started sprinting.

My uncle was right on my heels. "This makes no sense."

It made perfect sense to me. But I knew the prophecy. And I knew that I wasn't the messiah all the proselytizing vampires were waiting for.

As a kid, I never knew my father was a vampire hunter. To me, he was just Dad. The man who read me bedtime stories, who took me on archaeological digs, who made popcorn for *Saturday Night at the Movies* and did all the other things good fathers do. He was patient. Gentle. Kind. He only yelled at me once in my life—for going into the closet where he kept his gun. But he must have had another side because he was lethal. As a man, and as a vampire hunter, people praised him to the skies, and I never got tired of hearing it. But despite what was said, he couldn't have been the greatest vampire hunter ever. That honor went to Hyde. And his son was a blood drinker, a werewolf. If *he* became an orphan, he would be the one the prophecies spoke of, not me. And if he inherited his father's habit of killing vampires, of feeding on them, we might soon find ourselves on an endangered species list.

A shepherd or a scourge. A saint or a demon. The messiah would be one of these things. I couldn't let him become an orphan.

I rounded the corner with my uncle beside me. The air was thick with dust, the tunnel floor treacherous from all the fallen rocks. We scrambled to the entrance of Hyde's cave. He was still there, but the rock had slipped farther and forced one of his shoulders to the ground. His knees were underneath him. The rock seemed to have settled. I had no idea how we would get him out.

"Quickly, that rock over there," my uncle shouted. "Help me move it."

A large chunk of stone had collapsed from the ceiling outside the chamber. It wasn't in the way. I didn't understand why we should bother with it. I heard more cracking above and the roof fell down a few more inches.

"We'll set it beside him to hold up the stone, then try to slide him out."

That made sense. I nodded, then put my hands under it to test its weight. I wouldn't have been able to move it on my own, but with my uncle's help, we slid it into place beside Hyde. A few seconds later Luna arrived.

Hyde watched us. He was nearly pinned to the floor. Blood was dripping from his mouth and nose and ears. We were almost there. Then Luna took hold of my arm and yanked me backward. I wasn't expecting it, so I stumbled, arms flailing. Our feet got tangled up and I hit the ground on my back. Air shot from my lungs. Luna landed right beside me, but I didn't hear her. All sound was drowned out by a crack so loud, I'm sure it echoed right down to the earth's core. Then the roof of the tunnel at the entrance to Hyde's den plummeted to the floor.

CHAPTER 44

BLOOD DEBT

A cloud of dust shot past Luna and me. Tons of rock continued to fall. She took hold of my arm. She was shouting in my ear. The shock and noise had turned my eardrums into sirens. Nothing could get past their shrill ringing. But her thoughts were clear.

Get moving!

I stood, stunned. We'd come so close. I just assumed we'd get everyone out. That the story would have a happy ending. But that wasn't going to happen. Now my uncle and Hyde were buried together under a mountain of stone.

Luna started hauling me up the passage. *I don't want you to join them!*

I kept looking back over my shoulder through the hail of rock and dust and small stones, hoping I might see my uncle emerge, but it didn't happen. There was nothing I could do. We stumbled awkwardly, side by side, while the earth shook and the caves collapsed. We didn't stop until we reached the others. Then Ophelia took the lead. I carried Detective Baddon's son. Luna helped Charlie. The ground lurched. The rock above us cracked. It was as if the world were falling apart.

We hadn't run far up when Charlie stopped. "Entwistle's still up there," he shouted.

The tunnel roof lurched and fell. We barely got out of the way. I started to turn back, but Ophelia took hold of my arm and dragged me away. Her grip was iron. So was her voice: "I'm not losing you."

Eventually we reached a more stable section. The noise was far behind us. Then the tunnel roof began to slope downward, forcing us to crouch. We came to a fork. Ophelia reached up and touched the rock, then pointed to the right, where the ceiling hung even lower. She and the others dropped to their hands and knees. I had to do a crab walk with the boy balanced on my chest. I would have scraped my back raw if it hadn't been for Mr. Entwistle's body armor. Then the air grew fresher, and over our ragged breathing I could hear the babble of water. Not a trickle, but the Indian River. A few minutes later, we approached a cave dimly lit with morning light. Everyone stopped.

"Where are we?" Luna asked.

I'm not sure if anyone answered. I was squinting ahead, wondering where we would go. Ahead was daylight. And the river. A bulletproof aquatic car would have been handy.

"I guess we'll have to wait things out down here," Ophelia said. She retreated to a darker corner. We all followed. I lay down and practically sank into the cold stone. Relief calmed every nerve. Then I felt a warm presence beside me—Luna.

We made it.

We had. But others hadn't. Mr. Entwistle. My uncle. I wondered if there was some way we could dig them out. Heal them. But not Hyde. He was finished. A few days ago, this would have been cause for celebration. Music. Fireworks. Dancing in the streets. But his death seemed more like a tragedy now. Adam Baddon was a good man who loved his son. Now his boy was an orphan. *Perhaps the orphan.* The one who would control the future of our kind.

"What are we going to do?" I asked.

Ophelia was sitting up against the cave wall, staring at me. At the boy in my arms. "We're going to survive," she said.

Adam's son stirred again. His breathing came in short gasps.

"Do we even know his name?" Charlie asked.

Luna shook her head. "He doesn't sound so good."

I glanced at Ophelia. Her eyes were intense. Nervous.

"Can you help him?" I asked.

"I don't know." Something in her voice was off.

The words were barely out of her mouth when the boy stopped breathing.

I looked around at everyone. "What do we do?"

No one answered.

I grabbed his wrist. I'd seen doctors do this on television. I searched for a pulse, but couldn't find one, so I put my head on his chest. His heartbeat was weak. Irregular. It sped up to a frantic pace. Then it stopped.

"Is he dead?" Charlie asked.

I wasn't sure.

Luna was right beside me.

Do something!

But she didn't know what to do. Neither did I. I looked over at Ophelia. She hadn't moved. Her face was a blank mask. I stared into her eyes. They were out of focus.

"What do we do?" I asked.

She didn't respond.

"What do we do?"

My voice brought her out of it. She looked at me. Her face was uncertain. Scared.

"He's just a boy," I said.

"He's more than that," Ophelia replied. "We'll pay for this."

We'd already paid. Three lives had just been lost. And we had promised Hyde we'd look after his son. It was the price of our freedom.

Ophelia handed me the knife. She'd had a bad feeling about it. No wonder. It had killed Mr. Entwistle. It had almost killed me.

"It's fitting that it would be you," she said.

I steadied my hands and pulled the blade across my open palm. I gasped and made a fist, then moved my hand until it was overtop of the boy's mouth. Beads of scarlet blood dripped down inside.

"Don't touch him," Ophelia warned. "If he bites you, or infects you, you'll die."

After a few seconds, she put her hands over his heart and compressed his chest. She did this several times, then moved my hand away from his mouth and started pressing on his diaphragm.

"You need to breathe into his mouth," Luna said.

I agreed. I'd seen CPR on TV before. That was always what they did—blew oxygen straight into the patient's lungs.

"Don't go near his mouth," Ophelia snapped.

She continued to press down on his trunk, forcing the air out of his chest. Then she went back to compressing his heart. While she did this, I dribbled more of my blood into his mouth. While I watched and bled, his teeth lengthened. Then he tried to bite me. His movements were so sudden, Luna shrieked. I jerked my hand away. The boy was still unconscious. He'd done it in his sleep.

Ophelia moved back. I kept my eyes on the boy. His breathing strengthened. His face started to change. His blond hair lengthened. His forehead stretched back. His ears sloped to two sharp points. He looked almost elflike. Tiny, with fine features. A few breaths later, he started to change back.

"What is happening?"

Ophelia shook her head. "I don't know."

"Was he dead?" Luna asked. "Did he just die and come back?"

I nodded. He had. Just like me. Like the messiah. *A saint or a scourge* . . .

Charlie stumbled over. He was still unsteady on his feet. "Your blood did that? Does this mean he feeds on vampires, like his father—like Hyde?"

It appeared that way.

My best friend was incredulous. "Why did you save him?"

What could I say? For lots of reasons. Because he was an orphan, like me. Because I had failed to save his father, Adam. But mostly because Hyde was right, none of this was the boy's fault. I put my hand near the side of his neck and felt his pulse with the back of my fingers. It was strong now. Steady.

What does this mean? Luna asked me.

I thought about it—what the boy might become if we weren't careful.

It means when he wakes up, we'd better be really, really nice to him.

CHAPTER 45

IRON SPIKE ENTERPRISES—ONE MONTH LATER

We stood in the room, the four of us, shoulder to shoulder, not speaking. Even Charlie was dumbstruck. It lasted about ten seconds. That might have been his personal best.

"Sick!" he said. "Did you know about all of this?"

Not exactly.

Luna nudged me. *Out loud,* she reminded me.

"No," I said. "But I probably should have known it would be here. He had to keep this stuff someplace."

We were in Montreal, at Iron Spike Enterprises, my uncle's business headquarters. The building was practically a skyscraper. Every floor had its hidden secrets, but this room was pay dirt.

"So all of this is yours now?" Suki asked. She and Charlie were standing side by side, his arm over her shoulder, her arm around his waist. With each passing day she was more like the Suki of old. Confident. Bubbly. Fun. Spending time with Charlie had done her wonders. It might have been the one reason Dr. Abbott let her stay with us. Love cures all ills, as they say. It had done wonders for Charlie, too. I hadn't seen him this happy since last summer.

"Technically, the whole inheritance is in a trust," I told Suki. "But we can use whatever we need."

I looked around the room. We'd been doing a tour with Ophelia, floor by floor, room by room. It had ended here, in a weapons depot. All of my uncle's military equipment guns and grenades were here.

"Do you know what all of this stuff does?" Luna was staring at a rack of weighted nets that looked like spiderwebs.

Not all of it. Not yet.

She nudged me again.

I cleared my throat. "It looks like some kind of electrified netting."

I heard a quiet "Wow!" leak from Charlie's mouth.

If he thought this was impressive, the numbers in my uncle's bank account would have floored him.

Luna was playing with the charm on her necklace. She looked at me and winked. *A rich vampire messiah. Do I know how to pick 'em, or what?*

I laughed. But I wasn't rich yet. I'd get my inheritance when I turned eighteen. If I lived that long . . .

Don't be such a pessimist, she chided. *You have some pretty good help here.*

Pretty and good, I thought.

"Where did Ophelia go?" Suki asked. She was rubbing her neck. I half expected to see some teeth marks there, but both she and Charlie seemed to have agreed that it would be better to wait than risk infecting her now. Hyde was gone, but the danger of the Coven hadn't passed.

"She went to check on Vincent," Luna said.

Vincent was the detective's son. He was still in a coma. We'd moved him to the second floor of the building. My uncle had a full medical lab there, so he was wired up to an IV and a slew of machines that monitored his heart rate, blood sugar, and oxygen levels. The situation was stable, at least medically, but the rest was a bit messy. Issues surrounded the inheritance of his father's house and belongings, including the contents of the storage shed we'd broken into— the place where we'd found the wolfsbane. And Vincent still had family. Aunts, uncles, cousins, grandparents. Eventually they would have to be informed about his condition, but we thought it best to keep him hidden until we had a better understanding of whether he would be a danger to them. Or to us. He was in for some bad news when he awoke, and we all dreaded having to tell him. Ophelia was particularly troubled.

"Why the long face, Romeo?" Charlie asked. He'd wandered over to a rack that housed a number of impressive-looking assault rifles, and something that might have belonged on the top of a tank.

Why the long face? I didn't want to answer this question. We'd just done a tour of my uncle's garage. He had a collection of street racers and a number of motorcycles. And older prototypes of the rocket car that was now our main form of transportation. But I hadn't seen what I'd hoped to find—some construction equipment.

As soon as this thought passed through my head, I felt Luna close herself off. It kept me from hearing her thoughts. Our abilities were evolving. We could still communicate without speaking, but over the last month we'd learned to control what the other could hear. Whatever she was thinking now, she wanted to keep to herself. I understood. She thought I was in denial. They all did. Even Ophelia. I told myself that staying hopeful was better than grieving, but I'm not sure I really had a choice. My heart was just being stubborn. It couldn't accept that Mr. Entwistle and my uncle were really gone. They were vampires. All we needed to do was move a few million tons of rock from a very public provincial park, then give them some of the blood my uncle had pilfered from the Underground. There was enough to fill a swimming pool.

Charlie must have sensed what was on my mind. He looked away. Like the others, he expected me to be sad and thought it was odd that I wasn't, but I still wanted my happy ending.

"Is the body armor ready?" he asked.

I shook my head. "Not yet. A few more weeks."

"I thought Entwistle's stash was impressive, but this is the mother lode."

I had to agree. In the days before we came here, the five of us had toured Mr. Entwistle's safe houses in Peterborough. He'd kept extensive files, which included a contact that made specialized military equipment. We'd ordered suits for everyone. We also found blueprints for an Abrams tank he'd customized. But it was located in a hidden garage we hadn't yet discovered.

"You never answered my question," Charlie said. "Why the long face?"

I had a lot on my mind.

Luna smiled and slipped her hand into mine.

"Just thinking," I said.

"Thinking or worrying?"

"A bit of both."

Charlie surveyed the room. There was enough equipment here to outfit the Rebel Alliance. "How are we going to learn how to use all this stuff?"

"There's a shooting range on the third floor," Suki said. "You guys were in the gym when we found it. We could practice there."

I couldn't believe it. A shooting range. Charlie and I had missed that part of the tour. The exercise equipment in my uncle's fitness room was so impressive, we'd stayed behind to try it out when the girls went ahead. This place was like a spy school. The only things missing were the students.

Luna laughed. *Not anymore.*

"What is it with you two?" Charlie asked. "Always laughing to yourselves like that."

Luna raised her hands as if it were nothing. I didn't know what to say.

"All right, keep your secrets." Charlie wandered over to the far wall. A piece of equipment that might have fallen from space was hanging from the ceiling. "What is this thing? Some kind of photon torpedo?"

It looked more like a futuristic coffin to me, but I had no idea. "The equipment lists and operation manuals are all in the library," I said.

We'd hit that earlier in the tour. I was anxious to get back. I had noticed among the shelves some notebooks that might have been journals. If my uncle kept a log like my father, it might have some information about the Coven of the Dragon. It was time to find out how much trouble we were in.

"Well, let's go," said Suki. "This place freaks me out. I'm afraid to breathe too hard. Something might blow up." She cozied up beside Charlie and took hold of his hand.

"Where to?" Charlie asked. "There's a home theater on the fourth floor. I wonder what's playing."

"I was leaning toward a swim," she answered. "Ophelia says there's a pool on the roof beside a penthouse apartment."

"I think we should go back to the library," I said. "Check the catalogs and see what all this stuff does."

Charlie looked at me in disbelief. "Zack, it will take weeks to read through all that."

"Yeah, so we'd better get started."

As soon as I said this, my mind drifted back to the safe house where Charlie and I had been caught by the police. Where we'd found the letter with the prophecies, and the handwritten notes—that the End of Days was coming and that knowledge was our best defense.

Charlie looked at me. He seemed to know what I was thinking. He glanced around the room, then pulled a canister from a crate beside him. It was a thermite bomb. A smile creased his face.

"Knowledge is your best defense, huh? Well, not anymore."

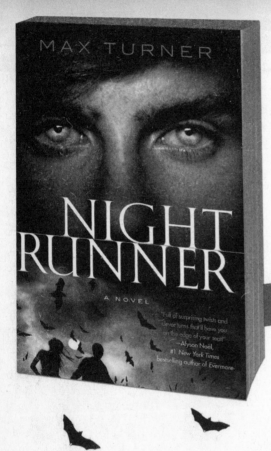
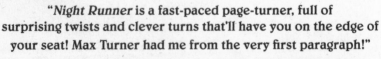